C0-AKR-104

MANILA TIME

MANILA TIME

Jack Trolley

CARROLL & GRAF PUBLISHERS, INC.
NEW YORK

First edition October 1995

Carroll & Graf Publishers, Inc.
260 Fifth Avenue
New York, NY 10001

Library of Congress Cataloging-in-Publication Data is available

ISBN 0-7867-0255-9

Manufactured in the United States of America

95 96 97   5 4 3 2 1

For my children,
Rob, Sara, and Tully,
who are bright and beautiful, magic,
and for their granny,
the best storyteller of all

ACKNOWLEDGMENTS

I am deeply indebted to Al Zuckerman, friend, teacher, agent, who contributed greatly to the form and fabric of this novel. Also, my thanks to Kent Carroll, erudite publisher, for his help with the polish and for suggesting a neat way of getting one of the bad guys to spill the beans.

MANILA TIME

ONE

Saturday night. Actually, Sunday morning. They had been lying in wait like chained dogs. Tommy Donahoo and Chip Lyons, confined to the captain's chairs of a battered burgundy/gold Dodge SE 250 Ram van, hidden by a cardboard windshield filler that said, EMERGENCY, SEND TWO BLONDES AND A SIX PACK, and taking turns looking through a hole in the O in the TWO. Donahoo's shift. Chip Lyons was taking a supper break.

Nobody would have suspected them. The van appeared derelict, abandoned. The paint was faded and splotched with rust. The left front wheel was off. Somebody would look and think it wasn't going anywhere. Except maybe to the junk yard. If they'd take it.

Donahoo shifted around, trying to get comfortable. He thought that this wasn't going to happen. It was almost two, an hour past the appointed time, and a midget submarine still hadn't broken the serene, stinking surface of the Tijuana Slough. Not that he actually expected a midget sub. He just thought, about now, that there was a better chance of a sub than what Chip Lyons expected, and also that maybe they should call it quits. Maybe they should go back to town and have a talk with Lyons's snitch, Ernesto Garcia Buddy Salinas. Maybe Buddy had gotten the time wrong? Or the day? Make that the night. The middle of the night. Donahoo thought that Buddy might have gotten the whole fucking thing fouled up. Maybe they were supposed to be at the Pink Floyd concert at Jack Murphy Stadium?

"It'll happen," Chip Lyons said. He was getting Donahoo's bad vibes, but that didn't bother him. He was upbeat and he was ready. He was wearing his baseball cap backward. He was wearing his gloves without the fingers. He was wearing his Dan Wesson 744V .44 Magnum.

"Sure," Donahoo said. He pronounced it *shoor*. He put aside the infrared camcorder and shivered down in his North Bay breaker. He wished he'd been smart enough to bring more coffee. It was April, and they'd been having April showers, and now the night wind was cold and damp, coming low off the Pacific, across the wasteland of Border Field State Park. Under other, lesser circumstances, he'd be packing it in by now. Nominally, he was in charge, he was the sergeant, but it was Chip Lyons's case, Chip Lyons's three months of undercover work, and Chip Lyons's snitch. Donahoo—special orders from the brass—was playing nursemaid to make sure things didn't get too out of hand at the close. Lyons was a certified hotshot, he had the commendations, he could build a case, like magic, out of smoke, and he could sell it, too, but he was inclined to lose things at the close. He needed watching. Special attention. Someone to take away his big Dan Wesson before he caused irreparable harm. Tell him, hey, that's enough, Chipper. You wanta kill just the bad guys. Not the material witnesses.

Donahoo, the nursemaid, Donahoo thought miserably, and he must do it carefully, subtly, so Chip Lyons wouldn't realize it was happening. They didn't want him pouting or off his chow. They wanted him razor-sharp and two hundred percent. It was his case, and if anybody could break it, he could.

Lyons opened his Wendy's bag. He took out two hamburgers, the 99¢ Double Stack, and the 99¢ Junior Bacon Cheeseburger. He put them on the dashboard upside down and started to dismantle them.

"What the hell are you doing?" Donahoo asked.

"I'm making a 212," Lyons said, smiling, flicking a quick look at him. "The Double Stack has mustard, ketchup, pickles, grilled onions, a patty, cheese, and another patty. The Junior Bacon Cheeseburger has mayo, raw onion, tomato, lettuce, two strips of bacon, cheese, and a patty. You take the dry, or bottom, buns off. You toss 'em." He was doing this as he spoke. "You put what's left together. The 212. You don't want all that bread anyway."

"Why the 212?"

"That's what it costs, with tax."

"The 212. You oughta send that in to Dave," Donahoo said, meaning Dave Thomas, the founder of Wendy's. "It would be a hell of a TV commercial. You taking the two hamburgers apart, and identifying all the ingredients—that's a long list, you know?—and putting 'em back together. And then you toss half the buns? 'You don't want all that bread anyway?' That's a great throwaway line."

Donahoo grabbed the cellular phone and pretended to be dialing. "I'm gonna phone Dave right now." He was looking at Lyons. "Hello, Dave? Listen, you don't know me, but I've got a poh-leece detective here, he's got a hell of an idea for a hamburger spot." Donahoo, watching Lyons, went through the whole routine, all the details, verbatim. Then he said, "Okay, they're your burgers."

Lyons finally looked at him. Donahoo pretended to hang up. He said, "He wants to do it himself."

"Well, fuck him," Lyons said.

"Exactly."

"Dave, he saw me work, he'd probably let me do it," Lyons said after a while. "Cop, magician, salesman. That kinda sums me up. Who I am. The Chipper." He paused, thinking about it. "What defines me, though, I gotta go with salesman, Tommy. That's my forte. It's where I really shine. You know?"

"Hey," Donahoo said. "You could sell a stool softener to a Mexican."

"Then buy this. It's gonna happen."

"Yeah, well, we'll see." Donahoo was giving Lyons all the rope he wanted. Actually, all the string. He'd run out of rope, now it was string, and Chip Lyons, he had a ball so big, he could take it somewhere, get it redeemed. He could trade it for some roller skates. Lemme outa here, Donahoo thought, getting desperate, but he knew he wasn't going anywhere. He was acutely aware of the politics involved and the fact that he had his own reputation to care for. If the case sank, *when* the case sank, Donahoo didn't want to go down with it, faulted because he went home too early. He wanted Chip Lyons to sink all by himself. Preferably in the pesthole that was at hand. The Tijuana Slough was the perfect place to dispose of the fucker, he thought. Donahoo could picture Lyons disappearing below the slough's placid sewage. Ploop! and the last thing he saw, the last thing anybody ever saw, was the glinting glass eye and the nose that could stuff a turkey. Farewell, so long, and goodbye. The end, and he, Donahoo, could return to more rewarding duties with the San Diego Police Department's elite Squad 5, better known as SCUMB, for Sickos, Crackpots, Underwear & Mad Bombers. He said, which was true, "I've got all night."

They'd been there since midnight, at the south reach of the slough, a rutted quarter mile up from Monument Road's dead end at Border Field State Park, and probably still within San Diego city limits, but possibly intruding on Imperial Beach. There was no way to tell for sure. The only line was on a map. Donahoo had mentioned this—jurisdiction was an act of faith for him—but Lyons didn't want to deal with it. He had said, "You get an Imperial Beach cop in here, the fat fuck'll blow it, Tommy. They'll spot his wiener campfire." End of discussion. Donahoo wasn't positioned to argue or overrule. It was Lyons's case. Donahoo wished now that they were closer to the close. Donahoo had a big man's inclination, sometimes barely restrained, to invoke physical solutions. He was an all-meat slab, six foot two, two hundred and thirty, and he had a natural brute strength. He hadn't honed it—he didn't have the speed, skill, or dedication of a brawler—but it still served him well. He could, when required, put most men down quickly, efficiently. Chip Lyons, a monkey fucking with an ape, would be gone in a blink. If, Donahoo mused, *if*—there was always this proviso—he could catch him without the goddamn Dan Wesson. The thing weighed just a shade under four pounds, but Lyons, a bundle of wires, full of electricity, was still the fastest draw on the force. Oh, and something else, Donahoo reminded himself. The guy had four kills, all of them debatable. A force record and a course record. They usually retired you after two borderlines. Lyons had somehow slipped through the net. No witnesses. Reluctant witnesses. Lying-through-their-fucking-teeth witnesses.

Maybe he'd have to catch him in the shower, Donahoo mused. Or put dog poison—who'd notice?—in his 212? He sighed and let it go, partly on account of the 744V, but mostly on account of himself. Everything about him was a shade oversize. He had a big head, big hands, big feet. Donahoo always looked like he might be carrying a rock. He had that kick-it-in knock-it-down look. There had been a time, before the busted, pushed-in nose, when he could have been called handsome, but now he had a veteran warrior's face. Wary, cold blue eyes under thick, bushy black eyebrows, a hard, solid, razor-blue jaw, and a wide, tough mouth. Even his graying hair was intimidating. He wore it long, it fell over his collar, unruly. He seemed, without effort, just slightly larger than life, and he could intimidate by mere presence. He seldom got to fight with anyone.

"It's gonna happen," Lyons said, finishing his hamburger. "Buddy, he's always been one hundred percent, okay? He knows the consequences, he gives me bad information. He's a pygmy now? He's gonna be a dwarf. He's gonna be all twisted and bent."

There'd been a moon when they arrived, a D cup sitting on the high, abrupt ridge to the south, where a sprinkling of faint lights marked some of the nicer homes in Tijuana and the border with Mexico. It had been bright enough to let them find their way without running lights and to get the van settled between a gutted flatbed truck and a busted Caterpillar. Now the moon was gone, leaving an earth that was two shades of black, the land mass, impenetrable, and the slough, which carried a blue-green sheen. It was very still, very quiet. Only frogs croaked. Literally, Donahoo thought. The slough had to be poison.

"Buddy's just naturally the nervous type," Lyons said. He put his garbage away and found the joint he had rolled in the dark, using a gum wrapper. He'd run out of ZigZag. "How I got him to tell me about this little rendezvous here? I stuck the DW in his mouth and pulled the trigger on an empty chamber. He pissed his pants. He didn't talk, he babbled. A little running brook."

Donahoo looked through the O in the TWO toward where (this when the moon was out) a concrete ramp slanted into the slough. He couldn't see the ramp now. He couldn't see anything but the sheen, which had come up from Tijuana, via the Tijuana River, and which was, frankly, shit. It would cook here and then it would find its relentless way to the ocean and Imperial Beach. Another thing the border patrol couldn't stop.

"So I figure, this is not a wasted mission," Lyons said. He ducked low, striking a wooden kitchen match in a cupped hand, his subsandwich nose suddenly grotesque in the flare, the glass eye flashing. He inhaled deeply. "Tonight is the night. You want some?"

Donahoo pushed it away. He wasn't opposed to a hit now and then. At the moment, he could use one. But not via a gum wrapper.

Lyons grinned. "The mother of invention . . ."

Donahoo said, "You'd smoke an oil-soaked rag."

They were waiting for a will-o'-the-wisp bad-ass Mexican, Primitivo, to show up for a meeting with an equivalent from San Diego, identity not known. They were hoping to get some video, that's all. Maybe, if they were lucky, some sound bites. Nothing more. Unless they got lucky, something dropped in their laps, this was just the first step in a long journey. Having a meeting wasn't against the law. But it might show, later, with other evidence, conspiracy. The first step, *if* it happened, but Donahoo didn't think it would, wouldn't have bet any money even two hours ago. Right away it was a long shot. There was no proof either existed. Yet-to-Be-Identified was so fresh a thought, he didn't have a file. He'd just been laid, like an egg, from the mouth of Buddy Salinas. He hadn't hatched yet. Primitivo's dossier wasn't much fatter. He was mostly a name being whispered in a disturbingly large and diverse number of criminal cases in San Diego. Crème-de-la-crème stuff. Heroin, white slavery, kidnapping, murder-for-hire. Activities that were directed from afar and bore the same brutal stamp. It was the kind of nightmare that San Diego law enforcement feared the most. A Mexican, from the safety of Mexico, ravaging San Diego, attacking like a pirate across a border that couldn't be defended, but which protected the invader. If Primitivo was real, he could make you wake up screaming, because you knew the kind of help you were going to get from Mexican authorities. Typically, cars that had been stolen in San Diego were being driven around openly in Tijuana. By the cops.

Donahoo wasn't sure about Primitivo. Maybe he was for real, maybe not. It didn't matter. He was legend, which was almost as good, maybe better. He'd been caught only once (this was part of the legend), for cheating on his driver's exam. Then, like a schoolboy, he had written the answers on his hand. Primitivo the legend.

He'd been rumored so long, he existed. He was accused of spilling blood in America's Finest City and he was on the shit list of people in high places. Lewis, captain, Investigations, wanted him. Saperstein, the police chief, wanted him. Purvis, the district attorney, he wanted him too. Even the mayor. So Chip Lyons, the magician cop, had been working his smoke and mirrors, trying to conjure hard evidence, and he sifted real fine. The smallest lead was followed. The dumbest tip checked out. Babblings from Buddy Salinas.

Understandable, but it wasn't going to happen, not tonight, Donahoo thought. He had a smart cop's list of reasons why not. In the first place, why would Primitivo leave Mexico, which didn't have conspiracy laws, to come up here to conspire? Here they could get you for conspiring to piss in the street. Why not have Yet-to-Be-Identified go to Tijuana, where they could conspire till their dicks fell off and nobody would look twice? Secondly, supposing Primitivo was that dumb, supposing *both* were that dumb, again why come here, why not choose a better place to meet, maybe a gentleman's club such as Pacers? He, Donahoo, he could have an Old Crow at Pacers, not have to secondhand-smoke Chip Lyons's gum-wrapper Humboldt Hurry. Thirdly, why one, correction, two o'clock in the morning, when by mere presence and movement they'd attract attention and suspicion? Decent people were in bed. They especially weren't hanging out at the Tijuana Slough.

Lyons passed the burned-down joint. Donahoo this time took a small, careful hit, handed it back. He tried to think of something positive. If, for example, Primitivo or Yet-to-Be-Identified, one or the other, had to get rid of something in a hurry should the border patrol show up, they could toss it in the slough. Now, that made a certain kind of sense. Nobody was gonna go in after it.

"Two o'clock," Lyons said abruptly. He'd been up and now he was down. "Something must have gone wrong." He took a last pinched pull on the dog end of the joint. "I don't believe this. You want to call it a night?"

For answer, Donahoo turned the key in the ignition. Nothing

happened. He tried again. Still nothing. Dead battery. He turned on the police radio. No green light. *Really* dead battery.

"Fuck," Donahoo said. "This wreck."

The disappointment shimmered on Lyons's face. "I'll go."

"No," Donahoo told him. "I'll go." He was starting to cramp up. He could use the walk. He pushed out. "It was gonna happen, huh?"

"He's been one hundred percent."

Sure, Donahoo thought. He'd never met anybody who was a hundred percent. Pygmy fags included. He paused to get his bearings. "Meanwhile, don't date any mermaids, Chippie."

"Chipp*er*."

"Yeah."

The Jaguar showed up maybe half an hour later. It came crawling along, parking lights only, and Chip Lyons heard the motor first, a cat's soft purr, and the tires bumping, losing it in the ruts. That was fast, Lyons thought. It was a good mile walk to the nearest place, a horses-for-rent barn, China Camp Stables. Donahoo should be just getting there. So this wasn't Donahoo?

Lyons put on his night vision glasses and rolled down the blackened driver's side window a couple inches. He picked up the camcorder and fitted it in the gap. He checked to make sure the camcorder was wired to the unobtrusive but highly sensitive directional microphone on the van's roof. He waited, his heart beating faster, the adrenaline pushing. If it wasn't Donahoo . . . ? Hello. He started rolling.

The Jag, a V12 sedan, showroom new, bumped around the last turn, came right at the camera for a moment, and then drifted away. It eased to a stop in the clearing in front of the van. Lyons, still rolling, twisted around, switched the camcorder to the hole in the O in the TWO. The Jag was positioned perfectly. He had it all.

The driver got out. He seemed to be alone. Tall, erect, he appeared fiftyish, maybe older than that, it was hard to tell in the infrared. For a moment he stood in profile, revealing strong, chiseled features, a trim mustache. He was wearing a peaked cap, a long scarf, a buckled trench coat. He had his hands stuffed deep in the pockets. He looked relaxed, assured, confident. He removed his hands briefly to rub them together. He was wearing smooth gloves.

Lyons was rolling. It wasn't Primitivo. He'd seen photos that were supposed to be of the Mexican. He had a fat, round face, cruel, pockmarked. He was short, powerfully built. So, Lyons thought, maybe you're not a lying fuck, Buddy Salinas. Maybe we do have a meeting going here.

The man moved. Another vehicle was approaching. Lyons turned the camera back to the slit above the driver's side window. Full headlights this time, bumping across the flats, up and down, seen and then not seen, coming at high speed. It showed around the last corner. The headlights were a blinding flash.

Instinctively, Lyons pulled back, fearful that he might have been spotted. He unholstered his Dan Wesson 744V .44 Magnum. He put it on the dash. He willed himself to relax. He aimed the camcorder through the O.

A Ford Bronco with BORDER PATROL splashed across it was suddenly in the frame. Fuck, no, Lyons thought. Not the border patrol. This was gonna blow it. For Christ's sake, *no!* The Bronco braked sharply behind the Jag. A passenger alighted, short, powerfully built. The cruel face was pocked. Lyons had seen photographs. This was the guy, Primitivo.

What the hell? Chip Lyons wondered. What the hell is this? *Border patrol?* He checked the camcorder. It was rolling.

The Bronco backed up, spun away, departed. Primitivo seemed surprised but not concerned. He appeared to shrug. Lyons held his breath. Primitivo and the man stood facing each other. Primitivo smiled and raised a hand in friendship. The man ripped his right hand from the trench coat, blindingly fast. He was holding a large pistol with a silencer. He fired four times in rapid succession. The first slug hit Primitivo in the face. He took the other three before he reached the ground.

Jesus, Lyons thought. Jesus, Jesus. He was rolling. He had it all.

The man separated his pistol from the silencer. He tossed them, in turn, far out into the slough. They went spinning away. He had a good arm.

Lyons was trembling with excitement. He could barely breathe. He couldn't believe it. He was getting everything that was happening. He had it all on tape. The beginning, the middle, and the end.

The man opened the Jag's trunk. He was working like this was a routine thing, something that he might have done, or practiced, many times. He removed what at first looked like a tarpaulin but which was actually a small inflatable boat. He placed it on the ramp at the water's edge. He dragged Primitivo's body alongside and rolled it on top. He inflated the boat with a small gas cylinder. Now Primitivo was in the boat. He took a tire rim from the Jag's trunk. He wired it to Primitivo's fat neck. All the time it seemed practiced, almost choreographed. He pushed the boat away, starting a small, eggbeater electric motor. He stood for a while, watching the boat's slow but certain progress, Primitivo being taken into deep water. Finally he raised an arm and pointed what looked like a remote control. There was a muffled explosion.

Lyons imagined that he could hear the complaining bubbles as Primitivo sank to the bottom of the slough. He had it *all*, he thought again. He had a murder charge that no one could beat. That was perfect. That was gold.

Donahoo wasn't away that much longer. Fifteen, perhaps twenty minutes. He arrived in a China Camp Stables pickup truck. He had a thermos of coffee and jumper cables.

"Anything happen?" Donahoo asked.

"Naw," Chip Lyons said. He took possession of the thermos. "This place. It's a fucking tomb."

TWO

There were a couple of ways home. Monument Road to Hollister Street and then a connection to I-5 or 75. I-5 was a straight twenty-minute run north to downtown San Diego and the Police Administrative Headquarters. Seventy-five, the Silver Strand Highway, skirted the west side of San Diego Bay, went through Coronado, then crossed back, over the Coronado Bridge, to join I-5 at Barrio Logan. Either route got them to the right exit.

Two ways, and Chip Lyons, grinning, not asking consent, took I-5. He said, when it was too late, knowing that Donahoo would have preferred the Strand, "You don't mind?" The glass eye winked. "I wanta make a pit stop. It won't take long, okay? In and out."

More string, Donahoo thought. The ball, it grew larger. He fed it now because he wanted to see how big it would get. He had the nagging feeling that the night's events were somehow incomplete. There was something missing here, he thought. Something missing or something wrong. The notion wouldn't let go. Lyons had been up, then down. Now he was up again.

"I could take a whiz faster."

Something, Donahoo thought again. Lyons ought to be in trauma. They were coming off a no-show stakeout. Bad information. Dashed hopes. A totally unproductive shift. And—this *is* magic— he miraculously turns it into a nice day?

Lyons grinned. "You're gonna like her. Rosie the Snake G-string."

Donahoo told himself he might figure it out if he was patient and went along for the ride. The old waiting game, he thought, not amused. The old waiting game and the old string game. He didn't have much else going at the moment anyway. He had this case, the Primitivo case, which hadn't really caught his interest yet, it was a real stretch, and he had the routine wraps of a couple kook's tours. He was putting away a guy who'd had a bottle capper, he'd open a Corona, pee in it, recap it, put it back. He was putting away an ex-navy frogman who had been pulling plugs on boats in the harbor. Both were going quietly. He hadn't had a murder case for quite a while. That was starting to worry him. Lewis, captain/ Investigations, what Lewis was always telling him, you're only as good as your next murder. That was probably true. Lewis was right about a lot of things, although he could be wrong too. Lewis was one of those toss-ups. He could come down heads or tails. Donahoo said now, softly, hiding his annoyance and disappointment at being denied the Strand, "Whatever." He had been looking forward to the peace he experienced in a swift passage beside dark water. He loved the sea, he was born and raised on it, up the coast a little ways, at Solana Beach. He hoped, someday, some way, to own a home on Coronado. He went there every chance, and this would be the best time, dead of night, the inhabitants in bed, no one to see his coveting look. The best time, but Chip Lyons, cop, magician, salesman, required more string.

"The Wham Bam Ice Trail." Lyons was still talking about the woman named Rosie.

Maybe it was sleight of hand? Handkerchiefs into pigeons, Donahoo thought. Frog into bowling ball. He couldn't figure it and he couldn't believe it. He gave it up. The sky was black and there was no sign of dawn. The freeway was slick from a passing squall. It was practically empty. Two trucks overtook them, passed in tandem. The van strained. Donahoo went to sleep in his captain's chair. Dozed off thinking that Chip Lyons was about as reliable as car repairs. He didn't wake up until National City.

"You coming in?" Lyons asked then.

They were stopped and Donahoo said it even before he was fully awake. He wasn't sure the van would start again. "Leave it running."

Lyons frowned. "What if somebody steals it?"

He said, "I don't think we're that fortunate." He looked around. "This is her?"

"Yeah."

"Tough neighborhood."

"Tough lady."

Donahoo thought that she had better be nails. They were at the end of a canyon cul-de-sac, facing back on six low, mean houses on a narrow, mean street. They all had graffiti on the walls and they all had bars on the windows. The canyon was being used as a dump. There was a refrigerator on the edge, waiting for somebody to push it over.

Lyons, sounding defensive, said, "So it ain't Coronado."

Donahoo got out with the camcorder. He hoped it would be the first house. It had a Yugo in the carport and a small stake-bed truck in the driveway. He'd always liked women who weren't in a hurry.

The other houses had big cars built for fast getaways. The first house, the one he was hoping for, looked older than the others: it had a larger yard than its neighbors, mature trees, a grove of eucalyptus and a big oak. It was on a slight rise at the end of the street and it would have a sweeping canyon view. It had a fireplace chimney and it had shingle siding. The other houses were stucco cracker boxes.

Lyons led the way to the first house. He went on a slant, from the side, through a narrow picket fence, between a low, sickly privet and across a steep, overgrown lawn. He went with the assurance of knowing the route. Donahoo picked his way after him. The lawn had lumps in it.

A woman had the door already open. Just wide enough for a panel of her face. Sleep-filled eyes and a mouth without lipstick. She must have heard the van arrive. She said, "What are you doing here? It's four in the morning."

"Manila Time," Chip Lyons told her. "Open up."

She backed off and he pushed inside. Donahoo waited for a moment, forgotten. He considered going back to the van. He felt unwelcome, an intruder. He should have stayed in the van, he thought. But he'd look dumb changing his mind now. He went inside, into a small, narrow, dark hallway. It smelled of cooking. The lingering smells of fish, garlic.

Chip Lyons was kissing the woman. His hands were inside her thin pink silk bathrobe.

Jesus, Donahoo thought. He wasn't good at odd-man-out. He hated it. He hated watching. He started to leave.

The woman pulled away. Her white body flashed.

"This is the Snake," Chip Lyons said, grinning. "AKA Rosie G-string." He said, "This is Tommy Donahoo."

"Gestring," Rosie said. She pronounced it *jest-ring*. She closed her robe and looked at Donahoo. There was a bruise high on her left cheekbone. Someone had clipped her recently. She said, not quite a question, almost, though, "You're a cop."

Lyons said, "He's a sergeant."

She said, surprised, "Oh." She noticed the camcorder. "What's this?"

"We're gonna take pictures."

"You're gonna take a hike."

Donahoo didn't say anything.

"Maybe we could go into the living room?" Lyons suggested. "You got a light you could turn on? Some soft music?" He said, "You got a drink or something?"

Donahoo looked at Rosie. He decided, despite the white skin, that she was Mexican, a compelling mix of the Spanish, the Indian. He thought she'd be in her early thirties. A tall, thin, voguish, very beautiful woman. She had big, dark, slanted almond eyes, faintly smoldering, and a full, pouting, sensuous mouth. It glistened even without lipstick. Her hair was long and straight and blue-black. Her face was shaped like a heart. Donahoo thought she had a lot going. She was electric.

She said, "Help yourself."

"The usual?" Chip Lyons wanted to know.

"You got Old Crow?" Donahoo asked, a question for Rosie.

She shook her head and went into the living room on long legs, moving like a model without trying, long arms turning on fat, squat lamps with tasseled shades, dimming them. Lyons went in another direction.

"Just ice," Donahoo called.

A door banged. Donahoo thought of following Lyons. Not very seriously though. He was watching Rosie. She was working through a stack of compact discs. He wondered why she would have anything to do with Chip Lyons. She was a beautiful woman. He was a garbage can. With the lid off.

Rosie selected a CD. She put it on. Willie Nelson. "Stardust." She was aware of Donahoo watching her. She said, "Do you have a question?"

"Yeah," Donahoo said. "I was wondering—maybe you know?—the time difference between San Diego and Manila? If we were on Manila Time—would that be a more appropriate time to call?"

"I dunno," Rosie said, looking now at Donahoo. "I think what The Great One means—" She stopped, took a breath, straightened her hair. "I think he just means it's party time." She said, "Any other questions?"

"Why do they call you the Snake?"

"I shed. Anything else?"

Donahoo put the camcorder on a hall table. He went into the old-fashioned living room with its false beam ceiling, wainscot-high wood panelling, and brown-on-brown field and stream wallpaper. He thought that the furniture must belong to someone else, her parents, or perhaps her grandparents. Overstuffed brown velvet sofas trimmed with wooden curlicues. An oak rolltop desk and companion filing cabinet. An antique upright piano that seemed too old to play. A television set with a round screen. A pendulum clock in a yellow wooden case. The CD player was the only modern piece.

"May I?"

"Help yourself."

Donahoo chose a sofa chair. It was old, worn. The brown velvet nap, in pressure places, had rubbed away completely. It was comfortable though. He sat down gratefully. It had been a long night and he wasn't happy with it. He still had the nagging feeling of it being incomplete. There was something missing. Or something wrong.

Lyons came in with the drinks. He passed them around. He said to Donahoo, "What do you think?" meaning what did he, Donahoo, think of Rosie Gestring.

"She's fine," Donahoo said. He meant it. It had been a long time since a woman had excited him with her mere presence.

"Yeah," Lyons agreed. He raised his glass in a toast. He took a small, quick sip. "I gotta use the facility. You mind?"

Nobody did. He left.

Donahoo took a long pull on his bar bourbon. He looked around the living room. The pendulum clock was staring at him. Four-twelve. He wondered what the hell was going on.

"So, you're a sergeant?" Rosie said. Now that she had a drink—it was clear, probably vodka, probably straight—she was more pleasant, almost hospitable. She found a cigarette in a small carved box. "You work with . . ." She was looking for a light.

"The Great One," Donahoo said, finishing it for her, not quite sure why he had said that.

She smiled crookedly. He'd made a friend, he thought. Maybe.

"On occasion," he added. He didn't know why he said that either. Just to set the record straight? He drank some more bar bourbon and watched her look for a light. He wished he still smoked. He could be looking for a light too. It was a good delay factor, when required, he thought. It let you get your thoughts in order. It put up—what? A smoke screen?

Lyons's voice drifted in anxiously. "Come on, *come on*."

Donahoo thought, Now he's talking to himself?

Rosie asked, "What kind of work?"

"Well," Donahoo said. He had a problem talking about Squad 5. There wasn't anything secret about it. There was a problem though. If he told her half of it, it would sound like he was bragging. If he told her all of it, he would sound like a bigger idiot than Lyons. Sickos, crackpots, underwear and mad bombers. Maybe twenty percent of our cases have something to do with underwear, ma'am. Panties, garter belts, stockings. For some reason, some kind of underwear. It just happens. It's strange. He said, "Police work."

"How interesting." She lit her cigarette. She blew smoke. She got a magazine. "Officer."

"What do you do?"

"I buy/sell. Antiques."

"That's your truck outside?"

"I hope so."

Chip Lyons's voice rose in another room. "Bullshit."

Donahoo looked at the clock. Four-fifteen. "Have you got other company?"

"I hope not." The magazine was *Redbook*. She was pretending to read it.

A toilet flushed.

Donahoo thought that maybe he'd better tell her about the squad after all. Or maybe he should tell her what a lucky cop he was. How he solved the Purple Admiral Murder Case. The Stardust Donut Shop Murder Case. How, with a lot of help from his friends, he wrote finis for the Balboa Firefly, and, along the way, stole a bit of glory from Chip Lyons.

Lyons came into the room. He was pumped up, anxious.

Donahoo finished his drink. "Are we going?"

"Give us a little time, huh?" Lyons complained. He looked at Rosie. He made a movement with his head. He said to Donahoo, "Relax, willya?"

Rosie tossed the *Redbook*. She got up and left the room. Leaving, she said to Donahoo, "Officer."

"You don't mind?" Lyons said to Donahoo. "This won't take long. In and out. The Wham Bam Ice Trail. Fix yourself another drink. Listen to Willie." He said, grinning, "Okay?"

Willie had just finished "Georgia on My Mind." Now he was singing "Blue Skies."

Donahoo didn't say anything. He stared into his empty glass for a while and then he got the camcorder and quietly went out. The guy, he really was a magician, he thought. Flick of cloak, puff of smoke. The Chipper does it all.

Donahoo waited in the van. He had a headache now. He had a bump on his head. Crossing the yard, unfamiliar territory, especially in the dark, he had banged his head on a low-hanging birdhouse, some dumb Hawaiian thing, it had a hula dancer painted on it, she was dancing with her hands. This place, it wasn't for him, it was for Lyons, Donahoo thought. Lyons wouldn't walk into the damn thing. He wasn't tall enough to walk into it. He was too fucking short. Donahoo couldn't figure it. Why Rosie Gestring would have anything whatsoever to do with Chip Lyons. What would explain that? The guy's dick, it had to be as big as his nose, Donahoo decided. That didn't make him any happier. He slumped down and closed his eyes and wondered if he could go back to sleep. He wondered, the van's motor running, if he'd get asphyxiated, and he wondered what Willie Nelson was singing now, singing for him and for Rosie Gestring, which was pronounced *jest-ring*. "Someone to Watch Over Me"?

THREE

The Jaguar videotaped at the Tijuana Slough was registered to a John Morley, address 14 Pannikin Drive, on San Diego's prestigious Bankers Hill. Chip Lyons was thrilled when he saw it. Fourteen Pannikin Drive, part temple, part church, was a two-story stone structure which, with grounds, spawled over half a block, with panoramic views of the bay, downtown, and Balboa Park. Except for the stained glass windows, it might be mistaken for a bank, a courthouse, or perhaps an overblown library. The entrance was classical Greek. It had the low, inverted V roof atop four tall pillars, and wide stone steps leading up to high double doors. Upon closer examination, though, an informed person might notice, in the façade's rendering, suggestions from Carlo Maderno's work in 1600s

Rome, and, in the golden angel blowing a long trumpet from atop the roof, Ricchino's alternative upper tier design for the Milan cathedral. There also was the cornerstone, which declared it was conceived to the glory of God, as the First Church Soldiers of Christ. Mostly, in one of several manifestations, it had been, the records showed, the Rodale Gallery (Fine Arts, Restorations, Appraisals), and later it was the Lyric, an amateur playhouse, and subsequently Heavenly Treasures, a thrift shop, before becoming what it was now, a private residence inhabited—be still my pounding heart, Chip Lyons thought—by a millionaire murderer who was about to be nailed to the cross.

Lyons was waiting just inside the front door. The maid—or was it the elevator operator?—had told him the boss would be home any moment now. Ten o'clock. He usually came at ten o'clock.

From where? Lyons couldn't get anything else out of her. She was high on something. She was acting really crazy. She was working a closet, pretending it was an elevator, sliding the door back and forth, saying, "Going up," and "Second floor. Home furnishings. Wall coverings," and "Third floor. Beds, mattresses, enemas." She was smiling and saying, "Notions?"

Fucking buggy black, Lyons thought. He shook his head despairingly and popped some more speed. He'd almost taken a shot at her when he broke in. She had scared him badly, sliding the closet door open, yelling, "Going down!" He had considered locking her away somewhere, and then he had decided to keep things "normal" for Morley. Nothing out of place when the boss came home. Business as usual.

The guy, he was an eccentric, okay? Lyons stood waiting inside the door and thinking that was part of the charm and also the luck of the draw. He'd had an hour to examine the house, prowling it like a thief, calculating its riches, and constantly thinking, every turn, that finally and at last, he had scored.

In the former nave, he had encountered a vast stained glass shell under a resplendent, soaring ceiling, faintly lit by spent sunlight, that was entirely devoted to orchids. He had been in a lavish living room that looked like a king's court and in a bedroom fit for a sultan. He'd been in a Roman bath that could garage a bus and in a personal gymnasium sufficient for a health club. He had found an office where, when he pushed the right buttons, the walls rotated, revealing, in turn, a big-screen entertainment center, a bar with a year's supply of Johnnie Walker, a walk-in vault, and an arsenal assembled for a professional assassin. A scope-fitted Parker-Hale M85 sniper rifle and an Anschutz Super Match Model target rifle. A Smith & Wesson .357 Combat Magnum and an S & W .38 Special Bodyguard. Two Leopold scopes, a 3 × 9 compact, a BR-36x target, along with an LA5 LaserAim sight.

The place spoke of money, blood and money, Lyons thought, waiting at the door. Blood, money, and madness. He peeked through a small hole in the stained glass window next to the door. He'd had several false alarms. Maybe this was him now?

Lyons couldn't be sure. The man was at a distance, walking up the hill, bundled against the cold, against the wind scooting from the bay. The marine layer cloud blanket was gone, lifted by the strong, steady offshore. It had stripped the corner's jacaranda of all its fairy bell blossoms. The man was scuffing through the mauve trash.

Maybe him? Yeah, definitely the guy in the video, Lyons decided. Only now he wasn't dressed as smartly. He was wearing an old bomber jacket, torn and faded jeans, and scruffy running shoes. He had a dark wool cap fitted low over his forehead. He reached the stairs and started up.

Lyons felt a stab of doubt. The killer, yes—but not John Morley? The guy, fuck, what if he just works here? Lyons thought. Borrowed the car. What if he's a fucking *nobody*?

The man was unlocking the door now.

Lyons thought of changing his mind. He could still go either way. One more second to make his choice. He thought briefly, tranquilly, about Donahoo. No worry there. Donahoo had other duties. He was at the VA. Lyons felt the speed gear in again. It gave him a little whack. The guy, he's an eccentric, Lyons reminded himself. Go with it. There was a bag of kumquats at his feet. He kicked it out of the way.

The door pushed open. The man entered. Lyons shoved the big Dan Wesson in his face. He showed his badge.

The man stared in shock and surprise. He needed a shave, his jaw was gray, and his eyes were puffy, sleep bugs in the corners. He needed a cup of coffee and he needed a shower. Lyons thought that he looked like a killer, all right. Up close, he looked a lot like a soldier, an officer. Scottish regiment. Guards. From a long line of pricks. Last ones out of the caves. He'd be fifty, but the kind who looked forty, still lean, still tough. He had good, strong features, they were holding up. His eyes, the best thing about him, the white/blue wolf's eyes, were empty and silent, scare the shit out of somebody. His mouth was generous, firm. He still had most of his teeth, if yellow, and, under the low cap, which didn't quite hide the dent in his forehead, he still had his silver/black hair, cropped short like his silver/black mustache. He said finally, slowly, "What's this all about?"

They all wanted to know, Lyons thought. They all had variations of that question. What's this all about? What the *fuck* is this all about? What the fuck is this all about, *asshole*? He turned him around and made a quick frisk, encountering sinewy muscle on every portion of an athlete's body. There was no weapon. He took a wallet. He turned him back. He wanted to see his reaction when he told him.

"It's about last night."

There was a flicker of concern. Not fear, not worry. Just a small suggestion of disquiet. He removed his cap. Definitely an old soldier. It was the kind of dent made by shrapnel. "Then I think I want a lawyer."

"No, you don't."

"I think I do."

"Trust me. You really don't." Lyons looked into the icy blue/white eyes. If he had a second chance to change his mind, it ran out about now, he thought. The eyes were empty and the face was an inscrutable death mask. He was looking at flesh and blood and he was looking at stone. If he, the Chipper, had a brain, he would break and run, he thought, but he knew it was somehow already too late. So he had to rush along. And he could do that. He hadn't been to bed. He'd been up all morning, thinking about this, planning it. He was on speed. He could rush. He said, "Who's the loopy?"

"Who?"

"The black."

"Trudy? Don't worry about her. She's harmless."

"Who is she?"

"Trudy Goody. The maid."

"Who is she?"

"A fuck."

A fuck, Lyons thought. He could identify with that. He flipped the wallet open and found a driver's license. The man's photo was on it. The name was Nicholas Quillan. Lyons felt his stomach turn. Alias? Or . . . ? He hesitated. The bomber jacket also worried him. It didn't fit a couple ways. And the faded, ripped pants. The scuffed trainers. The guy was in rags. He was supposed to be in an Italian suit. He was a fucking crime lord. The label was supposed to say Giorgio Armani.

"This is you? Quillan?"

"Yes."

"Nick?"

"Yes."

"You're not John Morley?"

"No. He owns the place."

"And you are?"

"The custodian."

Lyons's stomach did another flop. He didn't believe it. Not for a second. But he still thought, yeah, that would be his luck, the guy was a fucking janitor, he didn't have a can to shit in.

"Let's find out."

Lyons picked up his bag of kumquats. He made a motion, directing Quillan into the orchid greenhouse, which was formerly the church's nave. The temperature changed abruptly, becoming warmer, humid. They moved through it, toward the bedroom, situated in what had been the chancel.

"You ever drive Morley's Jaguar?"

"Occasionally. To charge the battery."

"That's what you were doing last night?"

"You're sure I don't need a lawyer?"

Lyons put the license back and checked the bank cards, credit cards, and other ID. Nicholas Quillan on all of them. Maybe forty dollars in cash. A couple receipts for small purchases. Only one photo, a bamboo cage, the door hanging open. He closed the wallet and tossed it to Quillan. "You live down the hill, huh?"

"Yeah. The Grand Hastings."

Lyons knew the place. It was six blocks away, an old apartment hotel, units for as little as four hundred dollars a month. But it had a certain style. Columns and gargoyles. An upscale rat hole.

"Am I under arrest?"

"What's your hurry?" Lyons tried to think it out. Quillan could be telling the truth. He could be a hired gun, working for Morley. His duties could include house sitting. And he might not have a dime for charity. Jesus, it was never simple, he thought. You started down the open road, and then it suddenly twisted, turned, zigged, zagged, doubled-back. It had potholes and detours and slippery stretches and lines you crossed at your peril. It had dips.

"I'm getting a little tired of this."

"Don't be a jerk." On the other hand, the guy, he could be living a double life, Lyons thought. Nights, he disappears into the Grand Hastings, just of one of the gang, lost among the pensioners and law students, the other weirdos and whackos. Days, supposed custodian, he lives a life of rare privilege, the sole master of 14 Pannikin Drive. Morley doesn't exist except on paper. He's a total fake in a shit-from-Shinola world. In which case Quillan is worth millions. But which was it?

"I'm not sure you're a cop."

"We're even."

They were almost at the bedroom. Lyons paused to inspect an orchid. He'd never seen anything like it before.

"Vanda burgeffii, a hybrid," Quillan told him. "From the Far East."

"It looks . . . complicated."

"You see what you see."

Lyons inspected it more closely. He saw a lot of things. All kinds of images came to mind.

"It's a specimen plant."

"No kidding?" Lyons snapped off a spike and stuck it in his lapel buttonhole. "Very nice."

Quillan looked at him with his wolf's eyes. He didn't say anything.

They went into the bedroom. It was a huge room, but the bed still took up most of it, set like a boxing ring in the center of an arena. An enormous ceiling fan with wide mirrored blades was overhead. Lyons had tried it out. It had ten speed settings. In the first, the blades, slow motion, barely moved, but they would add to the activity of those below. The low headboard was a bookcase filled with erotica. At the foot was a wide-screen television system with built-in stereo and VCR. The bathroom, *the baths,* were on one side, the gymnasium on the other. The far wall was a row of closets filled with a man's carefully chosen wardrobe. Suits, jackets, slacks, robes, sportswear. All very fashionable. All very expensive. Below, row upon row of footwear, also the best.

Lyons had been flicking through the clothes when he first encountered Trudy Goody. Now, as if on cue, she slid open a closet door. She was a pretty little thing with a puckish face and dancing dreadlocks. She rewarded Quillan with a big smile.

"Going up?"

"Maybe later," Quillan told her.

Trudy looked at him as if she had been slapped. Her eyes filled with angry tears. She pulled the door shut.

"You always go up for her, huh?" Lyons asked Quillan. He tossed him the bag of kumquats. "Fill your mouth. Don't chew, don't swallow. Just keep 'em in your mouth."

Quillan stared. "You're kidding."

Lyons pointed the Dan Wesson at his captive's skull. He snapped the safety. "Snack bar. Before the movie."

Quillan slowly filled his mouth with the kumquats. Lyons waited and then produced his videocassette. He held it up for a quick inspection, as if that kind of validation were required, and then inserted it into the VCR. He said, "This is called 'Manila Time.' You're the star."

The TV's wide screen flashed with the Jag's headlights. Lyons watched Quillan. The whole time, the whole run, he didn't watch the video. He didn't have to. He had watched it a dozen times already. He knew it by heart. Every scene memorized.

The Jag coming. Quillan getting out, waiting. The Jag's driver, unseen, staying inside. The border patrol wagon coming. Primitivo getting out, smiling. The border patrol wagon leaving. Quillan killing Primitivo, four rapid shots. Quillan putting the body in the raft. Quillan sending the body out into the Tijuana Slough.

Quillan stared, unable to speak. Lyons, watching Quillan, not the video, thought Quillan's eyes would have to speak for him. Lyons had done this many times before. He would put a gun to a man's head, force him to fill his mouth, stuff in an orange, or an apple like a pig, and then make him watch something intensely personal unfold. Watch someone fuck his woman. Or harm someone dear. Always, the eyes told Lyons what he wanted to know. They told him what he could do. The liberties he could take.

Not this time though. Quillan's wolf eyes showed nothing. They were empty. Lyons thought they would show surprise and fear and desperation, and, if he were lucky, the willingness to do anything, to pay any price. But he saw nothing like that. There was nothing there. Empty, dead eyes.

Quillan spat the kumquats out. They scattered across the bedroom floor like orange marbles from a child's sack.

Lyons looked at them, rattled. He had an almost overpowering urge to break and run.

"You've got the wrong fellah," Quillan said. "Sorry." He rubbed his mouth. "I'm not buying." He said, "I'd like to, understand? But I haven't got the kind of money you want. I've got a few thousand dollars, I was saving it for a trip, to see my maw." He said, "You want to settle for that?"

Lyons shook his head. He was rattled and he didn't trust himself to answer. His brain was screaming. The chance of a lifetime, and he pulled a pauper? No, damn it. *No!*

"Trudy!" he yelled. "I need a jacket out here. Any kind of jacket. Pick a jacket, throw it out. You hear?!"

The closet door opened. A cashmere sport jacket was flung out. Lyons retrieved it and gave it to Quillan.

"What's this prove?"

"Put it on."

Quillan removed his bomber jacket. He pushed into the cashmere. It was a perfect tailored fit.

"I didn't know this," Quillan said calmly. He looked at himself. "I guess we're the same size."

"You and Morley? Amazing."

"I don't think it qualifies as that. He's average build. I'm average build. What's so amazing about that?"

"Trudy!" Lyons shouted. "I want a shoe. Any shoe. Pick a shoe."

The closet door opened and a tasseled loafer came flying out. Lyons kicked it to Quillan.

"This is ridiculous."

"Put it on."

Quillan unlaced a sneaker.

"Two average, *normal* guys," Lyons said shrilly. "One size fits all. You wear the same underwear. You fuck the same retard. The same loopy fuck? Is that what you're saying? You disgust me."

Quillan didn't look at him. He got out of the sneaker. He put it aside. He put on the loafer. Another perfect fit. "I didn't know this," Quillan said, but his heart wasn't in it. There was some dead time and then he gave up. "Okay. How much?"

Lyons didn't know. He wasn't sure. He knew, whatever he asked, he'd have to stay with it though. He couldn't come down, back off. He could never retreat. Not with this sonofabitch. This cold cocksucker.

"How much?"

Lyons had been planning to ask for two hundred thousand. Cash, small bills, fives, tens, twenties, no sequential serial numbers, circulated and recirculated.

"Damn you! How much?!"

"A million."

Quillan laughed now. "A million? What the hell you smoking? You know what you can do." He said, "Fuck you."

"No. *Fuck you,* Nick. You're the fuckee here. I'm the fucker and you're the fuckee. The fuckee/payee."

"Fuck you."

"Fuck you!" Lyons said shrilly. "I've got you by the nuts, and I can mush 'em, motherfucker. I can take you in and I can charge you with murder and there's no way you can beat the rap. No possible way. You're dead." He stopped to get his breath. He had difficulty regaining control. He waited for a moment. "Unless that's all your life is worth, don't offer me small change, Nick. Get with the program."

"A cop millionaire? You're too greedy. People will notice."

"I've got to split it with my partner."

"You got a partner?"

"You watch TV?" Lyons demanded. He had forgotten to mention Donahoo. "All cops have partners." He was grinning again. He was enjoying himself. He was over the hump. "Shit, he's even real, Nick. He's not your cardboard Morley."

Quillan slanted a look at him. He didn't say anything.

"What is it? Have we got a deal?"

"Yeah."

"Good." Lyons took a breath. One last hurdle. He had to make it sound convincing that time was of the essence. "Nick, I'm going to need some money like *now*, understand? The video is my only chip. If you decide to screw me, I can't turn it in late, after the fact, say, 'Look what I found.' I've got to turn it in today or I can't turn it in at all. I turn it in late, they're gonna say, 'Hey, something smells here, you got a snuff tape, how come it's late? So there's no way I can do that. Today I've got an excuse. I slept in? But it's the last day it works, Nick. Tomorrow it won't buy me a doughnut."

Quillan looked at him.

"I *will* turn it in though," Lyons assured him. "If you fuck me, I will fuck you. Believe it."

"You need a down payment?"

"Exactly."

"How much?"

Lyons considered. There was the vault in the house. And there'd be bank accounts. More than one. He thought he'd go for his original figure. If the thing started to fall apart, he wouldn't have to come back. He'd just keep going. "Two hundred thousand."

"Today?"

"This morning. By noon. We've got a couple hours to put it all together. I'm happy. You're happy."

Quillan was silent for a while. "The rest?"

"This week. By Friday."

"And I get?"

"The video and all copies."

"I'm supposed to trust you?"

"What do I want with a copy? If I'm ever caught with it, I go to jail. I don't want a copy."

Quillan made a gesture of surrender.

"Now, just a couple loose ends," Lyons said, getting the cassette. "I don't want any surprises. Who drove you to the slough?"

"You can't see him in the video. What's the difference?"

"Who is he?"

"My main man."

"What's his name?"

"Taylor. Jimmy Taylor."

"Okay. And the border patrol?"

"Chaffee. Willard Chaffee."

"Just the one?"

"Yeah. Just him."

"If I ran a check, his name would come up, Willard Chaffee?"

"Yeah. No surprises. What should I know about your partner?"

"First, he's watching you," Lyons said, grinning. "Last, don't do anything to make him mad." He put away the big Dan Wesson. Four pounds of overkill. "Seriously, he's not like you and me, Nick. He's mean."

Trudy yanked open the closet door. She was pissed.

"I'm going down," Quillan told her. He managed a thin smile.

Wow, this was so great, Chip Lyons thought. A million bucks. He was going to live a fairy-tale life. He'd known it since the loafer fit, huh? He knew how the prince felt with Cinderella.

FOUR

The Veterans Affairs Medical Center in La Jolla is atop a hill. From the upper floors, depending on which wing, what pod, you can see, if not forever, a long way. You can see across the garment of the earth. Its button forests and its ribbon canyons. Washed by the sea and placed to dry in the sun. Back fresh from heaven's laundry room. A bright new uniform for your last parade. You can think about wearing it, how it will look on you, under pewter sky and gunpowder clouds, the earth's green mantle, those buttons and ribbons, the last decorations you're going to get. This is a teaching hospital, and one of the things it teaches, by its nature, is how to die.

Father Charlie was slowly learning. He'd been at it for two

months. He'd get it right soon though, Donahoo thought. He was so frail, a broken-bowl skull on scattered twigs, sucked together by yellow wrinkled paper flesh, he'd pass any day now. He, Donahoo, he would come into this gray room, and the gray bed would be empty. The bowl and the twigs would be gone. There'd be new sheets and they'd be turned down. Waiting for another soldier.

Donahoo stood staring. This waste, it had looked like him once. The big head, the big hands, the big feet. The arrogance and the purpose. Also, an eye for the ladies, despite his vows. A regular cuckolder finally denied a parish. He, Donahoo, had been almost a man when his mother, Kathleen, also on her deathbed, confessed that the cocky corporal in the faded photograph wasn't his father, and that the responsibility and obligation actually lay with a certain priest.

"How's your love life?" Father Charlie asked. A standard question. It really worried him.

"What love life?" Donahoo said, also standard. "Where am I gonna find a good woman these days? You remember when you had to put a ring on her finger? Now she wants it in her left tit. I dunno."

Bird, the nurse, a very pretty blonde, a large presence in a slight body, arched an eyebrow while pushing her wares. "You gotta take your meds now."

Donahoo looked at the pile of pills in the little white paper bucket. Cardizem 60 for Charlie's wayward blood pressure. Lithium 300 for his sinking spirits. Codeine 30 for the pain.

"You gotta take 'em," Bird said. "While I'm here." She was small, wiry, intense. She reminded Donahoo of Chip Lyons. That kind of manic commitment to the task at hand. She wasn't going anywhere until the pills did. She was just like Chip Lyons. The Chipper and the Chirper, Donahoo thought. "Open wide."

Father Charlie took his medicine. The bunch, one gulp. He drank the water only because it was there. He didn't need it to wash things down. A Catholic gullet, Donahoo thought. Swallow anything.

"Good boy."

"I try."

Bird did a few unnecessary things. A straightened magazine, a crumpled candy wrapper in the wastebasket, an adjustment for the curtain that pulled around the bed.

Donahoo, watching, thought he had a dirty mind. Here, of all places, he was imagining her sitting on his finger, and he was making her sing for him. A happy little Bird, singing his tune. She'd have the pipes. He'd bang the drum.

She looked at him and left. In parting, an anguished look.

There was no way to save Charlie. No cure for old age. He was there because he'd been a chaplain for a while. And because the monsignor didn't want him within four miles of a nun.

Donahoo waited for the door to pull shut. Then he got out the flask. Produced it ceremoniously. Old Crow. Poured a quick two fingers, which he downed fast. Poured a smaller portion, which he left. Put the flask away. All fast.

Charlie reached for his gladly. He said, a lie, "Better days." The whiskey went down like the pills. Sure as his deceit.

Donahoo washed the glass. The Old Crow was part of the ritual of their visits. They needed something to mark the occasion. Whiskey, like good food, forbidden, was a foregone choice. It legitimately helped Donahoo. It offered the illusion of helping Charlie. It couldn't, not at this stage, harm him.

"Actually, there could be some fire left," Donahoo said, returning with the glass. He put it on the nightstand. Normally, he could tell lies with the rest of them, the small lies that suited the occasion, but he didn't lie to Charlie anymore. He said, "I met a lady last night. Rosie Gestring, AKA the Snake, AKA the Wham Bam Ice Trail."

"Sounds like a crook."

"Maybe she is," Donahoo admitted, wondering, the first time, about that. Maybe, maybe not. Chip Lyons, twirling through his make-believe police state, handed out aliases like lollipops at Halloween. Most everybody got one. "Anyway, I liked her." He considered briefly. The twigs hadn't stirred. "It's been a long time since I liked anybody. I was, you know, wondering if that was permanent—the condition?—running empty? And, uh . . ." This was hard for him. "I guess I was glad to find out that I'm still capable."

"Of love?"

"Of liking somebody."

Charlie finally looked at him. Raisin eyes shifting in raisin skin. Barely peering above their sockets. "Maybe it's just a hard-on?"

Donahoo shook his head. He knew the difference. He could get to The Star Bar, drink their buck-and-a-half bourbon. He could let the girls sit in his lap, hold them by their hard little tits. He could make them squeal. Make them ask, Watcha want, you beeg bugger, Donna-who?

"You've been misled before."

"Naw. I could always tell."

"What's this *like* business?" Charlie said, a new direction. "You don't have to, you know. Love thy neighbor, that's a crock. Your neighbor can be a jerk. You've got a cop's disease, wanting to like people. You meet so much scum, people you hate, you get carried away, wanting to compensate, you start making bad choices. You don't have to like anybody. It's not required."

"Sermon for the day?"

Charlie sighed softly. A hand fluttered in dismissal.

"Hey, I listen to your problems," Donahoo complained. He settled in the big chair he'd brought in specially for himself. He pretended to be looking for some list he'd made. "The eggs taste like turnips. You can't see Mount Soledad. You can't get a nurse to wash your peenie."

"I never said that."

"You got somebody?"

Charlie smiled. "What does she look like?"

"Pretty."

"Not beautiful?"

No, Donahoo thought. Monica was beautiful. Everybody thought so. Everybody said so. People would come up to her, strangers in the supermarket, and they would say, "Pardon me, but . . ." and they would tell her she was the most beautiful woman they had ever seen.

"Okay. Sexy?"

"Yeah. But not especially. That's not it."

"Then what? Personality?"

No, Donahoo thought again. Hardly. But his mind was still on the previous question. Presh Logan, she was the siren. The mysterious, enchanting, *electric* Madame Zola. The sex machine. Inside, there was a motor somewhere, batteries. She had shown him the switch. Put his hand there.

"Well? What is it?"

Donahoo didn't know. In his whole life he'd been happy, *satisfied*, with two women. Monica, who had been his wife, and Presh Logan, who, very briefly, had been his dream lover. Two women, and they weren't coming back. Unlike him, they'd found their way, and their places. Monica, beautiful Monica, was sitting in a rocking chair, holding a cat, looking in the mirror. Presh Logan was dating an apartment manager who didn't carry a gun. Both were happy. Or at least happi*er*.

"You're not gonna tell me it's her mind?"

"I don't think so," Donahoo said, smiling. "We barely spoke." He was suddenly uncomfortable. "It was, you know .." He tried to think. He gave up. "Anyway, it doesn't matter. She's Chip Lyons's girl. I don't even know why I'm telling you this. She's Chip Lyons's girl."

"You're serious?"

"Yeah. I met her with him. Last night, after a stakeout. This morning, actually. We dropped in."

"Jesus Christ."

"These things happen."

"She's sleeping with him?"

"I don't know how much sleep they get."

"You're a goddamn menace."

"All I said was I liked her."

"Why?"

Donahoo didn't know. He got out the flask. What did he see in Rosie Gestring? Rosie the Snake, the Wham Bam Ice Trail? He said, "If I had to describe her, I'd say she was full of fire, and anger and need. Does that explain it?"

"Promise me something," Charlie answered. He sounded like an old Victrola. Worn record, scratchy needle, and he wanted rewinding. "You've got to promise me something."

"Name it," Donahoo said, although he had already promised too much. He had promised to come here every day, and he had promised, sworn an oath, to be there when the old man died.

"Tommy," Charlie said. He sounded delirious now. "These women. They're tearing you apart. They're killing you." He said seriously, "Give your word. No more women. Can you do that, Tommy? No more women."

"Sure," Donahoo said. He pronounced it *shoor*. He thought it didn't count if you said it that way. It didn't, did it? He wondered as soon as he said it. If he could cheat a dying old man that way. And who would punish him? And how?

The mindless questions clawed at him. The religion he denied and the fear of being wrong that would never quite go away. After this, Donahoo thought, looking at the begging bowl, he wouldn't know any more priests.

FIVE

Quillan clung fiercely to Trudy Goody. Their lovemaking was over, but he couldn't bear to release her. She was, he thought, the one sure thing in his world, which was in dark danger. He clung to her, and when she stirred, he said, "They weren't babies."

"You always say that," Trudy answered wistfully, in a tired whisper. "Every time."

"You believe me?"

"Yes."

Quillan, holding her, his lean muscular arms enfolding her softness, wondered if she really did. He thought, as always, that you'd have to be there, like he had been there, thinking, *knowing*, that every day was your last day, and watching the locals do it. The boys, they were fifteen, maybe through to twenty, they didn't last much longer than that, and the girls—well, yeah, they were maybe twelve and up, huh? But they were *not* babies.

Trudy stirred again. "You want anything?"

Yeah, Quillan thought. Exoneration. His mind was in a little grass shack, in Tegucigalpa, in Honduras. It was fixed on the burning image of his pal, Taylor, who was under orders to kill him, Quillan. The CIA brass thought it unseeming that one of their faux colonels was ravaging underage girls. He, Quillan, had been sent down to torture and kill, not to rape and pillage. He'd had plenty of time to get it straight.

Taylor let him off. He killed another guy, put him in what was supposed to be Quillan's grave. He showed him, Quillan, how to get to Belize, and where to catch a boat that was going to Jamaica. Taylor, his pal. Taylor, who, earlier, had sprung him from a bamboo cage in Vietnam. He owed Taylor.

Quillan finally let go. He said, "Everybody was doing it."

"I know, honey," Trudy told him. "I know."

Quillan rolled away and looked up at the enormous ceiling fan slowly rotating above them. They were still but they seemed to move. They flicked around in the mirrored blades.

"You're sure?" She was asking again if he wanted anything.

"No, I'm okay."

Trudy left the bed. A small, thin, soft black girl with touseled dreadlocks and a crooked smile. She was pretty, very pretty, but not a beauty, Quillan thought. She was smart but not wise. Faithful but not honest. He wondered why he wanted her so badly. Why he put up with all her craziness. Didn't mind her addictions.

The sex? Naw, Quillan thought, watching her black ass escape. She was actually running. She vanished around a corner. No, the sex was average. On a scale of a thousand, five hundred. It was something else. The way he felt when he was with her. Safe.

Maybe that was love, huh? Quillan thought. Safety? Safe in the arms of your lover—who said that? He didn't know but he thought it was true and he was sure it applied to him. He'd taken a lot of women, young and old, big and small. Some beauties and some so ugly there wasn't a word for it. He'd also—a penchant arrived at late in life—gone to the sheets with some males of the species. But he'd never felt safe. Never felt conscious of it as a part of the act.

Trudy was different. He couldn't explain why. All he knew, he went in her, and he was safe there. In Trudy Goody.

Love? Maybe, Quillan thought. Why not? He had never been in love before. Maybe it was about time.

Even at a great distance he could hear the shower suddenly pounding. There were no doors between bedroom and bathrooms. There were just crooked halls. He accepted the need for perimeter doors but had as few as possible inside. He didn't like doors. In Vietnam, he'd been in that cage, the bamboo cage, for a long time, and he'd sat a mere two feet away from the door. He was so hungry sometimes he'd pick through bird droppings for undigested seeds. But what he remembered most about that cage—what he hated most—was the door and the closeness of it.

Quillan got up. He pulled on a silk robe. He'd thought that he'd come a long way. The Green Berets in 'Nam. The CIA in Central America. Down and out in the good old USA. And now, back on top, an emerging crime lord in a city so ripe for the picking, it almost made your heart stop. He was going to be king of the hill. He was going to be the General. Hell, he *was* the General.

Yeah, Quillan thought. And then some prick cop with a big nose and a glass eye walks in and spoils it all. Some prick cop and his prick partner hiding in the weeds. With a video that crucified him.

He went to the bar, which consisted of a bag of ice, a bottle of Johnnie Walker Black Label. He fixed a drink. He could feel the nails in his hands. The spike holding his feet. Aw, Jesus, he thought. How do I get off this cross?

He wandered into the bathroom. Trudy Goody poked her head from the shower. She looked at him, sharing his bewilderment, his pain.

"You gonna use Taylor?" Trudy asked.

Quillan nodded. He always used Taylor.

SIX

The promised rain was a mist. It couldn't be seen, but with the car window down, Donahoo could feel it on his face, and it gathered, eventually, on the windshield. He had the wipers on Mist. He'd have had them on something slower if the Crown Victoria had something slower. It was a light mist.

Donahoo wanted it to rain. Up on the hill, at the VA, it had smelled like rain, he was sure it was going to rain, he'd gone home and gotten his raincoat, but it hadn't rained. If it rained, it might clean the place up, he thought, wash some of the shit away, but this wasn't rain, it was mist. Donahoo wondered if he was ever going to get what he wanted. He was still fiddling with the Chip Lyons riddle. Something missing or something wrong. Maybe both?

"Most people, they're losers," Lyons was saying from under his baseball cap. "They're doing nothing and they're going nowhere. They've built traps for themselves. You know why?"

"Not really," Donahoo admitted. He didn't have any idea. There was a time, he had a couple of theories, but they were cheese now, they had a lot of holes in them. He didn't know. He moved slowly in inchmeal traffic. The Gaslamp Quarter was in strangled flux. Day workers were heading out. Early Bird diners were heading in.

"They won't take a chance."

That's it? Donahoo smiled. More cheese. He should have smelled it coming. The Chipper was a chance taker. He'd step in front of a train just to annoy the brakeman.

"It's true," Lyons said. "You look out there, polyglot world, you think it's black and white, red, brown, but there's just one color, yellow. They're afraid, most of them. They haven't got the balls for a do-or-die run. So they're stuck."

"I guess," Donahoo said. He didn't feel like arguing.

"I know."

Donahoo, letting it go, he didn't want to argue, wondered how Chip Lyons knew so much when he, Donahoo, didn't know anything. He used to know some things, but not anymore, he thought. He used to know about good times/bad times. Not anymore. Now they all sort of just melded. You had to pick moments, not times, and you had to be quick about it, else they'd be gone. He used to know about women. Not anymore. He'd somehow forgotten how to make them happy. Had somehow forgotten how that worked. All he knew, at the moment, was what he was doing, which was looking for Buddy Salinas. The empty night at the Tijuana Slough still annoyed him. He had a question for him. You miserable cockroach snitch. How come nobody showed?

"Life, it's to be lived, enjoyed," Lyons pronounced. He felt blindly for the orchid in his lapel, confirming that it was still present. Vanda burgeffii, a hybrid. He wouldn't say where he got it. "You ever read that poem 'Next Time I'd Pick More Daisies'? That's my Bible." The baseball cap slipped lower. "I've got some time coming, you know, vacation? I thought I'd take it. You're not gonna miss me, are you? Tell me you're not gonna miss me."

"I'm not gonna miss you," Donahoo said. He took the Crown Victoria on a wide turn that set it east on E Street from Horton Plaza. He was working a grid. Back and forth and up and down in the Gaslamp Quarter. First, Second, Third, etc. D, E, F, G, etc. "But I miss you now."

Chip Lyons, in the slump position, baseball cap pulled over baseball nose, wondering about the worst/best things in life, he might be present physically, but his mind hadn't reported for duty. Donahoo thought he must be playing somewhere with the sugar plum fairies. He was goofing off major supreme paramount big-time. "You wanta tell me about it?"

"Huh?"

"What it's like there?" Donahoo said. "Paradise, while I'm stuck here, driving a Ford? What are you doing now? Willing women. Nymphomaniacs. While the best I'm gonna do, all night, *maybe,* is Buddy Salinas. Maybe you'd like to tell me, what it's like in paradise, Chippie?"

"Chipp*er.*"

"Okay. But what's it like?"

"I was thinking about Rosie the Snake G-String," Lyons said, pushing up. He took off his baseball cap and shoved it on the dash. He looked like he didn't appreciate being interrupted. He straightened his thinning dirty-blond hair. He sniffed and then he brightened. "Now, there's a fuck, Tommy. Her cunt's so hot, it could jump-start a tuna boat."

Shoor, Donahoo thought. The comment, the idea, annoyed and then angered him. The truth was, when he hadn't been thinking totally about Buddy, he'd been thinking, sometimes, about Rosie Gestring. She had been briefly, before she disappeared with Lyons, a candle in the night. He had, yes, warmed to her presence. He said, almost against his will, "I thought you said she was an ice trail?"

"For other guys."

"Fuck."

"All the time."

Shoor, Donahoo thought again, and now he was hurting. He closed his mind to an unwanted picture. Rosie Gestring with Chip Lyons. The sex act. Variations of. Jesus Christ, he thought. It was time he got his own woman. He was losing it. He was living in the past. All he had was fucking memories. His ex-wife, Monica. His last—and final?—love, Presh Logan. He slept with them in his dreams. Fucking memories. He said, "Are you ready to go to work?"

Lyons smiled without conviction. He got his baseball cap and put it back on. He looked around, a general adjustment, not really interested. He said, "Yeah, yeah. Buddy Salinas. Where art thou, Buddy?"

Donahoo checked his watch. They'd come on at four, another night shift. It was ten to five. Almost an hour for the hotshot to wake up. Normally, you couldn't hold him down with bricks. Normally, he was out of control.

"Gimme a minute," Lyons said, aware of the scrutiny. "We'll get settled here. I know this guy . . ." He made a show of adjusting his jacket to hide the Dan Wesson 744V .44 Magnum. "He's got a route, you know? Here, there. He always goes to the same places. But the problem is, it's at different times."

Donahoo waited. He could use the help. He'd been driving around in circles. The Gaslamp Quarter revisited. And revisited again. The city's initial site, it wasn't a large area, about eight blocks deep, six wide, but it had a lot happening, it was experiencing a rebirth. A hundred or so ornate turn-of-the-century brick buildings had been restored and dozens more were being worked on. It bustled with enterprise, swarmed with life. Professional offices, lawyers, architects, engineers. Hotels and work/live lofts. Restaurants, cafés, bistros. Shops and boutiques, art galleries, bookstores, antique shops, thrifts. Produce warehouses and farmers markets. Donahoo thought it was the most vital place in the city, he liked it, enjoyed it. It had a special look, feel, and flavor. It reminded him of Greenwich Village and Bourbon Street. The plight of the displaced bothered him though. Before restoration, the Quarter had been skid, row harboring the dregs of society, and now they were being forced out—the price of a bed kept going up—but there was no place for them to go. They were sleeping in doorways. They were standing on corners asking for change. They were wandering around dazed and talking to themselves. Donahoo, driving in circles, kept seeing more and more of them, and he wondered what the plan was, were they supposed to wait them out? Keep squeezing the knot tighter, harder, and they'd die? That could be the plan. There had to be a plan, and that could be it. Or, another possibility, maybe a better plan, they were under control, so just give them enough to exist, keep them as color? Maybe they were doing that. Maybe, on the Model-T-Ford tours, they pointed them out as attractions, the sad people and the bad people, the raving drunk gutter preachers, the five-dollar hookers. The nickel beggars and the crumb snatchers. The car parkers. They were all here, and they were colorful. He'd seen a guy with a propellor on his head. But he hadn't seen Buddy.

"We been to Pleasureland Peeps?"

Donahoo swore. "Yeah, and we've been to the Foxy. Wake up, willya?"

"Really?" Lyons laughed. "Take it easy. We're gonna get settled here . . ." He frowned. "Wait a sec. Wait a sec. What day is this?"

"Monday."

"*Monday?*" Another laugh. "Well, we're fucked. He's not here Monday. He's never here Monday."

Donahoo thought, Here it comes. The bugger, he's been blowing this off, and now he's going to torpedo it?

"Monday he's got a ballet lesson."

Donahoo looked at him. It was so ridiculous, it was possible. Propellors were possible. "Ballet? Bullshit."

"No. Really." Lyons grinned. "You read his file? He's a fag, acey-deucy. Fags, they like to tippy-toe." He laughed. "It keeps 'em higher off the ground. The rats outa their ass."

"That's why?"

"Yeah. They hate rats. Buddy, I was trying to make him talk once, I got this rat, you know, I was shoving it up there, and he went absolutely fucking crazy. He freaked . . ." Lyons was suddenly holding the Dan Wesson 744V. "Pull over."

Donahoo pulled over.

"You see those temporary signs over there?" Lyons asked. "Tow away zone, no parking, tree trimming?" He asked, "What else do you see?"

Donahoo took a moment. "No trees."

"No trees," Lyons repeated. He got out of the car. "Let's check it out." He was holding the 744V like a spear. It was pointed in the air.

Donahoo looked around. E at Sixth, across from the Jewelers Exchange. Trees all along E, but not for the half block stretch fronting the Exchange. Towaway signs there, on the sidewalk. A cleared getaway lane in rush hour traffic? Donahoo reached for the radio. The Crown Victoria's windshield exploded. The sound came a nanosecond later. Automatic assault weapon.

Chip Lyons was shouting, *"Cover me!"*

Donahoo rolled out of the car, out into the street, away from the direction of fire, which had come from the Sixth Street side of the Exchange. He unholstered his Colt Model Python .357 Magnum. "Where the hell are you?!"

"I'm going in!"

"Don't!" Donahoo shouted. "Stay out! Take cover!"

No response. Donahoo was still rolling. The Crown Victoria was still taking fire. He went around a big Mercedes 420SEL that had braked to a stop. He came up on the other side. The driver, a woman, was frozen stiff. He reached in and pulled her out. He held her low, pushed her away, back down the street, into the cover of the cars to the rear. All traffic had stopped. Vehicles were being abandoned. People were running, yelling. E was clogged at Sixth.

No movement. Sixth Avenue, one way from the north, was also jamming up. The Crown Victoria was shredded. The automatic weapon fire stopped.

"Chipper?" Donahoo called. No response.

Donahoo peered over the hood of the car he had commandeered. Lyons was a moving target in the Mercedes insignia. He was running into the middle of the intersection, no cover. He was still holding the 744V like he was going to throw it.

"*Chipper!*" Donahoo screamed. It was a suicide run.

The Exchange's E Street–side door kicked open. A man came out wearing a black jump suit and a ski mask. He was carrying an automatic rifle. He was dragging a big canvas bag. He looked around desperately. His vision was impaired by the ski mask.

Lyons reacted first. He kneeled, fired. The man went down like he'd been hit by a cannon. The rifle clattered on the sidewalk.

"The pump!" Lyons exulted. He resumed his forward movement. The 744V was moving up and down like a barbell. "I got him in the pump!"

Donahoo slid into the Mercedes. The key was still in the ignition. The motor was running. He got behind the wheel and slowly eased toward the intersection. He had to do something. He was sure there were others. The initial fire had come from the south, maybe from the Exchange, but more likely from the street, from Sixth. The downed gunman couldn't have moved from one place to the other that fast. So there was at least one other guy. He might have fired from the building, but, more likely, from the street. It was low fire.

He moved closer to the intersection. He thought he should have returned to the Crown Victoria, to the radio, and then immediately dismissed the idea; the riddled Ford was an established target. He was safer starting over with the Mercedes. He looked around for a black-and-white. Normally, the Quarter was filled with them. But, of course, not now. They'd be selling tickets before they saw a black-and-white.

Sixth Avenue traffic was shut down. The lead vehicles in each of the street's three one-way lanes had been abandoned. He looked north down the block for some sign of disturbance. Drivers were either holding in their vehicles or out on the street and moving away. The to-be-expected jam. The usual cars, pickups, vans. A couple delivery trucks. An armored car.

He scanned the west wall of the Jewelers Exchange. Eight floors. At least a hundred windows. The other guy/guys could be anywhere. Donahoo felt vulnerable. But not as exposed as Chip Lyons. Lyons was walking over to his kill. He was taking it slow, putting on a show. No protection, he could have been naked.

Hotshot, Donahoo thought, looking around, studying the traffic jam, silently counting the windows in the Exchange. Most of them were half open. All those places to shoot from. No lights on in the whole place. A dark, misty day but no lights. He hadn't noticed that before. There were lights on at the Plaza Suites. Lights at Mr. Neon, Inc. But the Exchange was dark. No power. Somebody had killed it. So we've got a gang here? We've got a fucking gang here, Chipper. He thought, armored car?

He looked back up Sixth. The armored car had moved out of the stalled traffic and onto the sidewalk. It was coming down the sidewalk, picking up speed, moving like a wayward tank. He shouted, "Armored car!"

Chip Lyons turned to face it. He squeezed off two quick shots. He was using a peashooter now. The armored car kept coming. It was going to get him and it was going to squash him.

Donahoo floored the Mercedes. The big sedan hit the armored car like it had been catapulted. Its front end closed like an accordion. The armored car fell on its side, then, slow motion, onto its roof, rear wheels spinning wildly.

Lyons was screaming, "Six o'clock! Six o'clock."

Donahoo got out of the wrecked Mercedes. He was rattled but okay. The air bag had taken the full impact for him. Lyons, holding his gun with both hands now, was swinging back and forth, working an arc from the armored car to the Exchange.

"Six o'clock!"

Donahoo had to get his bearings first. He looked at the armored car, which, the parts that he could see, the rear and a side door, remained closed. He looked at the Exchange. A second masked man had exited, leaving by the main entrance, on Sixth. He was holding a hostage as a shield, a young, terrified woman. He had an automatic rifle at the base of her skull.

The man shouted, "Back off or I kill her. I mean it. Back off!"

"I can make the shot," Lyons said, softly now.

Donahoo said, "No. That's an order."

"I can," Lyons insisted. "He won't expect it. He's not looking for it." He said urgently, "Distract him. Move away, get his attention. I can do it."

Donahoo pointed his Colt Python at Lyons. "I swear to Christ, hotshot. You kill the girl, I'll kill you."

Lyons grinned. "You don't have the nuts."

The man shouted, *"Back off!"* His weapon rammed at the base of the woman's skull, he moved along the building's wall, toward the corner, toward E Street. He was going to try for an abandoned car. The woman begged, "Help me!"

The man edged closer to a cluster of waiting cars. He was going to make it. "Back off, back off."

The woman was pleading, *"Don't shoot."*

Lyons fired and missed. The man disappeared behind a car. The woman remained in the open, screaming. Lyons probed, sighting over the 744V. He muttered, "What the fuck?" The shots came from nowhere. Two quick bursts. They ripped through his stomach. He gasped and fell.

Donahoo stepped over him, went past the overturned armored car, went out into the intersection for a better field of vision. He looked down the lines of stalled vehicles. The gunman was running away from him. He shot him in the back.

Now, suddenly, finally, there were cops all over, coming from all directions. They had Lyons's kill. They were circling the armored car. They were closing on the guy Donahoo had just shot. It was all over.

Chip Lyons was holding his stomach. Blood was running between his fingers. Donahoo went to him and looked at him. He knew immediately that nothing was going to save him. There were a lot of sirens now and one of them would be the paramedics, but they couldn't plug those holes. He closed his eyes in despair and anger. You idiot, he thought. You begged for it.

"Tommy," Chip Lyons whispered. "I'm outa here."

Donahoo kneeled beside him. "Don't talk now."

"Listen. I've fucked you."

"No. I'm okay."

"Listen . . ."

"Take it easy."

"I'm *dying*, asshole," Lyons said. The glass eye belonged in the skull of some carrion bird. "Listen."

Donahoo leaned closer. Lyons tried to speak, but he couldn't get the words out clearly. "Primitivo . . . hooli-gans . . ." He closed his eyes and gave up. He seemed to smile. "I'll . . . see you soon, Tommy."

Donahoo stared. He couldn't believe this had happened. Finally he felt for a pulse. Nothing. He took possession of the 744V. Then he reached over and took the orchid. He had wanted it all afternoon. It was strangely formed, and Chip Lyons, who would never pick another daisy, had claimed to have seen a lot of strange things in it. An alien from outer space, coming in on five wings, holding a shovel. He'd seen a bee and he'd seen a mermaid. He'd seen Elizabeth Taylor's enfolding bosom. It had a lot going for one flower. Donahue saw in it—you see what you see, he thought—a transmutation from plant to beast.

SEVEN

Donahoo, when it was over, went home to his cat, Oscar, and his solace, Old Crow. He didn't know where else to go or what else to do. Almost all of his friends were cops and he couldn't think of one who'd miss or mourn Chip Lyons. He didn't want to join them in a round of noncommiseration. There would be enough bad taste on display tomorrow. His other options were just as deficient. He had a favorite bar, the Waterfront, but it was a good-time place, inappropriate. There was Gus & Company, the Library, a chess tournament that never ended, but Donahoo wasn't capable of that kind of concentration tonight. He had some beaches, places he liked to walk, Garbage Reef, Wind 'n' Sea, Solana Beach, but he was physically exhausted too. There was no real refuge. And he didn't have a woman. Not anymore.

He was going a little crazy. Chip Lyons's last words kept hammering at him. *I've fucked you. I'll . . . see you soon.* The Chipper's absolute final statement, and the guy, he had said it like he meant it, Donahoo thought. The Chipper, he sounded serious. Like he really, truly, meant it, he wasn't kidding. It was scary hearing that kind of announcement from an about-to-be corpse. It made you wonder. Did he really know something? Donahoo thought it shouldn't bother him. A guy, he's going away, he might say anything, it could mean nothing. Maybe he just wants to shake your tree one last time. It shouldn't bother him, but it did. The Chipper, he could be going to hell, Donahoo thought. He'd been a bad cop. He was a candidate.

Donahoo wondered. He didn't believe in hell. He had bagged that as a bad idea a long time ago. It didn't seem to help at the moment though. In times of crisis, put to the test, the same shabby question revisited. What if he were wrong?

Yeah, he was going just a little crazy, Donahoo thought. He was worried that the Chipper knew something he didn't know. He was worried, if he was supposed to join him, what it said on the ticket.

Home was the Arlington, an aging three-story stucco apartment building on a canyon in Uptown, a small neighborhood north of Balboa Park, skirting Hillcrest. Donahoo had lived there for three years, since his divorce, choosing it mainly because the rent was reasonable. He didn't see much of his sergeant's pay. Monica had demanded, and had somehow been awarded, substantial alimony. He also felt obliged to allot a monthly stipend to Charlie. Something had to give, and he wasn't home much anyway, it was mostly to sleep, so he had settled on the Arlington. The other reason he had chosen it, California 163 twisted through the canyon, and there was easy access, on/off, north/south, within a block either way. He was minutes from downtown or connections with several interstates, I-5, I-8, and I-15. The farthest place he ever wanted to go was under an hour. There was a lot of water. San Diego Bay, Mission Bay, and the open sea from Border Field State Park to Oceanside harbor.

Hundreds of beaches, Imperial to Cardiff-by-the-Sea. Miles and miles of canyons to explore. Tecolote, and San Clemente, and Los Penasquitos. There was the vastness of Mission Trails Regional Park and Cleveland National Forest. There was Mexico. Tijuana and Baja. He was at the hub of a small but ample universe.

"Pussy," Donahoo said to Oscar, going straight by to the wheezing fridge. He hauled the Old Crow out of the freezer. He found a glass and poured himself a double. He drank it standing there. He wondered how he might have done it better. He went down the list. Chip Lyons, there had been no saving him, that kamikaze. The Chipper, he was electric, high-voltage, and there wasn't any switch, no plug. You couldn't stop him. You had to kill him. Somebody did.

Donahoo went down the list. Shooting a guy in the back. Some ex-marine named Harold Powell. In the back and through a lung. Well, Donahoo thought if Powell had been coming at him, he'd have shot him in the front. It was Powell's choice. Donahoo thought he could have tried for the knees, but that was a long shot. He had to stop the guy. He was a robber, a kidnapper, a killer. That put him on the Most Wanted. Donahoo went down the list. Maybe the Mercedes 450SEL? He might have screwed up there.

Yeah, but who cares? Donahoo decided. What could they do? They could sue. They couldn't send him anywhere he didn't want to go. He put his mind to the other thing that was really bothering him. He ought to make a special effort to reach Rosie the Snake G-string. He had tried to phone her from the hospital but she wasn't listed in Information. He'd have asked a squad car to go around but he didn't know where to send it. He didn't know her address, he didn't know the name of her street. Lyons had been driving. He hadn't paid any attention. He just knew she was on a canyon somewhere in National City. He didn't know if she watched the news. If she watched the news, she knew Chip Lyons was dead. If she didn't, maybe she didn't know. He thought somebody ought to tell her. She might want to know. She might care. Donahoo thought that was why he should try to get in touch with her. She might care.

The phone rang. Donahoo screened. It was Monica. "Tommy? Are you okay? Jesus Christ. I just saw it on the news. Call me."

Donahoo stood drinking and staring at the phone. Don't worry, li'l darling. The alimony is intact. Two more years. He thought he ought to check his messages. The red light was flashing. There might be a call from Presh. It was possible. She might have seen the news too. Might have seen it and might have wondered. Might have cared?

Shoor, Donahoo thought. He finished his drink, poured another. He set it aside and got out of his coat. He put the coat on the sofa. He didn't hang it up anymore. There wasn't anybody to tell him to do that. He was getting messier all the time. He barely kept in underwear.

He looked for the orchid. It was gone. He must have let go of it somewhere, probably at Mercy Hospital, there'd been a crowd in Emergency, or maybe he'd lost it later at Police Administrative Headquarters. He'd been carrying it in his hand, he didn't want it crushed. He must have put it down somewhere. The wild rush of events?

The loss dismayed him. He had been planning to press it in a book, if an orchid could be pressed. He had intended to put it in the fridge and then look that up, how to preserve an orchid. He had wanted to do that tonight. It was how he wanted to spend the evening, quietly, with Oscar, and Old Crow, and Vanda burgeffii, from the Far East. The loss left him suddenly alone. He was looking for something structured. He didn't know what was wrong with him, he ought to be in some sort of mourning, somebody he had known, worked with, was dead, he should feel bad about that, but what he felt was free. He didn't have to play nursemaid anymore.

Jesus, he thought. He had to stay put. If he went somewhere, he really could get crazy, start celebrating, get drunk, have a party. He had to stay. He winced as he looked around the small studio, which, because of its size, appeared to be in more disarray than it actually was. There was just the one room, a square box. All the wall space was in use. Entry door, fireplace, bar kitchen, bookcase/entertainment center, door to bathroom, Murphy bed, slider to balcony. Monica, the one time she'd been over, to see what damage she had wrought, had dismissed it with a word, *inadequate*. Donahoo had to admit it wouldn't work except for the high ceiling and the expansive view. The balcony hung over the canyon wall that slid into a semitropical forest at the north side of Balboa Park. He could cook a hot dog out there and pretend he was in Costa Rica.

The phone rang. Donahoo screened. It was Barney, a neighbor, upstairs. "Donahoo? Are you screening? I know you're there. I've got some radishes for you. I'm coming down."

Donahoo pushed the rewind and started at the beginning. The whole squad reported in a row. Gomez, drunk, "I love you, amigo." Montrose, "Whoa, I dunno, Sarge. Take care." Palmer, "Hey, the fucker, he deserved it, right? See you tomorrow." Cominsky with a worn Chinese proverb, "It is better to light a candle than to curse the darkness." There also was a call from Lewis, the captain, Investigations, to whom Donahoo reported when he wasn't reporting to Police Chief Saperstein. Lewis had shown up at Mercy Hospital. Now he was saying, "Me again. We've got an eight o'clock with Saperstein. Be early." Monica's call was next. Donahoo killed the tape. No Presh.

Presh Logan, AKA Madame Zola. Donahoo had met her the year before, he'd been working a case, the Balboa Firefly, in her neighborhood, Balboa Park. They'd gotten together and he'd taught her, at her request, how to shoot. The very next day, no other choice, she had been forced to use that newfound skill. She had shot and killed a man. She hated having to do that. She suddenly hated guns. She hated people who used them. She couldn't be with a cop. And she left. End of story.

Well, not exactly the end, Donahoo thought. He'd known her only long enough to fall in love. He'd known only the good parts, none of the bad. So when he lost her, it was total loss. There was no balance to the thing. It was all sorrow.

"You know why it hurts so bad?" Donahoo told the cat, Oscar, which had been Monica's cat. "They give you something marvelous and then they take it away. It's like, you know, you're a bird, and they give you the sky, and then they take it away. Let me put this on your level. If they gave you tuna, took it away, how would you feel? Would you settle, in your heart, for mackerel?"

No Presh. Donahoo opened the door for Barney so he wouldn't have to open it for her later. He was going to sit down, he didn't want to get up again. The double shot of Old Crow was settling in nicely. He hadn't eaten since yesterday, and he didn't plan to rectify that, although there were radishes coming. No Presh, but there was, could be, a Rosie? Donahoo immediately put that from his mind. The guy, he's not cooled down yet, you're thinking of stealing his girl. You are going to hell. Donahoo tried to remember when he believed in hell. He could recall being with a nun, Sister Somebody. She was laying it on, he'd burn forever. He believed her, and he believed in Santa Claus, and he believed in the Easter Bunny. People were always lying to him. They said if he ate his crust he'd get hair on his chest. It didn't work for him. But it worked for the little girl upstairs. It worked for Lenore Ericson.

The phone again, another neighbor, Cody. "Tommy? You screening? Don't go away. I'm coming over."

Donahoo drank his bourbon and waited. He kept thinking about Chip Lyons and going to hell, and he kept thinking, even though he knew it was wrong, about Rosie the Snake G-string, the Wham Bam Ice Trail. He couldn't get them out of his head. Chip Lyons saying, *Listen, I've fucked you*, and saying, *I'll see you soon, Tommy*. Donahoo drank his bourbon and wondered why the guy would want to say that. He thought he had been fucked plenty of times, but it had never killed him.

Until now? Donahoo drank his bourbon. Lewis was the only one he'd told about Chip Lyons's dying testament. "Any last words?"

Lewis, he was the kind of cop to ask that kind of question, and he'd asked it at Mercy. Donahoo had told him all of it. *Listen. Primitivo. Hooli-gans.* Lewis had looked wise. He had said, "Well, for the moment this doesn't have to go anywhere else, Tommy." Donahoo had looked at him. Except for Saperstein? Donahoo hadn't said the words. He had just formed them in his mind. But what he was thinking had to be clear to Lewis. Yes, it might not go anywhere else, but two other people still had to know about it, God and Saperstein. Lewis, in answer, had nodded solemnly.

Barney knocked and came in with a plastic bag full of radishes and a couple cans of Bud. She always bought her own. She couldn't handle the hard stuff. "You okay?"

Donahoo smiled for her. "Not a scratch."

"The news said you rammed a tank."

"An armored car."

"What's the difference?"

Donahoo gave her that one and discovered he had finished his drink. He hadn't planned very carefully. He was going to have to get up after all.

"Radishes," Barney said, showing him the bag. "Want one?"

"Not now," Donahoo said. "Just put 'em in the sink, please." He gave her his empty glass. "Would you mind taking this with you?"

"Not at all."

"Would you mind bringing it back with some Old Crow in it?"

She smiled and made the trip. Usually, she wouldn't wait on him. She was where he'd gotten the idea about staying put. She sat down, that was it. Donahoo thought she was a nice, if asexual, lady. She was short, round, with a little-girl's apple-cheeked innocence, even though she had to be forty. She had freckles and orange hair. Donahoo thought she looked like the Campbell's soup girl, back when Campbell's soup had a girl. She was in her sixteenth year, the longest reigning tenant at the Arlington. She had a top-floor apartment with access to the roof. She grew vegetables there which she never ate. She hung them in plastic bags on Donahoo's door-knob. Or, like today, a time of crisis, she sometimes delivered. She was a bookkeeper somewhere. She seemed to move around a lot. Maybe she had a route. She was wearing bib overalls at the moment. She always did at harvest time.

"You ever shoot a guy before?" Question from the sink.

"A couple times," Donahoo admitted.

She came back with the Old Crow. "I always wondered. I didn't ask before, it was private. But now, you're on the TV, that kinda opens the subject up. You're public domain."

"I got this guy in the knee once," he told her. "I figured, you know, that would bring him down."

"Did it?"

"Oh, yeah."

"And?"

"Another time I shot another guy in another knee."

"And?"

"That's all."

"You shot two guys before, and you shot them both in the knee?"

"There's no time to think. I guess you'd call it a knee-jerk reaction?"

Barney smiled. "Are you bullshitting me?"

Donahoo smiled too. "I wish I was."

Cody came in, not knocking. "You know you were on the news?" he asked, not waiting for an answer. He went straight for the bath-room, where he hid his own stock, a quart of vodka, Vons, in the toilet tank. His wife, Vera, didn't want him drinking, she said it ruined their sex life. She poured out everything she found. Cody retaliated by hiding the stuff. He had a basic month's supply in what was supposedly the extra propane tank for their barbecue. He had a quart in Donahoo's toilet tank and another under the hood of his Buick. For emergencies, he kept some in the enema bag hanging on Vera's bathroom door, he'd confided that once, he was drunk. Donahoo thought that Cody would probably drink about half as much if she'd just quit hounding him. Cody had a tendency, natural enough, to want to drink it up before she found it.

Gomez called. He was still drunk. He said on the machine, "Listen, amigo, I can't stand it, I'm coming over."

"Who's that?" Barney wanted to know.

"A cop."

"Can I stay?"

"Sure."

Cody came smiling from the bathroom. For a boozer pushing sixty, he looked pretty good, like Steve McQueen. He was medium height, but he seemed bigger, he had a barrel chest, and he moved with authority. He'd flown carrier fighters for most of his career and he'd never given up the naval aviator image. He had a brush cut, the hair sandy blond, and a sea-blown tan, and all the crow's-feet a guy gets squinting into adversity. He dressed mostly in khaki. He was wearing a khaki shirt and pants now. He had aviator sunglasses hanging off a shirt pocket. He had his bottle and a paper cup, folded, which he was opening up, poking into place, making a suitable vessel. He said, "Have you played the song yet?"

Barney said, "No."

"When you gonna play it?"

Donahoo thought. He'd had three drinks, which was really six. He should have played it a long time ago.

"I'm ready," Cody said. He sat down on the sofa beside Barney. He put his hand on her knee. She took it off. "I think I know how you must feel."

That would be for about half a second, huh? Donahoo thought. Barney was fast. He got the record. The song was "I Wonder Who's Kissing Her Now?" He used to play it on account of Monica. Now he played it on account of Presh. He wondered if he would ever play it for anybody else.

Cody put his hand on Barney's knee again. She took it off again.

"Do I detect a lack of interest here?" Cody asked. He was always using the word *detect*. He had been, briefly, after cracking up three carrier landings, in naval intelligence. That hadn't worked either. He'd caught a captain petting with a petty officer and was dumb enough to report it. He'd crashed and burned.

Donahoo thought, it had been on his mind all night, that he ought to make that special effort, to try to reach Rosie. National City wasn't the biggest place in the world. If he got in his car, drove around in circles, looking for landmarks, he was bound to find her place sooner or later. He could look for graffiti on the walls, bars on the windows. No, change that, look for something unusual, an old refrigerator. No, there were a lot of old refrigerators. Look for ...? Donahoo wondered what he was looking for. He wondered, but he was afraid to ask.

Cominsky called. He said on the machine, "Fuck it, let's curse the darkness. I'm on my way."

"Can I stay?" Barney asked.

Vera came in. She looked at Cody. She said, "I give up."

He was having a party, Donahoo thought. He had truly tried to avoid it, but he was having a party. He put the record on.

I wonder ... who's kissing .. her now.
I wonder .. who's teaching ... her how.

Cody wiped at a tear. One drink, he was gone. "You gotta play it, don't you?"

Donahoo nodded solemnly. Wouldn't be a party without it.

Later, sometime after midnight, Donahoo, quite drunk, and chauffeured by Cominsky, who was designated driver, finally found Rosie Gestring's house, which was on Ethel Place, off Mary Lane, in National City. He went up the side way, careful of the birdhouse, and knocked on the door. There was a long wait. Then Rosie Gestring opened it. "You again?" she said.

She was as Donahoo remembered. The door open wide enough to show just a panel of her face. The sleep-filled eyes and a mouth without lipstick. This time though—perhaps he was imagining it?—there wasn't the anger. She seemed more at peace.

"Did you know the Great One was dead?" Donahoo asked.

"Yeah. I saw it on the news." She closed the door.

"Do you care?"

The door opened. "Frankly, Officer, I don't much give a shit." The door closed.

Donahoo thought that the bruise on her cheekbone was healing nicely. He went back to the car.

"Well," Cominsky said, "what did you find out?"

"What I wanted to know," Donahoo told him.

EIGHT

Quillan and a whore were in a back booth at Club Hemingway, a small, dirty café on Avenida Paseo de los Heroes in Pueblo Amigo, which at night was a particularly dark and lonely section of Tijuana. They had finished dinner. Quillan was nursing a Tecate. The whore was drinking a bad margarita and typing a novel—the start of one— on an old Underwood chained to the table. She hadn't gotten very far. *Her mouth was curb red,* was what she had written, in Spanish. Quillan's partner, Taylor, who had been at the wheel of the Jaguar at the Tijuana Slough, was the other member of the dinner party, but he was briefly absent now. He had gone to the toilet.

"Do you like it?" the whore asked in Spanish, showing what she had typed.

"It's half mine, isn't it?" Quillan said. He had helped her with it. He could have helped her more. He knew Spanish, he was fluent, but he never let the Mexicans he met in Tijuana know that. To them, he was just another gringo who didn't know the lingo. Quillan didn't mind. He would listen to them talk, and pretend he didn't know what they were saying. He learned more that way.

The whore stumbled through a translation. "Her mouth was curb red." She was very pretty, with large, dark eyes, a small, perky nose, a full, ripe mouth smeared with bright red lipstick.

Quillan thought she would be prettier if her hair weren't dyed orange. He said, lying, "I like it."

"Really? Thank you." This in Spanish.

It was late, near closing time, and the café was almost empty. The kitchen had been closed. The waiter—there was just the one— was asleep standing in a corner. The bar was still going though. There were a dozen people at it, laughing, boisterous. A drunk was singing about somebody's suicide.

Quillan and Taylor were the only Americans in the place. It had been designed to attract Americans—the name, the old typewriters chained to the tables, the huge blowup photograph of Ernest Hemingway, titled "Papa"—but that hadn't worked. Few Americans came to Pueblo Amigo, fewer still ventured into Club Hemingway, and those who did were more interested in drinking than writing. Nobody ever entered the annual writing contest for the best imitation Hemingway. Nobody ever won the trip to Paris. The whole thing was a bust.

Failure, Quillan thought. He knew about it. He had failed himself a few times. He was frankly fucking tired of it. He didn't want any more of it. If he went down again . . . ? Shit, he'd eat a shotgun first, Quillan thought. He'd do that. Blow his brains out. Just like Papa. But not before taking a few bastards with him. Including the border patrol prick Chaffee. Including, with a tear, the bumfuck Buddy Salinas.

Quillan sighed deeply, thinking of how hard he had worked to gain what he held, thinking of how easily it could be torn from his grasp. He tried to think of his successes, but that didn't help. They served only as reminders of what he could lose.

Rank, for one thing. Now, after three momentous years in San Diego, carefully creating what he considered to be an untypical, very much above average criminal organization, he was starting to be known as the General. People were calling him that, behind his back mostly, but sometimes to his face, and he liked it a lot. It was something he deserved but had been denied in an exemplary military career. In the Special Forces, in 'Nam, he'd been a major, that was as close as he got, despite heroic exploits. With the CIA, in Thailand, and later in Central America, they called him a colonel, he carried papers to prove it, but that was just so the enemy might treat him better if he was captured. Like him, like the agency's whole operation there, the rank was a lie, bogus, a fake, part of a dark pillow sham covering black deeds by dirty men, all in the name of God and country. He never was what they said he was, Quillan thought bitterly. He was what they made him. A killer, a torturer, a rapist. A thug and a pig. They taught him all of the devil's skills and then they put him in a hell where he had to use them or die. They taught him, finally, their last lesson, that he could be any fucking thing he wanted to be, ranks were just tags, there for the taking, and so, when they kicked him out, he took general. He simply took it. He was the General. He had Taylor mention it around when they got settled in and started making contacts in San Diego. Let the word drop to the right people in the right places. Quillan, he's called the General. And it caught on. It was coming back to him. He heard it, more and more. The General. No army. But so what? He didn't need any army to kill.

Taylor came back from the toilet. He sat down and looked at what the whore had written. "What is it?" Taylor asked. "An autobiography?"

Quillan smiled. "A critic."

The whore had a ready translation for that. *"Critico?"*

"The best job ever," Quillan told her, but he said it for Taylor's benefit. "Imagine being paid to criticize? I had a woman once, she coulda made millions. Smile, Taylor."

"Do you like it, critic?" the whore asked in Spanish.

"It stinks," Taylor said. He was in a bad mood. He said, "Where the fuck is he?" meaning Willard Chaffee, the border patrol officer who had driven Primitivo to his slaughter.

Quillan shrugged. He wasn't worried. Chaffee, he'd show up. They owed him money. The man was driven by greed. He was like everybody else. He was like the bumfuck Buddy Salinas.

"It's getting late. I don't like it."

"You don't have to."

Money, and what it could buy, Quillan thought. He was still working on his list, what he could lose and never get back. He tried to stop obsessing, but he couldn't. He could lose 14 Pannikin Drive. Quillan could remember coming upon it, duffel bag bulging with plunder, money from the cocaine they'd brought up from Belize—"more money than a horse can shit," Taylor had bragged—and he didn't want some Dick-and-Jane house, he wanted a castle. Until he saw a Greek temple.

Fourteen Pannikin Drive. That was it. Quillan had to have it. When he walked through that temple/church's front door, walked into what was understood, now, to be a private residence, a home, he was swept by a sense of opulence, of raw power. There was that unmistakable authoritarian quality, and it was, for him, impossible to resist. Quillan sometimes cringed when he thought of what he paid for it and how much he still owed, but it had proved a good investment. The front door didn't get used all that often. Taylor, his associates, the men who worked for him, and also any delivery people or tradesmen, they all used the rear entrance. It was only an important visitor, usually a foreigner, someone who would be impressed, or who needed to be impressed, who was greeted at the front door, and it paid off then. They came through that door and they knew they were meeting somebody important. They knew they were talking to a guy who really had his shit together. Quillan smiled now in memory. There was a Jap who came in, he knelt.

"Can I have another drink?" the whore asked.

Quillan gave her the money and indicated that she should go and get it. He didn't want to awaken the waiter. The way he felt, the less he saw of him, the better. Quillan, when he came to Tijuana, he never went to the same place twice. He didn't want to be known as a regular anywhere. This had its drawback. He never got the good service afforded a known customer. On the other hand, if anyone was ever asked to describe him, they had seen him only once.

"Thank you."

"You're welcome."

The whore was learning English. She couldn't carry on a conversation, but she knew some words and phrases, she could ask some questions. She had discovered, early in her young career, that the boys in the barrios didn't have as much money as the marines from Camp Pendleton. She could say, "Would you like to have a good time?" She had learned that first. Even before "Can I have another drink?"

Both men watched her go. She had a nice, still-slim body. She had a good ass and attractive legs. She was wearing a short lime-green skirt, as short as a tutu, overly tight hot-pink panties. The skirt flounced with her every move. Outside, standing on a corner, it would lift in the slightest breeze, rise above her waist. She was wearing a black tank top and shiny black high heels. That's all she was wearing, except for a lot of cheap, gaudy jewelery.

Quillan called after her. "Bring some more Tecate." He used about as much Spanish as he ever used. "Tres Tecate."

Taylor lit a cigarette. His eyes got a faraway look. He said, "You ever think of just . . . fucking off?"

"No," Quillan said. "That won't work. Think it through. The guy, he's got the video, Taylor. If we run, he's gonna get pissed, show it. They'll put it on *Unsolved Mysteries,* there'll be posters up in Webbi Shebeli. They'll have fifty million people looking for us.

That's what happens, the TV gets a snuff video. They play it forever. We're fucked. We've got to stay, get the video, buy it, steal it. There's got to be a way." Quillan sucked at his beer and said, "Nothing we can't handle," stressing the *we.* "Shit, we've been in corners before, huh?"

Taylor puffed on his cigarette. He was about Quillan's age, but he appeared older, a tall, thin, wasted man in a too-large summer suit. It hung on him like he was a hanger. His face was narrow, crowded. It looked squashed. His eyes were too close together. He had a squished mouth. He had bad teeth and never smiled.

"We've *got* to handle it," Quillan added.

Taylor looked at him. He puffed on his cigarette. He still didn't respond.

"No choice."

"I suppose," Taylor said finally. There was a long silence. He looked around the smoky, almost empty café. The whore was still at the bar. "I just don't figure how I'm on the video."

"Well, you are," Quillan told him. "I saw it, okay? The fucker showed it to me. It's you at the wheel, no argument. They got you dead, same as me." He drank the last of his beer. "They've got some new infrared that turns night to day."

"Sure, but the Jag's dark windshield, you can't see inside in daytime, how can they see inside at night?"

"I don't know. Science, for fuck's sake. I'm telling you, it's a clear shot of you, Taylor. I've seen Doris Day fuzzed better. Accept it. They made you. You're in this, same as me. And I don't appreciate you looking for holes. You understand?"

"What's that mean?"

"It means, when we get the video, when you see yourself, you're gonna thank me, Taylor."

Taylor looked at him. He didn't say anything.

Quillan, if he had a friend, it was Taylor. They were blood brothers. They had spilled a lot of it together. Taylor, he'd been

Quillan's sergeant in the Green Berets, in Vietnam and Thailand. Later, in Central America, he'd been faux major to Quillan's faux colonel. They had killed more than necessary. It had gotten to be a game. The other bond between them was that Taylor had twice saved Quillan's life. He'd sprung him from a Viet Cong's bamboo cage in 'Nam, and he'd let him escape instead of killing him, as ordered, in Honduras. Quillan would forever remember the defining moment in a little grass shack in Tegucigalpa. Taylor with a cocked .45 Colt. He, Quillan, staring, asking, "What's the brass got against me?" and Taylor saying tiredly, "Well, maybe if you'd stop fucking babies."

"You're in," Quillan said now, meaning for whatever price was exacted by Primitivo's botched execution. He was going to say more. He was going to say, "You can't get out," but the whore was coming back, and behind her, at the door, just coming in, he could see Chaffee.

"I told you not to worry," Quillan said.

Taylor could see him too. He stared for a while, then looked away, uncomfortable, uncertain. He said, "If he fucked us, why would he come?"

"The same reason we stay, Taylor. No place to run."

The whore arrived with her margarita and the Tecate. Quillan got her to sit on his lap. He nibbled at the back of her long, slim neck. He fondled her full breasts and rubbed her warm crotch. Taylor sat watching impassively.

"Is that him?" the whore asked in Spanish, seeing Chaffee.

"Yeah."

"He's attractive."

"You gotta say that. They're all attractive. Otherwise, you'd go nuts, huh?"

Chaffee came over to the booth. Quillan shoved a Tecate at him in greeting. He indicated one of the empty chairs. Chaffee smiled his thanks and fell into it. He had come directly after finishing his border patrol shift. He had stopped only to change. He was out of uniform, in casual clothes, a white knit cotton sweater, no shirt. Blue jeans, deck shoes.

"Happy days," Chaffee said, popping his beer can. He was a big beefy man, the linebacker type, a blond giant. His hair was thinning but he still came across as a lady's man. A knowing glint in the crinkly blue eyes. Big, friendly, toothpaste smile. He said, smiling now, looking at the whore, "Where did she come from?"

"She's going soon," Quillan said.

Chaffee couldn't hide his disappointment. "Oh."

"But she's not going far."

The whore downed her margarita. She smiled good-bye to Chaffee. She slipped off Quillan's knee and disappeared under the table.

Chaffee took a moment. He grinned. "How far is she going?"

Taylor got up and pulled the booth's curtain shut. Quillan took a white envelope out of his pocket and pushed it across the table. Chaffee opened the envelope and counted the money inside. Five thousand dollars, in fifty-dollar bills. He nodded, looked at Quillan, tried to locate Taylor. Tried to find him without making it apparent he was looking for him. "It went well?"

"Yes and no," Quillan said. He wasn't worried about what the whore might hear—she had other things on her mind—but he still avoided using names and places. "The guy who had to go, yes, he's no longer with us, but now we've got some cops with us."

Chaffee pulled the envelope toward him. He frowned. "Cops?"

"Yeah, they were hiding there, at the place, two of them, and they made a record, on film, of the whole thing."

"You're kidding."

"No. They got it all, the pricks, and now what they want, they want a million dollars."

Chaffee let out his breath. He said softly, "Jesus."

"You can imagine my distress," Quillan told him, leaning back. "I don't have that kinda money lying around. I gave the point man something down, a kiss and a promise, but they want the rest right away, otherwise they're gonna fry my ass, and where am I gonna get it right away, so I'm looking, you know, for contributions?"

Chaffee released the envelope. "I don't know what to say."

Quillan looked at him. He could see in his face what was happening. The whore had his pants open. She had him out all the way. She was sucking him. And Chaffee, he had mixed emotions, huh? He was in two places at once. He was afraid he was going to immigration hell while he was going to cocksuck heaven. He wasn't dealing with it very well. That was the idea.

"The other problem," Quillan said. "Who would set me up for this?" He leaned forward solemnly. "Who'd be so fucking greedy, he'd go for a piece of this kinda action?"

Chaffee said, "Hey . . ."

"Maybe you, huh?" Quillan said, answering his own question. "Who else knew? Who else was there? Who else was in such a fucking hurry to get away?" The wolf eyes stared, empty. "It's hard to believe. We've done business a long time, Chaffee. You've always been treated fairly. You've always been paid promptly, in full. You've never been jeopardized. I know it's not you. How could it be you?"

Chaffee's eyes bulged. "It wasn't me."

Quillan didn't know whether to believe him or not. He had no proof of anything. He had no more proof it was Chaffee than he had proof it was Buddy Salinas. But it wasn't something he wanted to chance. A guy, he screws you once, he'll screw you again. So why take that chance? It wasn't worth it. "You're a lying fuck."

Taylor's arm came slashing over and down. He plunged an ice pick into Chaffee's heart. Chaffee cried out, an anguished, muffled animal scream. Quillan stuffed a balled napkin in his mouth an instant after Taylor struck. Chaffee reached for the pick but his hands fell away. He slumped back in his chair, eyes glazed, mouth agape. The napkin fell out.

Taylor parted the curtains and was gone.

The whore said in Spanish, "What is it?"

Quillan lifted the tablecloth, pulled it over Chaffee so that he looked like a ghost sitting there.

The whore scrambled out from under the table. "Mother of God. What have you done?"

Quillan counted some money in front of her. Ten fifty-dollar bills. Five hundred dollars. He gave it to her.

"Is he dead?"

Quillan also spoke in Spanish now. "Does it matter? If you want to keep the money, keep your mouth closed."

The whore, staring doubtfully in disbelief, put it in her purse with trembling hands. "Mother of God."

Quillan borrowed her lipstick. He drew a face for Chaffee's ghost. Big round eyes and a big round mouth. Then he rolled up the paper on the typewriter, typed some more bad Hemingway. This time it was in English. *When he came, he left.*

The whore stared dumbly. She didn't know what it said or meant. She was deathly afraid. Quillan, smiling, took her by the arm, guided her through the booth's curtain. The waiter was still asleep in the corner. No one at the bar was paying any attention.

"Let's go."

The whore nodded, face down. Quillan guided her. "You're okay."

Taylor was standing at the bar. Quillan, frowning, wondered what was wrong with him, he was supposed to be in the car. The bill had been paid in advance, with a generous tip. They were supposed to just walk out.

Taylor grabbed Quillan's arm as he passed. The whore pulled free and went outside. Quillan let her go. A late-night news program was on the uncertain television set. A reporter was giving a breathless account of a cops-and-robbers shootout in San Diego. A cop had been killed. Investigator Chip Francis Lyons. There was an inset photo. There was another cop involved. Sergeant Thomas Donahoo. His photo.

Quillan was looking at the photo of Donahoo. He was thinking of what Lyons had said about him. *He's not like us, Nick. He's mean.* Quillan thought that would be pretty fucking mean.

"You think we're off the hook?"

"I don't see how," Quillan answered. "That guy. Donahoo? He's the partner. He's been in this from the start. He's got the video. Or he knows where it is. Why would he quit?"

"More money for him?"

"He takes it all."

Taylor nodded. He waited for Donahoo's photo to flick away. "He looks tough."

"So I hear," Quillan said.

They went out. The whore was standing there in shock. Quillan took repossession of her. They hurried across the street to a rubbish-strewn parking lot. There was an old Cadillac positioned for a quick exit into the next street over. Taylor pushed behind the wheel. Quillan got in the back with the whore. She was trembling.

Taylor gave a quick glance as he pulled out of the lot. "What's wrong with her?"

"She saw a ghost."

Taylor shook his head. He knew what that meant. It was an old routine. A familiar Quillan modus operandi.

"Hey," Quillan said. "Let me see you smile, Taylor."

The whore trembled. She was sobbing. "Mother of God. How could you do that?"

Quillan pulled her to him. He put her orange head in his lap. He unzipped his fly. "Well, for starters," he said—he was enjoying himself—"I'm not the Mother of God."

NINE

They were sitting around Saperstein's office, waiting for Saperstein, and all trying to talk at once. Donahoo and Lewis and Squad 5's investigators, Gomez and Montrose, the celebrated team of Spick and Spook, and Palmer and Cominsky. They were all trying to talk, except Donahoo, who was just listening, and maybe also Lewis, who looked like he had tuned out. He had a cow look he sometimes got.

My guys, Donahoo thought. The proud men of SCUMB. Nursing hangovers, waiting for Saperstein, and trying, if not very hard, to think of a suitable epitaph for Chip Lyons's tombstone.

" 'Here lies Chip Lyons,' " Gomez was saying. " 'What kind of lie would you like to hear?' "

Donahoo thought that was pretty good. Gomez, the thin man, the accessorized detective, the Beau Brummell chihuahua. He was the squad's "Mexican Connection" and probably its best detective. Donahoo thought so. He liked the way Gomez went by what was in his heart. His emotions directed him. That, seemingly, would be a contradiction in police work, but it worked for Gomez. For him, it was not so important *how* a crime was committed, but *why*, Motive was everything. Always, he looked for that first, a fierce little dog of a man, proud, strutting, combative, always testing his leash. Pencil mustache, slick ink hair, string tie, white shirt, shiny patent leather ballroom sippers. He had a purse somewhere. Maybe he was sitting on it so he'd look taller. What kinda lie would you like to hear?—that showed some thought, Donahoo thought.

"I don't think so," Palmer said. He turned a thumb down. He looked at Gomez, asking for an argument. Palmer, small like Gomez, but physical, a fighter. He'd fought professionally as a featherweight before becoming a cop, and it was in his blood. He still looked like he might be entering a ring. A butch haircut and a ferret's glint. Puffed-up chest, arms akimbo. He had a fighter's attitude. He carried a mouthpiece. Donahoo thought if he had a favorite, it would be Palmer, not because he was the best cop, but because Palmer was the most like himself. Palmer was stubborn and Palmer was lucky. He also had an off-the-wall quality that meshed nicely with the runaway hysterics of his partner Cominsky. They were oddballs looking for oddballs. Donahoo thought it was a good thing in the SCUMB business. Some dippiness on *our* side. Palmer stared at Gomez. "I gotta give it a no."

"Or," Montrose said immediately. "Or." He was acting like he might have a winner. He had a pay-me expression. " 'Here's the Chipper, gone to his rest. His last day . . . was his best.' "

Again, pretty good, Donahoo decided. Palmer was being too critical. Last day, his best. A nice degree of ambiguity. Definitely a contender. Donahoo looked at Montrose kindly. He ranked him number two. Like Gomez, Montrose's main contribution was ethnic, he had solid connections in the black community, but he was also a superb investigator. Unlike Gomez, he dealt only in facts. Donahoo had never seen emotion play any role in Montrose's work. He was a stone. When he made a case, it was concrete. It would be nice if there was a bit of heart in there somewhere, but there wasn't. If there was, he'd be number one, not number two. Montrose, the movie star, the faux Jamaican. He sure was a black beauty, Donahoo thought. He was pretty, he was big, a natural athlete. He took his clothes off, he looked like a god. He was getting one of those high asses but he was still beautiful.

"I don't think so," Palmer repeated. He was dumping on everything. The hangover had to be killing him.

"You can take it two ways," Montrose protested.

"The problem," Palmer told him, his thumb working. "I gotta give it a no."

"May he rest in piss," Cominsky suggested.

Oh, now, there's a winner, Donahoo thought. He briefly considered interceding on Cominsky's behalf before Palmer could squash him. The guy needed a pat on the back once in a while. Rest in piss. Wow. Donahoo turned his kindly look to the often-maligned Cominsky. Palmer's partner had the appearance of a real ding-a-ling, a tall, thin, birdlike creature, uncertain, gawky, weird. He wore checkered suits with wide lapels and an expression Lewis said was maybe not vacant but sure absent often. They could never be sure about his degree of attention. Donahoo thought he should intercede but he didn't. It was important that he keep his distance. Cominsky had a tendency to build a kind word into far more than what was intended. He could misinterpret hello. Cominsky, the geek, no one ever figured him for a cop, or for much intelligence, but he did have his moments. His strange thought processes could lead you to the far reaches of a twisted mind. He meant where no one else meant. Lewis again.

"No," Palmer said. The thumb. "Too derivative."

"Who appointed you?"

"I'm a natural for it."

"Oh, yeah? Why?"

"My brother-in-law's in the navy."

Cops, Donahoo thought. Cops. No matter who had gone down, they would be doing this, indulging in this grotesque mockery, or some form of it. The venom wasn't all directed at Chip Lyons. A lot of it, yes, but not all of it, because there was more at work here. They were also mocking death. It was their way of dealing with the closeness of it. Chip Francis Lyons, the Chipper, he hadn't been close to them, he hadn't been close to anybody, but his death was. It had brushed so close, they felt it. They knew that only benevolent fate spared them from having their own guts on the street. They knew it could be them next time. They were cops. They were targets.

Bad jokes couldn't change that, but maybe they helped, Donahoo thought. The verdict was still out. They hadn't helped him yet. Maybe they weren't offensive enough? He was at the rear of the room, leaning back in his chair, balanced against the wall, purposely distanced from the graceless savagery. Of all of them, he'd had the worst hard-on, hands down. He'd had a real case against the Chipper. So he didn't want to appear unseemly. He would admit to having a nice day though. And he was hoping, now, for more of them. He knew what made the sky blue. The Rayleigh scattering. But a good mental set helped.

Being chief, Saperstein had the best office, the biggest picture window, the nicest view. It was only ten past eight, but the sun was already halfway up the sky, dappling Golden Hill, Barrio Logan. It was shining on the concrete rainbow that was the Coronado Bridge. It was coming in the window and it was warming Donahoo. He couldn't help thinking that he was free at last. He didn't have to baby-sit anymore. He could close his eyes and watch the chains fall away. The smoke clears from Chip Lyons's pyre. The loose cannon is gone. And, rising from the ashes, renewed, the phoenix of reason and moderation. Free at last, free at last, Donahoo thought. God help him, finding satisfaction in that, the guy still not in the ground, but there it was, how he felt, and he wasn't going to suggest he'd soil a hankie anytime soon. Besides, Chip Lyons wasn't killed, he committed suicide, Donahoo thought. He had asked for it. Fuck, he sent out invitations.

"A huge boulder," Gomez suggested. "It's so big, there's no way he can get out. That says it all. Who needs words?"

Palmer gave it a thumbs-down. "You ever seen a bare stone? There's always some writing."

"The epitaph," Lewis began. Donahoo glanced over in surprise and mild alarm. The beefy, unkempt captain normally didn't participate in this kind of revelry. He had only a couple more years to go and he wanted to retire, not so much in honor, but just in dignity. Donahoo wanted that for him too. Lewis had invested too much piss and wind to risk it by acting silly. Please, remember who you are, Donahoo thought. You're a captain. A Petronius head on a Barney Rubble body having trouble keeping your pants up but you do hold command. Lewis was smiling. This, special occasion, was going to be an exception. "The epitaph reads, 'We all Chip'd in.'"

"Now, that ain't bad," Palmer decided.

"You suckhole," Gomez said, outraged. "You think that's better than 'Here lies Chip Lyons'?"

Donahoo wondered if, as sergeant, and given Lewis's lead, he should now submit an entry, and if, perhaps, he should rise above the rabble, set an example of gentlemanly conduct. How about "Chip Lyons. Man of rare gifts. He could charm a fly out of a toilet." Naw, Donahoo thought.

"Listen to this guy," Palmer said, sneering at Gomez. "You beaner? You has-beaner?"

Lewis said, "Girls."

"He started it."

Saperstein came in, a dark, efficient whirlwind depositing debris—car keys, attaché, the *Union-Trib*—and Donahoo came off the wall. There was a snap, the chair hitting the floor, which Saperstein chose to ignore. He said, a lie, "Gentlemen." He said, a bigger lie, "Sorry I'm late." He carefully removed his jacket, an Yves Saint Laurent pinstripe, and placed it lovingly on a polished wooden hanger. It went then into an eighteenth-century Sheraton-style armoire, joining several other suits and jackets, including a tuxedo. The ornate walnut wardrobe in an otherwise spartan office was the one acknowledgment of his exalted position. Saperstein was a dresser. He could change here for any occasion. Besides the hanging garments, there was a drawer full of fresh shirts, another drawer of socks and underwear. There were four kinds of shoes, sneakers, loafers, brogues, black and pointed. He was ready for anything. He was just back from the mayor's office. Tonight was the Consular Ball. He was looking at Donahoo the whole time. He said, "The Chipper, he got the guy through the pump, huh?"

"Yeah," Donahoo said. "One eye, but he could see heaven."

Saperstein smiled, a bookkeeper's smile, not a cop's smile. He was all ledgers and he had that way a guy gets when he's the only mechanic in town. He smoothed his close-cropped hair and adjusted his tight vest and rolled up his shirt-sleeves, two turns, precise, even. He sat down and poked his dark horn-rimmed glasses into place. He rearranged several freshly sharpened pencils, the only items on his desk in addition to a yellow legal pad, a calculator, and a phone. The calculator was the gun he didn't wear. He had started his police career in Purchasing. He had never worked the street. He didn't have Lewis's old cop's Jell-O gut. He was tall, thin, cutting-edge. He looked smart, and he was. He had ambition. He was chief and he wasn't fifty. He still had other places to go. Everybody thought he'd be going. He had what it takes. Intelligence, dedication, organization skills, political savvy, and the capacity to make grown men cry. "You, Tommy," he said—he was looking at Donahoo—"on the other hand, why is this, you can't shoot a guy in the ass?" He sighed elaborately. "Do I have to put this on a blackboard or something? You shoot a guy in the ass, it's funny. You shoot him in the back, that's bad press. So let's go over it one more time. It's okay you blow a guy's fucking brains out. But never, ever, shoot him in the back. *Comprende?*" He said, "It's a good thing—we got a break here—the Chipper got the other guy in the pump."

Donahoo wondered where he ought to start on that one. Maybe he could go to the morgue and get a corpse. Saperstein could section it for them like a side of beef. Places to shoot that were politically correct, places that were funny, etc.

"Do I hear an answer?"

"Next time, the brains," Donahoo said. "But meantime, we've got a suspect, we can talk to him."

"About what?" Saperstein demanded. "Why he wanted dia-monds? He's gonna get engaged? He's got eighty-six fiancées?" He glared back at Donahoo. "I've got a dead officer here. Don't try to make any points this morning. Do you know how much a new Mercedes 420SEL costs? It costs sixty grand." The rest was for Lewis. "He's got a Crown Victoria. He can ram anything he wants with it. But, oh, no, he borrows a Mercedes. A German car fanatic."

Lewis, an effort, leaned forward, shoved a report across Sap-erstein's desk.

"It's not over," Saperstein told Donahoo. "The woman you dragged out on her ass, she's suing, okay? She's claiming trauma. Her lawyer's talking a couple million dollars. So don't try making points." He picked up the report. "What's this?"

"The story."

Saperstein put the report down. "The story is what the PIO put out. The story is in the paper. Officer, *heroic* officer, dies saving woman hostage. *Sacrifices self* to save woman hostage." He looked at the report. "Is this better than that? How does it get better than that?"

Lewis took it back. He said, "For the record, the deceased is a local thug, Raymond Newton, AKA Ray Newsom. Ex-marine. He's got a long rap sheet, mostly penny-ante stuff, assault, car theft. This was his first venture into the big time."

"We think."

"As far as we know," Lewis agreed. "The guy Tommy winged, Harold Powell, no aliases, no prior record, recently separated from the Marines at Camp Pendleton. Honorable discharge. He was a tech sergeant, supply. Originally from Missouri." He went to the report for more. "The guy in the armored car, Lloyd Winters, no aliases, no prior record, recent arrival, from Michigan." He checked something. "Uh, another ex-marine."

Saperstein was starting to show an interest. "Three white guys?"

Montrose, ever alert for racial slurs, said, "What's that got to do with it?"

"Spook," Saperstein said, not looking at him. "You got a fat ass. It's on account of your ancestors stored fat there to be used as food between successful hunts. Now, many generations later, your ass could satisfy two sittings at the Hometown Buffet, and you're asking me what's that got to do with it?"

Montrose stared blankly. "I'm not following that."

Donahoo said, "Spook, shut up, willya?"

"They were using 7.62mm SAM Crossfires," Lewis continued. "I don't know where they got 'em. They're not talking. That is, as you know, a law-enforcement weapon." He paused so briefly, it could be barely appreciated. "The armored car is from Mexico. It was stolen a couple years ago in a shootout in Durango. Don't ask me how it got up here. They're not talking."

"All ex-marines. Three white guys? What did they do? Meet in the service? I thought they had desegregation?"

"I guess." Lewis flipped a page. "Hostage is fine. No problem there. We recovered all the loot. They had about half a million in sparklers, assorted trinkets, knickknacks. It was all in the one sack." He looked up. "The D.A. is making a case. We're outa here."

"Except for the woman with the run in her stocking and her car at the wrecker's?"

"Except for that."

"Okay," Saperstein said, frowning. He considered for a moment.

He was tugging at something. Or it was tugging at him. "You gotta admit, it's unusual. Normally, there'd be a Hernandez in that mix. There'd be a Tyrone."

No one challenged him.

"Well," Saperstein said. "What difference does it make? The Chipper is gone, it doesn't bring him back." He brushed a dry eye. He focused on Donahoo. "Tommy, it's up to you now, I want you to solve the Chipper's case for him. You stay on it and you get it done. I want you to bring in Primitivo."

Donahoo wasn't prepared for it. He felt like he'd been run over. Blindsided while dreaming of better times. "Me?"

Saperstein looked over his glasses. "What have we got here? An identity crisis?"

"Give me a break," Donahoo said, scrambling. "The guy is a will-o'-the-wisp, ignis fatuus. We've never seen him. He's rumor. We've got a picture it could be somebody else. We don't even know if he exists. He could be a figment of Lyons's imagination."

Saperstein looked harder. "Everybody wants this guy. The mayor, the D.A. Everybody. So let's bring him in, okay? No excuses." He said, "Let's do it for a fellow officer slain in the line of duty."

Donahoo couldn't believe it. "One for the Chipper?"

"That's the spirit." Saperstein considered, let it pass. "Oh, and you've got a new partner, Cominsky."

Donahoo couldn't believe that either. He said it without thinking. His voice was an octave higher than usual. *"Cominsky?"*

"What's wrong with Cominsky?"

Oh, fuck, Donahoo thought. Cominsky was looking at him the way a nun looks at Jesus. "Uh . . ."

"You got a problem with Cominsky?"

"Of course not," Donahoo said, looking at Lewis, who was suddenly looking at the ceiling. "I'm thinking of Palmer here. You're taking away his partner." He was looking at Lewis for help. "How's Palmer gonna get along without Cominsky?"

"We're getting him another partner," Saperstein said. He turned to the others. "This is numero uno. I want the whole squad working on it, exclusively. Drop everything else. Everything. No exceptions. If it's important, give it to Lewis, he'll reassign. I don't want anybody working on anything except Primitivo."

"What about my poison rum case?" Montrose complained.

"Drop your poison rum."

Gomez looked like he had been speared. Either he couldn't speak or he was afraid to ask. He was very close to solving a series of indignities perpetuated against the Cabrillo monument. In the latest scandal, someone had put a pair of bloomers on it.

"Drop your pants, Gomez," Saperstein said, one of his finer moments.

There was polite applause.

"Okay," Saperstein said. He had saved the best for the last. "Moving right along here. I know how you gentlemen felt about Chip Lyons. I know how the rest of the department felt about him. He didn't have all that many friends. He wasn't your best mixer. But, be that as it may, he was a cop, and he was a shooter. He wasn't afraid of the firing line. He took four guys out before they took him."

"Five."

"*Five*," Saperstein said, happy for the reminder, "is, in my opinion, a straight shooter. I had breakfast with the mayor. He agrees with me. We've got a public relations windfall here. A bonanza. San Diego's toughest cop goes down fighting. An example for all of us in the never-ending battle against crime. We're not gonna have a funeral. We're gonna have a parade." He looked around expectantly. "How does that grab you?"

"Hey, that's terrific," Donahoo said. He wondered about the fates. He used to be lucky, he thought. Now he couldn't win a coconut, they were giving away hula dancers. "We could invite the Shriners. They could toss water-filled condoms."

"That's been done to death," Palmer said. He gave it a thumbs-down.

Donahoo grabbed Lewis in the hall as they were filing out of Saperstein's office. He steered him off to the side, away from the others, who were heading back to the squad room. Donahoo pinned him. Gomez and Montrose, Palmer and Cominsky, they kept going. They looked back but kept moving.

"You know I can't work with Cominsky," Donahoo complained then, his voice a rasp. "You see the way he looks at me? That's pure adoration. How am I going to work with somebody—he looks at me like a dog?"

Lewis pulled up his pants, which had fallen lower than usual. He opened his case file and sorted through it. Occasionally he glanced up, looking over his glasses solicitously, wonderingly. "Maybe we could change his name to Spot? Get you transferred to K-9?"

"You've seen how he looks at me?" Donahoo demanded. "You would—you weren't staring at the fucking ceiling."

"Here it is," Lewis said, pulling out a report. "You might want to make this a priority. Last night—early this morning, actually—a border patrol officer was murdered in Tijuana. He was in a bar—Club Hemingway?—with a couple Americans. They put an ice pick in his heart."

"Have you seen his lapels? He could use that jacket for a sleigh. It's embarrassing."

"I'd get on this right away," Lewis said, putting the report in Donahoo's hand. "It's a long shot, sure, but Primitivo—he's involved in alien smuggling?—that puts him on a collision course with the border patrol. Maybe there's a connection."

"He buys all his clothes at the thrifts," Donahoo complained. "He buys his *shoes* at the thrifts. He takes them to a bowling alley, gets them zapped. That oven they use for rental shoes? He gets them put in there. A double zap."

"Also," Lewis said, extracting another report. "I'm having second thoughts here. You might take a closer look at the *Semper Fidelis* Gang. What are three ex-marines doing with an armored car stolen in Durango? If they wanted an armored vehicle, they could have stolen it from Pendleton, it would be an easier snatch." He pressed it on Donahoo. "Another long shot. Another Mexican connection."

"You've gotta do something."

Lewis sort of rolled his eyes. "What is your problem?"

Donahoo said it. "The guy loves me."

"*Loves* you?" Lewis said. He glanced around, making sure no one had heard that. Gomez, Montrose, Palmer, and Cominsky were far down the hall. They were almost to the squad room.

"In the nicest sense, you understand."

"Oh. I think I know what you mean. It's in the way one guy will look up to another guy. In the way that he admires and respects all that he embodies. Both as a human being and professionally. Et cetera."

"Something like that."

"I can't imagine you handling it."

Donahoo almost screamed. "Jesus Christ, Lewis. We're talking about Cominsky."

The beefy captain, Detectives, twisted away, causing his pants to slip again. He pulled them up with an effort.

"Please," Donahoo said. He was begging.

Lewis smiled and started down the hall. Donahoo let him go. He watched helplessly for a while and then changed his mind and chased after him. He caught up to him at the open door to the squad room. Lewis took refuge in the doorway.

Gomez, Montrose, and Palmer were working at their desks, pretending to be oblivious. Cominsky glanced over expectantly, as if he wanted to be the next to see Donahoo.

"Lewis, I am begging here," Donahoo said softly.

"I don't care."

Cominsky pushed up. He started over.

"How can you not care?"

"I dunno. But it's easy."

Cominsky joined them. "Well, Sarge," Cominsky said, beaming. "Where do we start?"

Donahoo thought that they weren't going to start, but if they did, they'd start with the wardrobe. The yellow checkered suit had to go. The Ruth Gordon silk tie.

"I've got a couple of ideas."

Cominsky, the geek, Donahoo thought. He looked like a gawky bird. He looked like a goofy scarecrow. He looked like both. There was that kind of contradiction. It was very disconcerting.

"What do you think about doing a sting?"

"A sting?"

Donahoo's phone was ringing in his cubicle office. Palmer went to answer it.

"This is perfect for Montrose," Cominsky said confidentially. He looked around. He lowered his voice. "He pretends to be a mobster in from the East. He wants to take over, but Primitivo is in the way. So he puts out the word that he'll pay two hundred grand to anyone who can find, and rub out, Primitivo. Then—"

Donahoo stopped him. "Have you mentioned this to Montrose?"

"No."

"Good," Donahoo said. "It's too risky." He was looking at Cominsky's pained expression. "We don't want to endanger anybody on the squad. We'll use somebody from SIU."

Cominsky brightened. "That's why you're the sarge."

Palmer signaled that he was transferring the call. Lewis started to leave again. Donahoo motioned for him to stay. He wasn't finished begging. In the process, he dropped the files Lewis had given them.

Cominsky bent to get the scattered papers. Donahoo physically stopped him.

The phone on the desk inside the door rang. Donahoo picked up. "Sergeant Donahoo."

"Is this Investigator Lyons's partner?"

"Was," Donahoo said. He shooed Cominsky. "Investigator Lyons is no longer with us. He died yesterday, the line of duty."

"Yeah, I saw that on the tube," Quillan said. "Interesting." A pause. "This is Captain Video. The guy you've got nailed to the cross. You wanta do lunch?"

Oh, good, Donahoo thought. A cop got killed, there was always some prick out there, he wanted to celebrate. "No."

"Dinner? We need to talk."

"No."

"I'm buying."

"Then how about taking me bowling?" Donahoo was thinking about Cominsky and his thrift shoes. He was thinking about the bowling alley double zap that killed all the cooties.

"Do you know who you're talking to?" Quillan asked.

"Captain Video," Donahoo told him. "You need to come up with a better offer. Meanwhile, fly up your ass." He slammed down the phone. "Fucking ghouls."

Lewis was edging away. Donahoo called after him. "Listen, what we were talking about, maybe I didn't explain it properly. That kind of thing, it can get out of hand, interfere with police work. Can you see how that might happen?"

Lewis paused. "What bothers me. I've been wondering. If Saperstein is angry when he's changing suits—does that make him a cross dresser?"

"You're good," Cominsky said.

"Yeah, but your partner, he's so much better," Lewis said. He was leaving for good this time. "Always remember that."

Donahoo called after him. "You disgrace the uniform."

Cominsky grinned. "Pretty strong stuff."

"It was said in jest."

"No," Cominsky said. "I mean Captain Video."

Donahoo looked at him. It was impossible to tell, and he had only himself to blame. It was once Donahoo's theory, now ravaged, in shreds, that it sometimes took a crackpot to catch a crackpot, and that was the reason—the only reason—Cominsky was on Squad 5. Donahoo thought that he shouldn't ask, but he was going to anyway. "What about Captain Video?"

"You don't wanta let a guy like that go, Sarge. The guy might be acting the whole thing out. Wearing the cape? It would be real interesting to meet that kinda weirdo."

Free at last, Donahoo thought. He picked up the files he had scattered on the floor. Free at last. He wondered—the thought terrified him—if maybe he had been better off, *safer*, with the Chipper.

TEN

Quillan hung up. His wolf eyes burned bright. He moved away from the pay phone, left the corner, got off the sidewalk. He stood in the street. He was still wearing his bomber jacket, torn jeans, scruffy sneakers. He looked like he hadn't slept for a while. He looked tough, he had a two-day beard now, his hair was tousled. Taylor's Cadillac sedan came along and stopped. He got in, the backseat. The Caddie moved away.

"Cops," Quillan said. He said, spit in his voice, "Irish cops."

The Caddie, rattling, made a sharp turn, from 32nd onto Ocean View Boulevard, passing through a stretch of save you now, save you later, the Comprehensive Health Center and the Greater Trinity Baptist Church, heading west toward downtown from Logan

Heights. It was a '78 Eldorado. AC, PS, PB, power seats, windows, locks. They all worked. The seats were leather. But it still looked like the disaster it was. Paint faded. Body dented, rusted. The cabriolet vinyl top in tatters. Next to the AAA sticker on the back bumper a sticker that said GHOUL SPOON. The county, in a new program, would pay seven hundred dollars to get it off the street. Private sale, it might bring five hundred. That's how bad they wanted the junkers gone. Junkers were trash and trash drove junkers. Most of the time, anyway. That was Quillan's theory too. The you-don't-look-for-a-wolf-in-a-rat-hole theory, applied to cars. Now, after Chip Lyons getting aroused by the Jag, smelling big money just by the mere sight, it wasn't a theory anymore, it was a religion. Quillan would never forgive himself for taking the Jag to the Tijuana Slough.

"He told me to fly up my ass," Quillan said after a while. He was silent again. Then he said, sounding, for him, oddly plaintive, "I can't believe this, he wants a better offer, Taylor."

"What kind of a better offer?"

"He didn't say. He hung up."

Taylor, at the wheel, didn't look back. He watched ahead, alert for careless drivers, cops. "More money." It was presented as a fact rather than offered as a possibility. "The guy wants more money, Quillan."

"Yeah, well, I'll kill the fucker first. Who does he think he's teasing? I'll pull his dick off. Through his asshole."

"How much, you think?"

Quillan said, "You deaf? I'm not going up."

Taylor looked in the rearview mirror.

"Yeah," Quillan told him. "Watch it." He had a bar in the back. It consisted of a bottle of scotch, Johnnie Walker Black Label, a tumbler, and a bag of ice. He was the only one drinking. He poured a glass and spread out. He tried to think. "I mean it. I'm not in the mood."

Quillan watched the street go by, thinking you could see everything but the ocean on Ocean View Boulevard. He came up often, not just to make safe pay phone calls, but to scout around, look for new girls, smart guys, different scams. He'd found Trudy Goody on Ocean View Boulevard. Even in rags her smile had been irresistible. He smiled briefly himself. In the rags, perhaps more so?

Logan Heights was black, a ghetto. The Mexicans, evicted long ago, were barricaded below now, in Barrio Logan. The Caddie was passing through three life zones, escaping past the poor, and the desperately poor, and the beyond hope or salvation poor. The last held the others down and back. One culture, savagely rent, Quillan thought. The only constants were the graffiti and the basketball hoops, the churches. There were a lot of churches. The Caddie went by Manna, Church of God in Christ, Gerald D. Miller, Pastor. Quillan wondered what kind of prayers were said in there that weren't answered. It was tough, Logan Heights. Black blood, running red. They were destroying each other. The 3A bus, UCSD Medical Center, was routed along Ocean View Boulevard. So it could double as an ambulance, Quillan thought.

Taylor gave him a look and let him be. He watched the road.

Quillan didn't know who he was mad at most. Himself, Donahoo, or Primitivo. Chaffee, in death, or Buddy Salinas, who wasn't going to live much longer. Primitivo, probably. The Mex jerkoff, he wouldn't listen to sweet reason, Quillan thought. He just kept coming and coming and coming. He was like that fucking bunny banging that fucking drum. He wouldn't stop. Primitivo *had* to be killed. No other choice. Otherwise, he would have eventually taken over, taken it all. The illegals, the extortion, the white slave. He'd have taken the drug trade. Everything.

No choice, Quillan thought again. That, or just surrender San Diego, throw in Tijuana too. Which he couldn't, wouldn't, do. So he had to take him out. His only mistake—his *fatal* mistake—was in thinking he could do it himself and get away with it. Quillan had thought Primitivo would just disappear from the face of the earth. He, Quillan, he would be suspect in some quarters, of course.

That couldn't be helped now that guys were calling him the General. Even guys who didn't know him were calling him that. So, of course, Primitivo gone, there would be talk, because he, Quillan, the General, he was the beneficiary. There would be talk, naturally. But no proof. No way to definitely connect him. Except that Chaffee had sold out or Buddy Salinas had snitched. One or the other. And now there was a video that could put him on death row. How could that happen?

Yeah, well, if you're dealing with people, Quillan thought. If you're paying money into a greedy hand. If you're rubbing Vaseline into a tight asshole. Everybody's human, huh? He cursed himself and he cursed his decision to use the Jag. The Caddie couldn't be traced. Stolen car, stolen plates. A mystery vehicle. But the Jag pointed straight to 14 Pannekin Drive. It was a laser.

Quillan agonized. What was he? Guilty of snobbery? That had been the farthest thing from his mind when he arrived in San Diego. Then, he wanted power, and the careful exercise of it, that's all. He saw a city that was a small town and ripe for the plucking. No Mafia, just warring Asian gangs, die-for-a-nickel Mexicans, all of them too greedy, too brazen, too undisciplined, or just too fucking dumb. Cops overwhelmed by street crime and the drug trade. Nobody in charge.

He'd seen an opportunity, Quillan thought, almost smiling, and he had been careful about it. He didn't stay in anything long enough to get caught. He would make a drug deal, make a killing, and then he'd get out, stop. He'd wait six months, pick another drug, a different connection, another way. He'd put together a system for smuggling aliens and let somebody else run it for a by-the-head fee. He'd arrange a major robbery maybe once a year. A casino, a payroll, an armored car. Something fairly spectacular with a decent payoff but carefully planned and executed, and, always, without personal risk. He was a distant behind-the-lines, in-the-bunker, out-of-harm's-way commander. His foot soldiers didn't know him. He'd also arrange maybe a kidnapping a year, some rich bitch snatched easy as stepping in dog shit, nobody hurt, modest ransom. He'd do a murder-for-hire at real arm's length. The killer would come in from the East. He'd never, ever, meet him, Quillan. The only thing he got close to and stayed with was the white slave. He was in jeopardy then because he liked to check them out personally. He liked black women and he thought he might be in love with Trudy Goody. He never could get enough of her. He also liked Filipinas. He'd bring in some Filipina girls, put them right to work, a bar downstairs, rooms upstairs. He'd pick the best girl and give her a cookie-cutter operation and take an ongoing cut. He had Filipina bars going all over. Five, no, six of them. Quillan almost smiled. He was losing count. Too many Filipina girls. And the one and only Trudy Goody.

"What are we doing?" Taylor asked.

Quillan told him, "Thinking."

Pick and choose, very carefully, mostly at a distance, mostly through others, and bang the drum slowly—that was his secret, Quillan thought. Doing it better than any other wise guy. With patience, always patience. Watch for the fruit ready to drop. Never rush in. Never overstay a welcome. So what went wrong?

Primitivo. He wasn't planned for. He came out of nowhere—out of a foreign country—and he wanted it all. He wanted the dregs and he wanted the crème de la crème.

"About what?"

"I'll tell you."

Quillan tried to think. He had four days to raise the rest of the money. Eight hundred thousand—or, now, whatever Donahoo, the greedy bugger, was going to stick him for. A million-plus, and he had no idea how he was going to manage it. Picking and choosing had a drawback. It limited income. He was broke at the moment, high living, heavy expenses, and he was house poor, a fortune sunk into 14 Pannikin Drive. The mortgage was more than the market value. He couldn't find a cash buyer on short notice and he couldn't borrow any money on it. The $200,000 initial payment to Lyons had taken most of his hands-on cash. He didn't have other major assets that were liquid. He had called Donahoo hoping he could take a meeting and find an advantage and talk the lug into dropping the price. Hey, your partner's dead, you don't have to split it—that's what he'd been to hoping to say. So let's be reasonable, huh? Knock off half a million. You'll still be walking with as much as you had before. Be reasonable, give me some time, a payment plan, and you've got what you wanted, fellah. What do you say?

How about bowling?

Jesus, Quillan thought. What was with these haywires? Did they know something he didn't know? He'd thought Chip Lyons was hardball. This guy, Donahoo? He was unreal. He'd thrown a big kiss-off. Cool and fast. It just whiffed by. You hardly saw it. So now what? How to counter? The guy had all the aces. Shit, he had all the cards.

"Well, I'm mad," Taylor said, pushing it. He wanted this settled. He didn't fancy driving around in circles while the sky fell down.

Quillan was starting to sweat. He tried to think. He had to wiggle out. Find some hole to crawl through. "Maybe he's yellow?" he said, the first straw that came to hand. "His partner is dead. He doesn't want to do it himself. He puts the price so high, we just break and run? He don't have to deal with us anymore?"

"I doubt it. He don't look the scared type. If he changed his mind, you'd be arrested by now, in the can on murder first, and they'd probably have me too. The guy's got nothing to gain by walking away. He knows he could get mangled if he did that."

Yeah, Quillan admitted. This thing, it had begun, and it had a life of its own, and it had to be resolved one way or the other. You don't show a killer the evidence that will convict him of murder and then just let it hang over his head forever. The killer, he's going to come after you, settle the thing. A cop would know that, Quillan thought. A cop, especially.

Quillan drank his whiskey. Why wait? Kill him now? He said, another straw, "We could always waste him."

"Yeah," Taylor agreed. "With pleasure. And then they're gonna find the video in a safety deposit box. No thank you."

Quillan closed his eyes. No way out. He didn't have the money. He couldn't get it in time. No possible way he could raise a million-plus in four days. Donahoo was asking the impossible. Donahoo, like Lyons, stupid, greedy, was going to put him in a vise. He was going to squeeze, and, when it was over, nobody would have anything.

"I keep thinking, the only answer, it's to pull a job," Quillan said. "But how do you put something that big together that fast? That kind of job, it takes forever, all the planning, all the arrangements. It's nothing that happens overnight." He said, "We could grab Prince Charles, sit on him till the queen dies, then we've got the King of England, but you see how that takes time?"

"Maybe there's another way," Taylor said. "Donahoo has something of ours. Maybe we should get something of his." He glanced in the rearview. "Then we could trade?"

Quillan frowned. He loved the idea. He was frowning because he hadn't thought of it himself. He said slowly, "Put the snatch on someone near and dear to his heart?"

"I'm sure we could find somebody."

"A wife and kids?"

"We could make it a standoff," Taylor said. "He's got us by the balls. We've got him by the balls."

"And the first one that blinks?"

"No. The first one that yanks 'em off."

ELEVEN

The sign on the filigreed arch over the street said WELCOME TO TIJUANA, THE MOST VISITED CITY IN THE WORLD. Yeah, Donahoo thought. But notice nobody stays? They ought to put up another sign: THE MOST DEPARTED CITY IN THE WORLD.

It was true, given a chance, the whole fucking place would leave, he thought. Illegal immigrants, they kept leaving, running the border. They kept leaving and being caught and being sent back. There were stories of illegals, they had been sent back twenty, thirty times. Donahoo wondered if the back-and-forth illegals were part of the visitor count. He thought that probably was how Tijuana arrived at its record, most visited. He thought he shouldn't be too critical though. Visiting Tijuana and saying you'd been to Mexico was like visiting Watts and thinking you'd been to the United States.

"The whore's name is Doxanne," Chincuanco said. He finished his Dos XX and put the bottle on its side on the rickety, fly-blown table, to show that it was empty. "But it's not her real name. Her real name is Mary Luz. Mary Luz Guardado."

Donahoo said to Cominsky, "Why don't you buy Detective Chincuanco another beer?"

"Got it," Cominsky said. He looked for the waiter.

"Get it," Donahoo told him.

"She was very upset by what happened," Chincuanco said, meaning Doxanne, her reaction to Chaffee's murder.

"You don't think she had anything to do with it?"

"No. I'm sure. She was merely a pawn."

Donahoo gave Chincuanco a look. He wasn't sure what that might mean in this context.

"A distraction."

"She didn't lure him to his fate?"

"No."

They were at a sidewalk café, Pablo's, in a small district known as Calle Primero, or First Street, within a few blocks of the border and on the path that tourists, when on foot, took to get downtown, to Revolución. The place swarmed with beggars and street vendors and the smell of outdoor cooking. Carne adobada, a sweet, greasy, highly seasoned porked cooked on a vertical spit, melded with tacos, caldo, and churros.

Donahoo was aware mostly of the constant bargaining. Everything was priced more than it was worth. Nobody paid the asking price. They always bargained. They were supposed to bargain. It was part of the culture.

An old woman pleaded. "Señor. It takes a long time to stuff a frog."

Donahoo smiled. The frog was a toad. Donahoo had been put on to Chincuanco when he called the Baja California State Judicial

Police inquiring about the Chaffee murder. Donahoo had suggested meeting at Grupo Homicidios. Chincuanco had proposed lunch at Señor Frog's. They had compromised on Pablo's. Donahoo saved two dollars every time Chincuanco drank a beer. Otherwise he was not very pleased with the afternoon. It was slow, hard slogging. The Mexican cop gave up information like he was surrendering his honor. It pained him and he charged for it. Nor did Donahoo think that the information had any value. Despite Lewis's hopes—and they were Lewis's hopes, not his own—a contemptible killing in a grubby bar seemed a long reach for clues in the hunt for Primitivo. Why would Primitivo want to kill a crooked border patrol anyway? The guy, if he was crooked, he'd be gold. You could whiz a truckload of cocaine by him. He could make you a million dollars with a wave of his hand. Donahoo thought this was probably all a waste of time. And money.

"I am interested mainly in descriptions of the suspects," Donahoo said after Cominsky had left. "What about sketches of them? Did you have a police artist do drawings based on her recollections?"

Chincuanco laughed. "We don't have a police artist in Tijuana."

"But you have an identification kit?"

"You mean multiple drawings of various facial features to reconstruct descriptions of suspects?"

"Yes."

"No."

Donahoo let it go. He thought he had heard all the horror stories and then he always heard another. It was a poor region. They didn't have the money for forensic niceties. All of Baja was served by a one-man crime lab. It wasn't served well.

"Do you think I could talk to her?" Donahoo asked, meaning Doxanne.

The Mexican cop rolled his empty bottle toward the sheet of paper he'd brought. "What for? You can read my report."

"I have. There's not much in it."

"Really? What's missing?"

"I have some questions you don't seem to have asked her."

"So tell me what they are," Chincuanco said. "Perhaps I can ask them for you."

Donahoo thought Chincuanco was young to be a detective. He could not be thirty, his face was smooth, like a fat ripe plum. There wasn't a line on it. No bags, no crinkles. His smooth hair was jet black. His dark eyes sparkled. His teeth, when he smiled, showed very white and strong.

Donahoo said, "What would be involved if I were to ask the questions myself?"

"With me present?"

"I would need you. Why would she talk to me otherwise?"

Chincuanco considered. Despite his relative youth, he had a large, soft gut. It hung like a pregnancy in his maternity-shaped blue serge suit. "Just to cover my time? A hundred dollars."

"Fifty."

"Seventy-five."

Donahoo thought you were supposed to bargain. "Sixty."

"Okay."

Donahoo got his money clip. He peeled off three twenties. He put them in Chincuanco's empty glass.

"*Gracias.*"

"Don't even think about."

"It's a poor country. We have to do what we can."

"I know."

"When would you want to meet her?"

Donahoo said, "What's wrong with now?"

"Nothing," Chincuanco said. He put the money away. He indicated a woman sitting several tables distant. "Shall I ask her to join us?"

The popular belief was that all Tijuana cops were crooked. Donahoo didn't believe this. Some, yes. Many, perhaps. But not all. Donahoo couldn't accept that a whole police department might be corrupt. He felt certain that here, as anywhere, as wherever one might look, there always would be an honest man. If one looked hard enough, at least one honest man. It sure wasn't Chincuanco though. "Yes, please," Donahoo said. "Ask her."

Chincuanco pushed up and went to get Doxanne. He returned at the same time as Cominsky. He made a brief introduction. Mary Luz Guardado, AKA Doxanne. Then he put her in a chair and put her at the table.

Donahoo wondered if his tits were being pulled. Doxanne didn't look like a girl who would sit under a table performing fellatio while a guy was getting his heart picked. He thought she was a very attractive woman who could be anything she wanted to be and that she was dressed this way (a Chincuanco trick?) only so as to look like a whore. She was wearing a neon-green jump suit and matching peaked cap and draped with an enormous scarlet feather boa. She could be arrested for being loud.

Chincuanco, smiling, said, "Doxanne says she will be happy to talk to you without my being present."

"Does she speak English?"

"Not very much. It is inadequate. But I have taken the liberty of providing a interpreter." Chincuanco, smiling, made a little bow, his soft gut hanging like a smuggled balloon. He took his Dos XX. "This is all unofficial. I'm sure we can agree it never happened. Adios, amigos."

"Good-bye," Donahoo told him. "And thank you very much." He looked around. A boy, he'd be ten, perhaps eleven, but very worldly, wise beyond his years, had suddenly materialized. He looked like he'd make a good lawyer, Donahoo thought. The eyes of a defense counsel. A prosecutor's smile. His face and hands were dirty and his clothes were rags. He was holding a small carton of Chiclets. The cellophane had been removed and he was selling the individual packages. Donahoo asked, "Are you the interpreter?"

"Very much." The boy slid onto Chincuanco's vacated chair. He looked Doxanne over carefully. He smiled his approval. "I charge ten dollars. In advance."

"Are you related to Detective Chincuanco?"

"Perhaps."

"Where did you learn English?"

"From my sister." The boy turned from his inspection of Doxanne. "Would you want to meet my sister?"

"No thank you. I like French girls."

"My sister, she's French."

Donahoo smiled. "You know that one, huh?" He gave him the money. He said, "Cominsky, why don't you get Doxanne a margarita?"

Cominsky said, "You wanta run a tab?"

Doxanne rearranged her boa. Her English was tentative. She switched to Spanish. The boy translated for her. "How did you know . . . I like margaritas?"

"It's all," Donahoo began, and then he stopped, because of the boy. He was going to say it was all a good whore ever drank. Margaritas could be diluted, minimum alcohol, zero alcohol. They could be all sour water and a mark would pay full price. "You look like a discerning lady to me."

The boy translated. He had trouble with discerning. Donahoo helped him. Doxanne asked, "What does *discerning* mean?"

"It means you like margaritas."

The boy translated. Doxanne smiled.

Donahoo reviewed Chincuanco's one-page report. Chincuanco had read it to him and Donahoo knew enough Spanish to grasp the basics now. Willard Chaffee, American National, officer in the U.S. Border Patrol, murdered in Club Hemingway. Weapon, ice pick. Left with tablecloth over head to look like ghost. Suspects, two American males, age forty to fifty. Material witness, Mary Luz Guardado, AKA Doxanne. Deceased rumored to accept *mordida* from illegals.

Willard, the rat, Donahoo thought. A border patrol officer on the take. He put the report aside. He indicated to the boy that he should begin translating for him and for Doxanne. He said, "The two Americans—how did you meet them?"

"On the street. The sidewalk."

"They picked you up?"

"Yes."

"And then?"

"We went to some bars."

"Several of them?"

"A lot of them."

"You kept on the move?"

"Yes. Until we ended up for dinner at Club Hemingway. They said this man, this Chaffee, he would be coming later, and it was his birthday."

"You were going to be the birthday present?"

"I was going to be the birthday surprise."

"And you were?"

Doxanne flicked her boa. "It's my job."

Cominsky came with an extra large margarita. The glass was the size of a soup bowl.

"Thank you very, very much, a lot," Doxanne said in English. It obviously was something she had memorized.

Cominsky said, "You're very, very welcome."

Donahoo thought they were made for each other. Cominsky, finally taking a hint, was not wearing his yellow checkered suit today, nor his Ruth Gordon tie. He was wearing solid colors, a robin's-egg blue jacket, pumpkin slacks. He was wearing a T-shirt that said SAVE THE ALES.

Donahoo's questioning resumed with the boy translating.

"The killers—did they argue or fight with Chaffee?"

"One of them talked loud."

"He was angry?"

"Yes."

"What about?"

"I don't know."

Donahoo tried another way. "Were any names mentioned?"

"A person's name? No."

"Where any places mentioned?"

"No. Not that I remember."

Donahoo thought that he could understand that. She was busy at the time. "Was anything said that stayed in your mind? Anything unusual?"

"A million dollars."

"Excuse me?"

"A million dollars. The mean one—the one who made the ghost?—he said it. A million dollars. I remember him saying that."

Cominsky said, "That's a lot of money."

"Yes, isn't it?" Donahoo agreed. "What was the connection? Do you know why he might have said that?"

"No. He was talking very fast. I didn't understand anything else."

Donahoo considered. A million dollars? He wondered how many illegals might be sneaked across for that. He could imagine Primitivo being interested in such a sum. "Could you describe the killers for us?" Donahoo asked.

"Oh, yes," Doxanne answered, sipping at her drink. She was looking at Cominsky. "They were Americans."

Cominsky grinned. "We better get a sketch artist in here."

"Tijuana hasn't got a sketch artist," Donahoo said, frowning. It was his witness. He had paid sixty bucks for her. It was his interpreter. Another ten. "It hasn't got an identification kit either."

"No problem. We'll take Doxanne to San Diego."

"No thank you," Doxanne said, smiling. She flicked a look at Donahoo. The boy was translating furiously. "This one? He'd keep me there. He'd charge me with—how do you say it?—a helper to the murder?"

"Accessory. I wouldn't do that."

"You won't get the chance."

"No problem," Cominsky said. "We'll bring the sketch artist here. I can have him down here in a couple hours."

"Uh, uh," Doxanne said, still smiling. "Chincuanco, I owed him a favor, I said I'd talk to you, but just this once. That's all. Whatever you get, you get now, okay? This is it. How do you say it? The conclusion."

The boy was translating feverishly. He didn't know *conclusion.* Donahoo figured it out. The end.

"You're leaving Tijuana?"

"Yes. Guadalajara. My grandmother's. The mean one? He gave five hundred dollars not to talk. I can't wait to leave."

Tijuana, Donahoo thought. The most departed city. He waited to hear from Cominsky. He was waiting to hear her leaving was no problem.

"No problem," Cominsky said. He went away.

"He's a nice man," Doxanne said. She sipped her drink and watched him go. "He is—how do you say it?—unusual?"

"Yes. Very unusual."

"He's your boss?"

"No. I'm the boss. I'm a sergeant."

"Well, he has the ideas," she said, her eyes turning back. They fell briefly on the report. "Does it say what he wrote?"

"What who wrote?"

"The mean one."

Donahoo came alert. "Tell me."

"After they killed Chaffee, he typed it on the typewriter, to enter in the Hemingway contest. 'When he came, he went.' The mean one bragged about it later. He said he expected to win. The prize is a trip to Paris."

"That does sound like a winner, all right," Donahoo said. "Maybe I'm looking in the wrong place. I should go to France." He smiled, to let her know he was joking, but Doxanne wasn't paying attention, she was looking at Cominsky.

Cominsky was helping an old man through the intricate maze that was the table arrangement at Pablo's. Even at a distance his profession was apparent. He was clutching a large sketchpad and a fistful of pencils.

No, Donahoo thought. *No.*

Doxanne was full of admiration. "He has the ideas."

"This is Torres," Cominsky said, introducing his artist, who had a disconcerting resemblance to Picasso. He was perhaps sixty, a weathered, bright-eyed gnome in a worn, baggy suit. All his clothes were too big for him, including his shoes. He smelled very strongly of beer. "He's a screaming genius. He can draw your picture in a minute. He's what you call . . ."

"A caricaturist," Torres said for him.

Donahoo said, "Cominsky. Jesus Christ. That's cartoons."

"I don't give a shit, it's a *likeness,*" Cominsky told him. He produced a sketch of himself. Torres, with a few magical lines, exaggerating his most prominent features and faults, had captured the essence of Cominsky. It was Super Geek. "Is this me or is this me?"

Donahoo had to admit it. "It's you."

"Thank you." Cominsky sat Torres down next to Doxanne. "Honey," he said, "you tell him what the bad guys looked like, and Torres here, he'll draw 'em, okay?"

The boy translated. Doxanne's straw slurped at the bottom of her soup-bowl margarita. "Sure."

Donahoo said, "This isn't going to work."

"How do you know?" Cominsky said. He sat down next to Torres and across from Doxanne. "Sarge, get the little lady another margarita, willya?"

Donahoo came back half an hour later. He'd taken a leak, he'd taken a walk, he'd checked out the liquor prices. He'd gotten cross-eyed thinking how this had to be a worse time-waster than prayer. He wasn't going to come back at all, but he decided that would be kind of childish.

Torres had completed two drawings. He had them captioned. *American #1. American #2.* They sat waiting for Donahoo's reaction. Doxanne was sucking on a fresh margarita. Two empty glasses, *bowls,* were piled in the center of table. Cominsky and Torres had put away half a dozen Dos XXs. The boy was working on his second Coke.

Donahoo picked up American #1. The guy, he'd be forty, maybe older, and he looked like a soldier, an officer, Donahoo thought. He looked hard, mean, dedicated, and he had the close-cropped hair, the military mustache. He had a dent in his forehead that could have been made by shrapnel. It was the eyes that stopped you though. Wolf's eyes, empty and silent.

"Is this him?"

"Yes," Doxanne told him through the boy. "The mean one. Who would be Hemingway."

Donahoo got American #2. Fiftyish. He looked wasted. Like he might be sick. He had a narrow, crowded face. Eyes too close together. Mouth pinched. Like American #1, he was memorable, Donahoo thought.

"This is the other guy?"

"Yes."

Jesus Christ, this was ridiculous, Donahoo thought. A drunken Tijuana street artist drawing murder suspects for the San Diego Police Department. On the basis of information from a neon cocksucker drinking margaritas like soup. And the whole thing is being translated by a ten-year-old Chiclets salesman. Saperstein would blow a gut.

"Do you think it's going to work?"

Donahoo handed the drawing back. He wasn't going to fall into that trap. He said, "How would I know?"

TWELVE

Quillan thought that you could tell a lot about a guy from picking through his garbage can, but the genuine revelations, the real skinny, were in his medicine cabinet. Quillan carefully sorted through the scant arrangement in Donahoo's. Electric razor, aftershave, deodorant, toothbrush, toothpaste, comb, hairbrush. Scissors, nail clippers. Jar—*big jar*—of Extra Strength Tylenol. Plus a couple stray Band-Aids. The absolute bare basics.

Detective Perfect, Quillan mused. Nothing's wrong with him, except he gets a headache once in a while. No prescription drugs. No sleeping pills. No cold remedies. No ointments or salves. No Mylanta. No Kaopectate.

"Whatcha got?" Taylor called.

"A supreme being," Quillan told him. "No fungus between the toes. No bleeding asshole." He closed the cabinet door. "When it's good, it's good, huh?" He pulled the shower curtain the way he found it. "This guy, if he made a list, the ten most important things in life, what would be at the top, soap and toilet paper."

"Come here."

Quillan took a last quick look around the bathroom and then rejoined Taylor in the living area of Donahoo's tiny studio apartment in the Arlington. They had picked the lock and they had been inside about five minutes. If a neighbor saw them, they were wearing overalls, FRITZ PLUMBING. If Donahoo came home unexpectedly, they'd have the talk that Quillan wanted. Quillan was sure that Donahoo wanted to talk too. He just didn't want to talk yet.

"This may be something," Taylor said, handing him two framed photographs. "They were in a drawer, facedown, the bottom."

Quillan took them. A ravishingly beautiful blonde smiled at him from the first. It was signed *With love and squalor, Monica.* The woman in the other photograph was striking rather than beautiful, with long black hair, deep dark eyes. She looked mysterious and she looked sexy. The inscription said, *That will be twenty dollars, please. Madame Zola.* Below that it said, *Love, Presh.*

"What do you think?"

"Not current," Quillan said, handing them back. "If they were current, they'd be on a wall, not upside down in a drawer."

"There aren't any walls."

"Okay. On a table."

Quillan checked around. It looked like a bust, he thought. Detective Perfect, no problems, and, by all appearances, no significant other, either. No wife, no children. No woman of the moment. Just a big, dumb Irish cop. Shiny pants and clown-size shoes. Bank account running empty.

No wonder Donahoo was going for it all, Quillan thought. He's too perfect. No problems, and nothing else. Nothing, period. The guy, he's in the prime of his life, and he lives in a box, not a home.

He drives a Toronado and he buys his suits at Sears. He comes home to a crabby cat. "Pissy pussy," Quillan told Oscar. Donahoo, he wanted the big score, he could take it, and take off, anytime, Quillan thought. Nobody was going to miss him.

So now what? Quillan shook his head. It had been a good idea—a fine idea—but it translated to squat when there was no one to kidnap. What the hell were they supposed to do? Put a snatch on a neighbor?

"We're fucked," Quillan decided. "Star-crossed. It ain't gonna happen." He considered taking the place apart as a way of shaking up Donahoo. Maybe kill the cat? Donahoo would come and he'd know that they'd been there. He'd know that they were tough like him. Quillan looked at Oscar. "You wanta have some fun?"

"No. Let's get outa here." Taylor was putting the photographs away. He had an extra in the stack. "Why get the guy's guard up? The way this is going, we may have to kidnap *him*, Quillan. You ever think of that?"

Quillan frowned. That was another good idea he should have thought of first. Put the fucker on the rack. Make him tell where the video was. Have him not mention bowling. He said, "Who's that?"

"Some baseball team."

Quillan took it. The girls baseball team at Loyola Marymount University. The coach was a priest. If it wasn't for the collar on backwards, the guy, he could be a cop too, Quillan thought. He was a real big guy. Big head, big hands, big feet.

"The priest, he's in another picture, isn't he?" Quillan asked, looking around. He crossed to a desk and a grouping of oval photos in small silver frames. He'd had one of them apart already. A couple identified, on the back, as Kathleen and Mike, and who seemed to be Donahoo's mother and her second husband, both deceased. There were death certificates in the desk with those first names.

"What good is a priest?"

"People, they've been asking that for years, Taylor." Quillan picked up one of the small silver ovals. The same priest as in the baseball picture, but maybe thirty years older. He was trying to smile. It wasn't quite there. Quillan fiddled open the back. There was a name and a date. *Father Charlie Donahoo. 6–10–92.*

"Who is he?"

Quillan put the photo back in its frame. He was trying to think. Donahoo's check stubs made regular mention of a Father Charlie. Donahoo sent him two hundred dollars a month care of St. Paul's Mission for Men in Desert Hot Springs. Alone, that meant nothing, but according to the papers in the desk, Donahoo was born Thomas Carville. He changed his name to Donahoo when he was twenty—*after* his mother's death. And Donahoo the priest bore a good resemblance to Donahoo the cop.

"Want to hear something wild? This priest—he's Donahoo's old man."

"You find some drugs?"

"I mean it. The fucking priest is his fucking father." Quillan picked up the phone and dialed Information. He got the number of St. Paul's Mission for Men in Desert Hot Springs. He called there and asked for Father Charlie Donahoo. He was put on hold and transferred twice before getting someone in authority. He got the information he wanted and hung up.

Taylor was waiting expectantly. Quillan told him, "He's in the VA, La Jolla."

"He's sick?"

"Yeah. I don't know what with. They wouldn't say." He thought for a while. "Well, we've got a choice, huh? We can grab Donahoo or we can grab Father Charlie. Take your time here. Which would you say sounds easiest?"

"Oh, great," Taylor said. "What do you think we'll get—putting the snatch on some sick old priest?"

"Gee, I dunno," Quillan said, thoughtful. "An Act of Contrition, ten Hail Marys? Attend a different church?" He gave him a little fake punch. "Smile, Taylor."

THIRTEEN

Donahoo thought he had a little déjà vu coming. There were a couple of ways they could go home. I–5 or the Silver Strand Highway, taking him through his coveted Coronado. Donahoo stayed on I–5, committed to Chula Vista, National City.

Cominsky looked up from his sketches of American #1 and American #2. "What's going on? You always take the Silver Strand, Sarge."

"I thought, you know, we could check on Rosie Gestring."

Cominsky grinned. "The Wham Bam Ice Trail?"

"It's right on the way."

"Hey, go for her."

"I'm not exactly going for her."

"Yeah, but you're gonna get her, Sarge. Don't worry about that. You think she's gonna say no to you?"

Donahoo said, "Okay."

"There's a choice between you and Chip Lyons?"

"Okay. Okay."

"I mean, for Christ's sake," Cominsky said. "Lyons is dead."

It looked like she was home. The Yugo was in the carport, it hadn't moved. The truck, a cabinet in the back, was parked around the side. The venetian blinds were open, catching the last sun. Donahoo parked at the end of the street, beside the old refrigerator that was waiting to be pushed into the canyon. He sat watching the graffiti-laden house for a while. It looked so . . . what? Forlorn?

"You want me to wait?" Cominsky asked.

"Please," Donahoo said.

Rosie the Snake G-string. The Wham Bam Ice Trail. Donahoo wondered why she lived there and why she lived alone. You'd think she'd want a nice apartment in a good neighborhood. You'd think she'd have a roommate for company and the protection that afforded. You'd think . . . what?

"This won't take long."

"Hey, take all the time you want."

"I'm just going to talk to her."

"Yeah, but if you get lucky, don't worry about me."

Donahoo pushed out of the Crown Victoria and followed the path that the late Chip Lyons had blazed, on a slant, from the side.

Cominsky called after him, "You watch. She'd fall down for you, Sarge."

Donahoo pressed on. Through the broken picket fence and the sickly privet, and up the steep, lumpy, overgrown lawn. He ducked the birdhouse.

Rosie came out to meet him this time. She looked ready to leave anyway. She was wearing a man's jacket, the sleeves turned up, and the collar up too. A man's striped shirt and a man's tie loosely knotted. Sweat pants and running shoes. She left the door slightly ajar. "You again?"

Donahoo was blank. "You going for a walk?"

"No."

"I thought, the way you're dressed, you might be going for a walk."

"No. I'm going for a drive. Can I help you?"

"Yeah."

Donahoo thought her eyes were definitely her best feature. Big, dark, slanted almond eyes in a heart-shaped face. They were embers, promising warmth, warning of fire.

"How?"

"Uh, well, actually, I was just passing by," Donahoo said awkwardly. "I thought I'd stop. See how you're doing."

"I'm doing fine."

"Good. These things, sometimes, they can be a shock, and it doesn't hit you till later."

"I'm doing fine."

Donahoo thought that was true. She was a lot more attractive than he remembered. She was wearing makeup, just enough, soft pastels, and she had her hair up in a loose, wispy bun. The bruise on her cheek was almost healed. She smelled faintly of jasmine.

"Me? I'm not so sure," Donahoo said. He was trying to think of something to say. He'd had a script, what he was going to say, he had it worked out in his mind, but he'd lost it somewhere coming across the lumpy lawn. He thought it must have bounced right out of his head. Hit one of those lumps, and blooey. He said, "I've never got used to getting shot at. And, you know, it's not easy, losing one of your own."

"So you're not doing fine?"

Donahoo looked at her. Jesus, she was tough. If he patted her down, he'd probably find brass knuckles. Feel around in those sweats and get a switchblade. "Oh, I'm doing fine."

"Good. Thanks for coming by."

"Well, hold it. What I was going to say, Lyons, you know, the Chipper, we can go around calling him an asshole, but he was a pretty good cop. I think you ought to know that. They're not gonna give him a funeral."

"What are they going to give him? A parade?"

"Yeah."

"You're kidding."

"No. I swear."

"Jesus Christ. This I gotta see."

"Well, you could, you know. I think it's Friday. Anyway, it'll be in the paper."

"Where? In the entertainment section?"

Oh, whoa, Donahoo said. He wondered if Cominsky could see him now. He obviously wasn't going to be invited in. He'd better get this over with. Segue here. You don't have to sit down. Just brace yourself. "I was wondering . . . how you would feel about . . . going to dinner or something."

"With you?"

"Yeah."

"Like a date?"

"Sorta. To a restaurant."

Donahoo waited for her answer. She was looking at him critically and it seemed to him that she was debating with herself. He felt like he was a slab of meat in a butcher's case, and that she was trying to decide if he was good, select, choice, or prime. She was taking a long time.

"It's nice of you to ask," she said finally. She was looking at him and meeting his gaze. "It really is, and I appreciate it, but I just . . ." She hesitated. "I'm sorry. No."

Donahoo felt a surge of disappointment. He had come expecting a turndown, but then for a moment there he was sure she was going to say yes.

She smiled an apology. "I've gotta run. Good-bye."

"Uh," Donahoo said. He was hurting and he wasn't sure why. If it was being turned down, or if it was that and also, in the background, squirming somewhere in the dark recesses of his skull, Chip Lyons. "Do you mind if I ask a question?" He let her turn back. "Why?"

"Nothing personal. I just don't like cops. In my experience they're nothing but trouble."

Donahoo made a gesture. How to fight or overcome that? He said, "Well, good-bye, then," and started away, but the other part of the equation was still bugging him. He stopped.

"I've really got to go."

"I know. But just tell me something. If you don't like cops—what were doing with a prick like Chip Lyons?"

She thought for a moment. For the first time, the anger was back, and the hurt. "I think you just answered your question," she said, looking away. She reached behind, pulled her door shut, locked it. She headed for the carport and the Yugo.

Donahoo stared after her. What did that mean? What was that supposed to mean? That Chip Lyons had a big cock or something? It was so goddamn special, that's why she put up with the ugly bugger? He waited until the Yugo was backing out of the carport. She was making a point not to look at him. He waited, she still wouldn't look, and then he left the other way, across the yard, angrily dodging under the low-hanging birdhouse. He thought, inanely, that she needed a guy, somebody to fix the place up, cut the grass. She wasn't making it on her own.

"Presto, right?" Cominsky asked when he slid back into the Crown Victoria.

Donahoo ignored him. He got on the radio and got patched through to Gomez.

"Amigo," Donahoo said. "What I want you to do. Hustle over to the funeral parlor and take a look at Chip Lyons's dick."

Gomez took a while before replying. "His penis?"

"Yes."

"You want me to look at Chip Lyons's penis?"

"Yes."

"What do you want me to look for?"

"For about two seconds. Otherwise people will wonder."

Cominsky said, "And they think I'm weird."

FOURTEEN

"You don't remember me, do you, Father?" Quillan said. He put his offering, a potted begonia, on the bedside table. "Willie Russom. You had me for a couple weeks, August '88. Took me outa that Desert Hot Springs furnace. Bath and bed, three squares. You'd forget, sure. Only natural. There's a lot of guys go through St. Paul's Mission. But it's something I'll never forget. Help, when you need it, that's the best kind. Now I was just passing here—I've a buddy down the hall—and I saw your name on the door. I says, 'Well, Jesus. I know a Charlie Donahoo.' I go back to my buddy. Explain the situation. He didn't want a begonia anyway."

Charlie spoke for the first time. His voice was a croak. "I don't like 'em either."

Taylor said, "Maybe we'd better be going."

"*Shut up,*" Quillan said, giving him a look. He needed some time to make the adjustment. He was human, he couldn't just turn it off. He'd come in planning to take the guy, kidnap him, hold him for ransom. The videotape or he goes in the toilet. And the guy, he was in the toilet, they'd be flushing him any moment now. It wasn't going to work, forget it. But he needed some time with his intended prey. He couldn't just walk away. He said to Charlie, "What are they holding you for?"

"Senility."

Quillan managed to smile. "That's something comes around, huh?"

"I suppose."

"You hang in long enough? It yours?"

"Yeah."

Quillan could feel Taylor's eyes boring into his back. They should be going, he knew that. A nurse could come in, ask questions. Their unauthorized visit could get back to Donahoo. It could piss him off.

Taylor said, "Come on . . ."

Quillan waved him off. He'd seen this a hundred times on TV, he thought. A guy is dying and a cop, he doesn't give a shit, he's trying to get some crucial information, and all he cares is, he gets it before the guy dies. Quillan thought he was just like that cop. He didn't give a shit. He said to Charlie, "How's Tommy?"

Charlie's raisin eyes found him. "You know Tommy?"

"Oh, yeah. He visited you at the mission when I was there. Then I ran into him a couple three times down here. We had a mutual interest in firearms. He sure could pick the ladies, huh? That Monica."

"You met Monica?"

Quillan paused on shaky ground. He didn't know where Monica quit and when Presh started. He said, "To die for."

Charlie nodded, a slight, barely discernible movement.

Taylor was slowly moving for the door. Quillan said, "Sit down, Taylor." He said, "Tommy. Who's he squiring now?"

"Nobody."

"Oh, I doubt that," Quillan said, laughing. "A man who's had a Monica? Who's had a Presh? He's not gonna stop now. So don't tell me nobody. That's just not true." He picked over the begonia. He pulled a wilted leaf. He put it in the trash. "Tommy. I know him. He's got himself a pretty lady."

"Well, he could have, he wanted," Charlie said, the words an effort. "That's for damn sure. He was in here yesterday, telling me about her, some new one. His usual hard-on. He saw things in her."

"Oh? What's her name?"

"Rosie the Snake G-string."

Quillan gave him the same look that he'd given Taylor.

"The Wham Bam Ice Trail."

The same hey-settle-down look.

"Yeah, she sounds like a crook, huh?" Charlie said, smiling faintly.

"What's her real name?"

"It beats the hell outa me."

"You don't know it?"

"No."

Taylor said, "We'd better be going."

"You don't know her last name?"

"Never heard it."

"Rosie the Snake G-string? The Wham Bam Ice Trail? That's all you know?"

"Ain't that enough?" Charlie's fading voice was a whisper. "So I made him promise. 'For God's sake, quit, Tommy. Women, they're killing you.'"

Quillan leaned close. "That's a tough thing to ask. You think he'd keep that kind of promise?"

Charlie closed his raisin eyes. "I dunno."

Quillan put a hand on Charlie's stick arm. He thought this was a terrible way to die, of old age. It took so long, and, being old, you'd have so many regrets. You'd spend . . . what? Months, years with your regrets.

"We'd better go." Taylor again.

Quillan nodded. He wanted to wait, watch the guy die. The guy was a real disappointment, too old to be worth kidnapping, and he couldn't remember somebody's last name. Quillan wanted to wait, but he knew he couldn't. The guy, he could last two, three, four more days. There was no telling.

Donahoo was across town, at Mercy Hospital, in Hillcrest. He again was doing this for Lewis. He didn't see how the *Semper Fidelis* Gang, the three ex-marines who robbed the Jewelers Exchange, had any possible connection to Primitivo, but he didn't want to ignore Lewis's counsel, get Lewis annoyed. He needed Lewis—Lewis's sympathy and Lewis's support—in his labyrinthine relationship with Saperstein. Lewis, who knew Saperstein better, who *understood* him, and who didn't have quite so much trouble kissing his ass, Lewis was invaluable in helping him, Donahoo, chart and stay that course. That's why he was a captain. To keep the course. To know where they wanted to go, and to see, as best he could, that they got there. Safely into port, and not down with the scurvy, huh? Not too many hands lost. And, Donahoo thought, still reeling from the Tijuana sojourn, he needed Lewis's help if he had any kind of chance of dumping Cominsky. That was the reality. Without Lewis, no chance. With Lewis, maybe a one-percent chance. Not much of a chance, but Donahoo, he clung to it, he didn't have anything else. You take what you can get, Donahoo thought.

He came to the door he wanted, it had a sign, NO VISITORS. A uniformed cop was supposed to be on duty, but there was no indication of him. He was probably taking a smoke somewhere, Donahoo decided, unperturbed. A guard wasn't necessary. Waste of taxpayers' money. The patient wasn't going anywhere. He was in serious condition.

Donahoo pushed the door open. A fat, soft, pale man with a butch haircut and bug eyes was lying prone on the high hospital bed, staring at the ceiling. He had an oxygen tube in his nose and an IV in his arm. His round face shimmered with fever. Pain showed in the bug eyes. Donahoo thought that if there was a chart at the foot of the bed, the way there used to be a chart, the line would look like a Wall Street crash. Harold Powell did not appear well.

"Hello," Donahoo said. He moved closer and showed his badge. "Poh-leece. Here to ask a few questions."

Powell raised his head an inch. There was a flicker of recognition. "You're the guy who popped me?"

"Yeah."

"Your picture was in the paper."

"Yeah. I saw it too."

Powell fell back. "You're not supposed to be here."

"Yeah, well, I'm like you, Harold," Donahoo said. "I don't care about the rules either. Fuck 'em." There was a small white vase holding three pink carnations on the bedside table. The kind of bouquets that are paid for in Duluth and put together in Barstow, or, in this case, San Diego. Sent from afar, anyway, Donahoo thought. There was a note the size of a business card. *To Harold. Love, Mom.* Donahoo put it back. "How you feeling?"

"Lousy. They can't get me stabilized."

"You've got a fever?"

"I'm burning."

"Maybe it's an infection?"

"Get outa here, willya?"

Donahoo pulled up a chair and sat down. He thought that even at the best of times the guy wouldn't look like a marine. He'd been in twenty years though. Career man. Retired at forty. What had ruined him was twenty years sitting behind a desk. Supply guy. "What's the doctor say?"

"Does it matter?"

Donahoo shrugged. He had come to terms with his guilt. Two in the knee, one in the back. Nothing to be proud of, but nothing to be ashamed of either. The thing was, when you were trying to stop a guy, he was usually running away. Donahoo thought he'd better ask his questions. There'd be a nurse poking in anytime, pointing to the sign, calling him a Nazi. "The Jewelers Exchange caper. You want to talk about it?"

Powell shook his head. "I'll tell you what I told the other cops. Nothing."

"You're not interested in a deal?"

"No."

"Why not?"

"I've got nothing to deal," Powell said tiredly. "Newton's dead. You've got Winters. Nobody else was involved. Nobody helped us plan the thing. It wasn't an inside job." He signed. "Also, you recovered all the loot, so what's there to deal?"

Donahoo tried to think. Not much.

"I'm gonna plead guilty, save the expense of a trial, get a lesser sentence," Powell said. "That's the only deal I'm making. No information involved." He sighed again. It sounded like bubbles popping. "You saw the sign? Leave me alone."

"Okay," Donahoo said. "Just one more question. How come—"

The door pushed open and an orderly entered, pulling a gurney. He was a big black, built like a linebacker, a shaved head. He said, "Time to go."

Donahoo stood up. He checked the orderly's ID. He was getting vaguely worried about the cop's long absence. "Where you going?"

"None of your business."

"He's going to the VA," the orderly said. "He's got no insurance, just his veterans' benefits, so he's outa here. No mercy at Mercy. Gonna go to La Jolla." He looked at Powell doubtfully. "You up to traveling?"

Donahoo said, "You're sending him without the cop?"

The orderly shrugged. "He can go along if he wants to."

Donahoo rendezvoused with Cominsky at the nursing station.

"Nothing," Cominsky told him. "The guy's a clam. He's antisocial. He doesn't talk to the nurses, and he doesn't talk in his sleep either. No visitors. Nobody's even tried."

"You talk to the guard?"

"Where is he?"

Donahoo grinned. He could imagine the cop coming back, the room empty, his prisoner gone. He could imagine him trying to explain. Well, Jesus, you wanta smoke, you gotta smoke outside. You gotta go two blocks. It's unnatural.

Cominsky was waiting. He had his sketches of American #1 and American #2. He wanted to put them up on the wall in the squad room.

"Powell's being transferred to the VA," Donahoo told him. "I'm going to go over there, talk to him some more, then visit Charlie. I'll grab the bus home. It goes right by my place. You take the car. Go back to the station." He said, "Oh, and find the cop, tell him what's happening, get his butt over there, otherwise he won't have one."

Cominsky had his sketches. He looked filled with guilt. Letting his partner take a bus. "You're sure?"

"Cominsky," Donahoo said. "Please. Good night."

The ambulance pulled out of Mercy. When it reached the street, it stopped for a moment, the driver checking for traffic. Donahoo was waiting there. He opened the unlocked rear door and climbed inside. He pulled it shut behind him. The ambulance moved away.

Donahoo grinned at Powell. "You're supposed to say, 'You again?'"

Powell's voice was a whisper. "You again?"

The ambulance driver glanced back. Donahoo gave him a little wave. The driver smiled and hit the siren.

Powell whispered, "Am I dying?"

"No," Donahoo told him. "They just like to run. I get that way myself sometimes. Turn on that old siren. No reason—just turn the fucker on."

Powell nodded and closed his eyes.

"I almost bought an ambulance once," Donahoo said. "It was at one of those city/county auctions. They were practically giving it away and it would have made a helluva camper. Only sixty thousand miles and the brakes had hardly been used. How many times have you seen an ambulance stop?"

Powell smiled faintly. He didn't say anything.

"I'm trying to remember," Donahoo said. "Not too often."

"That don't mean they're not using the brakes. You see 'em approach an intersection, they slow down. That's brakes."

"Not hard brakes."

"It's brakes."

Donahoo pushed in closer. "You sound like a pretty smart guy. Here's my question. Why would you be so fucking dumb as to rob the Jewelers Exchange?"

Powell looked away.

"That's fucking dumb. That's *really* fucking dumb. You gotta go into six, seven offices to make it worth your while, and when you get outside, you're in a traffic jam. One-way streets. Gridlock."

No response. The ambulance lurched, changing lanes. The siren wailed.

"I'll tell you what," Donahoo said. "You answer that question, that one question, I'll leave you alone. If you don't answer it, I'm gonna be on your case so long, you're gonna be so tired of me, you'll wish you were DOA at La Jolla."

Powell opened his bug eyes. His voice was a whisper, but the pride in it was unmistakable. "We could have done an easier job. Real big. Real easy."

"What job?"

Powell shook his head.

"Why didn't you do it?"

"We're marines," Powell said, smiling. He closed his eyes. "You said one question."

Donahoo settled back for the ride. He thought that sounded . . . what? Awfully patriotic of the guy? He's a marine—*was* a marine—and there is/was a crime he wouldn't commit.

What kind of crime? Donahoo held on in the swaying ambulance. A real big job, he thought. Real big, and real easy. He thought it was a dumb time to run out of questions.

Quillan and Taylor were coming out of the VA. Donahoo was going in. They all recognized one another at the same time. Quillan and Taylor recognized Donahoo from the TV and his picture in the *Union-Trib*. Donahoo knew he was looking at the caricatures called American #1 and American #2.

Quillan had the advantage. He had his hands shoved into his bomber jacket and he was already holding his gun there. He'd started doing it—walking around with a gun in his hand—since being caught off guard by Chip Lyons.

"Hold it," Quillan ordered. For a split second he showed Donahoo the gun, a Smith & Wesson .357 Combat Magnum. He shoved it back in his jacket pocket. "Where it's pointing, it can blow your nuts off, okay? Turn around."

Donahoo turned around. He couldn't believe what was happening. They were at the main entrance to the VA. People were brushing by them, going in and out.

"Now it can sever your spine," Quillan said. "Taylor, get his piece."

Taylor stepped in front of Donahoo and quickly relieved him of his Colt Model Python.

"Now get the car, Taylor."

Taylor pocketed the Python and headed for the parking lot. During the whole process no one had paid any attention to them.

Donahoo thought he had heard the voice before. The phone call from the ghoul. "Captain Video?"

"Yeah, I know, I can fly up my ass," Quillan said. "And you can stick your head in yours. Here's what I was trying to tell you, and I suggest you listen carefully. You don't listen, it's the last fucking thing you'll ever hear, and that's a promise. I'm not the money tree. I can give you half a million—what you were gonna get in the first place—but I can't give it to you all at once. You're gonna have to take installments."

Donahoo said, "I don't know . . ."

"Shut up!" Quillan said. "This isn't negotiable, so just listen. Half a million dollars, that's all. Take it or leave it."

"You dumb . . ."

"Shut up! The payment plan is a hundred grand a month. You'll get the first tomorrow. I'm gonna call you, we'll set a time and place, do it. I give you a hundred grand—it shows I'm serious. You give me a copy of the video—that's your show of faith. When we walk outa there, I'll have you the way you got me, in a criminal act."

"Asshole. What video?"

"Okay," Quillan said. "I'm so tired of you. You fucking creep, you say one more word, I'm gonna kill you. One fucking word, you're dead. I'd love you to call me on it. *One word.*"

Taylor came up with the Cadillac. He leaned across and pushed the back door open.

Quillan prodded Donahoo. "Get in."

Donahoo got in. Quillan followed closely behind. He had the Combat Magnum out in the open now. The muzzle was a couple of inches from Donahoo's skull.

Taylor pulled away. He headed down the hill, leaving the VA. "What's happening?"

"This *prick*!" Quillan shouted. "I swear to God. I'm gonna waste him."

Taylor swerved to avoid an oncoming car that had strayed into his lane starting up the hill. "You're gonna fuck us."

"We're fucked anyway." Quillan put his gun into Donahoo's ear.

"Jesus," Taylor said urgently. "I don't know. Can't we get this sorted out? You said it yourself—there's no place to hide."

"We'll take our chances." Quillan tightened on the trigger. "You're going, motherfucker. Good-bye."

Taylor yelled, *"Not here!"*

Quillan eased off. "Okay. Find a place."

Taylor looked in the rearview. The car that he had narrowly missed was turning around. It was coming after them.

Quillan noticed. "Who's that?"

Taylor shrugged. He floored the Caddie.

"Ford," Quillan said. "Crown Victoria. Maybe it's a cop car. That's all they've got."

Taylor had to stop at the bottom of the hill. There was no way through the cross traffic. The Crown Victoria pulled up alongside.

"Hey, Sarge," Cominsky yelled, waving.

Taylor said, "Fuck, don't do it, Quillan."

"Open your door," Quillan told Donahoo. "Get ready to jump."

The cross traffic opened. Taylor jammed the Caddie in front of Cominsky in the Crown Victoria. He took off at high speed. He maneuvered into an open lane. The Crown Victoria followed.

Quillan waited until Cominsky was closing. "Okay, jump," he said.

Donahoo leapt from the speeding car. Cominsky braked, swerved, hit him. Donahoo went flying.

Cominsky got out, stricken with fear, remorse. The Caddie was history. It was already lost in traffic. He rushed to Donahoo's side.

He was crying as he checked Donahoo's vital signs. "Sarge, Sarge," he kept sobbing. "Holy Christ. I didn't mean it."

Donahoo managed to push him away.

"Oh, God, you're alive," Cominsky said. He looked him over frantically. "What's broken?"

"I dunno."

"Where does it hurt?"

"All over."

"Can you move?"

"No. What the hell you doing here?"

"I got feeling guilty about you riding the bus. I'm sorry."

"Just get me to a hospital, willya?" Donahoo said.

"We're at a hospital. We'll have an ambulance in a minute."

"No. They won't take me here. I'm not a vet. We've got to go all the way back to Mercy."

"Fuck that," Cominsky said. "We're here. You're going here. Don't move." He said, "You know who those guys were? The guys in the pictures!"

Donahoo nodded and held on to him. "Yeah, and listen, I found out something. The *Semper Fidelis* Gang was gonna pull a big job, only they turned it down on account of they're patriots."

Cominsky was trying to pull free. "Who cares? They're not gonna pull it now."

Donahoo said, "So maybe somebody else is gonna pull it?"

"Hold that thought. Don't move."

Donahoo grinned. He could move, maybe. He just didn't feel like trying. He raised his head to look at himself and saw an orchid on the road. Even in his dazed condition he recognized it as a Vanda burgeffii.

Cominsky was on the radio. He was ordering an ambulance. He was talking to headquarters. He was patched to Squad 5.

Donahoo wondered where the orchid came from. He'd thought he had lost it for good. He must have stuffed it down in a pocket or something. It must have popped out when he got hit.

Cominsky came back. Donahoo pointed to the Vanda burgeffii. "I found my orchid."

"I don't think so," Cominski said. "Your orchid, it would be wilted by now."

Donahoo thought that was probably true. It would be as flat as him. So the orchid must have come off American #1. But how the hell did that work? What did it mean? "I'm getting a little confused here."

"Take it easy," Cominsky said. "You can get confused later." He got his jacket folded and under Donahoo's head. He covered him with his slicker. "That was Gomez on the blower. He was over to the funeral parlor. He got a look at the Chipper's weewee."

"Oh? What did he say?"

"It's no biggie."

Donahoo smiled. Finally, a ray of sunshine, he thought, but he knew, in his heart, what it really was—another mystery.

The Caddie hurtled away. It weaved through traffic. Three blocks and it was on I–5, heading south at high speed, toward downtown San Diego. Taylor tossed Donahoo's Python.

Quillan cooled down. He willed himself to relax. That was a close call, he thought. But he felt safe for the moment. He said, "I should have killed him, you know."

Taylor looked in the rearview. "Kill a cop? That's nuts. We're pissing in the wind here, Quillan. We oughta settle it. No more talk. Throw the money at him. Pay him."

"How?"

"Do a job for somebody. There's always Joe Bong."

"That slant."

"His money's good."

Quillan shrugged. He didn't know. But he thought, next step, he ought to get some money, good or bad. He ought to have it ready if

Donahoo ever decided to deal. If there wasn't a deal, he might still need the money, to hit the road. So he needed it either way.

"I say we talk to Bong."

"Okay, okay," Quillan said. Now it was Taylor's decision. If it went wrong, he could take the blame. Me? I'll just take money, Quillan thought.

"I mean, what else?" Taylor asked. "You saw what happened there. Donahoo, he don't give a shit. You're gonna kill him and he don't give a shit. The guy is fucking steel. He's like a fucking Cong. You do it his way or it don't get done. He'd rather die than fold."

"Yeah, yeah."

"Yeah, well, scrap the kidnap idea, okay? Even if we've got him without a cop driving in the next lane, what really changes? You saw what happened. He ain't gonna talk unless we pay him. We gotta do like I said, Quillan. We gotta throw the money at him." Taylor looked in the rearview. "We gotta get off the merry-go-round. I'm not feeling good."

"I'm ready to puke myself," Quillan admitted. He thought that they really had been going in circles and that none of it made sense. Donahoo, he was playing pull my finger, and he couldn't be that dumb, even if he was a cop. Surely they had to write exams or something. Especially a sergeant?

"Who would have figured it?" Taylor complained. "The guy's got nobody. Nothing and nobody. Not one thing of human or material value. How do you take something from a guy who's got nothing? It isn't natural, all the guy's got, he's got a cat."

Agreed, Quillan thought. Unnatural. A guy with nothing. Quillan struggled with that concept and how it applied to the negotiations that went around and around and never concluded. Was that why Donahoo faced death readily? Because he had nothing? That simple? Then it came to him like one of the final questions in life's exam. You ever think—the way he's been acting?—he hasn't got the video?

Aaaargh, Quillan thought. The guy, he wasn't that ballsy. Was he?

FIFTEEN

Lewis put the orchid back in its glass of water. He said, "Vanda burgeffii? From the Far East?" He picked up Donahoo's cat, Oscar. He scratched its ears. He said doubtfully, "You wanta hang a guy with a pansy?"

Donahoo cast what he hoped was a who-me? look from his Murphy bed. He was on treacherous ground, but he had to walk it. Even run, if necessary. He had agreed not to mention some things that Lewis thought better left unsaid. Chip Lyons's assurance of an impending meeting in the Great Beyond. And, now, last night, American #1's offer of half a million dollars for a mystery video. Lewis had pounced on the latter like he'd jumped on the former. He had said, "Uh, Jesus, you must have gum on your shoe, be

---

walking in shit, you come in here smelling again?" He had said, "Let's make a deal. I'll hold my nose if you'll seal your lips." And he'd said finally, "That's an order. Follow it, Tommy."

Donahoo hadn't argued then. He wouldn't have won if he did. It was disturbing, probably damaging, definitely embarrassing information to throw at a captain, Investigations. It was understandable why Lewis might want to play cat and bury that kind of shit. They could dig it up later. It would always be there. It wasn't going to go away. But Donahoo hadn't made any promises about Vanda burgeffii. It was in the open. The one piece of the Chip Lyons puzzle that had escaped Lewis's shroud. It was on the table, up for discussion, and it was his, Donahoo's, deliverance. He could talk it up, and he could get everybody thinking about it. He could say, 'Hey, here's a piece of a puzzle, see if you can find some other pieces.' Then it wouldn't matter so much what Lewis had confiscated. There were always pieces missing. That's what made a puzzle. He just needed the one small piece—Vanda burgeffii—to get them all thinking. Gomez, Montrose. Palmer, Cominsky. Get them all wondering about the Chipper. If he was a crooked cop, and, if so, how crooked. Donahoo wanted them to have a head start on that track. It could help down the line and he no doubt could use some help if he ever made it that far.

"I take it that's a no," Lewis said. He'd been waiting all this time for an answer about hanging a guy with a pansy.

"Actually, it's a maybe," Donahoo corrected him. He wasn't going to back down. He wanted some consideration. He was home against doctor's orders. He had whiplash, four busted ribs, a bruised lung, a popped knee, a sprained wrist, and a mild concussion. He was wearing a neck brace. He had to walk with a cane. He was trying to run Squad 5 out of the Arlington.

Lewis seemed not to have heard. He dumped Oscar. "I've gotta go."

"Not yet." Donahoo struggled to sit up. He changed the who-me? look to a why-me? look. He fumbled for his cane. He went through the facial expressions routine of deserving a medal and being pinned with a cowplop.

"You don't have to see me out."

"I'd be less than a gracious host."

Lewis frowned, saying stay put. Donahoo pretended not to notice. He got his robe and twisted into it. All the time he kept watching for signs that Lewis might attempt to escape. When he thought about it, and he thought about it a lot, Donahoo believed Lewis was maybe the best cop in San Diego, but he also knew that Lewis had a flaw. It was when Lewis took his nose out of Saperstein's ass and tried to put his mind in Saperstein's head. It was when he tried to think like Saperstein thought.

Lewis jigged up his pants. A sign that he was really leaving.

"I want to solve a mystery," Donahoo said. He could picture Lewis's Petronius skull inside that of his demanding police chief Caesar. It was a bad fit, but it was stuffed in there anyway. Lewis thought Saperstein wanted, *needed*, the Chipper pure, and so, if possible, he was going to keep him pure. Lewis didn't want to hear any impure talk. Donahoo put Saperstein's get-well card, delivered by Lewis, aside. He thought he would burn it later, along with Lewis's card. "Chip Lyons was wearing an orchid. American #1 was wearing the same kind of orchid. A cop and a killer—the same orchid."

"Maybe."

"It fell out of the sky?"

Lewis didn't answer. He looked like his wife had just bought two tickets to the opera and she wanted to use them. Donahoo thought that he knew that look. Lewis hadn't wanted to come and he didn't want to stay. The visit was merely a courtesy. To express his sympathy. To drop off his dumb card. And Saperstein's dumber card. Now he was leaving. This wasn't anything he could sit through.

Cominsky said, "It wasn't the sky."

Donahoo examined Saperstein's card. There was a duck on the front. Inside, instead of a poem, it said, "Hurry up and get well."

Signed, "Walter." Donahoo said, "What I know, what I don't like, is that at either end of all this, like bookends, there's an unusual orchid first seen in the buttonhole of a cop who knew how to make things happen."

Lewis looked blank.

"I'm, uh, drawing a zero with Primitivo," Gomez announced, changing the subject. He was trying to protect Donahoo from himself. He examined the shine on his ballroom slipper shoes instead of looking at Lewis. "There used to be rumors, Primitivo was doing this, he was doing that. There was always that kinda talk on the street. Vague, but talk. Now nobody's heard nothing. It's like he fell off the face of the earth."

Palmer came out of the bathroom. He was zipping his fly, fighter-style. He had his chest puffed and his arms akimbo. He asked, "Did anybody ever do that?"

Donahoo checked Lewis's card. It had a dog on the front. Donahoo thought maybe Saperstein and Lewis got their cards together, from a pet store. Inside it said, "I told you not to chase cars. Lewis."

"Buddy Salinas, another zero," Montrose said. He popped a can of Coke. He bumped the fridge door shut with his between-successful-hunts butt. "I don't know where the hell he went. Nobody has seen him since . . . when? Your tip?"

"Chip's tip."

"Yeah, Chip, he had the last contact we're sure of, huh? Then . . ." To underline the disappearance, long black fingers walked off into space and eternity. "Nothing." A pause. "Maybe he's running?"

"Maybe."

"He could be dead."

"Another possibility."

Donahoo checked his other cards. They were nice cards. He looked at the present he'd gotten from Cominsky. It was embarrassing. Cominsky, the geek, had given him a new Colt Model Python .357 Magnum. He couldn't look at Cominsky. He thought it was just too fucking embarrassing.

"What I did find out though," Montrose said, glancing at Lewis. "No ballet lessons. Buddy Salinas, he may pull a posey's hose, but he don't fart with the fairies." He took a long drink of his Coke and now he was looking at Donahoo. "Everybody says that's bull. They all say the same thing. It never happened. No tippy-toe."

Donahoo flicked a glance at Lewis. More evidence. Chip Lyons, the weasel, he didn't want to find Buddy Salinas. He'd been laying a smoke screen. Lewis pretended a renewed interest in Oscar.

"Winters, our other *Semper Fidelis*," Palmer said quickly. He rejoined Cominsky on the futon that doubled as a sofa. "I don't think he's gonna talk. I've been to see him twice. He wants me to shit in my hat."

Lewis suddenly stood up. "Well, everything seems to be under control." He wagged a hand, a gesture of good-bye, or perhaps dismissal, in the general direction of Palmer and Cominsky. He pivoted, holding his pants, and wagged again for Gomez and Montrose.

"What are you telling me?" Donahoo demanded.

"You're a sergeant. You figure it out."

"I've been trying. I can't."

"A one-cell ameoba could figure it out."

Donahoo thought that he didn't have to put up with this abuse. He could have a relapse and go back to the VA. It would be safer there, the killers, Americans #1 and #2, if they were looking for him, they'd be looking for him here, he had checked out of the VA. So he could check back in under an assumed name. Juan Saul Ahmeeba. He could get that extra bed next to Charlie. He could say, "Charlie, the next time some guys come in, asking about my lady friends, tell them to mind their own business." Donahoo thought the other silver lining here, in addition to the Chip Lyons no-biggie lining, was that he hadn't told Charlie the last name of Rosie the Snake G-string the Wham Bam Ice Trail. Actually, she had so many first names, he forgot she had a last name.

"Dandruff could figure it out."

"Hey," Donahoo said. "Fat could. And apparently did."

Lewis stared at him. His expression was asking a question. Maybe you could jump in front of a truck next time? He pulled up his pants. He was definitely leaving.

Donahoo swung out of bed and limped after him. He caught him going over the threshold and held him in the hall. He pulled the door shut so the others couldn't hear.

Lewis shook him off angrily. "What the hell were you pulling in there? I thought we had a deal?"

Donahoo shook his head. "Not on the orchid. My orders cover the Great Beyond, American #1, and the mystery video."

"You kept your mouth shut about them—why not the orchid?"

"Because I couldn't hide it. Cominsky was there. He saw it."

"But you didn't have to make a big deal."

"Fuck," Donahoo said. "I've been doing my best here. Cominsky, he's my partner, he's doing balls-out work here, not to mention he probably saved my life, but I'm keeping things from him? He deserves to know. He's my partner."

Lewis sneered. "Your partner? A while ago he was a sleigh. You'd vote Republican to get rid of him. Now you're tighter than a fly's twat."

Donahoo said, "Lewis, I can't hide the orchid, okay? Cominsky knows all about it. He knows about Americans #1 and #2 killing Chaffee and he knows about *Vanda burgeffii. He knows.*"

"Yeah? Well, don't remind him. You're trying to make a federal case."

"You're trying to fly around it. You were twirling all over in there. You were doing everything but land."

"Okay. That's it. I'm outa here."

Donahoo got hold of Lewis's sleeve, pinned him. "Listen—you losing your memory?—the last orders from Saperstein were 'Get Primitivo.' And you recall what Lyons said—his last words? 'Primitivo.' "

"So?"

"One more time," Donahoo said. "Americans #1 and #2 kill Chaffee in Tijuana. The subject of money comes up. A million dollars. And the Mex cops think Chaffee took bribes from illegals. So there's our connection, maybe, to Primitivo. Now we've got Americans #1 and #2 trying to pay me half a million dollars for a video I don't know exists. They're a whistle away from killing me because I won't make a deal. Plus—*plus* here—the *Semper Fidelis* Gang, which has a link to Mexico, and therefore possibly a link to Primitivo, turns down a big job—a big, easy job—because they're marines. Translate that to patriots, flag and country, the stars and stripes forever, and we're talking about a military secret, or maybe a political assassination."

"Please," Lewis said. "You're scaring the shit outa me. You got one guy dead, one in the hospital, the other in jail. When do you think it's gonna go down?"

Donahoo told him what he'd told Cominsky. "We're not all patriots. Maybe somebody else is going to pull it?"

Lewis said, sounding full of sympathy, "I understand you had a close call, Tommy."

"Close?" Donahoo repeated. "It doesn't get any closer. Being here with you now, it's like an after-death experience, but enough about me. What about you, Lewis? How come you're so goddamn blasé about the mystery video? How come half a million dollars doesn't excite you anymore? I've seen you piss your socks when the Coke machine keeps a nickel. Suddenly half a million is loose change. What the fuck are you doing here?"

"Trying to leave."

"Okay, but just a reminder, the last place in Primitivo's date book, maybe, was the Tijuana Slough. Where, for about an hour, the Chipper was by himself, with a camcorder. Camcorders make videos. Some videos are very valuable. One in particular, if I had it, I could be going to paradise, Lewis."

Lewis stared. "Never mind the commercial. What do you want?"

"Lewis, Jesus Christ, I want to live, okay?" Donahoo gritted out. "I want this video shit taken seriously. I don't want it swept under the carpet or buried. I don't want vital information withheld from investigating officers."

"Such as?"

"Such as everything you want me to sit on. Such as Lyons being alone with that camcorder."

"Whose idea was it, he's by himself there?" Lewis asked. He already knew the answer.

"Mine."

"Did he offer to leave, let you stay?"

"Yes. But if I hadn't offered, he could have developed a sore foot, the conversation didn't get that far."

"It doesn't sound all that vital to me."

"How about the battery? The motor pool says it was a new battery. Somehow it becomes an old piece of shit battery."

"Guys are switching batteries all the time. It coulda been anybody."

"How about the dying words? The half million? The orchid? The ballet lessons?"

"Ballet lessons. Jesus Christ. Let me up, willya? The Chipper, he was pulling your leg, Tommy."

"Lewis. Listen. None of this is amusing. I was a nanosecond from being wasted. I was as close as anybody ever gets."

"Okay. You were close."

"Thank you. Now try to get close to this. These guys were talking about a million dollars when they killed Chaffee. Now they're talking about giving me half of that. So who do you think—seriously, put your mind to it, Lewis—who do you think might have been up for the other half?"

"That's what you want?"

"Yeah. I want to investigate Investigator Lyons."

"Tommy," Lewis said. "Let's try to put things into some kind of perspective here. I'm sure, in due course, there'll be an investigation, as there should be, by Internal Affairs. But right now we wanta look at the big picture." There was no one around. He looked anyway. His expression changed. He was going to ask a favor. He'd been waiting all morning to ask it, he just didn't know how. "Can it wait till after the parade?"

SIXTEEN

The Bo Thai Cafe. It was in Hillcrest, Sixth and University, a few doors down from the Thai Foon, which had started the trend. Now there was a Black Thai in El Cajon and a Thai Dal Wav in Ocean Beach.

Quillan and Taylor were in the Bo Thai's kitchen with the owner, a sleek, round, slit-eyed man, Joe Bong. Had he been a woman, he'd be Reubenesque. Being a man, he was a slug. Bong was half listening to Quillan. He was lifting the lids off pots and looking inside. Every lid released a different rich and foreign aroma.

"You want to work for me?" Bong said finally.

"Well, yeah, you can call it that, but it's more like cooperating with you, where it's mutually beneficial," Quillan answered, bent low. The ceiling was under seven feet and hung with strange cooking vessels and odd utensils. It was better suited to the mid-level Thai cooks darting around like rattled nannies minding bad children. "If I can help you out, you can help me out, I wouldn't call it work, I'd call it a good idea. You know what I'm saying? If it's a good idea, if it's good for both of us, it sounds good to me. Taylor here feels the same way. Why not?"

"What makes you think I need help?"

"There's always talk on the street, huh?" Quillan said. "That don't mean it's right. So it's not what I think. It's what you think." Quillan made a motion to Taylor. He wanted him to look in a pot. They might stay for lunch. It would be good politics if they stayed. "What I've heard—it doesn't mean it's right—somebody turned you down on a job. They didn't want to do it. Too big or something."

Joe Bong was suddenly interested. His slit eyes passed over him. Just the slits. The pupils weren't visible. "Who would turn me down?"

Quillan didn't know. He hadn't heard that part. The safest bet, he thought, would be to pick someone who couldn't deny it. He said, "What I heard—it doesn't mean it's right—Primitivo."

Joe Bong smiled. "Funny, what I heard, it doesn't mean it's right, Primitivo's on the missing list."

"Oh, yeah?"

"You never heard that?"

"I heard it. I didn't know you heard it."

Joe Bong smiled again. "What am I hearing? You get rid of the competition. Then you come in for the competition's job?"

Quillan stared at Joe Bong. He was ready to punch him. The Thai was third, maybe fourth on Quillan's list of wise guys he was going to bury. The ranking changed like TV ratings. In Quillan's mind, it really didn't matter who was where though. Eventually, they'd all go. Like Primitivo, they were in the way. He said, "I wouldn't call it competition. I wouldn't call it a job. What I'm making here—I'd call it a courtesy call." He looked at Taylor. "You heard enough?"

Taylor said, "So the Mex fuck is missing? Maybe he's using his frequent flyer miles? Golly whiz."

Joe Bong considered for a moment. Then he went back to his pots.

Quillan thought he ought to mush him, he really ought to put the slant in the pot, except he had a big enough war going already. He had Donahoo, who might or might not have a video. He said, "We're not killing the competition here. This ain't New York. This ain't New Jersey."

"I know what it is."

"Well, then?" Quillan demanded. He didn't know as much as he needed to know and he never would. The county was divided into an unknown number of ethnic gangs. Hispanic gangs, black gangs. Chinese, Cambodian, Korean, Vietnamese, Thai. Each had its own agenda. There was no organization, no overall control. If, one day, he were to pull this diverse army together, rule over its awesome power, he had to stay in touch with the brigade leaders, pretend that they were equals. He had to play a waiting game, strike when it was appropriate, not when it pleased him. "This is a courtesy call, Joe. Don't make it something else."

The slits returned, paused. "You think I'm competition?"

"Naw," Quillan said easily. "If I went against you, no contest. Me and Taylor, we'd open the Mike Thai Sahn, huh? 'Love us or we'll fuck you.' Listen, Joe, I like you, I've heard a lot of good things about you, but don't hand me this kind of fucking bullshit, I could change my mind."

"Tough guy."

"You know it."

Joe Bong considered. He was short, five six, and formed like a pie, the crust could be pushed in anywhere, but there was also a menace about him. It was in his face, the cruel, twisted mouth, the sneering hawk nose, and the eyes that couldn't be seen. His skin was a polished cherrywood. His hair was cut short like the bristles on a black pig. "You want to be friends?"

"I don't want to be enemies."

Taylor looked into a steamer. He screamed and dropped the lid. It clattered over to Quillan's feet.

"Rats," Taylor said, ashen. "The fucker's cooking rats."

"Jesus," Quillan said. He bent, got the lid. "I heard of cats."

"They're rats."

"Jesus." Quillan looked into the pot. They were sitting in a circle. Ten little furry animals, little beady eyes, little pointy noses. His stomach curdled and he looked at Joe Bong. "You fucking slant. You're cooking rats."

"Bats," Joe Bong told him, smiling. The racial slur was lost in the moment. He couldn't hide his amusement. "Fruit bats. From Guam. They're a great delicacy." He took the lid. "See? They've got wings."

Quillan peered in again. The Thai was right. They looked like rats but they had black leatherette-like wings folded at their sides. "People eat them?"

"Guamanians," Joe Bong said, smiling. "They eat everything. The fur, the leather. They suck out the brains and spit out the bones." He put the lid on the steamer. "Actually, they're very clean. They eat only breadfruit. They live in trees. They never touch the ground."

Taylor finally found his voice. "The Guamanians or the bats?"

"Guam, 'Where America's Day Begins,'" Joe Bong said. He couldn't stop smiling. "Why they say that—it's on the other side of the international dateline." He motioned, indicating that they should leave the kitchen, return to the front of the café. "An interesting place. Strategically located. I visit friends there occasionally. The island is thirty miles long, SAC has nuclear bombers at one end, the navy has nuclear subs at the other. Not a wise place to be in the event of a world war. It probably would be the first to go."

They went into the café. It was crowded with people eating lunch.

There were a lot of Thais present, but other Asians too, and a scattering of Caucasians. It was vibrant and noisy. Joe Bong picked a booth for them. He sat on one side and indicated that his guests should sit together across from him.

"What's this got to do with Guam?" Quillan asked. He could sense that they had crossed some threshold. They were going to talk business.

"Nothing. Except you sometimes meet strategic people in strategic places. They go there to—look at strategic things?"

A waitress came. She was pretty in a flat way. She had a flat face and a flat chest. She also was a Thai, but unlike Joe Bong, her eyes, the pupils and the whites of them, were open teardrops, brimming with sadness. She didn't ask what they wanted. She said, "Please, what is your pleasure?"

Joe Bong ordered first and expansively as a way of showing that his guests could have anything they wished. He ordered a starter, Tod Mun Pla, ground fish with red curry, deep fried, served with cucumber salad, and a soup, Tom-Yum, prepared with squid, and which had lemongrass, mushrooms, chili, and lime juice among its ingredients. For his entree, he ordered a specialty, Love Boat Vegetarian, consisting of mock scallops, mock duck, glass noodles, and vegetables, all wrapped in foil and steamed. Quillan ordered the Three's Company—shrimp, pork, and chicken sautéed with vegetables and the house curry paste. Taylor asked for a Coke with the cap on.

Joe Bong put the menus away. He waited until the waitress was out of earshot. "I do have an opportunity," he said then, his voice low. "It may also be an opportunity for you."

Taylor was going to say something. Quillan stopped him. Quillan said simply, "Go on."

"I want to be frank with you. You are not the first choice. I had another party in mind, they turned it down, they had—what?—reservations. And then I thought of Primitivo, I had a preliminary talk with him, fairly detailed actually, but he has—what? Become a frequent flyer? You want chopsticks?"

Taylor spoke now. "Why you telling us we're third draft?"

"Why don't you let him talk?" Quillan suggested.

"Forks for my friends," Joe Bong called. He said, "I'd rather you got it from me than someone else. If you heard it here first, that avoids misunderstandings. It's important that we understand each other." He again lowered his voice. "I sent my people out. They told me they couldn't find Primitivo. They told me they heard a lot about you though, Quillan." The slit eyes settled. "General."

Quillan felt a small rush of sincere pride in a hard-won accomplishment. "I don't know what you're talking about."

"So here is my proposition," Joe Bong said, sliding over that. It was as if it was never said and never heard. "I need a heart stolen."

Quillan and Taylor exchanged glances. Taylor said, "Is the guy still alive?"

"Yes." Joe Bong smiled in appreciation. "But only for a few more days. He is near death in Mercy Hospital. He knows he is going to die. He has agreed to donate his heart. When he dies, it will be taken out of him, and it will be flown to Burbank, where a transplant patient awaits."

Quillan and Taylor both remained silent.

"Your assignment, if you wish to accept it," Joe Bong said, demonstrating that he was fully Americanized, he had watched *Mission Impossible,* "is to intercept the heart on its way to Lindbergh Field. Steal it and take it to Montgomery Field. A plane there will take it to a different transplant patient who has been denied a heart because he is such a poor risk." He said, "That's the only thing poor about him—the risk. Actually, he's very rich. Happy to pay almost any amount for a new heart."

Quillan had been holding his breath. "How much?"

"I was thinking—perhaps two hundred thousand?"

Quillan thought, oh, fuck, a miracle. He'd been thinking of

punching the guy, and the guy, he was solving all his problems, everything. He was giving him his life back. He asked, fearful that his voice might reveal his eagerness, "Do you know what a ballplayer gets paid these days? And he's not risking his life and freedom? He's just swinging a bat at a ball—and missing most of the time?"

Joe Bong said, "Don't ask me about sports. In my country, the big thing, it's kicking someone in the balls. You try to make a comparison, it doesn't compute."

"Different cultures?" Taylor suggested.

"That could be the explanation." Joe Bong was looking at Quillan. "Perhaps I could pay more. What do you think fair?"

Quillan considered. He had his price. He wouldn't do it unless he got it. He *had* to have it. It was what he needed. "Half a million."

Joe Bong said, "Too much."

"No, it isn't."

"Two hundred and fifty thousand."

"No. Half million. Or get someone else. I won't come down."

"You drive a hard bargain."

"I get a fair price," Quillan told him. He said, as if that were settled, "When's this likely to happen?"

Joe Bong gestured. He had accepted the price without saying so. "Tomorrow, the next day. Soon."

"You'll pay on delivery?"

"Yes."

"There'll be up-front expenses. We'll need something down."

"How much?"

"Fifty thousand."

"I anticipated that. It will be delivered this afternoon."

"Wait a minute," Taylor said. He had been silent all this time. "You're throwing money away here. Why? There's six guys within two blocks who'd bring you a heart for a couple grand. They'd kill the first fuck they thought had one."

Quillan looked at him. The wolf eyes, usually empty, showed contempt. "It wouldn't be compatible, Taylor."

"Yes, there's that, and there's more," Joe Bong said, looking at Quillan, not Taylor. He had taken Quillan's side now. He was arguing against himself. "There's timing, it's crucial. And how you take it out has a lot to do with how you put it back in. I think, everything considered, a very wealthy man, his life hanging by a thread, would be happy to pay half a million dollars to remain alive. In these circumstances, think about it, half a million dollars, it's nothing. That's for you. I have my share." Joe Bong finally turned to Taylor. "He understands he's getting professionals."

Quillan was waiting. His wolf eyes were again silent, empty.

Taylor said, "I suppose." He said, looking at Quillan, "Okay. I'm in."

"Excellent."

The flat waitress came with Joe Bong's Tod Mun Pla. Taylor's expression changed—he'd gotten a whiff apparently. He pushed out of the booth and headed for the toilet.

Bong asked, "Weak stomach?"

"Not for the things that count," Quillan said. He waited for the washroom door to bang shut. "You want to tell me what we're really stealing?"

Bong had a cucumber slice halfway to his mouth. It hung precariously. "Can't say."

"Then write it down." Quillan got a pen and passed it with his napkin. "Or I'm not going to snatch the fucking thing."

Bong put his bowl aside. He accepted the pen and napkin. He printed, block letters, XLA BMGS. He shoved it across the table.

Quillan studied it. Aw, he thought. A McGuffin. "What's this, tell me?"

"All you need to know."

"I want to know more."

"It's strategic."

No doubt. Quillan picked at his food. XLA BMGS. Strategic. He was familiar with strategic. The kind of stuff that upset the balance of the world. "What's the rest of it?"

Joe Bong didn't answer. When Quillan looked at him, wolf eyes, cold, empty, the fat Thai shook his head.

"I liked what you said before," Quillan told him. "If I hear it here first—that avoids misunderstandings."

Joe Bong's response could barely be heard. "It's the guidance system for a small missile. The missile is designed to seek out and destroy a single person."

"Do I know this person?"

"You misunderstand. No particular person. But one person out of many."

"A face in a crowd?"

"Yes." Joe Bong resumed eating. "Does that change your mind?"

Quillan wasn't sure. He felt strongly that he'd been fucked over while serving flag and country. He didn't think he owed any loyalty. Still? Was there someplace better?

Joe Bong was waiting.

Normally, yeah, the McGuffin probably would make him stop, Quillan thought. In the usual scheme of things, pass. But these were difficult times. Driven by desperation, and desperation made a lousy chauffeur—who said that? Quillan thought again that Joe Bong somehow divined secrets he shouldn't be privy to. He must suspect, for instance, how much he, Quillan, needed, maybe needed, half a million dollars. "It's not a problem."

A flicker of relief showed on Joe Bong's sleek slug face. "We're not sharing with Taylor?"

"No." Quillan tore up the napkin, put the pieces in his pocket. "There's stuff Taylor doesn't need to know." He had the strange feeling, almost frightening, that he was crossing over here, changing sides, going to the enemy camp. He thought that he could be signing up for the crime of the century, and that a dead cop was guiding his hand, pushing the pen for him. He said, "Strategic. Does that mean a heavy guard?"

"No. Not in this instance. It involves a site-to-site transfer within the same private company. They do it all the time and they don't make a fuss. If they don't tell anybody, then nobody knows about it. That's the theory."

"I'll need how many people?"

"Six, the most. Two, three vehicles. Nothing fancy. There'll be a rendezvous with a chopper. The chopper is my concern."

"What else?"

Joe Bong was writing another note on another napkin. He slid it across to Quillan. It said, *Kill Buddy Salinas.*

Quillan stared at it. Jesus, the slant, he knew everything, huh? Too much. Quillan thought he ought to be very careful about what he said and how he said it. He said, "That's my business. I'll be doing it for myself. If, which isn't possible, I was going to do it for you, there'd be no charge."

"That's how much I planned to play," Joe Bong told him.

SEVENTEEN

Room 308. The Hotel Arthur. A flop at Market and Eighth. Donahoo stood at the door, holding his new Colt Model Python .357 Magnum. He should have been home in bed. He wasn't well enough, or strong enough, to be back on the job, and every minute of the long day had underscored that. He hurt like hell. He was weak as new tea. But he was happy. If not duty, frustration had called, sent him into the streets, into the flea bags of the Gaslamp, looking for Buddy Salinas, and now he was pretty sure he'd found him. The hotel clerk, shown a photograph, had said, "Yeah, that looks like him," and an old geezer sitting in the lobby, eager to be a part of history, had said, "Mebbe."

Donahoo wondered if Buddy Salinas was alone or if perhaps he was entertaining. The clerk had said that someone else had been around earlier, asking for him. A strong, silent type who wouldn't take no for an answer, and who had gone up, checked for himself. A crisp, no-nonsense guy who had looked like he might be back. What made it more exciting, Donahoo had passed around the drawings of American #1 and American #2, and the clerk thought the strong, silent type bore a good resemblance to American #1. The geezer was iffy but agreed it was possible. Donahoo could hear just the one person breathing hard, but that didn't prove anything. Maybe Buddy was entertaining the strong, silent type. Maybe the strong, silent type was American #1. Donahoo wondered whether he should knock or kick in the door. He wondered if he *could* kick it in. It was a flimsy door. He hit it with his shoulder and it splintered.

Buddy spun around like a frightened cat. He was holding a folded shirt. He let it drop. "How'd you find me?" he blurted out, staring fearfully. He was high. Heroin, probably. He was sweating. Glistening beads were puddled on his forehead. He had a small green plastic suitcase open on the unmade bed. A small pile of clothes was next to it.

"Radar," Donahoo said, thinking that he could taste the fear. He could smell the sweat but taste the fear. "Do you know how many flophouses there are in the Gaslamp? Too many. My feet, they're killing me." He looked around, there was just the single room, a wall sink, no toilet. There was nobody under the bed. He put away his Python. He carefully closed the splintered door. More questionable damage in the relentless pursuit of justice. They could put it on his Mercedes 420SEL tab. "Where do you think you're going?"

"Going?" Buddy started taking stuff out of the suitcase. He had been putting it in and now he was taking it out. "I'm just moving in." He said, wiping his face with a pair of shorts, "That was tough about the Chipper, huh? Who'd have thunk?"

Donahoo leaned against a rickety armoire. He was hurting. He'd taken off the neck brace, it was killing him, he planned to wear it only at night, but he still needed the cane. He said, "Bullshit, you moved in yesterday, you paid a week in advance, now you're running, where you going?"

Buddy considered. The sweat was beading on his forehead. He had a tic in his left eye that Donahoo hadn't seen before. Maybe he always had it, Donahoo thought. Maybe it showed only under pressure. Donahoo wondered what had prompted the pressure. Him kicking in the door? Or something else? Probably something else. Buddy had been sweating for a while. His shirtfront was like a washcloth. "I'm waiting."

"What happened to you?"

"I got hit by a car. I'm waiting."

"You look like you oughta be in bed."

"I tried that. It didn't work. And I'm still waiting."

Buddy grimaced. He was about thirty, a couple years either way, but he looked much younger because of his size. He was smaller than Donahoo by half, not much bigger than a midget, but he was a small man, not a midget. He had never grown much. He had a child's body and a child's face. He had a child's voice. It was squeaky. He was Mexican, but he was very pale, like he never got out. He wasn't an albino, but his appearance did have some sort of buggered-genes explanation. His smooth jet-black hair and black marble eyes made him look even paler. It was like he had been dusted with talc. He was wearing a black suit with a white shirt and a red bow tie. Black bookkeeper shoes with the cap toes. He said, "Your mother sucks giraffes."

Donahoo, despite his condition, despite the pain, grabbed him by the lapels and lifted him up and flung him on top of the rickety armoire. He took the bed. He stretched out, pushing aside a copy of the *Union-Trib*. He said, "You're paid for a week, Buddy. You're gonna stay up there for a week. You're gonna sit there in your own shit, nothing to eat, nothing to drink."

"Fuck you."

"No, Buddy, *fuck you.* I'm gonna send out for Cokes, cheeseburgers, fries, but I'm gonna eat 'em, not you. You don't even get to lick the paper. I'm gonna get a girl in here, a hooker, she'd be perfect for you, an itty-bitty thing, she's called Minnie Mouth, but she's just for me, not you. You're not gonna snap a garter."

"Fuck you."

"I'm gonna turn the television around so you can't watch it."

"What do you want to know?"

Donahoo smiled. He liked Buddy. A small guy, but a lot of style. It was a shame what drugs could do to people, he thought. It put them in a rathole that smelled like yesterday's vomit. A cracked window overlooking a bus stop. Torn blinds and frayed rugs and a busted bed. Crooked pictures out of old magazines. Buddy, he was smart, he could have done better. He was supposed to be a genius with figures. He didn't need a calculator. He could do it all in his head. He could have been a bookkeeper but he couldn't sit still. He was always looking for his next fix. He left a trail like the tracks on his arms. He couldn't hide who he was or how pitiful.

Donahoo said, "Do you take ballet lessons?"

"What?"

"Ballet lessons. Do you take 'em? Yes or no?"

"Jesus Christ. You put me up here to ask me that?"

"Yes or no?"

"No." Buddy glared from his perch. "Ballet lessons. You gotta be nuts. That's what this is about?"

Donahoo wished he still smoked. It would be a good time to have a cigarette. He could collect his thoughts. Light up, blow a little smoke. Look through the curling, thinning, vanishing wisps— for the truth? "It's about Primitivo."

"What about him?"

"He didn't show up. Nobody else did either."

Buddy hesitated. Donahoo, watching, saw that. Buddy shifted uncomfortably atop the armoire. He was sweating. The fear was back, prompted by the question. He said, "So what?"

"So it was a waste of time. A waste of the taxpayers' money."

"So I'm sorry. I thought it was good information. If it wasn't . . . ?" He tried to smile. "I've been wrong before."

"No, you haven't," Donahoo said, watching. "That's what makes this so interesting. You've *never* been wrong. I've been through the Chipper's file on you. It says you were one hundred percent, Buddy. Triple A rating. Your word was gold."

"Files can lie."

"You're saying the Chipper was a liar?"

"Fuck you."

"No, *fuck you.*" Donahoo got the *Union-Trib.* "I'm in no hurry here. I'm happy. I've got everything I want. I'm getting paid to do this." He grinned. "If there's anything you want, don't ask."

"Fuck you."

"You keep saying that, but what is actually happening, it's the other way around, Buddy. You've got a problem. You're in denial here."

"Fuck you."

"Maybe I shouldn't say this, Buddy," Donahoo said. "But we've got a cop killed here? Charles Francis Lyons, the Chipper. The best cop in the department. Totally dedicated to his sworn duty. A paragon of virtue and an example to all who knew him. If you're not gonna do it for me, I think you should do it for the Chipper, Buddy. I really think that."

"Yeah? Well, fuck him too."

"You gotta know that this case was very important to the Chipper. When nobody showed at the slough, he got all bent outa shape, you know? He was like a girl her first time. All the wrong responses."

"Too bad."

Donahoo started reading the *Union-Trib.* He'd had a busy, pain-filled day. He hadn't stopped for a moment. All he knew was flop-houses. He didn't know what else was happening. He checked the headlines. HEALTH CARE IN TROUBLE. He thought that had already happened. WOMAN SUES CLINTON. That had already happened too. He thought of looking at the date. Maybe it was an old paper.

"I could sue you," Buddy said. "You're gonna hear from my lawyer. Illegal detention."

Donahoo was checking above-the-fold headlines. SLAIN BORDER PATROL OFFICER ON THE TAKE? He read the story. Tijuana. Willard Chaffee. Veteran officer with the U.S. Border Patrol. Ice pick in the heart in the Club Hemingway. Suspected of taking bribes to let illegals cross the border at points under his control and/or surveillance.

"Cruel and unusual punishment."

Donahoo was reading a vaguely worded suggestion that Chaffee might have been getting his nuts off at the moment of impact. Then he noticed, below the fold, end of the story, a small ink drawing, a skull and crossbones. Beside it a carefully printed warning. *You're next, lover.*

"You can't do this to me."

"Save it for your mother."

Donahoo resumed reading. Chaffee had been well known in Tijuana as a member of the border patrol. It was suggested that his murder might somehow be linked to his work. The San Diego Sheriff's Department was assisting Baja's State Judicial Police in the investigation. Sure, Donahoo thought. He said, "What do you know about Chaffee?"

"Huh?"

"The border patrol guy. He got nicked in Tijuana. What do you know about him?"

"Nothing."

"Bullshit. You've got a skull and crossbones here."

"Where?"

"Goddamn." Donahoo showed it. "Next to the story."

Buddy Salinas was sweating. "It must have come that way. It's not mine. I just grabbed it somewhere."

Donahoo pushed up. He was thinking now that there had to be a connection between Chaffee and Primitivo. Maybe Chaffee was supposed to grease Primitivo's way across the border for his meeting at the Tijuana Slough. Maybe he fouled up? Maybe he blew the meeting? Maybe he knew too much—that's why he was killed.

"This is getting interesting," Donahoo said. "You're the most reliable snitch in the third world. Suddenly, inexplicably, you're full of shit. Not only that, you're running scared. You're sweating like the Three Little Pigs. You're packing your suitcase for a long trip. You got two shirts in there. And you don't want to talk to me. Why is that?" He stared up at Buddy Salinas. "I think it's got something to do with Chaffee. What do you think?" He said, "Maybe we should go downtown?"

"No."

"No thank you, or no?"

Buddy shifted atop the armoire. Donahoo thought he looked like a distressed penguin. The slick black hair and the chalk-white face. The shiny black suit and the white shirt. The little black shoes hanging over the edge. A flightless bird trapped in fearful straits.

"I gotta tell you," Donahoo said, starting over. "I'm doing this in loving memory of Charles Francis Lyons, the Chipper." He put the newspaper aside. "This isn't your normal case anymore. This is a debt owed a fallen comrade. This is sacred duty. The Chipper, he's no longer here to complete his appointed rounds, so I'm gonna finish the job for him, Buddy. I'm gonna find that fucking Primitivo. And you're gonna help me."

No response. Donahoo reached into his coat pocket to get his secret weapon. He undid a ziplock bag poked with breathing holes. His hand emerged holding a big grey rat.

Buddy stared in horror.

"This is going in your pants, pal," Donahoo said. The rat

squirmed wildly. "It's specially trained—it was raised on shit—to go straight up your fag ass." He pushed closer with his arm outstretched. The rat was fighting to free itself. "One last time. You gonna help or not?"

Buddy, no warning, heaved himself from the armoire, bounced off the bed, hit the floor running. He crashed through the window with his arms over his face. He screamed.

Donahoo lunged after him too late. Buddy was through the shattered glass and gone. He plunged three floors to the sidewalk. He made a faint splat.

Silence. Then a woman screamed.

Oh, whoa, Donahoo thought. He stood for a moment, listening to the woman scream, blaming himself and trying not to. He'd known coming into the room that the little bugger was high on something, totally paranoid, scared stupid. But not *this* scared, he thought. Not this bad. Who would have figured this bad?

Donahoo told himself it wasn't just the rat. Buddy had been in a panic long before he saw it. He'd lied about packing to leave. He'd lied about the skull and crossbones, not having seen them, that was bullshit. And he was deathly afraid of going to jail. The only time he'd told the truth, when he was plainly sincere, it was about the ballet lessons. Which made Chip Lyons a liar. That part at least was settled. Lyons had been laying down a smoke screen. He didn't want him, Donahoo, talking to Buddy, anymore than Buddy wanted to talk.

He realized he didn't have the rat. It was in his hand, now it wasn't. Where the hell did the rat go? It just disappeared. He almost started looking for it. Yeah, this was his fault, he thought. *Partly* his fault. He went through the pile of clothes on the bed and the things in the suitcase. He was trying to concentrate, get the job done, freak later. He checked the bureau drawers. He looked in the armoire. No ballet slippers. No tights. It was *settled.*

He considered looking for the rat. This case, it was fucked, he thought. It had started badly and it was getting worse. He left with a last glance at the smashed window. Something else that could be put on his tab. He limped downstairs, hurrying as best he could. He thought he was getting awfully hard. He felt sorry for Buddy Salinas. It was his fault, *partly* his fault. But what worried him most was getting to the corpse before somebody stole the wallet.

EIGHTEEN

"I don't know about you, Tommy," Saperstein said. "You're losing your touch or something. You can't arrest a midget?"

Donahoo sighed. He'd known it was coming. He'd heard it coming off the elevator, coming down the hall. The Saperstein steamroller. He said, "He wasn't a midget and I wasn't arresting him. He was a small man and I was interrogating him."

"On top of an armoire?"

"*He* was on top of it."

"And you let him jump out a window?"

"First he jumped off the armoire. *Then* he jumped out the window. And I didn't *let* him. He didn't ask permission."

Cominsky, more geek than usual today—he'd gotten rid of

his ponytail in favor of a death-march haircut—said, "It's all my fault."

Saperstein glared. "How can it be your fault? You weren't even there."

"That's why it's my fault."

"A crackpot investigating crackpots," Saperstein said. "More genius." He was struggling out of his suit coat. He obviously hadn't been to his own office yet. Donahoo thought maybe he should feel honored. The guy had come straight from his car to jump on him.

Saperstein was only half out of the coat and he was already rolling up a sleeve. He looked at Lewis. "Get this back on track. This is what I want: More progress. Fewer dead midgets. Okay?"

Donahoo wished he hadn't stopped smoking. It was moments like this, he thought. He could get out a cigarette. He could light it. He could stick it in Saperstein's eye.

"You've got it, Chief," Lewis said. "You've seen your last dead midget."

"Thank you," Saperstein said. He got out of his coat and hung it over his arm. He cast a final withering glance at Donahoo, told him, "You should have stayed in bed, superstar," and strode out of the sickos, crackpots, underwear and mad bombers squad room. Blastoff heat patterns seemed to shimmer in his wake.

Gomez said, "Caramba! Who put the tamale up his ass?"

Donahoo said to Lewis, "Can I talk to you?"

Lewis looked wary now. He pulled up his baggy pants and stuffed in his shirttail. "Why?"

"Why?"

"You're doing it again."

"What?"

"Emphasis."

Donahoo looked around the squad room. Gomez and Montrose. Palmer and Cominsky. They were all staring. They had just finished the police chief show. They were waiting for the captain, Investigations show. Their antennae, if they had any, would be scraping the ceiling.

"'Shall we?" Lewis prompted.

Donahoo made a let's-huddle sign to his squad members, then led the way to his office, a small glassed-off cubicle in a corner of the squad room. They crowded in with their coffees. Donahoo took the sofa chair, leaving Lewis, as his superior officer, the swivel chair behind the desk. Palmer and Cominsky grabbed the two remaining chairs. Gomez and Montrose had to stand. It was crowded and uncomfortable. It was the way Donahoo wanted it. It induced brief, to-the-point meetings. He didn't have very many rules for success, but one of them was long hours and short meetings. He hated meetings, and now he was having a meeting with five, no six, guys, including himself, and they were all going to be jazzed, and it was going to be chaos. He was looking for some way to go and he was going to leave with six sets of directions. Too many guys, too many theories, too much grandstanding, he thought. He not only subscribed to the theory that a committee had designed the camel, he also felt certain that a committee couldn't find a camel. Normally, he dealt with the squad's members as separate teams, and, of late, sometimes one-on-one. He got closer that way, found out what they were thinking, not just what they were saying. He spent a lot of time with them individually and that closeness worked. Saperstein could scream all he wanted, SCUMB had the best cases-solved ratio in the department, better even than Homicide, where most of the time the killer waited to be arrested, crying and looking for the cuffs.

This morning, though, with Lewis on hand—Lewis present to get things *on track*—there had to be a meeting. There was the one scarred desk with piles of old newspapers and magazines hiding a computer terminal. Several photographs in cheap frames. Donahoo's mother, Kathleen, and his stepfather, Mike. His ex-wife, Monica, the goddess. His lost love, Presh Logan, the exotic. He kept Monica and Presh out here and buried them at home. When he got a woman over, *if* he got a woman over, he didn't want her asking, who are Monica and Presh? Father Charlie was also present, and, hidden away a bit, behind a diskette storage bin, barely visible, the cat, Oscar. There was a large bookcase, filled mainly with municipal, county, and state codes, police manuals, law enforcement books. Two four-drawer filing cabinets. Nothing on the wall except maps and a Marilyn Monroe calendar. Marilyn, her skirt up, going Whooo!

Donahoo looked at Lewis. The beefy captain made a gesture. It was Donahoo's squad. He, Lewis, was just putting it on track.

"Okay," Donahoo said. "Let's talk about Buddy Salinas." He wanted on track too, he thought. Or was that Track 3? He felt a little giddy. Not much sleep again. Buddy taking the leap—that, when the reality set in, had rattled the Murphy bed. Not his fault—okay, partly—he kept telling himself, but inside he blamed himself. He wondered if he ought to have some counseling. Maybe a couple of lessons in the fine art of armoire questioning. "Buddy was on the run. He checked into the Arthur Tuesday, a week's stay, and he was checking out again yesterday, Wednesday. In the morning, when he wasn't in, there was a guy around looking for him, maybe American #1. The guy may have waited in the room for him, then left. Maybe, maybe not."

Cominsky said, "Which connects us to Chaffee."

Donahoo looked at Cominsky and his new haircut. Cominsky's explanation for it was that he had asked a guy for the time and the guy had misunderstood and given him a dime. So he'd gotten shorn. He didn't want to be taken for some hippie bum.

"Maybe," Donahoo said about a Chaffee connection. He took a manila envelope out of a jacket pocket, undid the clasp, and dumped the contents on the desk. A tattered leather wallet, a money clip holding a few small-denomination bills, a handful of change, a cheap wristwatch, a plain gold wedding band, a pair of reader's magnifying glasses, a small bag of heroin, and a half-smoked pouch of cigarettes, Basics. A ball-point pen, black ink, medium point, Bic. A Greyhound bus ticket.

"Was he married?" Palmer asked. He stood up, assuming his standard pugilist post, chest puffed, arms akimbo. He picked up the ring and put it on his own finger, where it twirled loosely. It would fit a larger man. He answered his own question. "Not necessarily."

"I heard he was a fag," Gomez said. He slipped nicely into Palmer's vacated chair. He adjusted his fake black suede jacket and decided not to cross his legs. He was wearing a pair of gray slacks with a crease that barked at you. "Or do we give a fig?"

"Bisexual," Lewis told him. "Acey-deucy. Boy or girl. Your ordinary little guy and also a bumfuck and a cocksuck. You can read all about in the Chipper's files."

Donahoo went to another pocket and the *Union-Trib* with its front page follow-up on the murder of Willard Chaffee. He had taken it from Buddy's hotel room. It had the drawing of the skull and crossbones. He made some space and spread it out on his desk.

Lewis was watching. "The life and times . . ."

Donahoo nodded. Yeah. That was it. One pitiful little pile. All he knew about Ernesto Garcia Buddy Salinas. All there was left of the guy. Put it together with his clothes and it wouldn't fill a trash bag.

"A squat load," Donahoo said. He retrieved the newspaper. He showed the skull and crossbones, and the carefully printed warning, *You're next, lover.* "Except maybe this. I'm assuming Buddy's visitor left it. Buddy freaked when I asked about it." Donahoo got the bus ticket. "And except maybe this. Gary, Indiana. One way."

Gomez looked thoughtful. "He'd be awful lonely there. How many white midget fag Mexicans are there in Gary, Indiana?"

"Maybe we oughta check it out?" Palmer suggested.

Lewis said, "Not yet."

"I should have figured him for the jump," Donahoo told them. He had decided to never, ever, mention the rat. "The little bugger was in role reversal. He's a snitch and his lips are sealed." He went back to the newspaper. "This is all I've got. I ask him about it, and crash, he jumps." He paused. Could he do this? Be so less than truthful? "No, wait a minute. I threaten to bring him in and he jumps." He kicked it around in his head for a while. "Where are we here?"

"In Buddy's glass world?" Montrose wondered. "Hell, if you're gonna bring a snitch in, you gotta take that chance, Sarge. There's guys in jail that hate snitches worse than cops. You know that. You bring a snitch in and it's like you're signing his death warrant."

Donahoo looked at him. "For fuck's sake, would you mind?"

"He's got enough guilt," Lewis said gently. "He already shot a guy in the back this week. Remember?"

"Hey, it makes perfect sense to me," Gomez said. "Buddy takes a header, three floors? The suspense is over. He doesn't have to sweat out who's got the ice pick and when is it coming?"

Lewis conceded. "It has possibilities."

"Or," Palmer said. "Or." He picked up the bus ticket. "He's outa here, right? He's outa here *before* you kick in his door, Sarge. He's outa here before you start asking questions and making threats." He put the ticket back on the desk. "He's outa here, the hard way—Gary, Indiana?—because he's already marked for death. He knows if he stays, he's dead. So when you suggested he might be staying . . . ?"

"El splatto?" This from Gomez.

"I like it better," Lewis said. "There's this fine line here. Buddy is marked for death because he is marked for death. Or Buddy is marked for death because he might talk to Donahoo. The first takes precedence."

Donahoo looked at Montrose. "See?"

"Now," Palmer said. He was rolling. "Now, in this light, we look again at the murder of Willard Chaffee. We can presume— the skull and crossbones—that when Buddy read about Chaffee's murder, he realized that he, too, was going to be murdered. That's why he made the drawing. Wrote himself that warning."

There was a moment of silence. Then several of them spoke at the same time. "*He* wrote it?"

"Sure. It's very Freudian."

More silence.

"When we find Chaffee's killer . . . ?" Gomez began.

"Maybe it all starts falling into place," Lewis said. "Maybe we find the guy who had Buddy scared to death. Maybe we find the link that leads us to Primitivo."

Cominsky had picked up the *Union-Trib*. He was looking through it. Donahoo said, "What are you doing?"

"I haven't seen this yet," Cominsky said. He looked up and around. "I'm listening."

"How can you read and listen?" Gomez demanded.

Cominsky regarded him blankly. "You can't?"

"Chaffee," Donahoo said, looking at Gomez and Montrose. "Do we know anymore?"

Gomez gave a little shrug. "Not much. We just got started. But enough to know he coulda been a bad apple. What they're suggesting in the paper. He'd been in the border patrol a long time, almost twenty years, no promotion. That's almost unheard-of. He also had a couple reprimands for assaulting illegals. What saved him, apparently, was a special knack for the big arrest. He wasn't picking 'em off one at a time, he was catching large groups, ten, twenty. He was stopping migrations."

"So what are you saying? He was lucky?"

"Good intelligence."

"Or he's making deals with competing smugglers? Pay him off and you get through? Don't pay and you don't get through?"

"Or he was making deals," Gomez agreed.

Donahoo turned to Montrose. "Personal life?"

"Divorced. Two kids in school. The ex-wife had to take him into court to get her child support. He spent a lot of his off-duty time in Tijuana. He liked the bars. He liked the whores."

"He had a girl there?"

Montrose turned his palms up. He didn't know.

"Friends?"

"We just got started," Gomez said.

Donahoo looked at Palmer and Cominsky. "The Jewelers Exchange idiots? Anything new there?"

"They're not talking," Palmer answered. "Powell and Winters could be as dead as their pal Newton. Nothing."

"We leaned on 'em, Sarge," Cominsky said quickly. He was still picking through the *Union-Trib.* "Nothing fazes them. They don't care if it's hard time or it's early release. They're resigned to their fate."

"How about the armored car?"

Palmer said, "Mexicans stole it. Not them."

"Yeah, but how did they get it?"

"We still don't know."

"And we still don't know how it came across the border?"

"No."

Donahoo considered. "So does the Jewelers Exchange caper connect in any way at all?"

Palmer shrugged. "We just got started."

"Keep checking, you think?" Lewis said to Donahoo.

Palmer said, "I think it's a dead end."

Donahoo wondered. He was inclined to put everybody on Chaffee. But the idea of an armored car being smuggled across the border intrigued him. That would be like taking a cow into a restaurant. Sooner or later somebody was bound to notice. There was also the thought—he was playing long shots—that it might somehow connect to Chaffee.

"This Newton," Donahoo said. "They're gonna bury him, right? Go to his funeral. See what you can find out."

Palmer made a face. "Two funerals in the same week?"

Montrose said, "One is a parade, remember?"

Donahoo finished his coffee. He gathered up Buddy Salinas's belongings and shoved them in the manila envelope. He hesitated with the bus ticket. He wondered why Buddy would buy it in advance. If Buddy was in such a hurry, why would he buy a ticket, go home to pack, then go back to the bus depot? He had twenty dollars' worth of clothes in the suitcase. Not worth risking his life for. So why didn't he buy the ticket and leave?

Gomez said, "Are we through here, Sarge?"

Donahoo was thinking. Buddy didn't buy the ticket. Somebody bought it for him. Somebody gave it to him and said get out of town?

"Uh," Donahoo said. "Gomez, Montrose, you keep on Chaffee. Palmer, Cominsky, the *Semper Fidelis* Gang. I'll stay on Buddy."

"You going to Gary?"

He smiled. "Maybe. I've got a ticket."

"Here's something," Cominsky said. He showed Donahoo the *Union-Trib*'s crossword puzzle. "The same guy did it. The puzzle and the warning on the front page."

Donahoo took it. He studied it briefly. The same black ink. The same careful printing. There were repeated entries, XLA and BMGS, subbing for the correct answers to tough questions. Twenty-four across, four letters, "wife of Cuchulain." Now, that's a tough question, so he wrote in BMGS. Thirty-five across, four letters, "Sleuths, briefly." Maybe a tough question, so again he wrote in BMGS. Fifty-five down, three letters, "Split pea of India"—oh, for sure, Donahoo thought—the guy put in XLA. Imagine missing that? Maybe his mind was elsewhere? Donahoo handed it to Lewis.

"I dunno," Lewis said after a while. He handed it back. "Could be." He said, "Emer," and then, throwing it away, "Emer, the wife of Cuchulain."

Donahoo gave it to Palmer. "XLA. BMGS. See if you can figure it out."

Cominsky said, "Hey? Why not me?"

"Because you haven't got a brother-in-law in the navy."

Palmer pushed up. He was ready to go to work. Gomez and Montrose began a slow drift for the door. Lewis said, "You heard the chief. No more small persons who are deceased."

Cominsky was sifting now through the stuff in Buddy's wallet.

Donahoo waited for him to finish. He'd already been through it. Mainly receipts from fast-food joints. ID, bus pass, library card. Nothing much.

"Secret compartment?" Cominsky said. He removed a passport-size photo. He showed it to Gomez. "Well, I guess he really was acey-deucy, huh?"

"Vavoom," Gomez said. There apparently wasn't a word for her in Spanish.

They passed it around. Montrose whistled. Palmer moaned softly. Lewis managed to get an eyebrow up. He gave it to Donahoo. "Nice."

"Very special," Donahoo agreed.

Cominsky said, "Who the hell is she?"

"It's off some modeling agency brochure," Palmer said knowingly. "He took it to the john. It's a whack-off photo."

Donahoo studied the photo for a moment and then got the wallet. He put it back in the secret compartment that he'd missed. He made an excuse for himself. He hurt a lot.

Gomez said, "Are we through here?"

Donahoo nodded. They filed out, leaving Donahoo and Lewis. Donahoo finished putting Buddy's possessions in the manila envelope. Lewis sat watching. He made no move to relinquish Donahoo's chair.

"You wanted to talk?" Lewis said.

Donahoo looked at him. Now? He didn't think so. Before, maybe. But not now. He was over the hump. He was on the down side, sliding. He could handle this on his own. He didn't need personal counseling.

"What about?" Lewis said.

Donahoo made a production of closing the clasp on the manila envelope.

"Take as long as you like. But it doesn't get any better."

"Okay. Ballet lessons."

"Ballet lessons?"

"That's what I said."

"What did Buddy say?"

"The same thing."

"And you believe Buddy?"

"Yeah, well, there were no tights, no slippers, and nothing in the file, you know? So, yeah, I believe Buddy. Switch the time frame, I would have believed Buddy before I wouldn't have believed the Chipper."

"You don't think Lyons was joking?"

"No. I think he was buying himself a day. He was saying let's pass on Monday and come back Tuesday. I think the last thing he wanted to do was to have me talk to Buddy Salinas."

Lewis pushed up. He shook his head. He was like an old bull. "What was the question again?"

"What are you going to do about it?"

Lewis worked his way around Donahoo. He got to the door, backed in against it so he was blocking it. He said, "What did you want to talk about?"

"That was it."

"No it wasn't."

"Yeah, well, I also wanted to apologize. I got out of line yesterday. I'm sorry."

"Apology accepted. What did you want to talk about?"

Donahoo looked at him. He could see himself, another ten, fifteen years. Pulling up his pants, blocking doors. Doing the politically correct thing. It happened to everybody, he thought. It was part of the process. There came a point, a time. You got old. You burned out. All you wanted to do was retire with dignity.

"Will you look the other way?" Donahoo asked.

Lewis shook his head no.

"It would be just me," Donahoo said. "Me alone, unofficial. Poking around very quietly. I'll have a relapse and say I'm going back to bed. If it ever comes up, anybody asks, that's where I was, sick in bed." He said, he was pleading, "We're wasting time. I know it in my gut. I know it when I see XLA and BMGS. This thing is bigger than Chip Lyons, but he's key, the answer, and it's going to blow sky-high if we can't touch him. Saperstein's got to face the truth now. If he hasn't got a hero—he hasn't got a hero."

Lewis shook his head.

"Lewis," Donahoo said. "The guy's dead. I dig up his secrets, he can't complain, nobody's going to hear him. He can't yell to Saperstein. Let me look."

"You're a good cop," Lewis said. He opened the door, pulling up his baggy pants, stuffing in his shirttail. It had somehow come out again without any perceptible activity on his part. He had just been sitting there. "Not the best, not the brightest. Not the most endearing. But you are the luckiest, Tommy. You are one lucky cop."

Donahoo watched him struggle out of the office. "What makes me so lucky here?"

"You're lucky you never asked me that question."

Donahoo stared after him. Lewis, he wasn't crooked, Donahoo thought. Nothing like that. He just wanted to retire with dignity. He just wanted to wait until after the parade.

Lewis got halfway across the squad room and then turned around and came back. "Who was the girl in the picture?"

"Rosie the Snake G-string," Donahoo told him. "The Wham Bam Ice Trail."

"Who is?"

"Was. Was a dear and good friend of the Chipper."

Lewis looked at Donahoo for a moment. He suddenly seemed tired. He stuffed in his shirttail.

"Well, I guess you're a lucky cop too," Donahoo said. "Lucky and smart. You're so smart you didn't come back here and you didn't want to know that."

Lewis tried to say something, but it wasn't there. Donahoo let him go. Permission granted, Donahoo thought. Go to Saperstein's precious parade for the Chipper, Captain, Investigations. Don't tell me what you can and can't do. Tell it to the dearly departed.

Donahoo waited and then picked up the phone and dialed the San Diego office of the Federal Bureau of Investigation. He asked to speak to Special Agent William Galloway. He said, "Hi, it's me, I've picked up something on the street, what has to remain an unidentified source, it may be of interest to you."

Galloway said, "Oh, yeah?"

"This source thinks somebody is going to put the snatch here on some secret military device designated XLA BMGS."

Galloway repeated the letters. "And?"

"That's it. Maybe it scares you like it scares me?"

Galloway was silent for a moment. He said, "Well, thank you, Tommy." He said, "How's your love life?"

NINETEEN

Quillan was having a bath with Trudy Goody. He was washing her, he liked to do that. He liked to do it by hand, get his hands all soapy, and get her glistening clean. A black woman, they cleaned up better than anybody, he thought. You could put a shine on them.

"You're sure a pretty little lady," Quillan said drunkenly. "I like you a lot." He pawed around the bottom of the sunken marble tub as if he were looking for a lost bar of soap, and came up with a bottle of whiskey, Johnnie Walker Black Label. He unscrewed the cap and filled one of the glasses sitting in a row on the tub's top step. He got some ice from a nearby bag. "I like you better than anybody."

"Better than some pretty little man?"

Tears came to Quillan's eyes. Normally, he never showed emotion, but there was a point, when he'd had too much to drink, where the barriers eroded. He could cry then like any other human being. Not often, but sometimes. If he was drunk enough. The tears now were for Ernesto Garcia Buddy Salinas. He'd heard about his jump from the third floor of the Arthur. He'd wanted to kill Buddy himself, but that didn't make the loss any less. He had loved the guy. Quillan had a predilection for small men, which had come to him later in life, in a bamboo cage in Vietnam. They were occasionally his cellmates. He got the taste. "Aw, Jesus, why did you have to bring that up?" he asked.

Trudy Goody grinned at him foolishly. She wasn't drinking but she was stoned on something that swept away inhibitions just as readily as any whiskey. Some mix of drugs she bought up on Ocean View Boulevard.

"The guy's dead, okay?" Quillan said wistfully. "He's over. Can't you leave the dead alone?" He took a slug of his Johnnie Walker. He was lost in a wash of memories. "The guy, he was smart, you know? He was a wiz with figures. Do 'em in his head." The liquor dribbled. "But what a bitch."

Trudy Goody sang softly. She sounded like one of the Munchkins in *The Wizard of Oz.* "Joe Bong, the bitch is dead. The wizard bitch is dead."

"Aw, come on," Quillan told her.

There wasn't any door to the bathroom. Privacy was attained by a series of short halls turning off from one another. Taylor pretended to knock on the door that wasn't there. He said, "Knock, knock," and he said loudly, "Visitor."

"Who?"

"Crash Evans."

"Send him in."

Taylor went and got Crash Evans, who was waiting with the orchids, sweating in the humidity. He was wearing a baggy suit, a kind of uniform for him.

"He'll see you now," Taylor said. "You don't mind talking in the can?"

Crash Evans looked alarmed. "He's taking a dump?"

"No. He's taking a bath."

Taylor led the way. Quillan, in a whirlwind of activity, had already hired Wheels Duran, who was going to be driver, and Chinaman Lee, who was going to ride shotgun. Now, if the interview went well, and there was no reason why it shouldn't, he was going to hire Crash Evans, who was going to be run over. Evans was a seasoned pro in the fake injury/insurance claim racket. He could take a fifty-mile-an-hour hit. He didn't want to, but he'd done it.

"How's business?" Taylor asked.

"It could be slower," Crash Evans said. He always said that.

Taylor led the way through the bedroom and to the nonexistent bathroom door. He pretended to knock.

Quillan heard the rustle of them. "I'm pretending to invite you in."

They entered. Trudy Goody was laid out on a blue velvet chaise longue that was out of a whorehouse. Quillan had bought it for her when the city auctioned off the contents of an infamous brothel, Lacey's. Her white terry robe was open, and her legs were too. She was half comatose. A high offering on a low altar.

"Crash," Quillan said expansively. "How the hell are you?" He poured himself another drink and offered the bottle. "God, how long's it been? We were gonna bring the trucking industry to its knees. You had to get all fucked up in that tram scam."

"The trolley folly." Crash Evans passed on the drink and sat down on the closest of the two toilets. He was a rubbery little guy about the size of a jockey. He had a big head though. It was oversize for the rest of him and made him appear larger than he was. A shock of pure white hair and big, pensive dark eyes, bagged like a pelican's pouch, kept attention on it and away from the rubbery body. He'd be maybe forty, but he looked older, the wear and tear of his profession, and he also looked, a permanent feature, apprehensive. "A mashed femur and I didn't collect a nickel." He smiled faintly. "I should have seen it coming."

Quillan let go of Trudy Goody, saying, "Don't go away, okay?" He scooted closer to Crash Evans. "I take it you're interested in working?"

"Does a duck fuck?"

"You mind if I sit in?" Taylor asked. He chose the other john, which was actually a bidet.

"I need you to walk in front of a van, stop it, hold it," Quillan said. "It won't be moving too fast. Coming around a right angle at an intersection. How much would you charge for something like that?"

"I've got a rate card," Crash Evans said. He dug around in his baggy suit. He produced a worn, folded sheet of paper about the size of a playing card. "Flat fee, fifty thousand. Then I'm on the bonus plan."

Quillan got a towel, dried his hands. He took the sheet of paper. He studied it for a while. "Twenty thousand for each broken limb. If you get killed, a hundred grand to the Elks."

"The main things."

Quillan handed the paper back. "I think I can live with that." He looked briefly at Taylor. "We got a deal."

"I've got a contract here," Crash Evans said. "Pretty standard stuff." He dug around in his suit. "This protects both of us. It says I gotta perform and you gotta pay."

Quillan laughed. "Crime, fuck, it's getting legal." He said, "Smile, Taylor."

Taylor escorted Crash out. Then he returned to sit quietly on the bidet. After a while he saved Quillan from drowning in his sunken tub. He pulled him out, left him unconscious on the marble floor. He threw a couple bath towels over him. Then he got Trudy Goody and carried her into the bedroom. He lowered her onto the big bed. He turned on the mirrored fan, slow.

Trudy was still singing. ". . . the wizard bitch is dead."

Taylor thought that Quillan, he got drunk, or seriously into pleasure, he talked too fucking much. He really did.

"Miss Goody," Taylor said. He got on the bed with her. He got on his back so he could see their images in the mirrors, moving around together. "You know any other songs?"

Trudy crooned for him. "A, B, C, D, X, L, A." She got his fly open. "Taylor . . . can come . . . out to play?"

Taylor looked at the fan. Round and round. He wasn't getting an erection. He preferred white girls. Alabaster thighs.

"B, M, G, S . . . whaddya say . . . ?" Trudy Goody grinned at him foolishly. She gave up. "The heart's not in it."

"What did you say?"

"I said the hard's not in it."

I heard you the first time, Taylor thought. The *heart's* not in it. He was looking at the fan, going round and round. If not the heart, then what? What else might be worth half a million dollars. He was thinking of the jumbled letters, which could mean nothing or everything, but he was pretty sure they meant something.

XLA BMGS. Taylor thought that he was as good a hands-on intelligence guy as any that had served on the front in 'Nam, and that probably applied to Central America too. He had a nice knack for where the information was. He also knew how to extract it. So, if he got off his ass, he could probably find out what the jumble meant. He ought to find out, he thought. It might be profitable to do that. Then, if somebody was trying to fuck him, he could fuck them.

Taylor looked at the fan. Round and round. He thought he should be angry but instead he was amused. The whole thing—how it was unfolding, and where it could lead—was becoming very amusing.

It really was, he thought. Smile, Taylor.

TWENTY

Donahoo bought a bottle of Old Crow and drove over to see Rosie Gestring. He waited until six o'clock, when he thought she'd be home from her antiques business, or just about home. He thought he'd like to catch her when she was tired, no time to relax. If possible, he'd like to catch her going in the door, he thought. The woman, she's exhausted, she's fucking had it, and, before she can kick off her shoes, she hears this desperation-incarnate voice say, "Me again." Maybe she'd just fall down and say, Take me?

Rosie showed up at seven-twenty. The Yugo came down the street, blowing smoke, making a five-hundred-dollar rattle. There was a moment of hesitation in the form of a little lurch—she's spotted me, Donahoo thought—and then it turned and clunked up the driveway and into the carport. The motor died slowly.

Donahoo got his Old Crow. He got out of the Toronado. He went up the usual way, slanting across the lawn, careful of the lumps. He was halfway when he wished he'd taken the sidewalk and brought his cane. It was rough going with his bad knee.

She was waiting for him at the door. She was wearing a long black poplin trench coat with the collar turned up. She was standing under a twenty-five-watt lamp that was bright enough to attract bugs. It made her appear at once vulnerable and suspect and mysterious. She was holding a takeout bag, KFC. It smelled of chicken. She said, "Gimme a break, Officer."

Donahoo grinned. He thought she was so nice. He thought again how much he liked her. He said, "New approach. Police business."

"Oh?" There was a flicker of apprehension, dismay. The dark, slanted almond eyes held on him. He imagined they were begging. They were saying no and they were begging. The pouting, sensuous mouth was asking for mercy. "Here?"

"Well." He was holding his Old Crow. It was in a bag but it was pretty obviously a bottle of liquor. "I suppose we could go somewhere. We could go downtown. It's up to you."

"Downtown?"

"Yeah. That's what they call it."

She was looking at him. He thought again that she had a face like a heart. This time he thought it was broken. He'd somehow broken it.

"It won't take long."

"I hope not. Come in."

She fumbled with the lock and got the door open. She went inside and turned on the hall light. Donahoo followed her. Before, he remembered, he could smell fish, garlic. This time he could just smell the chicken.

"Original Recipe or Extra Crispy?"

"Original."

She pointed to the living room and kept on moving. He was going to follow her—he wanted a glass, some ice—but changed his mind. It disturbed him that she seemed so threatened. He thought he shouldn't contribute to that. Anymore.

The living room was familiar for its dated quality. The false beams and the wainscoting. The old-fashioned velvet sofas, the roll-top desk, the antique upright piano, the television set with the round screen. The fat, squat lamps with the tasseled shades. Donahoo had thought it all so strange at first but not now. The lady took her work home, that's all.

He picked a sofa and sat down and waited. He studied the brown-on-brown field and stream wallpaper.

She called from the kitchen. "What do you want with that?"

He yelled back to her. "Ice."

"That's all?"

"A glass."

He unwrapped the Old Crow. He put it on the coffee table. He got out Buddy Salinas's worn wallet. He located the secret compartment. He got out the photo that Palmer thought was a whack-off photo.

She came in with a bucket of ice and two glasses. The trench coat had been discarded somewhere. She was in a clinging dark blue silk dress with a revealing V. Her hair had been up. Now it was down. She had a cigarette which she lit while she was walking, head cocked. She did that with the ease that comes with long practice. She sat down near him, for convenience, not intimacy. "You look like hell. What happened?"

"A misunderstanding." Donahoo took his glass from her. He filled it with ice. Then he filled it with Old Crow. If he was only going to have the one drink, it was going to be good.

She saw the photo. It was on the coffee table beside the wallet.

"Is that me?" she asked.

Donahoo had some of his booze. "Yeah."

"A long time ago," she said, picking it up. She examined it a moment, then frowned. "Where did you get it?"

"It was in Buddy Salinas's wallet."

"Really? I didn't know he cared." She put it back on the coffee table. She said tiredly, "How is old Buddy?"

Donahoo stopped. He was going to say, "Not too good," but the tiredness in her voice, the resignation, stopped him. Instead, he said, "Where do you know Buddy from?"

"You don't know?"

"No. I don't."

"He's my brother."

Oh, Donahoo thought. It was the last thing he had expected her to say. There was no resemblance. None at all. He felt like a charlatan and a fool.

"Is he in trouble?"

Jesus Christ, Donahoo thought. The poor, dumb bugger. Not anymore. He got his glass.

"What . . . ?"

"I'm sorry," Donahoo said. "I didn't know. I had no idea." He looked at her. The mystery had been wiped away. She was as open as a wound. "I don't know of any easy way to tell you this. I'm sorry—he's dead."

She closed her eyes. She sat very still. The tears started. She didn't brush them away.

"It was a suicide," Donahoo said. He thought it would be best to get it all done at once. "The Arthur Hotel in the Gaslamp. He jumped out of a window. He died instantly." He took away the cigarette that was burning down in her hand. "Maybe you know. He had trouble with drugs."

She nodded.

"The reason I came," Donahoo began. He wanted to leave. "The kid had your photo. I thought maybe . . ." He got his glass. He took a good slug. "I dunno. Maybe you could help me on a case I'm working on."

She didn't answer. She found a handkerchief in her pocket and dabbed at her eyes. "What did you do with my cigarette?"

Donahoo got another one going for her. Their hands touched when he passed it. Even with his concern, he could feel a sexual contact, electric. He was shamed by it and yet gladdened.

"We could do this some other time."

She shook her head. "No. Let's get it over with."

"It can wait."

"No," she repeated. She inhaled deeply, looking at him curiously. The smoke drifted from her nostrils, gray ribbons. "What do you want to know?"

Donahoo wondered. Where to start? He wanted to hear about the bad things. But he wanted to hear about the good things too. Francis Chip Lyons, cop, magician, salesman, cocksman—he wanted that explained, yes. But he also wanted to know where she got her spirit and her courage and her style.

Donahoo, feeling like an idiot, said, "I guess I want to know everything."

"Don't we all?" Rosie said. She pulled her long legs up under her. "You can pour me a drink now." She again looked at him curiously. "Let me tell you what you already know. Dreams crumble, fools die."

Donahoo got her drink poured. He gave it to her.

"Thank you."

"This was yesterday afternoon," Donahoo said. "I'd been looking for Buddy since—" He thought about how much he should tell her, and decided she ought to know everything too. She probably knew it already. If she didn't, it wouldn't hurt her that much more. "Sunday morning. I came over with Chip? We'd been at the Tijuana Slough. Buddy said some guys were supposed to show up. You knew he was a snitch?"

"Yes."

"You knew he was gay?"

"I knew, when he was five, he fucked the tooth fairy. What you doing to me here?"

"Okay. The slough. Nobody showed. It was/is an important (I had to find out why. Buddy said it was just bad info, but he scared, packing to leave. We talked about that—" Dona stopped. She was looking at him. She wasn't going to help. "I I was going to take him in. He jumped."

She didn't say anything.

"No warning."

She was silent, still.

"I've got some questions," Donahoo said. "The photo, we k about. He's your brother."

"My half brother."

He looked at her. There was still no resemblance he could dis "Okay. When did you see him last?"

"Tuesday."

"What was the occasion?"

"He wanted money."

"And?"

"I drove him back downtown and bought him a bus ticket

"One way, Gary, Indiana?"

"Yes."

"Why?"

"His father's there. Not my father. His father."

"Okay." Donahoo got out the *Union-Trib.* He unfolded it showed her the Chaffee story, the skull and crossbones, the car(printed warning, *You're next, lover.* "Did this come up?"

She shook her head.

"No mention?"

"No."

He got the crossword puzzle. The repeated entries, XLA BMGS. "Did he talk about this? Make any kind of reference at

"No."

"You're sure?"

"Positive. What's it mean?"

"I dunno." Donahoo thought he was through here. She had a way of saying something, you knew it was the truth. He said, he was stalling, "Tell me more about the bus ticket."

"Why?"

"Because I'm a cop. Because I want to know everything."

She said, "Sure." She took a last pull on her cigarette and stubbed it out. The smoke drifted from her. "Did I know he was a snitch?" She laughed bitterly. "I never wanted to see the little bastard again."

Donahoo got his whiskey. He waited.

"I raised him, you know? Stood by him through all the shit. All the bad-boy stuff. And he sold me for a fix."

Donahoo watched the tears return. He'd spent a lifetime dealing with people in emotional crises but he'd never gotten used to it. He thought that of all the things you could do to a person, when you betrayed them, that was the worst.

"You didn't know Chip got it from Buddy, huh?"

Donahoo shook his head no.

"Well, you know now. Chip told me when he was here Sunday. He said we were over, he didn't need me anymore, it was Manila Time. And then he said—he was bragging, you know?—that it was Buddy who told him about me. He said Buddy sold me for a dime bag. Buddy. He's blood, family. And he lets that scum get that kind of hold on me—I've got to sleep with the bastard or I go to jail."

Oh, Donahoo thought, and then, finally, he did know everything. Her mistake, and his too.

"Don't tell me," she said in confirmation. She was looking at him in her curious way. "I seem to have fucked up here. I just assumed . . ." Her voice trailed off. She shook her head. "God. I thought Chip told you what he had—that's why you were coming around."

Donahoo shook his head no again.

"You didn't know? No idea?"

Donahoo kept shaking his head.

"Jesus."

"What did you do?" he asked.

"Wrong?"

"Yeah." He was a cop, he thought. He wanted to know everything.

"Well, you're going to find out, aren't you? Chip said it was easy to check. Fingerprints off a glass. Put 'em in a computer. Presto!— we all fall down."

"What did you do?"

"Wrong?"

"Yeah. Wrong."

"I killed somebody."

"Murder?"

"That's what they call it." She said after a moment, "My husband. He was beating up on me all the time. One day I just couldn't take any more. I shot him."

Donahoo got his whiskey. He looked at her. He couldn't believe it. "What are you saying? You're running?"

"Where?" Her eyes were suddenly dead. Her voice was brittle, "Now what? Valid confession. Let's make a deal. You got lucky today here, Officer. Rattled the lady with your death announcement." She said, "That's what you want? I can't stop you. I guess you get to fuck me."

Donahoo looked at her. He always wanted to, he thought. From day one. He got his stuff. The wallet. The *Union-Trib*. The Old Crow. He had planned to leave the booze, but the way he felt, he probably needed it more than she did.

"I, uh, think I've got everything I need, Miss Gestring," Donahoo said, pushing up. He pronounced it *jest-ring*. "If there's anything else, one of my men will be in touch." He started for the door. "Thank you."

He was out of the house, the door closing, only a crack left, when he heard her. She said, "Do what you gotta do."

It was dark now. Donahoo took the sidewalk back to his car. His knee was hurting him, his side, his neck. He hurt all over. Outside, inside.

Would he do that—let her off? He wondered how he could do that. He'd never done anything remotely close to that before. The breaks, when they came, were for minor things, not murder. He'd never given anybody a shortcut for a long haul. It wasn't in him. He was a cop, not a judge.

Donahoo felt like screaming. Lewis, he could look the other way. Lewis and Saperstein. They could pull society's security blanket through the wringer. In the name of larger, deeper issues, fray some edges, poke some holes. They could find a way to make things right when they were wrong. But he wasn't allowed to do that.

The old refrigerator was still sitting at the edge of the canyon. Donahoo pushed it over. It went crashing down, tumbling end over end, the door flying open and the bins and shelves spilling out. It went all the way to the bottom. Donahoo couldn't see it, but he could imagine what it looked like. Another mindless blemish on a fair city. He had often asked himself what kind of person would do that. Now he knew, he thought. It was somebody who didn't care.

TWENTY-ONE

Night in the Big City. Donahoo was sleeping. He was dreaming. He was in trouble. Internal Affairs was chasing him. He was running through some tall grass, screaming at the top of his lungs, "I wanted the Chipper—Saperstein said no!" and then he tripped over a refrigerator and they got him and they told him, "Actually, Sergeant, this is about you harboring a killer, Miss Rosie Gestring."

His phone was ringing. Donahoo awoke with a start. The dream was still fresh in his mind. It was so real, he thought. His cry for help echoed. He touched his face. He could still feel the sting of the tall grass.

The phone rang again. Donahoo looked at his watch. Ten-twenty.

He'd gone to bed early, around nine. He'd been asleep about an hour.

The phone rang again. The answering machine hadn't cut in. Donahoo knew who it was before he picked it up. It was just something he knew. He said, "Yeah."

"Captain Video here. Can you come out and play?"

"Let me ask the doctor."

"And bring a copy of the video. I want to make sure you've got one."

Donahoo could see a tidal wave coming. It was going to hit him and it was going to wash him away. "Get fucked."

"You haven't got it?"

"I didn't say that. I said get fucked."

"Fine. Then I'm outa here."

"Good. It can't be too soon for me. You trigger-happy moron. What are you asking for? A map?"

"Jesus Christ," Quillan said. "Here we go again. You must have a death wish the size of your ego. I'm telling you—one last time— stop fucking with me. If I'm going down, you're going first, prick. You're taking a sniper's bullet at two hundred yards. Your brains will be all up Broadway. I can do that, and I'm gonna, you don't wise up."

"Fuck you."

"Jesus Christ."

Donahoo, imagining himself that kind of easy target, anywhere he might go, said, "Why wouldn't I have a copy?"

There was a long silence. "Let me guess," Quillan said then, barely in control. "Maybe your partner didn't give you one? Maybe he lied about you being in on the shakedown? Maybe he's going to his grave with the fucking thing? Maybe that would explain why you've been acting so weird? Maybe you're putting me off while you try to locate it?" He said, "Dicko—before you get a dime—I want proof, okay? I want to see a fucking copy."

There it was, Donahoo thought. The magic word. *Shakedown.* It forever condemned Chip Francis Lyons, and, before this was over, it could kill him too. He could be dead, and no parade. He said, "You were going to waste me at the VA. Why would I want to risk that again?"

"It's no risk, you don't fuck with me, asshole. You don't push all the wrong buttons. What's your problem? I don't want to be fucked with. I just want to make a deal—*if* you've got the video. If you haven't got it, say so, I'll leave you alone. If you do have it, prove it, show me a copy. And don't try to fuck me around, that's over. You gotta know that's over. I don't want to be fucked with. I'll pay you what the agreement was. Half a million for you. Forget Lyons, he's dead, too bad. You don't get his share. You get your share. Half a million. Period. You'll see it Friday."

Donahoo thought he liked the part where the guy left him alone. It sounded good. But it couldn't last. If there was a video, it would surface sooner or later, in a safety deposit box, under a sofa cushion, wherever. Chip Lyons wouldn't have hidden it in a place where it would stay forever. He didn't know he was going to die. He'd have wanted fairly easy access.

"Which is it going to be?"

"Okay. You get to see it."

"Good. Leave now. Get in your car, alone, and drive over to the Sports Arena, nobody following. Circle around for a while. You're in the Toronado? I'll find you. Half an hour."

"I'll need more time."

"No. Half an hour."

The phone went dead. Donahoo hung up. He thought it wasn't a drive he really wanted to take. But he might never get a shot at the guy otherwise. They were talking half a mil here, and it wouldn't make sense, no sense at all—*if* he wanted it, *if* he was in on the shakedown—not to show up. He had to go. Otherwise the guy would know the truth, that he didn't have the video, but instead he was looking for the thing, and that he'd eventually find it. The guy could back off, and he might not come this way again, and a lot of things might disappear with him. Primitivo, for instance. Or, what was also possible, just as possible, the guy, in his frustration and anger, in his reckless hate, the guy might take a sniper's rifle and hide somewhere and wait for the right moment to pull the trigger.

Donahoo cursed Lewis for not giving him a free hand. With a search warrant he could have tossed Chip Lyons's apartment. With a court order he could have opened the guy's safety deposit box. With luck he could have had the video by now.

Instead, he had limited choices. Donahoo could hear Chip Lyons saying, "I'll see you soon, Tommy." He removed his neck brace. He thought that he didn't want an army. Too many guys and somebody would be spotted and that would blow it. He needed two, three guys. He called Police Administrative Headquarters and asked for Squad 5. He got Cominsky. He said, trying to be diplomatic, he didn't want Cominsky to think he wasn't first choice, "How come you're working so late?"

Cominsky said, "I'm just finishing a booklet here."

"Oh? What you reading?"

" 'How to Ride the Bus.' Morris has been acting strangely lately."

It never ended, Donahoo thought. A guy who called his car Morris.

"Whatcha need?"

"Anybody else there?"

"No."

"Where are they?"

"Tijuana. The dog races."

"They all went?"

"Yeah."

Donahoo hesitated. He didn't want Cominsky. This kind of thing, it wasn't Cominsky's bag. But he didn't want a stranger either. Some SIU guy whose heart might not be in it. He wanted somebody who knew what he was doing. He wanted somebody he could trust.

"What's going on?"

Donahoo wondered how he could possibly tell him no. Cominsky, he had just saved his life, even if he did run him over doing it. He'd given him a new gun. None of that card shit. A new gun. He was feeling better about getting the gun.

"Anything I can do?"

"Life's a bitch, isn't it?" Donahoo said. "Yes, I do need your help, Cominsky. Captain Video called. American #1. He wants a meet at the Sports Arena." He looked at his watch. "In about the time it takes to drive there. I'm supposed to circle around and he's going to make contact."

Cominsky said, "Uh, you're not going, are you, Sarge?"

"I have to."

"Well, let's think this through, huh? I mean, those guys, they were gonna kill you before, and they took your gun."

"I know. But you gave me a new one, so it's kinda your gun now, and they're not going to take it this time."

Donahoo imagined he could hear Cominsky thinking. "You're sure I'm right for this?"

"Hey, I'm not doing you any favors, Cominsky," Donahoo told him, he had just remembered. "You're the only one who knows what these guys look like. You've seen them in the flesh. You're automatic choice."

"That makes sense." There was a pause. "But, you know, it works both ways, they know what I look like."

"So disguise yourself."

"Right."

"Here's the plan," Donahoo said, feeling like an idiot, and also like he was putting his head in an oven. "When these guys make contact, no matter what they want, I'm not going anywhere except Blockbuster Video. That's where I'm going to be. Now, I want you to go down to the evidence room, and I want you to check out a video."

"Which one?"

"Any one. It doesn't matter. And I want you to bring it to me at Blockbuster."

"Any video?"

"Right. But wait till you see that I'm in there with these guys. Don't bring it to me if I'm alone. Okay?"

"Any video?"

"Yeah, Cominsky. Any fucking video."

Donahoo headed for the Sports Arena. He thought that there were a lot of things you couldn't do in half an hour. You couldn't put on a wire—not do that and be on time at the Sports Arena too. You couldn't get Squad 5 up from Tijuana. You couldn't think of a decent plan.

The problem, he thought, which was the problem from the start, he didn't have anything on American #1. He could maybe get him for threatening. He could maybe get him for assault. For inviting to jump from a car—that was a very popular charge. The guy might do a few months. He might do nothing. He, Donahoo, he could bring him in, but the guy could leave just as fast, a revolving door. He could make bail in five minutes. He'd be out in a phone call.

Then, Donahoo thought, and he knew this was a real possibility, he'd heard it in the death-rattle voice, loud and clear, the guy was going to load his sniper's rifle. The guy was a maniac. He wasn't going down alone.

So the plan was? Donahoo went over the problem one more time. If he brought the guy in, the guy would know (a) that he, Donahoo, didn't have the video, but (b) he was looking for it, very hard, and (c) he'd probably find it one of these days real soon, which meant (d) he should be iced before he found it. Donahoo thought that was the problem with bringing the guy in. It solved nothing and created more problems. Like a shorter lifespan. So what was the plan?

Donahoo thought he had to figure a way to buy some time. The guy had said Friday—the money would be ready Friday. So if time was ever going to finally run out, that's when it ran out. When the guy was standing there with half a million dollars, saying, "Here's half a million dollars." If you didn't give him the video then, there could be only one reason, you didn't have it. End of story.

Two days. They were available. And he needed them desperately. But could he get them? What could he say or do to convince the guy that he needed two more days—and that he wasn't going to fuck him?

Donahoo got on I-8 and headed west. He was ten minutes away now. The Rosecrans exit. Sports Arena Boulevard. Donahoo wished he still smoked. The plan was to play it by ear. The plan sucked.

Hotel Circle exit. Donahoo coasted by in the outside lane. He wasn't in a hurry. When he got there, too many things could go wrong, he thought. It was programmed to go wrong. If there was a seal guaranteeing disaster, they'd be plastered all over.

The Caddie came up alongside. Taylor honked to get Donahoo's attention. Quillan, in the passenger seat, had his window down. He yelled, "Toss it!"

Donahoo rolled his window down. "What?"

"The video! Slow down! Toss it!"

"I haven't got it!" Donahoo shouted. "It's coming from the station!"

"Toss it!!"

"You asshole," Donahoo shouted. "I said *it's coming.* If you want to see it, follow me." He speeded up. "Public place. I'm going to Blockbuster."

"No!"

"Yes."

Quillan grabbed the wheel and turned the heavy old Cadillac into Donahoo's Toronado. Donahoo wasn't expecting it. He was driving with one hand, feeling for his seat belt; he wanted to un-buckle in case he had to move fast. The Caddie ran him off the freeway. The Toronado went into the ditch, rolled. The Caddie kept going.

Donahoo went in thinking he was dead. Sixty miles an hour and no air bag. He was suddenly in an upside-down world. The pain was unbearable. Then nothing.

Blockbuster Video was sitting like a lantern in the dark. It was ablaze with light shining from two-story-high windows, the only place still open in the Loma Plaza Shopping Center. They were just now shuttering the adjacent Bookstar, a huge bookstore that now occupied what was formerly a movie theater, Loma. Book signings were advertised on the marquee. *Dr. Ronnie Edell, Sexually Satisfied Woman, 2 pm, Fri.*

Donahoo was delivered in a black-and-white. Farris, the fat traffic cop who was driving, who had been first upon the Toronado's demise on I-8, and who was being very reluctant about this whole thing, said, "You sure about this? You oughta be in the hospital. You're lucky to be alive." He said, "I'm serious. I need a report later." He said, "Think hospital."

Donahoo shook his head. "No, they'll think I'm taking advan-tage." He surveyed Blockbuster. No sign of any customers. The clerks were acting like closing time. He looked around the all-but-deserted parking lot and on both sides of Point Loma Boulevard. No sign of the killer Cadillac. The Morris Minor down the street was Cominsky.

Donahoo got out.

Farris asked, "You want me to wait?"

"No. I've got a ride."

Donahoo smiled his thanks and limped into Blockbuster. He wasn't worried about getting shot anymore. He was worried about—

what would be the term?—getting injured to death? He had a lump on his head the size of a big scoop. His nose was broken. Again.

Outside, the black-and-white drifted away reluctantly. The Morris Minor stayed put.

Donahoo showed his badge to the girl at the cash register. She was a very attractive Latina with a cascade of reddish-black curls. She looked bright, sharp. That would help. He said, "I was supposed to meet a couple guys here. They're kinda hard to describe. One's real mean-looking. The other's real sick-looking. You happen to see 'em?"

The girl smiled. She was relaxed, cool. "They're in here all the time."

Yeah, Donahoo thought. He looked around. The place was a fishbowl. The two-story windows wrapped half of the building. He could be seen from several vantage points. From two of the yards across the street, one thick with trees, the other with vines. From a hastily rented room in the Loma Lodge. From a parked car. Donahoo looked for cars. No sign of the Caddie. The Morris Minor hadn't budged.

"Uh," Donahoo said, turning back to the girl. "I'm doing some undercover work here. I want you to wait until I move away and then I want you to call this number for me, *unobtrusively*. Like it has nothing to do with me. Like maybe you're calling your mother?" He told her the number. "You're gonna get a pager. Leave a message. Tell him, 'Come here.'"

The girl nodded.

"Also," Donahoo said. "The guy'll be bringing me a video. I want to play it, out in the open if possible. You got a machine I can do that on?"

"Just the one here."

It was behind the counter, set well below eye level, for employee use only. It fed the six screens that were hanging from the ceiling in various parts of the store. Donahoo thought that would have to work. He smiled, thinking she was really pretty, she reminded him of Rosie Gestring, and then he moved away, checking out the store. He kept looking outside, but he couldn't see the Caddie.

The other clerk, a clean-cut young man, he looked like a what college student is supposed to look like, said, "Can I help you, sir?"

"Thank you," Donahoo told him, "but I am beyond help."

"Okay, but just ask if you change your mind."

Donahoo wondered if American #1 was watching from a distance. He tried to put himself in the guy's mind. He couldn't do it. The guy was . . . too unpredictable? Donahoo thought that was putting it mildly. The guy was a pinball machine. He was bing, bang. Lighting up all over.

The Morris Minor lit up, sort of. Headlights that were about as bright as the parkers on most cars. It came down the street and stopped in the red zone in front of the store. Cominsky got out.

Donahoo didn't recognize him at first. He was wearing dark glasses and a large mustache. Donahoo wondered where he could have gotten that so quickly, and then he thought, why, dummy, from his disguise kit, of course. He wondered how he could see at night in dark glasses.

Cominsky came into the store. He was holding a videocassette from the evidence room. He was holding it the way a man holds a purse. He looked at Donahoo. He said, "Not again?"

"Throw me the video," Donahoo said.

"Throw it?"

"Please. Throw it."

Cominsky tossed him the video. Donahoo went to the counter. He indicated, sign language, that he would like to use the player, and that he would like to be alone. The girl quickly moved out from behind the counter. She went to visit with the college student.

Donahoo did the business with the cassette. He again wondered if American #1 was watching. He hoped so, because what the guy was seeing, *if* he was watching, was an indication, if not proof, that he, Donahoo, had kept his part of the bargain, which was pretty good for playing it by ear.

The movie started. Donahoo thought he was asking for a little miracle here, in that American #1 would be close, but not too close. He didn't want him to be able to make out what was on the screen. It was called *Star Whores*. There was a black guy hung like Man o' War. A pretty little blonde in penis heaven. It was playing on the store's six screens. You could see it from the sidewalk, but probably not from the street unless you had binoculars.

"You said a fucking video," Cominsky said in reminder.

Donahoo watched for a while. He wondered how the hell the stuff turned anybody on. You see a guy, he's got a horse's dick, that's just going to make you feel inadequate, isn't it? How does that help? Tell me how.

"Now what?"

Donahoo looked around. No sign of the Caddie. American #1, Captain Video, he could be out there somewhere, but he didn't look like he was coming in, not tonight. Maybe he'd seen enough. The business with the video. Maybe the charade had worked. Donahoo hoped so. He again tried to put himself in the guy's mind. The guy, he could be seeing this, and he could be thinking, okay, this is a plus, a good sign. The guy could be thinking that he, Donahoo, was playing it smart, willing to show the video only in a public place, and he could decide, on account of the clerks, on account of Cominsky, on account of the black-and-white, to keep his distance tonight, to try again tomorrow. "Drive me home?"

"Sure."

Quillan and Taylor were watching from an upstairs room across the street in the Loma Lodge. They were trading back and forth with a pair of binoculars. They could make out Donahoo and Cominsky. They had observed part of the business with the videocassette. Cominsky tossing it to Donahoo. Donahoo taking it behind the counter. They couldn't see the screens though. Wrong angle. They were looking down on screens that were facing down.

Quillan said, "Either he's got it or he's a great bullshitter. Let's try again when it's less crowded." He was thinking ahead. "Or maybe when it's more crowded."

In the Morris Minor, Cominsky said, "Jesus, you're a mess," and then he said, "Did you keep the gun?"

Donahoo showed him. Yes, he did. He smiled. He tried to. His nose felt like his head. "Pretty good, huh?"

From somewhere, maybe somewhere across the street, it was hard to tell, Captain Video yelled, "Okay, wise guy, next time!"

Yeah, pretty good, Donahoo thought. He made a motion. Now let's get the hell outa here.

TWENTY-TWO

Saperstein was putting together, final touches, his parade for Francis Chip Lyons, the Chipper. He was using bent paper clips for what he called the various units. The San Diego Police Department Color Guard, first unit. The United States Marine Corps Band, Camp Pendleton, second unit. The San Diego Police Department, every man and woman, except for a skeleton crew remaining on duty, third unit. Instead of limousines, police cars, a dozen of them, together as the fourth unit. He, Saperstein, he'd be in the first car, along with the mayor. The D.A., the sheriff, second car. Other law enforcement officials and various government representatives in the following cars. Next of kin in the final police car. Then, the hearse.

"We assemble at Pier B," Saperstein said, getting some more paper clips. "We move straight up Broadway." He looked at Donahoo, and then at Gomez and Montrose, Palmer and Cominsky. They were arranged in front of his desk along with Lewis. "We move solemnly through the heart of the city. In twenty blocks we pass a representative cross-section, from the shiny high rises to the pitiful slums. A measure of all the people he served—keeping law and order in a clangorous society. Those on foot disperse here at headquarters, joining us later, their own arrangements. The parade's mobile units continue on directly to Mount Hope Cemetery."

He bent his paper clips. "You guys. You're going to be here, walking behind the hearse. Anybody who can't walk twenty blocks, I want to hear it now, I want to see a note from a doctor, I want to talk to the doctor."

Donahoo was only half listening. He was still hung up on *clangorous*. Then it struck him why it was all so unreal. He could hear Lewis giving him the word at Mercy Hospital. 'This doesn't have to go anywhere else, Tommy.' They'd made an unspoken agreement. Okay, except to Saperstein.

Only it wasn't okay, Donahoo thought. Lewis hadn't told Saperstein. He hadn't told him sweet fuck all. If he had, Saperstein wouldn't be telling him, Donahoo, to limp behind Chip Lyons's hearse. Not even Saperstein would ask that.

Donahoo thought this was the worst kind of horseshit, and he thought, it crossed his mind, that maybe Lewis was somehow in this with Lyons. He hated himself for thinking that, but he briefly thought it. It was the way cops thought. That was his excuse. He said, something else he couldn't resist, "You didn't tell him, did you, Lewis?"

Saperstein was in mid–paper clip. "What?"

Lewis looked at Donahoo. He looked sad. "Leave it, willya?"

Saperstein was back and forth. "What?"

"I think Chip Lyons was on the take," Donahoo said flatly. "I think it involved a murder cover-up."

Saperstein stared at him in shock and disbelief. His paper-clip parade was forgotten.

"I've got a case," Donahoo said, quickly laying it out for him. He hurt so much, he didn't care anymore. He wanted everything out in the open, up front. He wanted everybody to know everything. If the case was being deep-sixed, he wanted to hear it from Saperstein, not Lewis, and he wanted the whole squad to hear it too. He wasn't taking a dive by himself. He went down the list. The opportunity—Lyons's hour alone with the camcorder at the Tijuana Slough. The motive—the money he could get for whatever crime, probably a murder, he may have filmed. The evidence—the eagerness of Americans #1 and #2 to pay half a million dollars for the video. The scary part—XLA and BMGS. What the hell did that mean?

Donahoo went through it all with only one interruption. When he claimed he had a statement, American #1's assertion that it was a shakedown, Lewis grumbled, "Not a signed statement." There wasn't a peep from Gomez and Montrose or Palmer and Cominsky. They sat like they were carved from stone.

Saperstein listened in a kind of daze. A hand moved unbidden through the line of paper clips. The parade was demolished. He stared in dismay. Then he said to Lewis, "Is that what this guy has been telling you?"

"Yes."

"And what have you been telling him?"

"To fish, fuck, and forget it."

"But he won't listen?"

"He won't hear."

Saperstein was looking at Donahoo. "All of you, get the fuck out of here. Tommy, you stay."

Palmer got up and left, quickly followed by Gomez, Montrose, and Cominsky. "Lewis. You don't hear either?"

Lewis pushed up. He got his shirt in. He scowled—the limit of an old cop's insolence—and then left without comment.

"Where you going with this?" Saperstein asked when the door was closed. "How does it end?"

"I dunno," Donahoo admitted. "The national security aspect, I guess. XLA, BMGS. Palmer had some thoughts there."

"Oh? What were they?"

"X, that usually means experimental. LA, he didn't know. B, bomber, or maybe ballistic . . ."

"Very good. Here's some more. LA, Los Angeles. BM, bowel movement."

"You're not really interested in this, are you?" Donahoo said.

"Tommy, Tommy, Tommy," Saperstein said, all mockery now, he had recovered. "Where are your priorities?" He got his bent paper clips together. "You want to hear my favorite cop story? My favorite cop story: There's this black officer in New York. She gets in a gun battle in a barbershop. She shoots it out with three or four Mafiosa types, and she gets 'em all. It was wonderful, she's a hero. How come that never happens here?"

"No Mafia."

"Yeah, that is a problem," Saperstein admitted. The whole time he hadn't stopped looking at Donahoo. "But you know what I think? That little black broad probably did more for the New York Police Department than an honest commissioner." He started rebuilding his parade. "There's two things you gotta tell the public, Tommy. The system works. The cop works."

Donahoo said, "Yeah, but . . ."

Saperstein shook his head. "I don't give a fuck about Primitivo at the moment. I used to give a fuck about him, but at the moment I don't give a fuck about him, I really don't. Another thing I don't give a fuck about, I don't give a fuck about military matters, which, frankly, are out of my jurisdiction. That's FBI and CIA and XYZ and who gives a fuck. You following me?"

"I'm ahead of you."

"Good. Now, listen carefully. I've got a cop here, Chip Francis Lyons, who, if I can just get through this fucking day, is going to be buried as the town's biggest hero, bigger than Ted Williams, bigger than Tom Cruise. Which—let me stress this part—is going to pay off big-time for the San Diego Police Department. In better public appreciation. In improved morale. So what the fuck are you doing to me, coming in here saying he's a spy?"

"I didn't say he was a spy."

"You're saying he's a crook?"

"I'm saying it looks like it."

"Yeah, well, if he was or he wasn't, he's dead, okay? What are you going to do with the corpse? Put it in jail? You want a corpse in Chino, doing hard time, the spicks are spitting on it, they're spitting on a cop corpse, is that what you want here?"

"There are other aspects . . ."

"What?"

"The alphabet soup."

"Here's how you handle that. You call the FBI. You tell them what you've got. Say it's from a reliable source you can't identify. XLA, BMGS. How you handle that, you let them handle that." He said, "You called them yet? Call them."

Donahoo didn't admit having made the call. He didn't want it used as an excuse or reason for him walking away. It was such a small scrap of information that he'd given Galloway. And the FBI wouldn't have the gut feeling for it that he had. He said, "How do we know they'll act on it?"

"Tommy. Listen. I don't want this. Bury the fucking thing."

"The case? I can't do that."

"No. The part involving the Chipper. Bury that part. Bury it with the guy."

"That may not be possible."

"Sergeant," Saperstein said, he was looking at Donahoo. "I'm not telling you again. Get your shovel."

Lewis was waiting down the hall. He had a Coke and an attitude. He said, "I didn't tell him because he didn't need to know. People used to rain on parades. Now, with your example, they'll pour acid on them. Your contribution to the lexicon."

Donahoo looked at him and kept on going.

"I also knew he'd tell you to bury it," Lewis said. "That's part of the job description. Reading the boss's mind."

Donahoo stopped. "You mean kissing his ass, don't you?"

Lewis sucked at his Coke. "I'm sure some good can come of a remark like that. Maybe you're a body parts donor?" He said, "Get real, will you? It's not even your job, Tommy. Sooner or later, in due time, this all goes to Internal Affairs."

"Saperstein owns Internal Affairs. And 'in due time' may not be soon enough."

Lewis considered. He hiked his pants. "If you get something solid, talk to me," he said. He changed his mind. "If you get lucky."

The squad room had been vacated, except for Cominsky. Gomez and Montrose, Palmer, they knew absence was the better part of valor, Donahoo thought. Only Cominsky could validate a presence. He would have some weird reason. Weird—but a reason.

"What did he say?" Cominsky asked, meaning what did Saperstein say after they had left, his office door was closed, showdown in the inner sanctum, how-big-are-your-balls time.

"I forget."

"Yeah," Cominsky said. "That's what I thought he'd tell you. But I didn't think you'd forget already."

Donahoo looked at him. That was the reason he had stayed? To counsel insurrection?

"I thought, you know, I'm your partner, maybe there's something you'd like to tell me—what did *you* say?"

"Cominsky. I'm trying to remember here. I think I said I forget."

"Maybe you can't help it," Cominsky decided. "Maybe you're getting that Reagan thing, you know, Alzheimer's? They say he's gonna forget he was ever president, and then he's gonna forget his name. They say he's gonna forget where his dick is, and then he'll piss his pants. I feel sorry for Nancy."

"I beg your pardon?"

"You heard me," Cominsky said. He pushed up from his desk. "I think I'll take the rest of the day off. I'm not feeling so good." He got almost to the door and stopped. He was in a new outfit, a double-breasted suit, dark blue with a fine white pinstripe, and he looked rather elegant. He had a blue shirt and a yellow tie. "Oh? You wanted to know who Chip may have called from Rosie Gestring's on Sunday? The telephone company says the number belongs to a Margaret Lyons. She lives in the Sands Trailer Court over on Mission Bay. Unit six." He said, "But maybe you forgot you wanted to know?"

Donahoo said, "What the fuck do you know, Cominsky?"

"Nothing, I guess," Cominsky said. "Not anymore."

Donahoo watched him go. What was it Rosie Gestring said? Dreams crumble, fools die. Yeah, he thought. And heroes perish. "Cominsky," he said, he was talking to nobody, the guy was gone, "that's a nice suit, but your shoes look cooked, you left 'em in the oven too long." He went into his cubicle.

There was a note on his desk from Cominsky. It said the same thing. *Margaret Lyons. The Sands Trailer Court. #6. Mission Bay.*

Donahoo fingered the note. Margaret Lyons. That would be his mother? Probably, Donahoo thought. Every boy had a mother. He wondered what she was doing now. Probably getting ready for the parade. Getting all dressed up for the funeral of her hero son.

A parade down Broadway. Interment at Mount Hope Cemetery. It couldn't get much better than that.

Donahoo sat wondering what he should do here. It was a tough call. Fools die, heroes perish. He could end up in Traffic. He could be a meter maid.

Yeah, well, fuck you, Saperstein, Donahoo thought. You're all alone in your ivory fucking tower. I've got to live with Cominsky.

TWENTY-THREE

Mission Bay. Donahoo drove over in the Morris Minor, which was a loaner from Cominsky until he got a replacement for the Toronado. He was supposed to be on a sick leave and he wasn't authorized to have department transportation. At least it would keep him out of trouble, he thought. He couldn't catch a lawn mower in a Morris Minor called Morris.

Donahoo had talked to Cominsky about that. He had said, "You know, if you want to call a car by its make, you gotta put the *the* in front, Cominsky. You should say, for example, 'Do you wanta borrow the Chev?' You don't say, 'Do you wanta borrow Chev? Or, in my instance, I would have said, 'Do you wanta borrow the Toronado?' I would not have said, 'Do you wanta borrow Toronado.' You see what I mean?"

Cominsky had said, "Do you want it or not?"

Maggie Lyons was trying to choose between a long black dress and a short black dress.

Donahoo found her that way. When she opened her trailer home door, she had one over each arm, like she had been walking around with them, eenie, meenie, minie, moe.

"Oh, police," she said, squinting at Donahoo's badge. "Are you my ride?" She backed away to allow him to enter. "You're a little early, aren't you?"

Donahoo went in. It was a single wide, an early model, a lot of fiberboard and cheap linoleum and plush carpeting. It was homey enough though. She had fixed it up. There were frilly curtains and puff cushions and a world of knickknacks. There was a birdcage with a bird and a fishbowl with a fish. No sign of the sand through the yellowed picture window, but it was out there somewhere, the smell of the bay's sewage was in the room, just as it was outside. The Sands Trailer Park. Just the place for a boy's mother.

"Your ride, it's coming," Donahoo said, looking around. "I was just hoping—before you get away—you might answer a few questions."

"Oh? What about?" She didn't look much like her son. The resemblance, if any, was in her ruddy skin, the thinning hair that used to be blond but was now mostly white. Her features were petite, pleasant, set in a small, round, starting-to-sag face. Her blue eyes were crinkled.

Donahoo wished for a moment that he hadn't come. He didn't like her, he thought, and it was for no reason, except that she had hatched the bugger. She was a small, dumpy woman, shaped like a warped pear, no breasts but wide, round hips. She was in a cheap cotton print housedress decorated with tiny red and yellow flowers. It had faded from repeated washes.

"I also wanted to extend my sympathy. Your son was a noted officer. He is sorely missed."

"He worked with you?"

"Yes. On occasion. He was on my squad."

"What's your name?" She was squinting at him.

"Donahoo."

"Donahoo?"

"Yes."

"I don't recall that name."

"Well. We weren't that close."

Donahoo looked around. The living room was a narrow box. There was just a sofa, a coffee table, an easy chair for the TV. The photographs were stuck in with the knickknacks on built-in shelves. There were several of Chip Lyons.

"Happier times, huh?" Donahoo said, picking up one of the photographs.

Maggie Lyons nodded tightly. She looked like she might not approve.

Donahoo studied it. The Chipper as a tourist in the Philippines. Three very pretty young women were hanging on him. The glass eye and the big nose—they didn't matter. The girls were looking at him like he was a millionaire.

"He loved it there," Maggie Lyons admitted. "He was always talking about going back."

Donahoo returned the photo to its place on the shelf. "Manila Time?"

No answer. She was trying to decide which dress.

"I like the short one," Donahoo said. "It's more you."

"You think so?"

"Yes."

Donahoo leaned against the wall. He wondered how much time he had. It was almost noon. The parade started at two.

"I'm supposed to put something on a plaque," he said. "Something, you know, appropriate. But I'm not very good at that. I'm, you know, a cop, not a poet. It's hard."

"A plaque?"

"Honoring him."

"Why not just say he was a hero?" She was squinting at him again.

"Yes," he told her. "But it would help if I knew why. Your son—excuse me here—had what could almost be called an obsessive compulsion to be the world's bravest police officer. That's a rare thing. You don't see it often."

"And you want to know why?"

"Yes."

"Well, I don't see it as important," she said. She moved away with her black dresses. "You think the short one?"

"My choice, certainly."

"I don't know. It's kind of uniform-y."

Donahoo got another photograph. It would be Chip Lyons's father. He had the nose. It was a fist in his face. "Wear it. You'll look proud in it."

"What a nice thing for you to say."

Donahoo smiled for her. He put the photo back.

"Actually, that's the reason there, I suppose," she said. "He—his father—he wasn't a very brave man. Something happened in the war. He saved himself and he let others die. He was never the same. When he came home, he took to drinking, he was always depressed, despondent. He hated himself. It was awful to watch. It went on for years and then one day he killed himself. A whole bottle of sleeping pills. He just couldn't stand it any longer."

"And Chip spent a lifetime trying to compensate?"

"Something like that."

Donahoo thought he should ask his question now. "Chip called you Sunday morning. It would be about four A.M. Could you tell me what he wanted?"

She looked at him in surprise. She had put the dresses aside and she was holding a small black hat with a heavy dark veil.

"I wouldn't ask if it wasn't important."

"He wanted to borrow my VCR," she said, moving in front of

a narrow mirror attached to the back of the open bedroom door. "He wanted to catch me before I went to early Mass." She put on the hat and adjusted the veil. "He wanted me to leave it on the back porch."

"Didn't he have a VCR?"

"He said it was broken."

He lied, Donahoo thought. He wanted two VCRs, so he could make copies of what he had just filmed at the Tijuana Slough.

"Is there something wrong?"

"The prick," Donahoo said without consideration, he just blurted it out. He'd known from the start, he thought. From that first moment, Lyons announcing, "This place, it's a fucking tomb," he'd known there was something wrong, he just hadn't been able to figure what. Maybe he hadn't put his heart to it. Maybe he was in denial because Lewis was in denial. Maybe he'd always known that Saperstein would tell him to do his digging with a shovel.

Maggie Lyons turned away from the mirror. Her sudden tears were visible even behind the heavy veil.

"Nobody liked him," she said. Her little face screwed up. It was a pinched welt. "How does this look?"

Donahoo thought it looked like death.

"I wore it when we put his dad down."

"Then it's all the more appropriate."

"What do you mean?"

"Well, I was thinking, you know, we all fight our battles, and maybe, the way your husband hung in so long, maybe he was a hero too. Maybe they both were heroes."

"What a nice thing to say." She was squinting at him.

Chip Lyons lived—*formerly* lived—in a garden apartment complex on Georgia Street in North Park. It was very Southern California, eight separate but identical boxlike units, four in a row, just the two rows, facing each other across a small, poorly tended lawn and limp birds of paradise. Pink stucco walls and red Spanish tile trim along the edge of the parapet roofs. Narrow wooden casement windows protected by ornamental iron bars. Little, square houses that were set low, just the one concrete step at the in-an-archway doors. Not so much places to live as places to hide.

Donahoo found the one he wanted. Number 4, at the back. *C. F. Lyons* on the mailbox, which was empty. Somebody had advised the post office, tenant deceased, redirect. They'd also told the paper boy. There was only one *Union-Trib,* looking tired, yellowed, stuck in the lower branches of the withered cypress standing sentinel to the left of the door. Nothing else.

Death, they say it's getting complicated, but actually it's getting simpler, Donahoo thought. There was a time you'd have to stop the milkman, you'd have to stop the bread man, you'd have to stop the iceman. The Singer sewing machine man and the Fuller Brush man. Now all you had to stop were the Jehovah Witnesses.

Donahoo looked around. There was no indication that any of the neighbors had been alerted to his presence. He went around the side of the house, down a narrow, barely passable path between the wall and a high grapestake fence. There were three windows, all barred. He went around the back, into a small concrete-walled patio used for exercise and storage. It again was difficult to maneuver. Free weights, a bench. A dented smoker. A rusted ten-speed. With an effort he made it to the back stoop, to the door, which was ajar.

Hullo, Donahoo thought. It had been jimmied. The bar marks were like scars. He could stop worrying about not having a search warrant, he decided. He was investigating a burglary, possibly in progress. He unholstered his Cobra, Cominsky's present, and kicked the door open, so fiercely that a panel cracked.

"Police, freeze!" he shouted. The cocked Cobra fanned the gloom. "Hands on your heads!" He waited a three count and then entered. He walked into an eerie stillness. No movement, no sound. No audience for his theatrics. But the place looked like it was screaming.

Donahoo picked his way through. Kitchen, bathroom, bedroom, living room. He put the gun away and surveyed the carnage. He had never experienced this thorough a search of any premises. The house had been tossed by experts. *Everything* had been torn apart or broken. They hadn't been content to ravage just the furniture, clothing, and possessions. They'd ripped out light fixtures, pulled off molding, lifted paneling.

There was a pile of videocassettes beside a pile of the cardboard covers they came in. Someone had gone through them to make sure the labels were correct. Someone looking for the video taken at the Tijuana Slough?

Donahoo didn't doubt that for a moment. He sorted through the cassettes. There was a lot of Sylvester Stallone. Every Sly movie ever made, probably. Donahoo imagined Chip Lyons imagining himself as Stallone. Imagining himself as Rambo. Or maybe the Specialist. Anyway, a tough guy.

Jesus, Donahoo thought. What a mess. He was pretty sure they hadn't found what they were looking for. If they had found it, they would have stopped at some point, not continued forever. He picked up a pair of jeans. The pockets were turned out. They weren't just looking for the video. They were looking for anything that would help. A scrap of paper with a safety deposit box number. A key.

Donahoo sorted through the mess. He found Chip Lyons's VCR and he found what was probably Maggie Lyons's. There were a couple of starfish decals glued on it. She was the kind of lady who would be interested in starfish, living down on the sand and all. He stopped looking when he found a file, *Banner, Rosita.* It was sitting there like somebody left it for him.

He felt, the first time, like an intruder. He wanted to read it and he didn't want to read it. He took it out on the back stoop, where the light was better. Banner. That had been her married name. Her maiden name was Ayala. Her AKAs, bestowed by Chip Lyons, were Rosie the Snake G-string, the Wham Bam Ice Trail. God knows where she came up with Gestring.

There wasn't all that much in it. Just enough to keep a lady on her back with her legs spread, lying there and thinking, Hurry up and come.

Donahoo read it. The official documents said murder in the second degree in the shotgun death of Charles Banner. Sentenced 4/2/86 to ten years in Women's Correctional, Gary, Indiana. Escaped 10/16/88. Press clippings with a fuzzy photo said the defendant claimed self-defense. She fired one shot to protect herself from violent attack by her husband. She cited a long history of spousal abuse, testifying of repeated beatings that required medical attention, including hospitalization. The court considered her actions unwarranted and excessive.

Spousal abuse, huh? That apparently didn't cut much in Indiana. He did the arithmetic. If she went back, eight years remaining in her sentence, plus whatever they'd tack on for escape, unlawful flight. Eight-plus in the Women's Correctional. Even Chip Lyons would look good compared to that.

The dented smoker was sitting in front of him, Donahoo, staring at it, couldn't imagine being a bad cop, and he couldn't imagine feeling good about it. Don't think, he thought. He put the file in the smoker. He found a match and set it afire. He looked at his watch. It was too late to make the parade but he could get to the cemetery on time. He thought he ought to do that. Saperstein would be glad to see him, and he, Donahoo, he'd be happy to see Chip Lyons, hero, put in the ground.

TWENTY-FOUR

Dreams do come true, Donahoo thought. Chip Lyons's funeral, it had to be everything Saperstein wanted, and more. At least two thousand people were gathered on Mount Hope's grassy hillside. Most of the San Diego Police Department, representatives from other police jurisdictions, heads of various city departments, citizens drawn by all the publicity, and enough media for a celebrity murder trial. Remnants of the parade were scattered around. The SDPD Color Guard. A Navy Color Guard. The U.S. Marine Corps Band from Camp Pendleton. The brisk wind from the bay was snapping their flags. There was a festive flavor, and a somber tone too. Donahoo thought it was the Fourth of July and Veterans Day and

Thanksgiving and maybe even Christmas. You could have it any way you wanted it. Saperstein was having it all.

Donahoo parked the Morris Minor illegally and at a distance. He sat watching and listening for a while. They were at some indeterminate point in the graveside ceremony. Saperstein, with notes, was holding forth at a lectern, looking—Donahoo borrowed a term from Maggie Lyons—very police chief-y. He was in his new enforcement blue police chief uniform. The cap with the birdshit visor. The epaulets and the silver buttons.

"Men like Investigator Chip Francis Lyons, the Chipper," Saperstein was saying, his voice amplified by a sound system. "They don't appear often." He looked out on the attentive assembly as if searching for an equal, finding none. "They don't stay with us long enough."

Donahoo left the Morris Minor. He started down a long slope of lawn, walking into the wash of Saperstein's words, coming at him like waves, rising and falling in the wind at his back.

"A police officer doesn't go to work," Saperstein was saying. "He goes on duty . . . to protect and to serve . . . and every time he does so . . . he puts his life on the line."

Donahoo was looking for somebody he could stand with. Maybe the Chargers' cheerleaders?

"Chip Francis Lyons did more than that. He *drew* the line."

Donahoo was trying to find anybody in his squad. He'd take Cominsky.

"He drew it harder, wider, sharper . . . and he told the criminal element . . . the scum tearing at the fabric of our society . . . that they crossed it at fatal risk."

Donahoo spotted Gomez and Montrose standing off to the side. He veered and joined them. He said, sotto voce, referring to Saperstein, "What the hell is he doing?"

Montrose smiled. "I think he just made murder legal."

"For cops," Gomez added. "I dunno if it applies to off duty. He hasn't got to that part."

"Investigator Chip Francis Lyons . . . didn't know the word fear,"

Saperstein said, amplified. "In his dictionary, you found fealty . . . faithfulness, allegiance . . . and the next word was fearless . . . having no fear, brave. Fear wasn't listed. He drew a line through it."

"Jesus," Montrose said. "Does Webster's know about this?"

"Law, order, justice," Saperstein said. His voice boomed across the cemetery. "If there is no law, there is no order. If there is no order, there is no justice. If there is no justice, we are enslaved." He looked out over his audience. The tears glimmered on his face. "Law, order, justice. We cannot have one . . . without the other. Together they form . . . the foundation . . . of our free society." His voice was filled with emotion. "The law comes first. The men and women . . . who fearlessly uphold it . . . come first. Today . . . in America's finest city . . . we put to rest . . . the first among the first . . . Investigator Chip Francis Lyons."

Donahoo thought he recognized Rosie Gestring. For an instant, a face in a crowd, and then she was gone.

"I guess he's going to heaven, huh?" Gomez said.

Donahoo smiled for Gomez and patted Montrose good-bye. He headed back up the hill to where he thought he had seen Rosie Gestring. Saperstein was still speaking, but the sense of it wasn't fully registering. Lyons was going to heaven, but he wasn't in heaven yet, Donahoo gathered. Saperstein hadn't gotten to that part.

Saperstein was saying, "If there is a place for peace officers . . ."

Donahoo went back up the hill, searching the crowd. He thought Saperstein might be overdoing it just a tad. The Chipper, they were going to bury him with crayons, so when he got to heaven, he could draw lines.

Saperstein was saying, "Investigator Chip Francis Lyons . . . never once shrank . . ."

Which accounts for the nose, Donahoo thought. He went through the crowd. He wasn't certain he had seen her. Maybe wishful thinking? He was pretty sure though.

". . . from the awful choice . . . of that split-second judgment . . . that we as a society ask of our front-line defenders."

Rosie Gestring had left the crowd and was sitting against a pine tree, her long legs stuck straight out, as if she had just dropped that way. Her bag purse was open beside her. Some of the contents were spilled on the grass. It looked like she had gone through it hurriedly, searching for something. Probably a tissue, Donahoo thought. She was crying.

"You again?" she said, sniffing. She was dressed in a business suit, dark blue, conservative. Matching pumps and stockings. Her hair was up. She could be making a day of the occasion or simply taking time off from work. "Officer."

"I'm supposed to be here," Donahoo told her. "You? I dunno. I thought you'd have sat it out."

"I am."

"In a bar somewhere."

"Yeah." She patted the grass beside her, an invitation for him to sit down, and then went back to repairing her makeup. "I don't know either. What do they say? 'It ain't over till they throw dirt in your face?'" She patted the grass again. "I guess I just wanted to make sure it got done."

Donahoo hesitated. If he sat down, he might not be able to get up without assistance. His knee was really hurting again.

"It's not like he was a total monster," she said. "He didn't beat me or keep me locked up. He wasn't weird or depraved . . ." She blew her nose. "It was just . . . such a *fucking invasion*." She laughed at herself. "I've got a way with words."

Saperstein was saying, "The San Diego Police Department . . . will forever honor . . ."

Donahoo sat down next to her. He got a small vase out of his jacket pocket. It was plugged with a thimble-sized cork. He gave it to her.

She looked at him quizzically.

"I was over to his place today," Donahoo said. "I was looking for something else and I found a file he had on you. The conviction and . . . well. I burned it. That's the ashes."

She was looking at him. "You knew I was going to be here?"

"No. I was going to scatter them for you. But, since you are here, you can scatter them yourself, if you wish."

Saperstein was saying, "What is important . . . he chose to serve us . . ."

"Maybe we could scatter them together?"

"Okay."

Donahoo, grimacing, pushed up. Rosie was getting her bag together and didn't notice his difficulty. He took her hand, helped her to her feet. She smiled and didn't let go. They stood holding hands. Donahoo thought it somehow was a very natural thing for them to be doing.

"Where?" Her eyes were dry. She was smiling again.

He was lost. He didn't say anything.

She gave him the vase. He uncorked it, handed it back.

"Here?"

Fuck, he thought, we've got to get rid of these ashes. He didn't know what to say. He shrugged helplessly.

"Are you always this inept?"

"Yes. No."

She laughed. Donahoo thought he must be crazy. He was pretty sure he was in love with this woman, and it was the first time he had heard her laugh.

Saperstein was saying, "We face a time . . . of great challenge and peril . . ."

Donahoo saw the old Cadillac. It was the only vehicle moving in the cemetery. It came around the sweep of the road above the assembly, moving slowly between the lines of parked cars, as if on a reconnaissance. There was no mistaking it. An ugly raw metal smear ran along the whole right side.

"What's wrong?" Rosie asked.

"Take cover," Donahoo ordered, pushing her away. "Get lost in the crowd." He looked around. Gomez and Montrose had disappeared. There was still no sign of Cominsky and Palmer. "Do it. Hurry."

The Cadillac had stopped. Donahoo gave the bewildered Rosie another shove. She moved away, shocked, not comprehending. Donahoo started for the road. He could see the car's occupants clearly. American #1 in the passenger seat, as he had been on I-8, when he forced the Toronado into the ditch. American #2 at the wheel. Two unpredictable killers.

Donahoo couldn't figure why they had come to the cemetery. The last time there were this many cops together it was payday. But then he put himself in their heads. If he was going to use the video against them as evidence, he'd have done so long ago. They'd be behind bars. They remained free either because he didn't have the video or because he wanted to make a deal. They were thinking, their whole focus, Let's make a deal.

American #1 was smiling.

Maybe they were smart, not stupid, Donahoo decided. They could do business here as readily as any other place. The funeral service afforded a certain amount of protection for both sides. A gunfight would be in really bad taste.

Donahoo made it to the waiting Cadillac. Quillan and Taylor were looking at him amiably. They didn't seem to have a care. Donahoo thought they could pass for a couple of happy-go-lucky bums. The Caddie looked like they lived in it. The headliner was a sagging curtain. A rip the width of the front seat had been pinned together. The backseat was piled with blanket-draped possessions. A sign said HOME SWEET HOME. And it smelled of scotch.

"You got a girl?" Quillan said, smiling. He was looking past Donahoo.

Donahoo saw the binoculars on the dash. He turned away briefly. Rosie Gestring hadn't sought the safety of the crowd. She was standing out in the open. She was looking at him.

"She's just an acquaintance."

"Oh?" Quillan said. "I saw you holding hands. That must be Rosie, huh? Charlie mentioned her when we visited him at the VA. Miss G-string." He was smiling, yellow teeth. His wolf eyes were cold, empty. "Holding hands. That looks like more than friends to me, wouldn't you say, Taylor?"

Taylor said, grinning, "I say he's fucking her."

"You're wrong," Donahoo said, trying to control his anger. He looked at Quillan. "Let's get with it. Can we go someplace?"

"What's wrong with now?" Quillan was still staring past him. "You've got another Monica there? Naw, more a Presh."

Taylor grinned. "I guess you like her a lot?"

Donahoo looked around. Rosie Gestring seemed to be the only one at the funeral aware of his existence at the moment. The crowd was intent on Saperstein's soaring sermon. There was no sign of Montrose and Gomez or Palmer and Cominsky.

"You got the video?" Quillan asked.

"In my car," Donahoo told him, meaning the Morris Minor, meaning the evidence room porno movie, *Star Whores*. He thought that he was back at the beginning. The plan was to play it by ear and the plan sucked. "We're getting close to a deal here. You want to show me the color of your money?"

Quillan shook his head. "No. What we're doing here is establishing your good faith. Have you, or have you not, got the video? That's what we're doing now."

Donahoo thought things might be breaking for him. If he could establish a criminal transaction, money paid for what was *thought* to be evidence, even though it wasn't evidence, that might stand up. It was like a cop dressed up as a hooker. A guy might think he was going to get some pussy, but there wasn't any pussy. Was this the same thing? He wasn't sure, but it was worth a try. The no-pussy argument. It might work.

He said, "Lyons, the money you gave him, it disappeared with him. I can't find it."

"I'm crying here."

"Come on. Tomorrow you're paying me half a million. Today you can't spare a dime?"

"Nothing."

Taylor said, "Jesus, Quillan. Give the dick something."
Quillan's wolf eyes were on Donahoo. "I said no."
"Then I'll give it to him."

Donahoo waited. This is it, he thought. It's going down. It was all he could do not to look back at Rosie. He could imagine her still standing out in the open. He wondered why he always got involved with stubborn, headstrong, dog-ass-dumb women.

"I'm a partner in this bug-fuck," Taylor said. "Give him something."

Quillan considered. If he was angry, it didn't show. "How much?"

"Just walking-away money," Donahoo said quickly. "A first-class ticket to Zonguldak. A bag of quarters for the whores. If, come tomorrow, I've already got the getaway paid, I'm ecstatic. Is that twenty grand in your pocket? Or do you just get excited easily?"

"Give it to him," Taylor said.

Donahoo waited. Quillan reached into his jacket. His hand emerged with a manila envelope. He opened it to reveal a stack of hundred-dollar bills. He riffled through it for Donahoo's benefit.

"I'll be back."

"I'll be here."

Donahoo went to the Morris Minor. Rosie was still standing out in the open. Standing *defiantly*. The woman, she was dead from the ass up, Donahoo thought. At the moment he hated her. He got to the Morris Minor. He got *Star Whores*. He headed back to the Cadillac. He didn't look at her this time.

Saperstein was saying, "His favorite poem was . . . 'Next Time I'd Pick More Daisies.'"

Donahoo wondered how the hell Saperstein knew that. He must have known the Chipper pretty well to know that.

Quillan had his hand out.

"The money," Donahoo told him.

Quillan's other hand came out of his jacket. He had a bunch of bills from the envelope. He made a careful exchange—the money for the cassette.

"Good-bye."

"Not yet," Quillan said.

Taylor ripped away a section of the sagging headliner. A sawed-off shotgun fell into his waiting arms. He had it pointed at Donahoo's head in the same instant.

Quillan reached into the backseat. He lifted the blanket, revealing a VCR, a monitor. The wires ran under the front seat. Twelve volt, Donahoo thought. They were going to run it on the cigarette lighter.

Donahoo released his fistful of money. He fanned it across the roof of the Cadillac. He let the wind take it from him.

"Let's make sure here," Quillan said, picking up a plug at his feet. He inserted it into the lighter socket.

The wind took the money. Twenty thousand dollars in hundred-dollar bills. It took it out over, and into, the crowd gathered at the graveside, distributing it like a bonus from heaven.

Quillan leaned across the seat with the cassette. He shoved it into the VCR. Taylor was intent on Donahoo. But then there was a split second when his gaze strayed. He saw the money flying away. He said, "Hey?"

Donahoo dropped like a hawk. He fell, rolled away, twisting, turning. On his second turn he had the Cobra. He fired blindly at the Cadillac.

Taylor, momentarily blocked by Quillan, got off one blast, too late. Donahoo was too far away from him. He gave the shotgun to Quillan.

Donahoo, pausing, careful now, squeezed off two more shots. The second slug missed Quillan by inches. The Caddie's windshield shattered from the inside.

Taylor hit the gas. The Caddie roared away. Quillan fired two meaningless blasts. Donahoo responded just as futilely. He made several hits, but nothing happened.

Rosie Gestring was screaming, "Tommy, *Tommy!*"

Donahoo was reloading. He looked back at the graveside service. The hillside was absolute bedlam. Two thousand people chasing twenty thousand dollars. It was a circus."

Saperstein, amplified, was saying, "Donahoo . . ."

TWENTY-FIVE

Charlie was saying his prayers. Donahoo heard him when he entered the hospital room. His voice was strained and uneven but still strong enough to be heard. If not by God, at least by me, Donahoo thought. He paused, deeply touched by the moment. He had never heard his father in prayer before. "And God bless the monsignor, and Mother Superior, and Father Flaherty, and Burt Reynolds, and Hoyt."

Donahoo waited. He thought, as always, that Charlie's head had already become a skull, it rested on the pillow like an upended bowl, and his withered body had turned to sticks. His life beat faintly in him. Every day he seemed to get weaker. He didn't have much time left.

Charlie opened his raisin eyes, smiled faintly. "Hullo."

"Hi, there," Donahoo said. He moved over to the bedside. "How you doing today?"

"Saying my prayers."

"Yeah, I heard," Donahoo said. "But I didn't hear my name mentioned." He showed his package. "I brought you a present."

"You got early billing." Charlie started to reach for the package but his hand fell away. "A day for presents. Maybe you better open it for me."

"Oh? Who else has been bringing you presents? That nurse?"

"No. Hoyt."

Donahoo unwrapped his gift, remembering how he, Donahoo, acting through Charlie, had profoundly changed Hoyt's life at St. Paul's Mission for Men in Desert Hot Springs. Well, mostly Charlie had changed the kid's life, Donahoo thought. But he had helped a bit. Hoyt, not yet a man, still a boy, barely sixteen, was lost and bewildered, bent on self-destruction, when he showed up at the mission. Now he was a country music singer. He was just starting out. Nobody had heard of him, he liked to say, but you happened to wander into the right bar, you listened to him.

"That guitar you bought him?" Charlie said.

"You bought him."

"It was your money."

"Yeah. But it was supposed to go in the general fund."

"Which never missed the fifty bucks."

Donahoo shrugged. He revealed his present. It was a framed photograph. A younger Charlie, and a younger Donahoo too. Down by the seashore, Solana Beach. Clowning around like a couple of bricklayers. Charlie in one of Donahoo's skimpy bathing suits and with his collar on backward, that's all. They looked vital and happy and secure. They looked like they could live forever.

In the picture, the sun would never set, Donahoo thought. He held it for close inspection. "Remember this?"

Charlie nodded, smiled. "Those were the days, my friend."

Donahoo moved things around to make room on the bedside table. He set the photograph up.

"Looks good, huh?"

"It looks terrific."

Donahoo sat down in the large chair he had brought in for himself.

"How was the funeral?"

"Pretty good. Big turnout."

"How many, you think?"

"Two thousand."

"Wow. Popular guy."

Donahoo nodded. "To paraphrase whoever said it first. If you give people what they want, they'll come out."

"What else?"

Donahoo made a gesture that meant nothing. His life, it was turmoil, he thought. He didn't want to share it. That would only cause concern. He'd best just talk about times past. He'd like to talk about Rosie, but he'd made a promise, no more women, so that was out. Besides, he probably was reading too much, far too much, into a little hand-holding at a cemetery.

"It's quiet, huh?"

Yeah, *now*, Donahoo thought. He could still hear Saperstein screaming at him over the loudspeakers as he chased the Caddie off Mount Hope in Cominsky's Morris Minor. It was an incident that neither would ever live down. He, Donahoo, would be remembered for the most futile car chase in Southern California. Saperstein would be commemorated for saying the f-word at a funeral.

"You must be doing something."

Donahoo made another empty gesture. He was in a kind of limbo at the moment, not sure which way to turn, how to proceed. He was acting, or reacting, instinctively. Evading Saperstein. Catching his breath. Trying to get some sort of fix in the swirling tangle of evidence suggesting that Chip Francis Lyons was part of something bigger than a blackmail scheme. No plan, but a couple of priorities.

Saperstein—he had to stay clear of him for a while. He faced a war crimes trial with the guy. Supension, demotion. Meter maid. Lost and Found. It was too terrible to contemplate. Rosie Gestring—he had to explain and apologize for shoving her around. This whole thing, it started with somebody shoving her around, Donahoo thought. He wasn't angry at her anymore. He was vaguely worried about her. American #1, the guy with the wolf's eyes, had said, "Looks like more than friends . . ." and American #2, his pinch-faced pal, had said, "I guess you like her a lot?" They had her name. *Part* of her name. G-string, not Gestring. Did they have more? There was a chance, an off chance, of them having seen her arrive in the Yugo, but that would have been before they saw her with him. So they wouldn't have had any reason to take her licence number. And there were a lot of Yugos around. Not many of them running, perhaps. But enough to make tracing her difficult. Unless they were pros?

Charlie, as if he sensed something, said, "What about that Rosie?"

"What about her?" Donahoo looked around. He said, "Listen, uh, what did Hoyt give you?"

Charlie motioned feebly to his small radio/tape deck. "He brought me a tape he made. The guy's written a new song. 'Curious Ginger.' "

"Really? That's great."

"You want to hear it?"

"Sure."

"It's in there. Just push the button."

Donahoo leaned forward and pushed the tape deck play button. It started somewhere in the middle of the song. Donahoo was going to rewind and then changed his mind. Hoyt on his guitar. Hoyt singing.

> Curious Ginger, pressing her nose
> Seeing all the window shows
> Learning all the mannequin knows
> Nothing moves, but the time sure goes.

"What do you think?"

"Well, uh, it's good, I guess," Donahoo said. "But it's not very upbeat."

"I don't think it's supposed to be upbeat."

"That's possible."

Donahoo sat listening to Hoyt. It didn't get any better. It was a real downer. He remembered Hoyt playing for Presh when he took her to visit Charlie at St. Paul's Mission. That song, 'Never Gonna Pass You,' had been pretty much of a downer too.

"Gee, I dunno," Donahoo said. "How does that kid make a living singing sad songs?"

"He sings about what he knows."

> Curious Ginger, what you're gonna find
> Your daddy's deaf and the gods are blind
> Rocks from the mountains, they grind fine
> Nobody lives in the sands of time.

Donahoo sat listening. Hoyt, he was singing about dying, he thought. That wasn't very appropriate. He wanted to turn it off.

He got out the flask. He poured a quick drink for Charlie. He poured a faster one for himself. Nurse Bird was around somewhere. He'd heard her chirping in the hall.

"You going to be here?" Charlie asked. He was a bowl and some sticks.

"I promise," Donahoo said, upset, the first time, about the diverted fifty dollars. The kid was writing sad songs. That's all he sang. Like the one he sang for Presh that day in Desert Hot Springs. "I won't miss the ten minutes, I'm wasting here behind." The kid's first dumb song. It set the pattern. Donahoo said, "You've got my word, Charlie. I'll be here for you." He said, reaching for one of the sticks, "For me, too, huh? I want to be here for me." He couldn't get the dumb song out of his head. "I've lost so many years/Ain't never gonna find." That was sad.

Bird came in. She said, "We having a party?"

"No, we're listening to sad songs," Donahoo told her. He thought of her on his finger. He was trying to think of something happy. "Do you sing, Bird?"

She said, "You have any idea how many people ask me that?"

Donahoo didn't answer. He had his hand in his pocket. He was screwing the cap on the flask. He thought he could suggest a song for Hoyt. Bad day at the VA.

TWENTY-SIX

If what Tom Wolfe said was true, "You can't go home again," then he was driving in the wrong direction, Donahoo thought. He hadn't read the book. He loved the title though. He was afraid, if he read the book, he might discover that the title meant something different from what he thought it meant, and that would not only spoil the book for him, but it would spoil the title too. What Wolfe meant—Donahoo's interpretation of it—was that you couldn't do something, anything, that was really worth doing, twice. You couldn't go home again and you could climb Mount Everest only once. The second time wouldn't be the same. There wouldn't be that fear of the unknown and that thrill of discovery and that glow of victory. That's why nobody climbed Everest twice. Not to mention that it was a bitch of a thing to do.

You couldn't go home again and you got only one woman. There was some literary critic who knew that Wolfe wrote in longhand while standing up and using the top of a refrigerator for a desk, some smart guy who was going to say that his, Donahoo's, interpretation was obvious or dumb, but Donahoo didn't have the heart to look into the matter any further. It worked for him the way he had it figured out. One woman.

National City. Donahoo drove down Main Street and National City Boulevard. Roosevelt Avenue and Mary Lane and then to Ethel Place. The little cul-de-sac neighborhood was in repose. Those who went to work had already departed. Those left at home would probably sleep till noon. The stake bed truck was in the carport. The Yugo was snuggled behind it.

Donahoo parked at the end of the street overlooking the canyon. It wasn't quite eight o'clock, and the night's mist still lingered below, broken, drifting. The canyon's thick vegetation, the color of camouflage, poked in and out, looking alien and forbidding. The sun hadn't yet warmed the day.

Rosie Gestring. It always came back here, to her, this solitary woman, Donahoo thought. She pulled him like some magic lodestone. He couldn't resist her—the idea of her. He pushed out of the Morris Minor. He went the front way instead of taking the shortcut across the lawn. It was Chip Lyons's shortcut. He, Donahoo, had staked the front way.

She had the door partly open when he got there. She must listen for cars, he thought. Be ever alert for strangers, or danger. She was always waiting to say go away. It was like a replay of a movie of his hopes and dreams. The panel of her face. Sleep-filled eyes. No lipstick.

"What are you doing here?" she asked.

"Trying to prove Tom Wolfe wrong."

"Oh, God," she said, but she opened the door wider, let him enter. "Don't even try to explain that."

He went into the hall and the smell of coffee and breakfast. He stood trying to decipher it. Bacon. Toast, maybe eggs? Maybe hash browns?

"Now what?"

"I was just thinking, for a skinny lady, you're always eating. The first time I was here, fish. The next time, chicken."

"Yeah?" She put her blue-black hair up with a couple of quick twists. "Well, Officer, let's see how good you really are, what's it this time?"

"Easy. Bacon and eggs."

"Wrong. It's chorizo. And I don't think it was fish before, it was squid. What I'd bet, the only reason you could tell it was chicken was the bag. You want some chorizo?"

"I could use another coffee."

She crooked a finger and led him into the kitchen, which, like the hall and living room, belonged in another era. There was an old gas range, a green and white Garland, and an ancient white refrigerator, what was possibly the first Whirlpool. The sink and its fixtures and the Formica countertops and plank cupboards were obviously original equipment. Instead of a table, there was a small built-in booth, a squeeze for four, stuck against a blank wall. The light was in a round white bowl attached to the center of the pressed tin ceiling. The floor was covered with a gray linoleum decorated with pastel dabs that made it look like an artist's cleaning rag. It was the kind, no matter how deep the wear, the pattern remained. The window was over the sink.

"You own this place?"

"No."

"You're renting?"

"No. I'm buying it."

Donahoo checked out the frying pan. She wasn't lying. Chorizo.

"You're sure?" she asked, meaning did he want some.

"Yeah. I can't do that. I'd look like a sumo wrestler."

"You know what it is?"

"Chorizo. I know it's Mexican."

"It's pork. Pork salivary glands, lymph nodes, and fat from the cheeks and tongue. You can also get it in beef. But this is pork."

"Wow. But I still don't want any."

"There's other good shit in it. Vinegar, chili pepper, spices, flavorings."

"Like I said."

He got himself fitted into the inadequate booth. He watched while she got a cup and poured him some coffee. She gave it to him black.

"Well," she said then. "We can't ignore it forever. Somebody's gotta go first." She was sort of half-smiling. "You sure know how to fuck a funeral. They must be still talking about it, huh?"

He took a sip. "I guess."

"I couldn't believe it."

"Neither could I."

"So where did you go afterwards?"

"I, uh, tried to catch those guys, but they were just too fast for me."

"In your Morris Minor?"

He smiled. "Yeah."

"Is that your car?"

"No. Is that your truck?"

Donahoo watched while she finished cooking the chorizo. She was wearing a navy-blue bathrobe with white piping and matching blue slippers. It was a man's robe, but she looked very much like a woman in it. He thought that he wanted her, but he was glad it wasn't just sex, he was happy just talking to her, just being with her in her old kitchen.

"The reason I'm here," he said, sipping his coffee.

"I know why you're here."

Oh? He looked at her back. He wished she was turned around, facing him. He said finally, "Well, the other reason."

"I don't want to talk about the other reason. I want to talk about the reason. We can talk about the other reason later." There was a short wait. "We can talk about it later, Officer."

Donahoo considered. She was still turned away from him. Yeah, he thought. In the grand scheme of things, eight o'clock in the morning, the fates, the Lottery, Tom Wolfe—okay, later. He said, almost afraid to speak, "You want to talk about the reason now?"

"No."

"No?"

"No." She finally turned to face him. "I'm frankly all talked out. You're the first man I've wanted to go to bed with since the Kennedy administration. What say we just take this chorizo and jump in the sack?"

"Take the chorizo?"

"You're talking. We'll rub it all over each other."

Donahoo struggled out of the booth. "Jack or Bobby?"

"You're still talking. Both of them."

Donahoo waited in a brass bed. It was a real one, he noted, real brass, and a lot of decorative cast iron connectors, painted with a high-gloss white enamel. The bedspread was handmade, a crazy quilt, the colors bold, shimmering. The pillows were huge, feather-stuffed. The whole presentation was much more—Donahoo tried to think of the word—much more *alive* than his sedate Murphy at the Arlington. It had some varoom.

The bathroom door was open. The shower drummed in the cast iron claw-foot tub. Rosie was singing some song he couldn't make out. He thought it might be in Spanish. The water masked it. He thought he'd have to learn Spanish. Take some crash course somewhere. *Learn Spanish in six hours.* He'd seen that ad somewhere. Maybe in Consumer Fraud. Maybe at the D.A.'s office. He could give them a call. Get on the stick here. Spanish. He didn't want her talking behind his back.

She shouted, "What are you doing?"

He yelled back. "Waiting!"

The room was a mirror image of the rest of the house. It had the same wainscot-high wood paneling, the same field and stream wallpaper, and it was crowded with antique furniture, dressers and bureaus and settees. The only modern touch—modern and time-less—were the bamboo blinds. The day's light, southern exposure, entered now as faint slats. It would be brighter later. Donahoo knew how that would work. He had the same kind of blinds at the Arlington.

The shower stopped. "The chorizo ready?"

He lied. "Yeah!"

He wasn't going to peel the chorizo. It was sitting in an old china washbasin atop the bedside commode. It was going to stay there.

"I'll be right out."

"Good."

There were a lot of old pictures, old photographs. People who came with the furniture and who hadn't survived it. They stood and sat in stiff poses. The men wore hats and dark clothes. They had mustaches, beards. The women were in long skirts and white blouses. They wore their hair up. In their musty midst, alien, there was a larger black and white photograph of John and Robert Kennedy, sitting together in the Oval Office. They were in sofa chairs, across from each other, very close together, their heads bowed in private, painful conversation. Donahoo wondered what they were talking about. It could be anything. The Cuban Missile Crisis. Marilyn Monroe.

Rosie appeared eager and smiling. She had a big beach towel around herself and a smaller towel around her head. "Hi."

He was off somewhere with the Kennedys. "Hello."

"What are you so serious about?"

He motioned to the photograph. "I was thinking. I have this partner, Cominsky. He wears shoes like that."

She looked. "Jack shoes or Bobby shoes?"

"Bobby shoes."

She sat on the edge of the bed. "You want to dry my hair?"

"Sure." He loosened the towel, gently pulled it away. Her hair fell free like a shiny escaping animal. He caught it.

"How long have you got?"

"I dunno. You might be able to pry me outa here next Thursday."

He sat drying her hair, the crazy quilt pulled around him, hiding, he hoped, his urgency. He thought he'd come a long way here. Not in time, but in journey. He had traveled far. He wasn't eager to leave.

"My mom used to dry my hair," she said. "I'd wash it and she'd dry it, and she'd comb it. She loved to comb it. That's when she'd talk to me. She'd tell me how pretty I was. It seemed like we'd sit for hours. Sitting in the sun."

"Tijuana?"

"Yes."

Her hair was like black silk. He thought that he could weave it. He could make a purse to hold all his riches.

"We didn't have a house," she said. "We had a yard. You went through a gate in a wall. Behind the wall was a yard. We lived in the yard. My mother. Me."

"Not Buddy?"

"No. He came later."

Donahoo finished drying her hair. "Would you like me to comb it?"

"Please." She passed him a large red comb.

"Tell you how pretty you are?"

"Oh, yes."

Donahoo set the red comb into the black silk. He thought she was unlike any Mexican woman he had ever known. Her beauty, yes. Her hair and her eyes. Her spirit. But not her skin. Her skin was pale, almost white. It would damage in the sun, he thought. She would burn and peel. The Snake.

"I was a bridge girl," she said. "Not a street girl, but a bridge girl. If you cross the border on foot, you know the bridge you take, not over the river, but at the edge of town?"

"Yes."

"You know the children sitting on the steps selling Chiclets?"

"Yes."

"That was me."

Donahoo combed her hair. He got it all straightened, the tangles out, weasel sleek. There was a hand mirror on the commode. He gave it to her.

She looked at herself. He could see her image. The dark almond eyes in the face that was the shape of a heart. The eager smile was gone. She seemed engulfed by sadness.

"You're very beautiful."

"No, I'm not."

Donahoo took the mirror away. He put it back on the commode. He pulled the towel off her, revealing the long curve of her back, her slim waist and flaring hips. She stiffened in response. He hesitated, afraid to disturb her. He thought she was like a still-life, frozen with the room's other preserves, beyond his reach. He didn't know what he had done wrong.

"When I was young," she said, "I asked them to rub me with food, so I could eat it later."

Donahoo didn't say anything.

"It's true."

He still didn't answer.

"I don't want any lies between us."

Donahoo held her tightly while he flung the chorizo across the room. He turned her around, rolled her over him, under the crazy quilt. He held her fiercely and kissed her gently. He didn't know what else to do.

He told her, "There's nothing between us except what we put there." He said, "Of all the things you know, that's the most important."

She responded slowly, tentatively. He let go of her waist so he could take hold of her hair. He tangled his big hands in it. They kissed passionately for a long time.

Donahoo waited until they could no longer resist. Then he sank into her. Tom Wolfe, he thought, was wrong.

*   *   *

He awoke at noon. The sun was in the room, warmer than it ever got at the Arlington, which was where, for a moment, he thought he was. The bamboo blinds fooled him for a moment. They scattered soft bars, strips of light, strips of dark.

Rosie suddenly appeared. Her smile hung over him. Dark eyes sparkled.

He rubbed his own eyes like a child. She was propped up on an elbow, her head cupped in her hand. Her smile belonged on an elf.

"Okay," she said, taunting him. "What was the other reason?"

He was still half asleep. The other reason? He wished there weren't any. He wished there were only one reason, her, and that they could stay there together, never leave. He thought he would like that. Imprisoned by the soft shadow bars. Held forever. He gently brushed his fingertips across her swollen lips.

"Tell me."

"Yeah," he said. He couldn't wake up. He didn't want to. "Those two guys at the cemetery?" He found her hand, held it. "This is going to sound awfully self-serving. They, uh, thought you were my girl."

"I can think of worse things. What's the problem?"

"Well." He was waking up. He was trying to find a way to make it easier, for her, for him. "There's a possibility, a danger, that if they knew how to locate you, they might threaten to harm you."

"Harm me? Why?"

Donahoo looked at her. Full of fire, and anger and need. The one word, *harm,* had transformed her. He said, "If I don't do what they want me to do."

"Oh." Their eyes met. "In that case . . ." Donahoo thought that she was looking deep inside him. She was examining his very soul. "Then I guess you'd better do what they want you to do."

Donahoo knew he had to answer without equivocation. He wondered if he could promise her that. If, no matter what the situation, or how high the stakes, he would choose, first, to save her. Could he make that kind of promise? Or, the real question, could he keep it?

"Hey," he told her. "I've waited a long time for you." He took her into his arms and held her tightly. "I'm not going to let you go. Nobody's going to take you from me." He thought it was awfully soon to say but it was something she should know now. "I love you, Rosie."

He heard her whisper against his chest. "That was the correct answer, Officer."

Later, when he was leaving, kissing her good-bye, going out the door, she was suddenly afraid again.

She grabbed him by the sleeve. "Hold it, I hate lies. I don't want to start with one between us."

He looked at her, wondering what she meant, his lie, or hers?

"You remember when you asked me—the last time I'd seen Chip?"

He nodded.

"Well, it wasn't Sunday," she said, tears shining in her eyes. "He came back Monday." She composed herself with an effort. "Nothing happened. He just . . . wanted to talk, that's all. It was the same thing. He was really full of himself. He didn't need me or anybody else. It was 'Manila Time.' "

Donahoo's mind was racing. The videocassette. "Did he give you anything?"

"What do you mean?"

"A package—for safekeeping?"

"No. Of course not. I'd have told you."

"I know," he said, apologizing. He picked up the phone and started dialing. "We're going to have to search your house. Tell me now—do I need a search warrant?"

She looked at him. "Cops. Nothing but trouble."

"Yes or no?"

"Fuck, what is this, a test?"

"Yes or no?"

She tried to smile. *"Mi casa, su casa."*

TWENTY-SEVEN

It took them two hours. Gomez and Montrose. Palmer and Cominsky. Carefully taking Rosie Gestring's house apart and then putting it back together. Looking in every cupboard and drawer and nook and cranny. All the hundreds of hiding places in a big old house. All the secret corners.

Donahoo waited with her on the front porch. The morning had changed everything between them. He couldn't bring himself to be part of the search. He didn't want to touch her personal things, her private property, unless he had her direct, express consent. She would have to be present, and she would have to have the right, when she wished, to keep some things from him. That was the only way it could work, and of course it didn't, so he sat on the porch with her.

He asked, it was the second time, "How long was he out of your sight?"

"I told you," she said. She lit another cigarette. "Five, ten minutes. I was in the living room. I don't know where he was."

"You let him wander around your house like that?"

"I didn't want to be with him."

Yeah, Donahoo thought. He knew the feeling. He also knew he should apologize. It was something else he couldn't do.

She smoked her cigarette. She had gotten dressed for the occasion, a man's shirt with the tail out, blue jeans, sneakers. Her hair was in a ponytail. She had decided to pass on the antiques business for the day.

"When this is over . . ." Donahoo said. He sounded as if it was never going to be over.

"We'll see," she said, finishing it for him.

Donahoo got up and went out onto the street. He went to the end, to the canyon. He wondered if he could see his refrigerator. It was down there somewhere with the rest of the neighborhood's debris. He looked but he couldn't spot it. A slotted shelf caught on a dead branch. That's all. The rest was buried in the camouflage.

Earlier, she had said, "Cops tearing the place apart, what are the neighbors going to think?" and he had replied, "That you're one of them." He hadn't apologized.

There was a movement below. Someone, or something, in the tangle of brush, crashing through briefly. It stopped almost as soon as it started.

Maybe it was someone recovering the fridge, Donahoo thought. They wouldn't take it when it was up here, but now they wanted it. He thought that people made things difficult for themselves. If it was easy, they made it hard. Not always, but sometimes, he thought.

Gomez came out of the house. He called, "Hey! Compadre!"

Donahoo turned.

Gomez had his arms raised like he wanted to be crucified. He said loudly, "Nothing."

"You're sure?"

"Positive."

"Okay."

Gomez left the porch. Montrose, Palmer, and Cominsky came out of the house, filing past Rosie. If they spoke to her, Donahoo couldn't hear it. She flicked her cigarette into the yard. She got up and went inside.

Gomez was at his Chevy. "Anything else?"

Donahoo shook his head. "No, that's it."

"You staying?"

"For a while."

"There's a hidden camera in the bedroom. She's a movie producer."

"Oh, yeah?"

Gomez smiled and disappeared behind the wheel. The others arrived and piled in with him.

"It's not there, Sarge," Cominsky said, holding back.

"I know," Donahoo told him.

"I'm sorry."

"Me, too."

"It was a hell of a funeral, though. Wasn't it?"

"Oh, yeah."

"You wanta keep Morris?"

"For a while."

"You got him. Take care."

"The funeral, it's all we talk about," Gomez said. "It was beautiful." He said, "Well, watch the birdie."

Palmer said, "Say cheese."

Cominsky got in the back of the Chevy with Palmer. Gomez pulled away. They went down the street and turned. They disappeared.

Donahoo watched them go, alone. He wondered how anything could be this good and this bad. It should be one or the other. It shouldn't, couldn't be both.

He started back for the house, across the lawn this time, navigating the lumps. He was looking down and he almost hit his head on the birdhouse. He dodged and pushed it away. The faded hula dancer swayed. She was dancing with her hands.

Her lovely hula hands, Donahoo thought, and then he knew what Chip Lyons had said, it was staring at him. Not hooligans. Hula hands.

He reached into the birdhouse, felt the bottom, the sides. He reached up into the roof and took out the videocassette that was jammed into the V.

He shouted joyously. "Rosie!"

Donahoo didn't trust himself. He let her do it. Things that he normally could do without thinking but now he was too keyed up. He was sure he'd bust something. He'd somehow get the tape twisted. Or jam the machine.

Rosie darkened the room. The video started. Infrared picture. The Tijuana Slough.

"This is it?"

"Yes."

Donahoo watched intently. A Jaguar appeared. American #1. Then the border patrol wagon, dropping off a short, powerfully built Mexican. It had to be him, he thought. Primitivo.

"Always an angle," Rosie said, meaning Lyons. "What did he want for this?"

Donahoo silenced her with a touch. American #1 was killing the squat Mexican. He was putting his body into a raft. He was sending it out into the slough.

"What did he want?"

"A million dollars."

"What do you want?"

He turned unsurely. The idea hadn't occurred to him. Oh, no, he thought. Jesus. Don't do this to me. Yes, she killed her husband, she *had* to kill him, but don't make her bad, okay? Don't make her want to sell this thing. Don't let her even think about it.

"I want you, safe," he told her. He ejected the cassette and stuffed it in his jacket pocket. "This is going to put that fucker away forever. You won't have to worry about him, and I won't either." He waited. She was staring at him. He couldn't tell what was in her eyes. "The right answer?"

She smiled. "Yes."

"So was that."

Donahoo went to the phone. Suddenly he had a lot of things to do. He had to get a bulletin out on the Cadillac, Americans #1 and 2, armed and dangerous. He had to find out who was the registered owner of the Jaguar, get a bulletin on it too. He had to get a team of divers to the Tijuana Slough. Oh, and he had to get a cop over here, right away, he thought. He wasn't taking any chances. Until he got back, he wanted a cop sitting with Rosie. He wanted her protected.

He was dialing. He said to her, he had just remembered, "What's with the camera in the bedroom?"

"His idea."

"Chip's?"

"No, Bruce Willis's." She shrugged. "All part of the game."

"Well. Maybe you should pull it out of there."

She smiled, hugged him. "Can we use it first?"

"Hello, Lewis?" he said. "Guess what? I got lucky again."

"You found a way to fuck Saperstein?"

"How did you know?"

"The song in your heart," Lewis said.

TWENTY-EIGHT

Quillan came out of the canyon first. He hunched down, surprised to have reached the top so quickly, afraid of being seen by someone in the row of houses lining the cul-de-sac. He sprawled flat, hidden in the tall grass. It was like Vietnam, he thought. Thailand. Sneaking up.

Taylor slithered in beside him. "Anybody?"

"Shut up," Quillan said. He could see, fifty yards away, Donahoo getting into the Morris Minor, waving good-bye to the woman, Rosie G-string, who had turned out to be—not much detective work required—Rosalind Gestring. She wasn't in the phone book, but she was in the DMV computer. He had a connection at the DMV. "He's leaving."

"Donahoo?"

"Yeah."

"You're gonna let him?"

"It's the woman we want, ain't it?"

Taylor snapped off the safety on his automatic for answer.

Rosie went back into the house. Her mind was filled with thoughts of Donahoo. She ached for him. A cop, she thought. She couldn't imagine that she would ever fall for a cop. It was like sticking her hand into fire. Yet she had to do it. It was true what she had told Donahoo. It had been years—years and years—since she had wanted to be with someone. She had so much to give and he took it. He took her in his big hands, and he drank from her. She had so much to give, and she couldn't give him up.

She went through each room. The house looked disturbed, things out of place, but there was no sign, thankfully, of a thorough search. They had been careful to leave it as they found it. They knew how to follow orders.

Cops, she thought again. She wondered what kind of person it took to be a cop. They had to be hard, a shell, and, somewhere inside, violent. Bursting into someone's home and going through it piece by piece. Or, worse, putting them in handcuffs, putting a gun to their head. Killing them . . . ?

She closed her eyes. She knew what it was like to kill, she thought. She knew how that worked. A man who said he loved her was coming toward her with a belt. He was going to whip her like a dog. *Don't,* she said. She said that all the time, and he never listened. This time she pulled the trigger. So close, the shotgun took his face away. You couldn't make that up. Could you?

Taylor was in the kitchen doorway. He said softly, "Hello."

She was startled. She thought they had all left. She didn't recognize him, but that didn't bother her. She hadn't paid that much attention when Donahoo's squad came in. Actually, she hadn't wanted to look at them. She said, "Where have you been hiding?" His clothes were dirty and he was breathing heavily. He had a large gun shoved in his belt. He was staring at her strangely. She looked around the kitchen, flustered. She wondered if he wanted a drink of water. "Can I get you something?"

Quillan was behind her now. He said, "We didn't come for tea."

Quillan handled the interrogation. He grabbed her without warning and put her flat on the hard little table in the kitchen booth. He didn't say what he wanted or was hoping to achieve. He held her down from one side. Taylor on the other.

"You hear a lot of stories," he said then, lighting a cigarette. "People withstanding any kind of torture and not talking. That's how they show it in the movies. But it's not true."

Rosie stared at him, terrified. She couldn't speak.

"Jimmy Cagney, he was best, I guess," Quillan said. "I remember, the Germans had him, the SS probably, and they were torturing him, they wanted to know the date of D-Day, where the Allies were going to land, something like that, but Cagney, he wouldn't talk. He held out until the Allies bombed the castle where the Germans were holding him. It's a classic movie." He looked at Taylor. "I dunno. Was that *The Cross of Lorraine?*"

Taylor grinned for him. "If Disney didn't make it, I didn't see it."

"Anyway," Quillan said. He blew on the cigarette, creating a red-hot coal, "I'm speaking from experience here, and it doesn't happen that way in real life." He passed the hot coal in front of her face. It traced close to her eyes, her nostrils, her lips. "In real life, if I ask you the date of D-Day, you tell me. There's only one possible reason why you wouldn't, and that's if you didn't know it, okay?"

The answer was barely audible. "Okay."

"Yeah, okay," Quillan said. He put the cigarette aside. Taylor held her down while Quillan pulled off her sneakers, her jeans, panties. He put his hand on her vagina and manipulated her. He got the cigarette again. Another hot coal. "Now."

"You haven't asked her anything yet," Taylor said.

Quillan blew on the coal. "She hasn't volunteered."

"*Jesucristo,*" Rosie whispered, a prayer. "Please."

Quillan fell back, disappointed. Normally, they took longer to break. He would always remember one woman. He reamed her out and she wouldn't talk. He'd wake her up, ream her some more, and she wouldn't talk. Wouldn't tell where some Commie slopes were hiding. She was quite a woman, Ling Shong. Tougher than Cagney. A better dancer too. He'd first met her in a dance hall. She could dance like an eagle. The way an eagle flies—that's how she could dance.

Rosie said, "In the name of God—what do you want?"

Quillan wondered where to start. He wanted to know when Donahoo was coming back. He wanted to be ready for him. He wanted to know the exact dimensions of their relationship. If, as he suspected, as he hoped, Donahoo would trade the video for her. For her return—in one piece, unreamed.

"He's gone," Rosie said, the words spilling out of her. "He found the video. It was hidden in a birdhouse . . . in the yard . . ."

Quillan stopped her. "*Found* it?"

"Yes. He'd been looking for it . . . all over . . ."

"When?"

"Now. He just left with it."

Taylor said, releasing her, "He never had it till now?"

"No. He just watched it."

Quillan slammed his head against the table. He rose up bleeding. He cried in agony, "What the fuck have I done?!"

Taylor stared. His pinched face seemed to reflect the pain.

"I've convicted myself," Quillan complained. "If I'd have left him alone, he wouldn't have looked for it. Some fucking birdcage out in the yard ..." He grabbed Rosie. "It could have stayed there forever?"

"Some wrens laying eggs on it," Taylor said.

Quillan slumped back.

"Lady," Taylor said. "When you saw me, you were friendly. When you saw him, you screamed murder. Why?"

Quillan said, "Hey."

"You'd seen him on the video—killing Primitivo?"

She nodded.

"Did you see me?"

She shook her head.

"Now, wait a minute ..."

Taylor fired under the table. Quillan grunted and grabbed himself. He fell out of the booth onto the kitchen floor. He writhed in pain, gut shot.

Rosie screamed.

Taylor scrambled out of the booth. He stood over Quillan. He aimed the gun at his head. His finger tightened on the trigger.

"Finish me," Quillan said. "I don't want to go slowly." He said, gurgling, "You owe me that, Taylor."

"I owe you fuck all," Taylor told him. "Take your time." He went out the back way, the way he'd come in.

Rosie slid off the table. Half naked, she stopped to find her jeans.

Quillan rolled, grabbed her leg with a bloodied hand. He tripped her, pulled her down. He threw himself on top of her. He said, his breath sick, "We're doing this together."

A National City police department black-and-white rolled to a stop in front of the house. The cop at the wheel was alone. He double-checked his notes. He looked at the address. This was the place.

He got out, slamming the door, hoping that he might attract

somebody's attention. He had been on the force only six months. He still liked to be seen in his uniform.

He started up the path, checking out the other houses, watching for any sign that he was being noticed. He put his hand on his holster, held it there as he walked. Flick, it would be open. Lousy neighborhood, but a good assignment, he thought. Lady in distress. You couldn't get much better than that. He hoped she was a pretty lady. He was fantasizing now. She was going to be gorgeous. She was going to offer him a drink. They were going to end up in the sack. Another day in the life of—flourish of trumpets—Patrolman Gordie Taggart.

He arrived at the door. He knocked, no answer. He knocked again. Still no response. He considered going around back. He decided he should try the knob first. He did so, and the door opened.

He went inside, into the dark. He said, "Hello?"

Bloodied fingers, jabbed into his eyes, blinded him. Bloodied hands took hold of his head. In his last instant of life he realized that his neck was going to be snapped. He said, "Don't."

TWENTY-NINE

They were waiting at Ben's U-Gas on Pacific Coast Highway, a block north of Laurel Street, the first turnoff, southbound, for Harbor Drive and Lindbergh Field. They said they didn't want any gas. They wanted to wait for the mechanic. The attendant, whose name was Roy, even though the tag on his shirt said Ben, had mentioned several times that there wasn't a mechanic on duty, but they told him they'd wait anyway. They said if there was a charge for waiting, they'd settle later. Three of them. Chinaman Lee, Wheels Duran, Crash Evans. Two vehicles. A '56 Chrysler sedan that was tuned like a shortwave and hit like a tank. An ambulance purchased for one of those virtual songs at the San Diego city/county auction.

Quillan's squad, and it needed Quillan, it needed the General,

Chinaman Lee thought. So where was he? Quillan had put them together. It was the kind of stuff he liked. Doing the phone calls. Conducting interviews. Making choices. Revealing plans. Delivering speeches. All the things that went into creating a squad. Taylor, he'd been there for most of it, but he hadn't contributed. He had sat quietly on the sidelines. If he had a veto, he hadn't used it, or at least not in front of anybody. He was just the guy in the corner or on a bidet. A guy who watched, listened. Chinaman Lee wondered where Taylor was too. But mostly he wondered about Quillan.

Lee was at the wheel of the ambulance. He was wearing a jacket that looked paramedic. He was smoking a clove cigarette. Duran was sprawled on the hood of the shiny blue Chrysler. He was reading the comics in the *Union-Trib*. Crash was pacing back and forth in front of Ben's U-Gas. It was how he relaxed. Pacing.

"What do you think's going on?" Crash asked, making a turn. He was wearing his baggy suit. The pockets held balloons filled with fake blood.

Nobody answered. Duran looked at him, a flat, blow-it-out-your-ass look, then went back to his comics. He was Mexican, an Indian kid from Tijuana, he didn't know much English, the pictures helped him. He could really drive though. No fear. He could raise some eyebrows at Indy.

Lee had Quillan's cellular in the ambulance. There'd been one call so far. Somebody who sounded like he'd just got off the boat from Bangkok. Somebody who turned into a raving Bangkok basket case when he learned Quillan hadn't shown yet. Who said, finally, barely in control, "We've got confirmation. It's going to be removed. Stand by."

That had been almost an hour earlier. Asians, Lee had thought at the time. Their inscrutability was a myth. They screamed the loudest when things went awry. His father was the Chinaman. His mother was French. She'd been beautiful, but she had passed none of her beauty to him. He was a caricature of the Yellow Peril. All through school he was called a North Korean Jap.

"What are we supposed to do—Quillan don't show up?" Crash asked. He was making another turn. The fake blood gurgled. He had more balloons in his pants.

Nobody answered.

Lee lit another clove cigarette. One off the other. He was going to get a hole in his lung. Everybody told him that. He didn't much give a shit. North Korean Japs, they were just like everybody else, he thought. They had to die from something.

The cellular rang. Lee answered. "Yeah."

Bangkok Basket Case said, "Is he there?"

"No."

The panic rose again. "We're in surgery. Stand by."

Lee signed off. He sat smoking his clove cigarette. He showed no emotion. He had trained himself to be the exact opposite of his father in the expression of feelings. Once, practicing, he'd had a particularly exquisite orgasm, it hadn't shown on his face.

Crash, watching him, said, "This is weird. Imagine the guy who's waiting. He thinks he's gonna get a heart—then we steal it. How's he gonna feel?"

"Shitty?" Lee said. It was the first time he had answered one of Crash Evans's questions.

"How do you know it's an hombre?" Duran said. His look suggested that it could be a woman or even a child. He said, taunting, "So, when did you start to care, Señor Crash?"

Crash spun away, sounding, in miniature, like a swimming pool in an earthquake. That same kind of slosh.

Lee went through the motions of pretending to start the ambulance. Then, dead motor, he worked the gears, pretending now that he was moving it out. He hadn't driven the ambulance and wasn't supposed to. His job was riding shotgun. If he had to, he could drive though. He could do a lot of things. He was very sure of himself.

"Here comes somebody," Duran said. He turned a page, folded the paper. He was still in the comics. The *Union-Trib* had two full pages of them.

The old Cadillac came down the street and rumbled into Ben's U-Gas. It braked in front of the lube stall. Taylor got out.

"There's no mechanic," the attendant said.

Lee watched as Taylor came over to the ambulance. He wondered why Quillan wasn't with him. He wondered, vaguely, the question just coming to mind, if Taylor was taking over for Quillan.

Taylor reached in and got the cellular. He punched in Joe Bong's number. He indicated that Lee should scoot over and take the passenger seat.

"The General's indisposed," Taylor said, talking to Lee. "I'm talking over." He looked at Lee, then at Duran. "Which one of you is the fag?"

Lee wondered if he should let Taylor take command. If he knew more of the plan, he could do this himself, Lee thought. Then he thought, if he was going to do that, he should do it later. He told Taylor, "The one with his cock up your ass."

Taylor smiled for him. Lee couldn't remember Taylor smiling before. He had never seen so large a display of Taylor's bad teeth. They were broken, rotten. Lee thought that Taylor must be like that inside, decayed. When he later seized command from Taylor, *if* he seized it, he should remember, and beware of, that decay, Lee thought. Decay was slow death.

Joe Bong came on the line. His excited voice echoed faintly in the ambulance's cab. Lee watched as Taylor made a quick survey of the situation. Lee could imagine what Taylor was thinking. He had the men, he had the vehicles. He had a jump-off within a block of ground zero. Ben's U-Gas, it was key. The only place within a mile that they could control. That's all it took. Easy access, swift strike. It was doable. He didn't need the General.

"Settle down," Taylor told Joe Bong, looking at Lee. He put his hand over the cellular. "We got a code name for this guy? Maybe Mr. Excitement?"

"I prefer the Bangkok Basket Case," Chinaman Lee said.

THIRTY

The Tijuana Slough. Donahoo thought it was like the lady at the end of the bar. It looked better at night. In the harsh light of the day, whoa. The sewage-laden water was flat, still. The vegetation was low, skimpy. Tamarisk, willows, and bamboo along the edges. Marsh plants and cordgrass choking the middle. And, pervasive, the outhouse smell. It got better farther west, closer to the ocean, where the estuary began, but here at the slough, where the river's sewage first started to mix with tidewater, it was almost sickening.

Some rabid antienvironmentalist, wanting it all dredged out, so the river could flow free to the sea instead of creating a mucky deathtrap, had put up a large sign, WELCOME TO THE TIJUANA VALLEY. WHERE BIRDS FLY AND PEOPLE DIE.

Donahoo had to smile at the sign. Lost battle. Every level of government was committed to saving the place. The Tijuana Estuary was the state's largest, a refuge for more than a hundred and fifty species of birds, some of them endangered. Fish and marine life flourished. So the prodevelopment boys were stuck with the smell and the muck. The estuary and the slough were an inseparable package. They ran together, like love and pain.

He was standing on the spot where the van had been parked. He was picturing, in his mind's eye, the video, and the approximate distance from where the water started and where the raft had gone down. He was guessing—a half-ass educated guess—sixty yards. If he was wrong, he'd have an expert look at the video, make the calculations, but at the moment he didn't have an expert.

Sergeant Ben Jelley, head of the crime lab, was sprawled like a beached whale on the concrete boat ramp slanting into the slough. He said, "Tommy, you really know how to pick 'em, this place smells like a fart. Next time you find a map—where the corpse is buried—can it be under a lilac bush?"

Donahoo ignored him. He was watching the divers skimming out across the slough in their luminous multicolored raft. Forty yards. Fifty yards. Sixty . . .

"Now!" Donahoo yelled, waving. The raft stopped.

"How long has it been down there?" Ben Jelley asked. "Sunday . . . ?" He did the arithmetic on his pulpy fingers. "Five and a half days? Yo, ahhh." He tried to look back at Donahoo. His neck wouldn't turn that far. "Here's something else you can do. Next time, find him earlier, huh?"

Donahoo watched the divers. There were two of them. They put down an anchor and two orange marker floats.

Ben Jelley said, "I think they're afraid of speedboats." A sigh rattled in him. "Jesus Christ. There ain't been nothing on this water since . . ." He said, "Excuse me, this ain't water."

Donahoo watched the divers. If they found the guy—and, sooner or later, they *were* going to find the guy—he had a no-contest first-degree murder charge against American #1. If the guy was Primitivo, he had somebody that everybody, at one time or another, said they wanted. Lewis, Saperstein. The D.A. The mayor. They all wanted him, the legendary Primitivo. They *had* to take him. And, when they did, poof! Chip Lyons, hero, vanished. Hello, crooked cop.

"Me?" Ben Jelley said, trying to sound inconsequential, as if he weighed something less than four hundred pounds. "I'd have taken the video into Saperstein. I'd have shown it to him, played it on his new four-head VCR, the one with all the whips and jingles, it answers the phone, it brews coffee. I'd have said, 'You're the chief. Whatcha wanta do?' I wouldn't have come here balls out."

"Good," Donahoo said. "We don't want to scare the last of the wildlife."

"You always were a stubborn sonofabitch."

"Yeah, and lucky too."

Rosie came out of her house in the dead cop's uniform. Quillan was beside her, the cop's gun, a .38 Colt Special, rammed against her spine. They went down the sidewalk that way. They got in the cop's black-and-white. Rosie got behind the wheel. Quillan got in the back. Now he put the Colt at the base of her skull.

Her mind was in turmoil. It was swept with anger, fear, dismay. She shouldn't be here, she thought. This was none of her doing. She felt sure she was going to be killed. There was no escape. If he died, yes, then, maybe, but what she knew in her heart, he'd pull the trigger with his last breath.

"Where to?" she asked.

"I dunno," Quillan told her. "Just drive." He winced with the pain of the slug in his belly. "Find someplace that's wide open. I want to be able to see who's coming. Maybe a park . . . or a football field . . ." He said, "We get set up, you get on the blower, make the arrangements."

Rosie started the police car. She moved it away from the curb. "This isn't going to work."

"It'll work," Quillan assured her. "It's simple. He gives me the video. I give him you. Straight trade. Nothing complicated." He grimaced, caught his breath. "He's not gonna pull anything. He knows what'll happen. You're gonna tell him where the gun is—at the base of your pretty head. He fucks with me, you're a dead bug, your brains are on the windshield."

Rosie ground some gears and took the car down the street. It was a big, tublike Oldsmobile. It moved like a boat. When it got to the corner, it didn't turn, it came about. She drove it unsurely.

"Everybody's got somebody," Quillan said. "That's their weakness. That's how you get 'em." He tried to laugh. "And my strength."

"I hardly know the guy."

"But you do know him?"

"Yes."

"And you've fucked him?"

Rosie looked in the rearview. She couldn't see him. He was ducked down behind her. But she could feel his hot sick breath next to the gun's sharp muzzle.

"Then he's in love," Quillan said, trying to laugh. "I know the guy. I've been through his drawers. Pictures he keeps upside down. Monica, Presh, very beautiful women. He wants the best. He won't settle for less. The guy, he's a big, good-looking guy, two photographs. He coulda had more but he's got standards, huh? He waited for you—for *you*, Rosita."

"Rosie."

"Yeah, Rosie. I'm Quillan, okay? But you can call me Nick. I got a lot of names. I'm Nick in New York and Frenchie in Montreal. I'm hurting in Jersey. Jesus Christ. Fuck, shit, piss. I'm dying here, Rosie. Find someplace to park. How about a supermarket?" He bit on his free hand. "Maybe a roller rink?"

Rosie took the fat Oldsmobile onto National City Boulevard. She tried to look like a tough dyke cop who wouldn't take crap from a dinosaur on the rag. If she was stopped, if anybody started asking questions, it was all over, she thought. The guy was crazy. He was dying. He didn't care who he took with him.

"Everybody's got somebody," Quillan said, returning to that theme, it was his rationale for why this was going to work. "He's got you. You got him." He said, as if he were making conversation, a way to pass the time while they looked for someplace wide open, "Who else you got?"

"My mother," Rosie said, lying. Her mother was dead. But she didn't want to talk about death. She didn't want to admit that there was such a thing. "She's special."

"Who else?"

"My stepfather."

"Oh, yeah?" Quillan said. He pushed the gun so hard, she cried out in pain. "You wanta tell stepfather stories? I got one for you, Rosie. Hear this." He eased off with the gun. "I'm a kid. Seven, eight. We're going for a ride in his car. I let a fart, and he makes me get out, walk behind. Can you imagine that?"

Rosie tried to look at him in the rearview. She thought he was crazy.

"A nicer man woulda rolled down the windows," Quillan said, coughing up blood on her neck. He spat, wiped his mouth. "There's something wrong here. I'm a man of the world. I've done the samba in San Juan. I've chowed down in Changchow." He said, he was like a delirious child, "Don't make me die in National City."

Rosie thought maybe that was the answer. She would drive around in circles. She would keep looking and looking and maybe the crazy sonofabitch would die. She hoped so. She hoped he would die and that he wouldn't pull the trigger.

Taylor was on the cellular with Joe Bong. "Fruit Bat, relax, willya?" Taylor said. He'd given him that code name, Fruit Bat. Lee had suggested Bangkok Basket Case, but Taylor thought maybe that narrowed it too much. Fruit Bat, that could be anybody. If some-body thought it meant a Guamanian, well, let them look for one, you know? He said, becoming annoyed, "Nothing changes. The job gets done. You get what you want. We, *I,* get paid." He was aware of Lee watching, listening. He put his hand over the cellular's mouthpiece. He said, "You'll get yours, Chinaman."

Joe Bong kept talking. Taylor stood listening. Finally he said, "Okay." He switched off, put the cellular in his jacket pocket. Like Lee, he was now wearing a paramedic-type jacket. It was dark blue with a bright red cross in a round, white patch high on each sleeve. He also was wearing a name tag, STAN, ARGUS MEDICAL SERVICES. The ambulance had that painted on both sides and on the back, ARGUS MEDICAL SERVICES. On the front it had ECNALUBMA.

"We've got a go here," Taylor said, looking north up Pacific Highway. The van, when it came, would be in the curb lane, to facilitate a right turn onto Laurel Street. He would be able to iden-tify it from a block away. That would give them plenty of time. He said, "Crash, why don't you take a walk over to the corner now? Try not to spill anything."

Crash nodded tightly. He'd been getting edgier as the moment approached. "Wish me luck."

Taylor got in the ambulance. He settled in behind the wheel. He made sure everything was where it was supposed to be. It was like a truck, and he was used to trucks, he wouldn't have any trouble with it. American iron, not some pansy Jaguar.

His rare smile appeared again. It was amusing that snobbery, of all things, should be Quillan's undoing, he thought. Quillan, the General, who didn't have any class, never would, insisting on the Jaguar for the trip to the Tijuana Slough. He had wanted to go in style to meet and kill his enemy. But he didn't have any style. He didn't have any style and he didn't have any class. His whole world had come tumbling down for nothing.

Taylor smiled his rotten smile, thinking that he'd never have that problem, he knew who he was. He knew a lot of things this fine day. He knew he didn't have to worry about Quillan. He'd seen a lot of men with bullets in their bellies. They never got very far. A few steps and then they were on their knees. They got help or they died. They didn't show up to run a heist. No worry there.

No, and no worry about Joe Bong either, Taylor thought. No worry—absolutely no worry—about whether the slant would pay. The smile again. All he had to do was pull this off. Do the job. Nothing more. He knew a lot of things.

Taylor said to Duran, "Wheels, you're first."

Duran got in the Chrysler. The engine roared to life. It sounded like a train. Then it settled down to a gentle purr.

Lee slid into the ambulance next to Taylor. His face glistened.

"How's Ben?" Taylor asked, meaning the attendant.

"The guy's name is Roy," Chinaman Lee said, "and he's history."

There was a shout from out on the slough. "Bingo!"

Donahoo looked. One of the divers was waving to him. He walked down the ramp to the water's edge.

"Body!" the diver yelled.

Donahoo made a motion. Bring it in.

"That was quick," Ben Jelley said. "In this soup . . . ?" He heaved to his feet. "They must know braille."

The second diver surfaced. The two of them conferred briefly. The first went down again. The second inflated an auxiliary raft. It popped open like an air bag. The noise scattered small birds.

Jelley made his way back to the crime lab van. He had to get his black bag. He never got it until he was sure he needed it. His size, economy of movement was essential. Now, having to go back, the one trip equal to a dozen unnecessary appearances with the bag, there didn't seem to be any rationale for leaving it behind in the first place, but there was an explanation. Besides being a blimp, he was a gambler.

Donahoo stood watching. The divers conferred on the surface again and then dove together. They returned with a large black greasy object with a tire rim attached it. With an effort, they got both into the auxiliary raft.

Primitivo, Donahoo thought. A week earlier he'd had serious doubts about the guy's existence. He'd seriously thought that maybe, just maybe, Chip Lyons had made him up. Ignis fatuus, Donahoo could remember saying that to Saperstein, and now the guy's corpse was being delivered to him, on the equivalent of a platter.

The divers came ashore. They pulled their rafts up on the ramp.

"All yours," one of them said, walking backward in his fins. He put his diving mask back on and kept going. The stench was sickening. The sweet and sour watery-death gas smell of black/green putrid flesh feeding the slough's myriad of small carrion eaters. The body hung with crabs. It crawled with worms.

"Thanks," Donahoo said.

The other diver scooted by wordlessly. They had a pickup truck at the top of the ramp. They were going to change there.

Donahoo put a handkerchief over his nose and mouth. He went down to look. The large black greasy object was indeed a body, and five would get you five it was Primitivo. There was enough face left for a match with the photographs that were supposed to be of the Mexican. A fat, round, pockmarked face, cruel even in death.

"I love this job," Jelley said, joining him. "Imagine getting paid to vomit?" He opened his bag and removed a pair of rubber gloves. He snapped them on with surprising grace. A brain surgeon approaching a crowned head. "Subject is an Hispanic male. Five foot four to five foot six. Two hundred and twenty, thirty pounds. Approximately fifty years old."

Donahoo said, "Don't fuck with me."

Jelley grinned. He bent to the body, examined the head, stuck a finger in the hole between the eyes. "The first shot."

"Uh-huh."

Jelley opened the corpse's coat, unbuttoned the shirt, found a few more bullet wounds in the chest. "Insurance."

"I know he's dead. What else?"

Jelley went through the pockets with practiced skill. He produced a wallet, a pocket watch, a set of keys, a small knife. He found an ankle holster with a derringer.

Donahoo checked the wallet's ID. Luis Mendez. That didn't mean anything, he thought. If the guy was Primitivo, he wasn't going to broadcast it. "What else?"

Jelley was in the mouth. "He was afraid of the dentist. There's a cavity in here the size of Lake Erie."

Donahoo put the wallet in a Baggie. "Don't exaggerate."

"Everything is relative," Jelley lectured. "If this guy was the earth, this cavity, by comparison, would be Lake Erie." He said, "What's this?"

"What?"

Jelley had a hand now. He lifted it for Donahoo. "The guy's got stuff written on his palm. It looks like a shopping list."

Donahoo bent closer. More like topics for discussion, he thought. The list was in Spanish. *Drogas. Pornografía. Asesinato.* It filled the palm. Drugs, pornography, assassination. It went on and on. *Vencedor.*

Victor?

Donahoo stared at the word. It didn't fit with the rest of them. It was like you had a grocery list and you put *success* on it. They didn't sell success at Piggly-Wiggly.

Victor. It didn't compute.

Donahoo went back to the crime van. He got on the radio, got patched through to Palmer. He thought that there were wars and that there were victors in wars. That's what they said, anyway.

"I've got another puzzle for you, Palmer," Donahoo said. "It's a Spanish word, *vencedor,* which, when translated, means victor. I'm playing a hunch here. See if that could possibly connect in some way with XLA BMGS. You got it? Victor."

Palmer said, "How could it connect?"

"That's what I'm asking you," Donahoo told him. "What else do you wanta ask me?"

"Nothing."

Donahoo grinned. He was feeling pretty good. "Good-bye."

He left the crime van and headed for the Morris Minor. He felt good. He felt like flying home. He changed course and went over to the Imperial Beach cop who had been asked to attend in case they were in Imperial Beach and not in San Diego. The cop had a nice new Chevy. It looked like it could catch just about any lawn mower.

The cop said, "What do you think?"

Donahoo said, "I think we're in San Diego."

The cop said, "So do I."

Donahoo looked at the Chevy. If Palmer came up with something on *Vencedor,* he wouldn't be able to reach him in the Morris Minor, Donahoo thought, but Palmer could reach him in the Chevy. He could patch through. Also, Donahoo thought, if he needed to move fast, to act quickly on something from Palmer, he ought to be in the Chevy, not the Morris Minor.

"You mind if I give it a little test spin?" Donahoo asked the cop, admiring the Chevy. He gave him the Morris Minor's keys in exchange. He smiled. "In case I don't come back."

The cop accepted the keys unsurely. He tried to smile. "Yeah."

Donahoo thought he could make up some kind of excuse for keeping the Chevy for a while. He could always say he had an emergency.

"How far you going?"

Donahoo gestured vaguely. He thought he must be responding to some primitive foreshadowing boiling up from unknown depths. He thought, what he was doing here, he was stealing a fucking car.

THIRTY-ONE

There were a couple of ways home. I-5 or the Silver Strand High-way. Donahoo contacted Palmer with instructions on how to reach him and then decided to take the Strand. He'd coast through Coronado, take a look around the place, have that reminder of how good it could be if you were smart and rich. He'd drive down those wide, shady streets. Past those big, ritzy houses. Bikes sprawled on the lawn. A cocker spaniel. Carefree voices drifting. "Wanda? You seen my diamond cuff links?" "Those things? I gave 'em to the Goodwill." Donahoo thought he'd do that, and then he'd go home, take a shower, wash off the smell from south of the border, down Mexico way.

Palmer was suddenly on the radio. Static broke up the transmission but he sounded in a hurry. "... priority ... ahoo ..." Then,

"Respond, please." Donahoo was changing lanes. He'd made up his mind. He was going take the Strand. He punched in to Palmer. "This is Donahoo. Go ahead."

"We may have something," Palmer said. "I've been through all the Victors in the phone book." More static.

"Repeat."

"There's a Victor Combat Engineering Systems Center on Pacific Highway. No switchboard. An answering machine asks for an entry code. The line goes dead if you don't punch it in."

"Sounds like."

"Yeah. The FBI says it's high tech, super secret. They can't talk about it. Lewis is arguing with them."

Donahoo considered. "You think there's a connection between Victor Combat and XLA BMGS?"

"Don't you?"

Donahoo changed lanes again. He was going for I-5.

"Sarge?"

"Yeah, I do," Donahoo said. He really didn't. It was the longest of long shots. But then, he reminded himself, he was a lucky cop, and the way to stay lucky was to push it. Ben Jelley knew how that worked. You can't win if you don't gamble. "Tell Lewis to keep trying. I need to talk to these guys. They could have a problem here. Maybe they don't know it? Maybe they're vulnerable?"

"What? You want a meeting?"

"Yeah. Now."

"What if they say no?"

"Then get a warrant."

"A warrant? How am I gonna do that? And what for?"

"Talk to the D.A.'s office, Purvis. He'll think of something."

Rosie Gestring drove the stolen National City black-and-white into the vacant parking lot of Jesus of Nazareth Church of Eternal Life. She drove out into the middle of it and stopped. She cut the motor.

Quillan shoved the dead cop's revolver into the base of her skull. "Okay," he said, his voice broken. "This'll do. Get on the blower. I want Donahoo. I want the video. I want all the copies. I want them now."

"This is crazy," she told him. "It's not going to work. It's too easy for him to keep a copy." She looked around desperately. There were no other vehicles in the parking lot. No sign of anyone in the church office. She was alone with a mad killer. She said, "Let's just escape, huh? I'll take you anywhere you want. Mexico. Oregon." She was begging him. "We'll get that wound fixed. We'll switch cars. We'll hide."

"No. I want the video."

"He's a *cop*. Don't you understand? He'll keep a copy."

"No. He won't."

"Jesus Christ," she said. The gun felt like a cannon. She thought that any moment it would explode. "How do you know that?"

"Because he loves you," Quillan said. He shoved the gun into her flesh. "I want him. Get him."

Donahoo was headed north on I-5. Lewis was on the radio.

"This is coming together," Lewis was saying. "The Jag is registered to a John Morley, who is also known as Nicholas Quillan. I've got a bad fax mug shot here. He could be your guy."

"American #1."

"Yeah. The FBI has been eavesdropping on foreign nationals suspected of illegal arms activities in the United States. Quillan's name came up recently on the tapes. So the bureau started monitoring Quillan's cellular."

"And?"

"And there's something going down at the moment. A lot of calls on Quillan's cellular. It sounds like a robbery or something. They're setting up. The funny thing, though, it's Quillan's cellular, but the bureau isn't hearing Quillan, it's some other guy."

"Maybe Quillan's pal, American #2?"

"I don't see why not."

"My guys. I love it. Is there a connection with Victor Combat?"

"There could be. They're working on it."

"When will we know?"

"I can't answer that."

Donahoo swore. "Am I pointed in the right direction?"

"I think so."

Donahoo floored the Chevy. It was going down, he thought. Something, somewhere, within his range. He had a shot at it. XLA BMGS. X meant experimental. BM, ballistic missile. He didn't need Palmer to guess the rest. He could do that himself. LA, low altitude. GS, guidance system. When the dust settled, it could be looney asshole, geriatric smartass, anything to please Saperstein, but right now he had to live with himself. He was opting for an end-of-the-world scenario. It was the only thing that made the past week worthwhile.

Hey, he deserved it, Donahoo thought. He had worked for it.

The Chevy threaded through the freeway traffic like a wayward rocket.

Rosie finally figured out how to work the National City police car's radio. She also had the car's number, seven. She'd found it on a tag on the dash.

The dispatcher was a woman. That made her feel a little better. As good as she could feel with a gun at her head. She listened to the calls for a while.

"Dispatch," she said then, breaking in. "This is car seven. Acknowledge, please."

"Car seven," the dispatcher responded, sounding uncertain. "Confirm your number. I have an Officer Taggart assigned to car seven."

Quillan jammed the gun viciously. Rosie screamed in pain and dropped the mike. She scrambled for it.

"Forget the conversation," Quillan gritted out. "Tell the bitch what you want. *Tell her!*"

Rosie cut into another transmission. It was all a jumble. She wasn't acknowledged.

"You stupid cunt."

"You're *scaring me*!" she screamed at him. "How can I do anything? Every second . . ." She couldn't stop the flow of tears. "You're going to kill me?"

Quillan grabbed her by the hair. He turned her head to face him. Blood from his hand, which had been clutching his stomach, ran down her face, mixing with her tears.

"I am going to kill you—" he told her. His other hand held the gun. It was in her face now, cocked. "—if you don't get this done." The words gurgled in his throat. He released her. "Last chance. Do it . . . now."

Rosie got hold of the mike with both hands. She waited for a break in transmissions. "Dispatch," she said. "This is car seven. Officer Taggart is dead. My name is Rosalind Gestring. I'm being held hostage. I've got a gun at my head."

Quillan was reminded to put the gun back at the base of her skull. "Now you're cooking," he said.

Lewis on the radio again, frantic. He said, "We've got a disaster here. We're minutes away . . ."

Donahoo jammed the Chevy. "What?"

"This is so fucked," Lewis said. "We've got a nondescript van somewhere between Victor Combat and Lindbergh Field. No escort, lightly guarded, radio silence. Transporting, quote, in a small steel box, about eighteen inches square, something extremely vital to national security."

"My guys?"

"Are probably going to grab it. Maybe already have grabbed it. And you're the only one who knows what they look like." There was a break. "We've got units converging. But you're key. Be there."

Donahoo eased the Chevy onto the off-ramp for Pacific Highway and Lindbergh Field. "This thing in the box. How important is it?"

"It's the guidance part of some special missile. It can pick out one person in a crowd. It can bump a head of state."

"So it gets light security?"

"It's a private firm making an in-house shipment. It has its own procedures and they've worked till now. Where are you?"

"Closing."

Donahoo left the ramp and hit Pacific Highway. He tried to put his head into Americans #1 and #2. If he was going to grab a van somewhere between Victor Combat and Lindbergh Field—where would he do that?

Cominsky was on the radio. "Sarge," he said. He could hardly speak. "Rosie Gestring. She's on a police frequency. She says—" There was a break. "American Number One—the guy identified as Quillan? He's got her."

Donahoo stared at the radio in disbelief. He felt sick. "Quillan? How's that? He's supposed to be on this job."

"No. His pal's doing it. We've got an ID. Taylor, he's doing it. Quillan's with Rosie. He killed the National City cop sent over to guard her. He's got a gun at her head and he's going to shoot her. He says you've got to bring him the video, all the copies, or he's going to kill her, Sarge."

"Where?"

"National City. They're in a stolen cop car in a church parking lot. Jesus of Nazareth Church of Eternal Life."

"Okay. I know it."

"Sarge," Cominsky said, he was like a broken machine, he couldn't stop. "The VA called. Your father's dying, he's not going to last, he wants to see you. The nurse says he's going to go any moment, Sarge. He's had last rites. She says don't waste any time."

"Thanks for letting me know."

"And, Sarge . . ."

"Leave me alone."

"Okay."

Donahoo ran a red light. He didn't have much time to think about it. Points of the compass, north, south, west. Who should he be there for? The woman he desperately wanted to love? The man who gave him life? His country? He wondered what kind of idiot would think up that kind of test. How to choose?

Charlie, okay, he'd understand, forgive, Donahoo thought. Charlie would die content knowing he was doing his duty. If somebody explained it would be okay. Duty was a priest thing. But the rest was an impossible choice. How the fuck could they do this to him? He was supposed to pick? Save Rosie from a blood-crazed killer? Or make the world a safer place?

He thought, inanely, about Hoyt's song, about its desolate perspective. *Rocks from the mountain, they grind fine.* That was a fact, he thought. They were grinding him. *Nobody lives in the sands of time.* True. You live only now. For a limited and uncertain period. So you'd better make the best of it. Was that what the kid was saying? Donahoo thought maybe it wasn't sad. Maybe it was just honest and true. Do your best. That simple.

Rosie The Snake G-String. The Wham Bam Ice Trail. Jesus Christ. How could he abandon her? Let her die for the sake of some hellfire piece of machinery? He couldn't. It wasn't within him. Somebody help me, please, he thought. How does this work? The Chevy was screaming. He had to decide. He could make her wait, he thought. He could try to do both. Ask that of her. He could keep careful track and push it to the absolute limit and try to do both. Maybe he could do that. He was a lucky cop. He could try.

Charlie, I'm sorry, Donahoo said silently. Rosie, hang on.

THIRTY-TWO

Crash Evans was positioned on the northwest corner of Laurel Street and Pacific Highway. He was worried that someone might think he was acting suspiciously because he had passed up several opportunities to cross the street. Every time he got a walk signal, he'd back off, hold. He was getting edgier by the minute. He wished the van would hurry up. He wanted to get this over with. It was like giving birth, he thought. You knew it was going to hurt. But you did it anyway. Because you wanted to, or because you had no other choice. In his case, he had no other choice. The only thing he knew how to do was to walk in front of cars.

He lost another chance to cross the street. The red hand started flashing at him. He turned and looked back down the highway to Ben's U-Gas.

There was a visual signal. The Chrysler's hood was up. Then the mike in his ear crackled. Taylor was giving him instructions. "Ford Econo, white. Not the Dodge. The Ford Econo. Coming up."

Crash looked down the curb lane. He could see it coming. A plain white van. He quickly turned around.

The mike crackled again. "Confirm."

Crash pulled off his cap. He might be with a bunch of bastards, but they knew what they were doing, he thought. They didn't leave much to chance. Visual and radio—that was smart. He had to admit that was smart. He felt better.

The van came along. Ford Econo, white. The traffic light turned to green. The van slowed to make the turn. Crash was careful not to make eye contact with the driver. He steeled himself—and darted into the road in front of the turning vehicle.

There was a bump! Crash bounced off, screaming. The fake blood spilled into the street. The van braked, stopped.

Fifty yards back, the Chrysler, twisting in and out of traffic, jumped from the curb lane onto the sidewalk. It had a clear run now. It picked up speed.

The van's driver got out. He went to assist Crash. Before he could reach him, the Chrysler smashed into the van, knocking it on its side.

Duran tumbled from the Chrysler. Writhing, screaming, pretending a terrible injury, he rolled toward the van's rear doors.

A siren sounded nearby. The wail of an ambulance.

The van's driver backed off. He looked around unsurely, at Crash, at Duran. He yelled, "Kelly? You okay?"

Duran sent a smoke bomb spinning against the van. It spewed a white cloud.

The siren was growing louder. Taylor and Lee arrived in the ambulance. It pulled up within six feet of the van.

The van's driver was reaching for his gun.

Lee picked him off from the ambulance. One shot to the head. There was hardly any sound. The *pffft!* of a silencer.

Taylor leapt out with a shotgun. He used the butt end to smash one of the van's rear windows. He tossed in a tear gas grenade. He took a chain cutter from his belt and stood ready in the swirl of white smoke.

The courier stumbled out, retching. He was handcuffed to a square stainless steel box. Lee shot him in the head. *Pffft!*

Taylor bent to the courier with the chain cutter. The handcuffs parted readily. One quick snap of the powerful jaws.

Duran was already at the wheel of the ambulance. He shouted, "Let's go."

Taylor got the steel box. He put it in the back of the ambulance.

Crash, in extreme pain, soaked with the fake blood, staggered to the ambulance, dragging a broken leg. He flung himself inside.

"Come on," Duran said urgently. He turned on the siren. "Leave them."

Taylor helped Lee put the courier's body in the ambulance. Then they got the driver. They clambered in with his body.

Duran was pulling away as they yanked the doors shut. The siren wailed.

"Damn, damn," Crash cried. He was holding his broken leg. "This is really smashed."

"Why didn't you let us get you?" Taylor asked. "I was just telling Wheels. I never leave bodies."

Crash looked at him. He was in so much pain, he missed it. "Can you give me something for this?"

"I can put you out of your misery," Taylor said. He had the shotgun across his knee. He swung it and fired. The large-gauge pellets peppered a blood bag before ripping open Crash's chest. A wash of real and fake blood spurted from him.

"What the fuck?!" Lee screamed. His gun was back in its holster. He'd never draw in time. "What the fuck . . . you doing?"

Taylor spent a split second moving another shell into the shotgun's chamber. Whack, whack.

Duran glanced over his shoulder. He didn't have a gun. He never carried one. He said, *"Jesucristo."*

"You want it all?" Lee demanded, incredulous. "You're killing me? You're killing the Mex? For an extra hundred grand?" He pushed back fearfully. "You gotta be crazy. This isn't that big a deal."

Taylor pointed the shotgun at him. "You couldn't be more wrong, slant."

Lee stared at him. "It's not a heart?"

Taylor shook his head, no.

"Then what is it?"

Taylor smiled for answer. He seemed to be saying, guess.

"Well, fuck," Lee pleaded. "If it's something bigger ..." He was looking at the shotgun's approaching muzzle. "You're gonna need help."

"You've been very helpful," Taylor told him, firing.

Lee's chest ripped open. He fell back, clutching it. For an instant his eyes appeared to be repeating his accusation. "You gotta be crazy." Then he was dead.

Duran said, *"Jesucristo. Jesucristo."*

Taylor got the steel box and clambered into the seat next to Duran.

"Hey, man," Duran told him, sweating. "Take it easy, huh? You've got my share. You can have it all. I don't give a shit. Keep it." He said, not looking at Taylor, trying to concentrate on his driving, "Tell me what you want me to do." He was headed south on Pacific Highway. Traffic was stopping for him, responding to the siren, but some vehicles were staying in the street, not pulling over. He had to weave among them. "Just let me walk when it's over, man. I swear to God ..."

"Shut up."

"I got a kid, man."

"Shut up."

Duran flicked a look at him. He stopped talking.

Taylor put the shotgun aside. He cradled the steel box in his lap. He slipped out of his paramedic jacket and put on a baseball jacket. He put the steel box into a reinforced shopping bag from the Farmers' Market. He put the bag between his feet. This was perfect, and what was so marvelous, he had all the time in the world, he thought. He'd just hide out. Be patient, wait. Then—the coast was clear?—he'd go somewhere. China? Yeah, that was the best bet. But there were other places where he would be just as welcome. Iraq, Iran? Maybe Israel? He smiled. He could start a war. A bidding war.

"I'll make it easy for you, Wheels," Taylor said. "Drop me off here, then keep on going, okay? Drop me off and keep driving. Stay with this bucket for another couple miles. Then you can ditch. Understand?"

Duran blinked back tears of relief. He nodded. "Okay."

"You gotta do that though," Taylor warned. "I'm going to be following you. You ditch too soon—you're dead."

"I understand."

"Good. Stop here." Taylor, getting his shopping bag, hit a switch under the seat. He opened the door. "It's been nice knowing you, Wheels."

The ambulance slowed. Taylor jumped out hugging the shopping bag. The ambulance sped away, siren wailing.

Taylor got into a Ford LTD parked at the west curb three cars down from the intersection. It had been there since early morning. It had a parking ticket. He removed the ticket and got in. He sat watching the ambulance until it disappeared from sight.

Two miles, Taylor thought. Wheels Duran, Crash Evans, Chinaman Lee, the van driver, the courier—they'd all be blown to rat shit before the ambulance got that far.

Taylor thought it was a very nice plan, and what he liked most about it, it was his plan, not Quillan's. He had thought it up all by himself. No input from the General. A stand-by plan to be put in effect if he found proof that Quillan was lying.

Quillan, he shouldn't have lied, Taylor thought. He, Taylor, he'd been a strong right arm, a good friend. He'd taken Quillan from the bamboo cage in 'Nam. He hadn't shot him, like he was supposed to, in that little grass shack in Tegucigalpa.

Taylor sat thinking that Quillan had been wrong to fuck him. He thought, shit, you can't fuck Taylor, huh? So smile, Taylor.

THIRTY-THREE

Donahoo was speeding north on Pacific Highway. He could hear the wail of an approaching emergency vehicle. Ambulance, he thought. They were all different. Ambulances, fire trucks, police cars—each had their own anguished cry for attention. The car in front of him started pulling over. He kept going, picking up speed, taking advantage of the open road. This was a break, he thought. He could really make time for a couple of blocks. He thought, he was having crazy thoughts, that it was like divine intervention, letting him get this done, out of the way, so he could get to Rosie, get to Charlie. Divine intervention giving him a couple of precious extra minutes.

Lewis was suddenly on the radio. "Donahoo? We've lost it. The van was ambushed—Laurel and Pacific Highway."

Donahoo broke in. "What can you give me?"

The ambulance swept past him at high speed. The siren drowned out Lewis's response.

"Repeat."

"The driver and courier are missing. We're looking for a small stainless steel box."

"Do we know a vehicle?"

"Repeat, an ambulance," Lewis said. "South on Pacific Highway. We have units converging." There was a break. "It's been spotted from the air. We could have a warp here."

Donahoo was trying to find a place to make a U-turn. He braked to avoid a tan station wagon cutting in front of him. It was a Ford, an LTD. He caught a glimpse of the driver. It looked like American #2. It looked like Taylor.

"Your decision," Lewis said. "You can help. You can make ID. But if you want to break off . . ." He said, "It's up to you."

Donahoo swerved. He got on the tail of the LTD. There was another car between them, but he got a good look at the driver's profile when he adjusted the outside rearview. It was Taylor. Definitely Taylor.

Lewis said, "Let me know."

"I'm outa here, Lewis," Donahoo told him. "I'll be in touch later. I'm going to National City."

"I understand."

Donahoo turned the radio lower. He slowed, dropped back, let a few more cars get between him and the LTD. It had a telltale aerial on its roof. The kind recommended for use with police scanners. Taylor was probably listening to everything. Donahoo wanted him to think he was going for Rosie.

"Good luck, Tommy."

Yeah, Donahoo thought. He stayed two cars behind the LTD. He could predict where it was going. The Grape Street access to I-5. Then a straight run south to the border. Twenty minutes, and Taylor, he'd be in Mexico, no questions asked. He'd just sail through. You had a pass going into Baja. They didn't ask questions until you got into the interior. Past Ensenada. Taylor, he could hole up in Tijuana forever, sitting on his little steel box, waiting for the right moment to do what he was going to do. Which was sell out for more money than probably even he imagined.

The LTD got onto I-5. Donahoo followed it past the turnoff for the Coronado Bridge. Then he pulled over at an emergency roadside telephone. He got patched through to Lewis.

"We're screwed," Lewis said. "The ambulance blew up. We're still picking up the pieces, but it looks like the box is gone."

"Anything more on what's in it?"

"No. Just a guidance system."

Just, huh? Donahoo tried to imagine a missile that could pick out a man in a crowd. His mind filled with pictures, past and present, of presidents of the United States. Presidents and a lot of wannabe presidents. The guidance system in the wrong hands— would any of them ever be safe?

"I need a backup," Donahoo said. "Taylor's headed south on I-5. He's got a scanner, so you've got to arrange this off air, okay? Have everybody run silent till he's in sight." He gave a full description of the LTD. He said, "I'm taking him at the San Ysidro off-ramp. I'd try earlier, but I don't want to blow it. This gives you enough time to set up properly."

"Does he have the box?"

"I dunno. But who else?" Donahoo hesitated. "Rosie. She's . . ?"

"Screaming bloody murder."

"Quillan?"

"He keeps threatening to kill her unless you get there. He won't deal with anybody else but you."

"Keep stalling. Have Cominsky get a couple of videos for me— copies for Quillan. Tell him what worked before. And get me a chopper out of San Ysidro."

Donahoo went back to the Imperial Beach cop's Chevy. That was something else to fuck with his head, he thought. Taylor, did he have the box? He sat behind the wheel, torn. He'd done his job, most of it anyway. He could go help Rosie. But a thousand things could go wrong between here and San Ysidro. Taylor, he could turn off. Or he could switch cars. Or he could give the box to someone else. Or . . . ?

He thought of Rosie. It's not over till they throw dirt in your face. That's what she said. He pulled out onto the freeway and resumed pursuit.

A National City black-and-white quietly took up position in a Circle K across from Jesus of Nazareth Church of Eternal Life. Then, on the other side of the church's parking lot, in front of a vacant house, another black-and-white. A minute later and a third showed. It parked at the church office.

Quillan was aware of all of them. He said matter-of-factly, "We're being surrounded."

Rosie said, "Yes."

"How do you think they found us?"

"We *told* them we were here!"

"Oh, yeah."

She whispered it. "Jesus."

Quillan looked around, his head turning in slow motion, as if he were afraid, if he moved faster, it might fall off. He counted the police cars. One, two, three . . . now four. They were on all four sides. They had formed a box. He was in the middle.

"My favorite war story," Quillan said, slowly turning back to Rosie. "There's this director, he's making a picture, and he gets his draft notice, he's got to report for duty immediately. In the middle of the picture."

Rosie kept silent. Quillan's gun was still a cannon against her skull. She thought that he was losing it. His mind was drifting. He wasn't focusing on the situation. He was telling her dumb stories.

She thought that she was going to die, and it wasn't fair. She hated Donahoo. For getting her into this. For not coming. For not being here, as promised.

"So, this director," Quillan said, slurring. "He gets all the marines in this picture he's making, and he puts them up a coconut tree, no guns, no ammo. Then he gets all the Viet Cong, he puts them in a circle around the coconut tree, and they've all got machine guns, hand grenades, flamethrowers. The director films the scene, then he leaves. He says, "Let's see you get out of that." Quillan tried to laugh. It rattled in his throat. "Let's see you . . . get out of that."

Rosie thought that she hated Donahoo. Where was he? Where the fuck was he?

Quillan pushed the gun. "Try again."

Rosie got on the radio. "Dispatch. This is car seven. My situation—" She stopped. She was so shaken, she couldn't think of any other word. "—is deteriorating here."

"Tell your abductor he must wait," the dispatcher responded. "The officer you requested can't leave his present assignment. He's dealing with another emergency. It has priority."

Rosie screamed. "What can be more important?!"

"Repeat. You have to wait. We're estimating—this is only an estimate—half an hour."

"*Half an hour?!*"

"I'm sorry."

"Jesus." Rosie flung the mike away. "The sonofabitch. The bastard." She broke into tears again. "The sonofabitch. He's not coming."

Quillan slowly looked around. The same four police cars. They were waiting, the same as him. Everybody waiting.

Rosie thought about what Donahoo had said. "I'm not going to let you go. Nobody's going to take you from me." He had held her, and he had said that. He had told her that he loved her.

"Taylor," Quillan grunted, talking to himself. "Taylor, he's doing the job, and Donahoo, he's trying to stop him. That's the *other* emergency."

Rosie tried to compose herself. "What?"

Quillan said, "Fuck, if they know what's going down, we don't count no more, Rosie. We're the back of the line." He leaned forward. "Give him a time limit," he said harshly. "Ten minutes. If he's not here by then—don't bother coming."

"Ten minutes?"

The gun pressed harder. "If he loves you, he can make it, Rosie. If he doesn't, it's all over, you'll never cry again."

"I forgive you," Monsignor Cervantes said, talking to Father Charlie, but he was looking at Nurse Bird. "God forgives you."

Charlie said, a faint whisper, barely heard, "How do you know, Frank?"

"It's the nature of my calling," Monsignor Cervantes said. "I talk to God. He tells me these things. I have asked Him. He says He forgives you."

Charlie said, "I've talked to Him. But He's never talked to me."

Monsignor Cervantes smiled. "Well, that is hardly God's fault, now, is it? You have not been ..." He glanced to Bird. She was taking Charlie's pulse. "His most faithful servant."

Charlie nodded. An admission of guilt.

"Those who walk with God talk with God," Monsignor Cervantes said. He looked at his watch. He had other calls to make. "There will be a Mass for you at St. Francis Liberal. You still have friends there."

"Thank you."

Monsignor Cervantes almost made a motion, as if to suggest it was nothing. He caught himself just in time. "Well ..." He gathered himself. "You're in God's hands now."

"Yes."

Monsignor Cervantes drew Bird aside. "The police officer," he said, his voice low. He continued with difficulty. "His son. Will he be here in time?"

"Why don't you ask yourself, Monsignor?" Bird said. "You speak with God. You must know everything."

The Monsignor looked at her. The rebuke shimmered in his eyes. "You're not a Catholic girl?" he asked softly.

Bird said, "You don't know that either? I guess you don't know a lot of things."

"Tell him, Bird," Charlie said, using all his strength.

San Ysidro. The freeway exit was a mile away. Traffic was starting to slow.

Roadblock, Donahoo thought. They're shutting it down. They're closing it.

He was four cars behind the LTD. He had been that way for the whole run south. Now he changed lanes and moved up. He maneuvered until there was just one car separating him. He didn't care now if he was spotted. Taylor had no way to go except forward. A high steel mesh barrier fence divided the freeway's north/south lanes. The shoulder fell away to a deep ditch.

The radio crackled. "Fisherman. This is Skyhawk. We have a sighting."

Donahoo could see the back of Taylor's head. He imagined him reacting in fear and dismay. It was the first San Diego police radio transmission making even guarded reference to him.

"Skyhawk. Can you give us a position?"

"Affirmative. One mile north of exit."

The LTD stopped. Taylor leapt out with a gun in one hand and the steel box in the other. The shopping bag hiding it fell away in his haste. He started for another car.

Hostage, Donahoo thought. The bugger's going to take a hostage. He was out of the Chevy. He took careful aim with his Cobra. He didn't call out any warning. He just fired.

Taylor screamed and went down, shot in the right knee, crippled.

"Drop it!" Donahoo screamed. "The next one's in your skull. *Drop it!*"

Taylor looked at him. He didn't have a shot. He was down with his hands slammed on the pavement and his gun askew under it.

"*Push it away.*"

Taylor tried anyway. He got a grip on his gun. He started to lift it.

Donahoo fired. Two shots. Both in the chest. Taylor slumped to the pavement.

Everything was suddenly turmoil. People leaving their cars. People screaming.

Donahoo took possession of the steel box.

"I almost made it," Taylor said. He was dying. "I coulda had it all."

"Yeah, I know," Donahoo said. "Manila Time." It was starting to sink in. He had killed somebody. He'd never done that before. He didn't like the feeling. "I'm sorry."

"No, you're not," Taylor said. He was going. "Fuck you too."

Donahoo put away the Cobra. He started back for the Chevy. An FBI agent was running toward him. There was FBI on his cap, on his jacket. He was holding a gun at his side.

The agent was out of breath. He said, "Let's have it."

Donahoo checked the tag attached to his collar. The ID looked real enough. Now a second agent arrived. Donahoo recognized him from somewhere. He remembered having met him on a case. He surrendered the box.

The first agent took it. He said, still out of breath, "You're a little out of your jurisdiction, aren't you, hotshot?"

A San Diego Police Department chopper was fluttering down at the side of the freeway. The pilot waved.

"You can get picky later, Earl," the second agent said. "The guy's got a plane to catch."

THIRTY-FOUR

Jesus of Nazareth Church of Eternal Life. The National City black-and-whites forming a box around it suddenly moved away and left the scene. There was just the one car remaining in the middle of the parking lot. Rosie Gestring waiting with Nicholas Quillan. For a while all was silent. Then the clatter of a chopper.

"Here he comes," Quillan said. He had a cigar. He put it in his mouth. He didn't light it. He tried, gave up.

The chopper landed next to the church office. Donahoo got out and got clear. The chopper lifted.

Donahoo stood looking at the car. It was too far away to see either Rosie or Quillan. All he could make out was a dark shadow or shadows. He was facing the unknown.

The flight from San Ysidro had taken only a few minutes but it had seemed like hours. He'd had too much time to think about this moment. It had become, in his mind, an impossible situation which he could not possibly resolve. He had imagined a hundred possible scenarios, and they were all bad. He was too late, Rosie was dead. He was too late, and Quillan, dying, was only waiting to kill Rosie, so that he, Donahoo, would witness it. He was too late . . .

Jesus, Donahoo thought. For the first time in his life he hated being a cop. He hated killing Taylor. He hated starting this long walk.

The car horn honked. Donahoo headed out. He knew what he was supposed to do. He was supposed to give the video and a couple of copies to Quillan. In exchange he was supposed to get Rosie. That's how it was supposed to work. That straightforward and simple. That easy.

Oh, yeah, Donahoo thought. His mind was a jumble of the unthinkable. Rosie dead. Rosie being killed before his eyes. A long nightmare ride, both of them hostage to Quillan's madness, and all that goddamn impossible horror to go through, and then he kills her?

Donahoo reached the car. Rosie was turned away from him, her head against the side window. Quillan had his gun pushed against her skull. He was staring with his cold and empty wolf eyes.

Donahoo pulled open the door on the passenger side. He threw the video and two copies onto the back seat. He reached over and pried the gun out of Quillan's dead hand. He took the cigar out of his dead mouth.

"Say something," Donahoo said softly.

Rosie turned to face him. Hate radiated from her.

He reached for her tentatively. She pulled away in loathing.

"Listen, I'm sorry," he said. He was asking for forgiveness and he was trying to explain. He wasn't quite sure what he was saying. It was just pouring out of him in desperation. "I couldn't come sooner. I don't know why he'd do this to you. It's just such a dumb thing to do. He had to be crazy. What would make him think I'd give him all the copies?"

She said, the tears starting, "He said . . . because you loved me."

Donahoo looked at her. "Oh."

"I can't imagine why he'd think that." She stumbled out of the car and hurried away. "Can you?"

Oh, Jesus, he thought. He'd lost her. He said, "If you'd just give me a chance, I can explain, Rosie. It was national security . . ." He watched her go. She was headed for one of the returning black-and-whites. He said, "Gimme a break."

She didn't look back. "Fuck a tree, Officer."

THIRTY-FIVE

The VA Medical Center in La Jolla. Donahoo always knew this time would come. He would walk into this gray room and the gray bed would be empty. The bowl and the twigs would be gone.

"He died just before five o'clock," Bird said. "He complained about missing supper." She was fussing with the things on the bedside table. "Of course, he never ate supper."

Donahoo stood looking at the empty bed. He was thinking about broken promises. He had promised Rosie he'd be there when she needed him. He had promised Charlie he'd be there when he died. Two promises broken in one day. It didn't seem possible. It didn't seem right.

"He asked me to tell you something," Bird said. "That he loved you. And that he forgave you."

Donahoo looked at her. "For not being here?"

Bird shrugged helplessly. There were tears in her eyes. "Probably for everything."

Donahoo didn't answer. He didn't know what to make of that. The defenses rose without bidding. Everything considered, he'd been a pretty good son. He started to think that, then, he quit. He shook his head. He said, thinking about Rosie, "Well, I kept one promise anyway."

"No more women?"

Donahoo flushed. "He told you about that?"

Bird nodded. "We talked a lot. Mostly about Catholicism."

"Well," Donahoo said. "I'm glad you could share." He looked around. He had everything. It was all in one bag. Priests, the good ones, they traveled light. An empty attaché and a watch that didn't work. Some photographs. A pair of slippers. The radio/tape deck. Hoyt's song, "Curious Ginger."

"Your partner, Cominsky, he called," Bird said. "That made it easier, line of duty." She said, "How'd that go?"

Donahoo made a gesture. "Half and half."

She waited. She apparently wanted him to say it was really justified or something. He thought she was being pretty fucking intense under the circumstances, and he wasn't quite sure why. Maybe he had invited it? He was always looking at her, imagining her on his big finger, little Bird. She couldn't have helped but notice. He said, he didn't know what else to say, even though it sounded ridiculous, "What faith are you?"

"I'm a trisexual." She was looking back at him. "I'll try anything." She said, "Later, when you're feeling better, call me if you want, okay?"

"Uh. Maybe I will."

"Good."

Whoa, life goes on, Donahoo thought. A girl would find out about that, working in a hospital, a new lesson every day. And if she wanted to say something, she had to say it now, because if she didn't say it, he wasn't going to be back to hear it later. This was the last place he'd ever want to come again.

"Don't forget."

Donahoo smiled for her. He thought that he didn't know when he would get better but that he would get better. The VA, it was a teaching hospital, and one of the things it taught was how to get better. Find yourself a nurse.

Cominsky was waiting outside. In the scant time available, he had somehow managed to dress for the occasion. He was in black. Black coat, black suit, black shoes. Donahoo thought he would be impressed if it weren't for the red umbrella.

"Everybody, you've got their condolences," Cominsky said, banging the umbrella open. It was raining lightly, a passing shower. "We had a meeting on the fly. Saperstein says it's okay, he's not looking for you anymore, but he still thinks you should stay away for a while, give him some time to adjust." He put the umbrella over Donahoo. He guided him toward the parking lot. "Lewis says that would be okay by him too. He says take your time." They arrived at the Chevy. "Imperial Beach, on the other hand, says you bring this back today, or your ass is sand."

"My ass is grass."

"Not at Imperial Beach."

Donahoo looked at him. "What else?"

"The Chipper, they're gonna let him stay a hero, that's good PR, and you're not gonna be one, the government doesn't want the public to know how close they came to losing that steel box, which contained, I dunno, I guess you know, huh?"

"I dunno and it doesn't matter. What else?"

"Well, from what the FBI is saying, it was an inside job at Victor Combat. Somebody on the XLA BMGS project told some guy they still know only as Fruit Bat about the device's shipment. The Bat hired Quillan and Taylor. Quillan, he had a big house up on Pannekin Drive, it was full of those orchids, Vanda burgeffii, so that definitely links Lyons to Quillan, even though we can't find the two hundred grand he's supposed to have gotten from the guy. Quillan, he had a closet elevator operator, Trudy Goody, and she says he liked to talk, brag about his criminal activities, and also that he went both ways, he liked boys, and he was doing Buddy Salinas, so that explains that part. Other parts we'll never know."

"Closet elevator operator?"

"I think it's something to do with kinky sex. Maybe she *didn't* come out of the closet?"

"Makes sense. What else?"

"Oh." He raised his hand to shake good-bye. "I'm not your partner anymore. I'm back permanently with Palmer."

Donahoo looked at him. "Says who?"

"Saperstein, Lewis. They say you're the kinda guy, you don't want a partner. You're a loner. A loner with a boner."

"Yeah?"

"Yeah."

Donahoo got in the Chevy. He started it, drove away. Cominsky was standing forlornly in the rain, the red umbrella at his side, open and down, as if he were collecting raindrops.

Jesus, Donahoo thought. He couldn't believe what he was going to do. He drove back. "Come on, get in, we're going downtown."

"What for?"

"To talk to Saperstein. He can't take you away from me."

"You're the sarge," Cominsky said, grinning.

Donahoo got out the cigar he'd taken from Quillan. He bit off the end and stuck it in his mouth. He found a book of matches and lit one and got the cigar going. Its rich aroma filled the Chevy. Cuban.

The whole time, Cominsky stared, incredulous. He said, "Uh, I don't think that's good for you."

"Look at George Burns," Donahoo told him. "He smokes cigars

every day. He's almost a hundred years old, and the first time he gets in trouble, he slips in the shower. Now, does that tell you not to smoke cigars?"

"No. To stay outa showers."

Oh, boy. Donahoo wondered if he'd made a mistake. Cominsky, you tried to talk to him, he just got you all tangled up, after a while you didn't know what you were talking about either. Stay outa showers. The guy was a menace.

Cominsky said, "Rosie. What you gonna do about her?"

Jesus, Donahoo thought. Here we go again. How the hell did he know? He'd just been blown a kiss by Bird. It was all coming at him at once. It was disconcerting. Anything he said was going to be wrong. He said, "I dunno. I thought I'd give her a while to cool off. Then I'd take her up to Mr. A's, the city at her feet. Buy her some of those four-dollar drinks. Tell her how pretty she is. Comb her hair." His heart was broken but he was piling it on for Cominsky's benefit. He put the cigar back. He talked around it, "Just charm the knickers right off her. What do you think?"

"You know women."

"Yeah."

THIRY-SIX

Rosie Gestring moved through her house, nursing a straight vodka, her third. It was all over, she thought. Everything. Chip Lyons, Quillan, Donahoo. The nightmare was over. She had survived. She smiled, thinking of the cop who had dropped her off, he had been so considerate, chivalrous. He had held her hand and he had suggested that she might need counseling. She had told him that she needed a drink. He had said, "You're quite a lady." She had said, "Don't even think about it."

It was dark now. She put her glass down and went outside. She crossed the yard to the birdhouse. She opened the false bottom and removed the oilskin packet hidden there. She replaced the false bottom and took the packet into the house.

In the kitchen, she unwrapped the oilskin, counted the money. Two hundred thousand dollars, less the cost of two one-way tickets to Manila, which were at the bottom of the pile. Chip Lyons had said you could live for almost nothing in the Philippines. He knew where there were islands with white beaches and grass shacks. Food you could buy for pennies and people who'd be your servants for a couple of dollars a day. She'd get a refund on the tickets, she thought. Then she'd have an even two hundred grand.

She got her glass, refilled it. She tried to think of how many times she had gone to bed with Chip Francis Lyons. She arrived at a figure that seemed close and then divided it into two hundred thousand dollars. It came to ten thousand a pop.

That much? She smiled like a little girl selling Chiclets on a Tijuana bridge. Ten thousand, huh? She wondered what that made her. Rosie the Snake Gestring. The Wham Bam Ice Trail. The highest paid hooker in America?

Maybe, probably not. There was a lot of competition out there. She raised her glass in a happy, if solitary, toast. Fuck Manila, she thought, smiling.

It was Rio Time.

Excerpts, Testimony Before the Committee on Police Oversight

IN THE MATTER OF INVESTIGATOR FRANCIS LYONS ET AL

Special Agent William Galloway, Federal Bureau of Investigation, appearing at his own request, testified that Sgt. Thomas Donahoo had informed the bureau, in a timely manner, of the XLA BMGS information in his possession, and that the bureau, in hindsight, had not acted, in this instance, as swiftly and effectively as might be desired. He noted that the bureau is hampered in that it receives a large number of crank calls and that all must be evaluated and that this requires considerable effort and time, and thus manpower and resources are sometimes misdirected.

Lt. Bernard Mancuso, Internal Affairs, testified that evidence was developed suggesting Investigator Francis Lyons was blackmailing Rosita Gestring, a fugitive from the Women's Correctional, Gary, Indiana. It appeared that he was protecting her in return for sexual favors. Lt. Mancuso further testified that evidence was developed suggesting that Sgt. Thomas Donahoo, using files found in an illegal search of Investigator Lyons's residence, also blackmailed Ms. Gestring, again for sexual favors.

Sgt. Donahoo testified that contrary to Lt. Mancuso's suppositions, the Rosita Gestring formerly residing in National City, California, was not the Rosita Banner who escaped from the Women's Correctional in Gary, Indiana. He said he had reason to suspect, and his suspicions were later confirmed, that the Rosie Gestring file in Lyons's home was a fabrication. The criminal record was falsified. The press clippings were doctored.

Sgt. Donahoo said it appeared that Ms. Gestring and her half brother, Ernesto Garcia Buddy Salinas, conspired to have Lyons think that he had a hold on Ms. Gestring, while in fact he did not. Ms. Gestring, with no fear of arrest, since she was in fact not a criminal fugitive, would have been able to collect information—film from hidden cameras, tape recordings, etc.—showing Lyons was blackmailing her. Lyons's guard would be down. He thought that one word from him and she would go to jail. Actually, one word from her and he would go to jail. At some point Ms. Gestring apparently was able to convince Investigator Lyons that his only choice was to turn criminal. Again conspiring with her half brother, Buddy Salinas, she arranged for Lyons to be at the Tijuana Slough, so he could videotape Quillan's murder of Primitivo.

Chief Saperstein and Capt. Lewis commended Sgt. Donahoo for his work on XLA BMGS. Sgt. Donahoo said he would like the record to show that he was a lucky cop.

The hearing was concluded with no official findings or action.

Proceedings Sealed